The Watercolourist

BEATRICE MASINI was born in Milan. She is a
well-known and successful writer of books for children
and teenagers, translated into over twenty languages. She
works as an editor for an Italian publisher and has translated
many books for both children and adults. The Watercolourist
won the Premio Selezione Campiello prize and the Premio
Alessandro Manzoni award for best historical novel.

Oonagh Stransky has translated Pasolini, Saviano,
Pontiggia and Pope Francis. She currently lives in Italy.
www.oonaghstransky.com

Clarissa Ghelli is a practising artist, teacher and translator
of Italian literature. She lives in New York City.

Beatrice Masini

❧ ❧

The Watercolourist

Translated by
Oonagh Stransky and Clarissa Ghelli

PAN BOOKS

First published 2016 by Mantle

This paperback edition published 2017 by Pan Books
an imprint of Pan Macmillan
20 New Wharf Road, London N1 9RR
Associated companies throughout the world
www.panmacmillan.com

ISBN 978-1-4472-5774-5

1 3 5 7 9 8 6 4 2

A CIP catalogue record for this book is available from the British Library.

Printed and bound by CPI Group (UK) Ltd, Croydon, CR0 4YY

ore about all our books
s, author interviews and
gn up for e-newsletters
t our new releases.

The Watercolourist

She doesn't know. She doesn't know if this is love, this rubbing of fabric against fabric, this warm and rugged fumbling. Fingers. Fingers everywhere. Hands touching places no stranger's hand has ever been. A strained gasp. To want and not to want. Here, this, where, what, why. And now the pain: piercing, tearing, leaving her breathless; unceasing, insistent, like pain without compassion, a rasping of flesh inside flesh. *No, not like that, no.* But words are useless. Nothing changes.

Her other self, silent and composed, watches from afar. Her eyes are pools of pity. *Why pity? What if this is actually what it is like? What if it is supposed to be like this?* She doesn't know any more.

She continues to listen to the agony stampeding inside her, nailing her to the wall, snatching from her very throat a sound that doesn't belong to her. It isn't her voice; it is neither laughter nor lament. It is a horrible sound, the sound of a wild beast suffering, nothing more. *How long will it go on? Will it ever stop?*

And later, when it is finally over, the question lingers: is this love?

Six years later

There is a queue in front of Santa Caterina. She arrives in a rush and out of breath, tripping over her own feet, now and then turning around to look behind her. She stops and hides behind a pillar. She is not alone.

In front of her, a short, thickset fellow takes a quiet and unmoving bundle out from under his cloak and, without hesitating, places it inside the wooden pass-through in one smooth and careful movement. As if he has done it before. He doesn't linger but turns around and walks away, the hem of his cloak flapping at his back. Like smoke vanishing into the darkness.

Next is a woman who wears no bonnet. The dim light of the street lamp is bright enough to illuminate her face as she places her tiny, shaking, angry bundle in the sliding drawer. It is not a cry that emerges; it is a wail, a bleating. The woman hesitates, leans forward towards the infant and is herself almost swallowed up by the drawer. Her shoulders shake. She straightens up, turns around and walks off, bareheaded, poor, in tears. She is likely a seamstress, mending hems. She is very young, almost a girl. Not a maid, though. It must have been her first time but it probably won't be her last.

It is her turn now. She herself has nothing to entrust to the city's custody, nothing from which to free herself with anger, relief or sorrow. She knocks on the wooden door and waits. The door swings open and a large, ample woman comes out, wiping her hands on her apron. As it closes behind her, she leans against the doorway.

'You got the money?' she asks, without preamble.

The girl nods. She holds out a pouch, trying in vain to meet the woman's gaze.

'So, is she all right?'

'She's fine, fine.'

The woman snatches the pouch, her eyes downcast, and slips it into her open, damp blouse, her large breasts drooping like the ears of a dog. She spits on the ground like a man.

'She's healthy. She's fine. The supervisor went to see her last month. It's just that the woman died.'

2

'Oh.' The girl holds her breath. 'Now what?'

'Now nothing. She's been moved to another family. But don't worry, she's fine.'

'Is she big? Is she well behaved?'

She knows it is silly to ask such questions. This spitting, milk-oozing woman doesn't know a thing. She won't know if her little girl's skin has been ravaged by smallpox or if she has escaped the outbreaks entirely; if she has started drawing her first letters or if there is no one there to teach them to her. It is a miracle in itself that the woman is able to tell her that her daughter is still alive. And she knows that this, too, could be a lie.

The fat woman grows impatient.

'I have to go. I got seven new ones last night. Plus the ones from today. Three have died already. It's better that way, though, because I've got almost no milk left. I would have had to start feeding them cow's milk, and they would have died anyway. Cow's milk isn't good for little ones.'

The girl pretends not to hear the woman.

'I'll come again when I can. How is your child?' she adds politely.

'Ha! I've sent mine off to the countryside. Just like yours.' The fat woman laughs a horrible laugh, turns, opens the door and disappears back inside.

Alone now, the girl looks up at the moon without seeing it. Lowering her gaze, she sighs, adjusts her bonnet, and leaves. She doesn't cry. She stopped crying long ago. But her grief and doubt are an obsession and the woman's few words have done nothing to soothe them.

Part One

Inside the carriage there is the overwhelming smell of sweet vinegar, perspiration and possibility. Bianca looks out of the dirty window and sees the sprawl of Bergamo: its trees, walls and towers, red mixed with green, green mixed with red. Then a new scent, an earthy one. Probably from those low trees with slender trunks, thick foliage and supple thorns that claw at the sides of the carriage as they pass by. Springtime. The best season for travelling, except when rain transforms the roads into swamps. Bianca is lucky, though: hers isn't a very long journey. One night at an inn isn't enough to call it an adventure. She knows where she is going. There is no mystery involved.

All that brilliant green seems to force itself in through the window. The old woman travelling alongside her, enveloped in a cloud of camphor, starts muttering.

'What is there to see? It's just the countryside. Personally, I don't like the countryside. I prefer the city.'

The fragrance of camphor, mixed with the lady's bodily odours, which are intensified by the unseasonable heaviness of her black garments, grows stronger with every gesture and suffocates the smells of nature, ruining them. Bianca opens the window in search of fresh air and breathes in only dust. She coughs.

The old woman ties the ribbon of her hat under her chin. She keeps mumbling to herself, but Bianca has learned not to pay her any attention. She wishes she could push her out of the carriage door and leave her there, on the ground, enveloped by her own vile odour, in the middle of the fields that she so detests. That way Bianca could continue the trip alone and enjoy the silence that is not quite silence: the rhythmic pounding of hooves, the creaking of the carriage, the calling voices of peasants outside, the fleeting sound of women singing, a concerto of birds. As she travels, she becomes someone else, not the person she has always been. Not even the one *they* are expecting. She is in limbo. She always felt this way when she and her father journeyed together, too. Only their bond defined who they were. But now everything is different.

She looks down and picks a leaf off the sleeve of her turtledove-coloured dress. Bianca's path has been decided. A powerful magnet pulls the carriage towards the halfway mark of their journey. Some call it destiny, others duty. And even though she knows that dresses for travelling ought to be dark in order to hide the dirt, she has chosen a light one so that every trace of change will be evident. This is her last adventure. Once she arrives at her final destination, she will be who they want her to be, or who they *expect* her to be.

Maybe.

❧ ❧

The master, Don Titta, isn't there when she arrives at Brusuglio in the evening. He isn't in the living room with the rest of them, in any case. His three daughters sit on the sofa, all dressed in white, their dresses flouncing, their tiny black feet hanging down like musical notes. Donna Clara, the older lady of the house, is dressed in black from head to toe and, with her marble eyes, looks like a large insect in her shiny satin. Her beauty hangs stubbornly from her cheekbones. The younger lady of the house, Donna Julie, Don Titta's wife, is dressed in white. She smiles kindly, though somewhat vaguely, on account of her guest. Lastly, there are two almost identical boys who come and go endlessly.

The living room is pale green and filled with the light of dusk. It seems cool to Bianca after her long, sticky journey. She feels dirty, dusty and out of place. And so she simply gives a slight bow, which to some may appear rude, but the younger lady understands.

'I will have Armida attend to you at once,' she says with a hint of a French accent. 'Go upstairs now. You must be exhausted. We will have time together tomorrow.'

Bianca climbs the stairs and goes down a long tiled and carpeted corridor. She is shown to her bedroom. It isn't very spacious but it is charming, with a white and gold sleigh bed. There is even an unexpected luxury: a bathroom entirely for herself. Armida, a giant of a woman with a solemn but gentle face, has already run her bath.

Bianca tests the water with her fingers. She hasn't even taken off her bonnet and is already imagining herself submerged.

'Is it too cold? I'll bring you a pot of boiling water.'

The woman is halfway down the hall when Bianca stops her.

'No, thank you. It will be fine.'

Armida comes back with the quick step of an experienced domestic servant.

'Then let me help you.'

Bianca draws back, embarrassed.

'I can manage on my own.'

Armida smiles, bows deeply, and then walks back towards the staircase.

Finally Bianca is alone. She frees herself of her travelling dress. She kicks off her undergarments, now grey with dust.

She takes a million bobby pins out of her hair, steps into the bath and crouches down, her knees to her chest, enjoying the sweet feeling of her breasts against her bones. Then she relaxes and settles back. Water seeps into her ears, cancelling out all noises except for the deep, low sound hidden inside seashells. Bianca has only ever seen the sea at night: twice – once coming in and once going out. It was a yawning nothingness, ferocious, black, cloaked in fog and frightening. But she still likes water more than anything.

She resurfaces and leans out, dripping wet, for a vase of peach-rose bath salts. She sniffs the pungent scent of artificial flowers and then hears the children playing outside. The boys are running, kicking up gravel, and arguing over something precious. Their accent is almost foreign: soft and harsh at the same time. She doesn't like it.

She emerges from the bath, enjoying the shivers that run down her clean body. She takes a dry linen towel, wraps it around herself, and goes back into her bedroom. A tray has been positioned on a little table with crooked legs. There is some milk, two white rolls, a cold chicken wing and three plums. She sits on the soft carpet and dines, clean and half naked, like a goddess, the wind billowing the curtains as if they are the sails of a ship at sea.

჻ ჻

She meets Don Titta for the first time two days after she has arrived, in the afternoon. Before this, she has been uncertain what to do with her time.

'For that, you need to speak to him. He's the one who summoned you here, isn't he?' Donna Clara remarked drily, giving Bianca the impression that she disapproved of the entire project.

So Bianca takes walks in the park, intent on measuring the extent of its wilderness and discovering where it turns into moorland, which she has heard can be somewhat dangerous.

'There are wild dogs out there,' the housemaid warned as she brushed, or rather pulled at, her hair.

Bianca, fighting the urge to cry out in pain, imagined the moorland filled with extraordinary creatures like shaggy, ferocious bears. In reality, the only creatures that cannot be ignored are birds. Thrushes, skylarks, blackcaps and thousands of other tiny unidentified creatures fill the sky with their baroque songs.

As she bends down to examine an unknown flower, focusing on the pale green-veined striations on the white petals, she doesn't notice him approaching. At the sound of snapping branches she turns around sharply and freezes. She doesn't know what to do next.

To say that they have met then, though, is an exaggeration: she has simply seen him. He doesn't even notice her. He continues striding on, at a rapid pace. He looks like a giant: tall, thin, bony – sickly even. His head is bare, he wears no frock coat; he looks more like a villain than a gentleman. His shirt is not even fully tucked into his trousers. His clothes cling to his body with the same sweat that drenches his hair, making it appear darker than it probably is. He walks briskly, his arms swinging wide and his hands spread. He mumbles to himself. A poem, Bianca thinks. Perhaps this is how he composes them: he wanders through the woods and allows himself to become transfixed by divinity. Maybe it's even in Latin.

'So you saw him?' Armida asks the next day, in the matter-of-fact way of the domestic help, who see and know everything, as she brushes her hair, pulling a little less this time. 'He roams around like a vagabond, talking to himself. He calls out plant names. Blah blah blah here and blah blah blah there. He does it for hours on end. Gentlemen are truly strange.'

He isn't present for lunch.

'My son has gone to Milan to attend to urgent business,' explains Donna Clara, before starting her soup. 'Be sure to make yourself available when he's ready to speak to you.'

Bianca would have enjoyed chatting with Donna Julie, but after just two spoonfuls of soup, the younger lady pushes herself away from the table and rises.

'I have to attend to little Enrico,' she says apologetically. 'He's got a fever again.'

And just like that she disappears up the staircase, followed by a maid carrying a tray of treats for the ill child. The little girls come in from the nursery in single file in search of their mother, awaiting their after-lunch ritual: a sweet and a kiss. But she is gone. So they stand there like lost ducklings. Their governess hurries them away, paying no attention to the youngest one's shrill screech.

Bianca still confuses the girls' names. Even though there are only three of them, they all look alike. Pietro, on the other hand, sits at the table with the adults. His eyelids are heavy; he has prominent dark brown eyes. They are almost black, opaque and unreadable.

'Does the little red pony belong to you?' Bianca asks now, trying to make conversation with him. 'What's his name?'

But he just looks down at his plate in silence.

Bianca spends the rest of the day reorganizing her clothes, going back and forth to the laundry, and freshening the items that need to be aired out, which is pretty much all of them.

When she comes down that evening, the only person at the dinner table is Donna Clara. She gives no explanation for the absence of the others and limits herself to glaring at Bianca impatiently. The cook serves stewed quail. Donna Clara throws herself at the frail little bodies rapaciously, sucking on the bones and drawing out the tender, dark meat. Bianca hates game. It is meat that was once so alive and is now sentenced to rot. She eats two slices of white bread then peaches with lemon juice for dessert.

'You're a delicate little thing,' observes the elderly lady, licking her lips.

᠅ ᠅

The next day, Bianca sees the master of the house approaching from afar and gives a hint of a curtsey. She is worried that she is wasting both her time and his being here. With her standing there, in his way, he has no choice this time but to look at her, the pale thing that she is. But instead of stopping, he walks on. He isn't any more composed than on the first day she saw him. Again, he is mumbling his strange botanical rosary. She watches him grab hold of a large buzzing insect with a swift movement of his right hand and hears as he squashes it between his index finger and thumb. And then he is gone, his mumbling and rustling footsteps gradually receding. She imagines the bug's cartilage cracking and squirting its thick and greasy fluid onto his fingers as if they are her own.

᠅ ᠅

Enrico recovers and goes back to bickering with Pietro. The two boys are very similar, with Enrico being the more timid. He always has a sullen look, as though expecting defeat. Instinctively, Bianca prefers him. She watches him chase after

Pietro, who has taken possession of the pony and cart and is now flogging the animal mercilessly. The pony runs and runs, as though fleeing from the pain, kicking up wings of gravel down the driveway. When Enrico realizes that he is never going to be able to catch Pietro or the pony, he throws himself down on the grass in frustration. Bianca walks over to him, pretending to have seen nothing.

'What's the pony's name?' she asks.

'My brother says you're a foreigner and we don't like foreigners,' he replies defiantly.

'Listen to me. Do you hear what I am saying? I'm not a foreigner.'

'I'm not going to listen to you. You're a spy. You'll spy on me and then tell Mamma everything, even if it isn't true.'

'What could I possibly tell her? That I saw a little boy chewing on a blade of grass?'

'My brother is horrible,' Enrico continues bitterly. 'He always wins because he's bigger. When I get big . . . do you think I will grow up to be bigger than him?'

He finally looks up at her. In the light of day she sees that his eyes are greenish-grey.

'I think so, yes,' answers Bianca, looking him up and down. 'You may be smaller now, but if you eat lots and exercise, you'll end up taller than him, I'm sure.'

It could happen: Pietro has a fairly solid build with robust, sculpted legs but Enrico has the long, delicate bone structure of a foal.

'Then one day I'll beat him and get the pony back, since it belongs to both of us. That's what Papa said. But Pietro always keeps it to himself.'

'Do you want to tell me his name?'

'Furbo. I named him. Do you like it?'

'It's nice. It suits him.'

'Well, I'm leaving,' says the little boy, standing up and smoothing out the wrinkles in his trousers. He wanders off without saying goodbye. But after a few steps he turns around. 'I guess you might not be a spy.'

❧ ❧

Five days after her arrival and she has still yet to formally meet him. She doesn't know what to do any more. His mother keeps saying he is in Milan, but now and then he emerges from the woods and startles her, only to quickly disappear again. And so, Bianca decides simply to start working.

The little girls, all dressed in white cotton, are playing Ring-a-Ring o' Roses on the great lawn, their brown hair gleaming in the sunlight. She sets up her easel near the poplar tree, places a pad upon it, and opens the mahogany box that holds her pencils on one side and her charcoal sticks on the other. The sight has reminded her of a Romney painting she saw in England, on one of the stops along her reverse Grand Tour.

In that painting, three little girls and a boy, dressed in summer sandals and tunics, dance like tiny deities while an older sister plays on the drums, an annoyed look across her face. The older child is clearly from another marriage, while the four dancers are siblings. And undoubtedly this bothers the older girl tremendously.

'Lady Anne looks as though she'd rather be somewhere else,' Bianca said to her father, as they stood contemplating the painting in one of the sitting rooms of the estate, which was located in some idyllic corner of the English countryside that was itself a work of art.

'You are right,' he agreed, without lifting his eyes from the painting. 'One can only hope that she eventually married well.'

'What on earth do you mean?' Bianca cried.

'I'm only teasing,' her father said firmly. 'I only said it to see if you were listening. Although really, do you think that she had any other option?'

That memory is fading fast. She is here now, and the colours of this reality are different and fiercer than any painting. The whiteness of the little girls is almost too painful to look at against the full greens of the forest and meadow.

Donna Clara comes up behind her quietly, announcing her arrival by clearing her throat. Bianca is always startled by how thin she is. Once it might have been considered a virtue but now her figure seems almost comical. Bianca gives a slight curtsey without interrupting her pencil strokes.

When you are working, her father said, *never stop what you're doing just because someone tells you it's teatime.*

This echo lasts only a second; short but penetrating. And when she comes back to her senses, as if emerging from a trance, she readies herself to respond to a circumstantial comment with a circumstantial smile. Instead, Donna Clara just coughs.

'You're quite talented. My son has chosen well. He and his eccentricities . . .'

Bianca wipes her hands on a rag, pleased with the unexpected compliment.

Meanwhile, the girls have finished playing and come over to the easel, their tiny hands behind their backs. They look at the picture, curious but confused. Their governess apologizes quickly.

'They wanted to see your drawing, but . . .'

Of course they are disappointed. They expected to see clear representations of themselves. They shift their gaze from her to the piece of paper and back again, perplexed, waiting for an explanation or perhaps some kind of magic. They expect her to take a brush, dip it into her watercolours and fix everything.

'Those marks,' Donna Clara explains patiently to the girls, leaning forward a little, 'are the lines of your bodies. Miss Bianca has caught you in the moment. This is Giulietta, lifting her foot in the air. This is you, Matilde, and here is Franceschina, skipping. Your faces will come later. You aren't running away, but the moment is. Isn't that right?'

Bianca nods.

'All paintings start out like this – a sketch, a jumble of marks,' Bianca explains. 'Some stay sketches, others turn into finished paintings. Do you girls draw?'

'I can draw daisies,' says Giulietta, the eldest.

'One day we can try and draw together if you'd like,' Bianca hears herself say.

Donna Clara breaks up the group as if they are a brood of chicks.

'Shoo, shoo, leave Miss Bianca alone now and go back to your games. Oh, what good children,' she adds to Bianca as they run off. 'Angels from heaven, here to bless our lives.'

Bianca is surprised to hear such simple, affectionate words when just a moment earlier, in speaking to the children, she had used such a different tone. With newfound respect, Bianca watches as the elderly lady leaves.

⁂

The following evening he joins them at dinner. At last. He looks elegant, dressed in a light grey waistcoat. His face, in the candlelight, is no longer ghostlike. Actually, he looks like a truly healthy man who spends much of his time outdoors. He extends his hand to her in a modern half-bow. The children sit very still, delighted by their father's presence, and keep shooting him reverential glances. Donna Clara stares at her son feverishly, as if to keep him from disappearing again, turning away only to oversee the servants. Even Donna Julie seems more serene than usual and for once she stays at the table from the beginning to the end of the meal, without running off to take care of someone. Her charges are all present. She has fair skin, a braided bun of thick brown hair, and a long, delicate neck. Every so often she rests her elbow on the tablecloth in a childish, coy manner, before resuming her composed posture again as if it were a bad habit.

They have potato and leek soup, cold chicken in aspic, and a medley of shredded carrots and courgettes, all of which are truly pleasing to the eye. The meal ends with a blancmange with wild strawberry sauce. It is a meal for convalescents. Or for kings. Or for convalescent kings.

'The children picked the strawberries. They got incredibly dirty but it made them happy doing it,' says the young mother, rolling her Rs in the French way with charm.

He eats voraciously in a silence that is more intimate than solemn. He stares straight ahead, absorbed in his own thoughts.

'I have been toying with the idea of letting the children have a small vegetable garden,' he says finally. 'Beyond the shed, by the well, so that it's easy for watering. It is important that the children have a garden.'

'But the season is almost over. What could you plant? And really, Titta, next to the well? I think it's dangerous.' Donna Clara speaks assertively, pressing her napkin to her lips. 'I think I'll have another helping of dessert,' she adds. Her empty plate disappears and a new portion of blancmange arrives instantly.

'Your mother is right,' says Donna Julie. 'The girls barely know how to swim yet. And they're so fragile.'

'I hope you're not worried that they might get too much sun.

At least they would look a little healthier. They're as pale as linen,' the master of the house says. 'And you, signorina, do you have freckles? I imagine you were raised in the English manner.'

Bianca, addressed for the first time, wipes her mouth delicately on her napkin while thinking of her reply.

'In the English manner? I wouldn't know. I'd say I was raised rather rigorously. My father always had clear opinions when it came to children. I learned to swim when I was three years old. Everyone knew how to swim at the lake. My brothers and I spent all our time outside, in every season. During the winter they would dress me like a boy in leggings and trousers, to keep me warm and comfortable.'

Donna Clara raises her eyebrows while swallowing her last pink and white spoonful of blancmange. She licks her lips as a cat would its whiskers.

'My mother didn't entirely agree with his approach,' Bianca adds, looking at the older lady. 'But then she gave up arguing.'

'Is your mother English as well?' Donna Clara asks, her plump hands resting at either side of her plate.

'No, she was Italian,' answers Bianca.

'Oh, I'm sorry.'

'We had an English tutor,' Bianca offers, to fill the silence.

Donna Clara glows with approval.

'Just like our own Innes! He's away now, taking the waters in the Venetian countryside. He took a break from us, so to speak.'

'Did your tutor take an interest in plants?' Don Titta asks her. 'Or did you start to botanize on your own?'

His eyes are animated and observant. His tone soft and worldly. It occurs to Bianca that the forest ghost she has previously encountered could have been his crazy twin brother. Their physical appearance is the only trait that connects them.

She pauses for a moment before answering, weighing that verb in her mind – *to botanize*. She likes it tremendously.

'I started out on my own, when and where I could,' she explains. 'I would ask the names of flowers and trees, and then compare the leaves with images in books, and learn the scientific nomenclature. I used to own a herbal encyclopaedia. I did the kinds of things that all children do. And then, a dear family friend helped me learn a great deal more.'

She lapses momentarily into silence, distracted by the recollection of afternoons spent at Conte Rizzardi's home, with that smell of dust, old paper and tanned leather, a smell that would forever remind her of her fondness for study. The large estate and its domesticated wonders lay outside; theory was separated from practice by just a pane of glass. There were countless volumes of books – she used to call them the diaries of flowers – and they were ready to spill their knowledge and complex terminology.

'The flowers are not shown in the manner in which they truly exist,' the count had explained. 'It is only a representation. There is always a slight margin of difference between the way the eye sees and the hand draws.'

She recalls the old man's patience, the way he'd take her by the hand out to the vegetable and flower garden to see the originals.

Don Titta's voice brings her back to reality.

'If you could come by my study tomorrow morning after ten, we can discuss the tasks I would like to entrust to you.'

He then pushes his chair aside and stands.

'Would you please excuse me,' he says, and leaves the room.

The two boys wait for him to disappear down the corridor before imitating him and running off in the opposite direction, towards the French window, which opens onto the darkness.

The girls and the women remain seated. The younger lady is surprisingly animated, her cheeks flushed.

Donna Clara observes, 'Julie, my dear, you look quite rosy this evening. Have you started to follow my very own wine treatment? A nice glass of Marsala after a meal will have you wanting more, to be sure. You should try it too, Miss Bianca,' she says, turning to Bianca. 'It won't do you any harm. I'll call for some.'

The maid appears with a tray, decanter and tiny glasses. The liquid looks like aged gold in the crystal. As it touches Bianca's lips, it releases a burst of sun and almonds. It is heavy, full-bodied.

Donna Julie raises her glass to look at it through the light.

'What a lovely colour. Like an ancient coin,' she says, but puts it down. 'I apologize, Mother, but I just can't tonight. I don't need it. I am so pleased that he's doing better that I don't need it to feel well.'

Donna Clara flashes a piercing glare in her direction, as if to quiet her. Then she looks down and, without waiting for the maid to do so, pours herself some more wine.

❦ ❦

Donna Clara advises that Minna will serve as Bianca's personal maid.

'She's too delicate for heavy labour and needs to learn a trade,' she says, holding the girl's arm and forcing her to bow clumsily in front of her, intimating that Minna can learn her trade at Bianca's expense as Bianca herself is young and probably doesn't know any better. And with that she leaves the room.

Minna is just a young girl. She has pink cheeks and dark brown hair, which she wears in a bun with a few loose curls.

Her mouth is sealed shut with shyness. Bianca tries to meet the child's gaze, but it is as if a dark force keeps her chin glued to her chest. Bianca pretends not to notice. She continues to organize her clothes, something she hates doing because it reminds her of their inadequacy. Minna approaches her timidly, aware of her duties as maid, and begins to help put away her freshly laundered undergarments. Someone knocks at the door. Minna hurries forward to open it.

'Oh, it's you!' she says, glowing with happiness.

'May I come in?'

The person at the door is another young girl whom Bianca has noticed before, out walking with the governess. She is older, taller, but must be twelve or thirteen at the most, with lively grey-green eyes and freckles on her cheeks.

'I'm Pia, signorina, here to serve you,' she says.

There is nothing really for her to do. However, Bianca soon realizes that she has only come up out of curiosity. Pia looks around the room, peeking into the half-closed wardrobe as if hoping to uncover a mystery. Then she looks over at Minna, who has shrunk into a corner.

'You're a lucky one, aren't you?' she says with unabashed envy, running over to hug her tightly. Minna lets herself be hugged without moving her arms or altering her expression. 'You deserve kisses! That's what you deserve.' Pia plants one on her cheek. 'There, there, what good are kisses if we don't give them?'

The little one continues to stare at the floor, without smiling. Pia, satisfied, curtseys, offers her respects, and then leaves.

What a strange household, Bianca thinks to herself, *where maids have such independence*, but the scene has cheered her up.

Minna, meanwhile, comes back to her senses, stands up straight, and gives a deep curtsey, holding up each side of her skirt as the little girls have been taught to do by their governess.

'I am Minna, my lady, here to serve you. What would you like me to do? Shall I brush your hair? Shall I organize your clothes? Shall I put your hairbrushes in order?'

Bianca smiles.

'For now, nothing. You're free to go. I need to get my things ready and I like doing that myself. I will expect you tomorrow morning at seven, at the door to the garden.'

Minna looks at her, disappointed.

'But . . .'

'Go downstairs now. I'm sure they will have something for you to do in the kitchen.'

Minna mumbles something then turns and walks away, no further bows or farewells – insulted.

⁂

Bianca's meeting couldn't have gone any better. He ushered her into his study; a room of modest size, lined with books. There was no pale green, antique-rose or peacock-blue wallpaper here, as in the rest of the house. Instead, there were several ox-blood leather straight-backed chairs. A sombre pattern of brown rhombuses lined the walls and a black crucifix hung above the empty fireplace. He sat behind a large desk. She took a seat in front of him. They talked. They talked about botany, classifications, colours and chemistry. Bianca noticed right away that he was knowledgeable, passionate and precise. He only spoke of things of which he was certain. She could tell he was progressive on account of his ideas and the way he spoke about implementing them.

'Some people here think I'm crazy. I'm the stereotype of a

city gentleman obsessed with foreign ideas and with domesticating nature. But we mustn't ever stop. We mustn't rest. The countryside hasn't changed for centuries, and yet progress affects it just as much as it affects all of us. And it is precisely for this reason that I feel it is my duty to experiment.' Then, as though he had been too solemn, he added with a furtive smile, 'It's also a lot of fun. It helps keep my mind on something. Otherwise, things get too stirred up in here.' He motioned towards his temple before brushing back a strand of hair from his forehead. His hands were elegant, she noticed: he had long fingers, delicate wrists, and manicured nails. 'I'm no theoretician, don't be fooled,' he said, trying to read Bianca's stare. 'But I know what soap and water are for, I know it is proper to wash and be clean.'

They shared a brief laugh, and then, somewhat more seriously, they passed on to more concrete topics of discussion: numbers, deadlines and her fee. They discussed everything that had been previously written out in black ink on white paper. There were still some wrinkles that needed smoothing out. He addressed each clause of their agreement carefully, as if he was worried he might offend her. She thought it might be disagreeable for him to discuss such topics with a woman. But she proceeded calmly and agreed a deal which, at least in premise, would be profitable for both parties. Except for one, rather important, detail.

'Sir, it's almost summer. This year the season is extraordinarily hot and it seems that the heat will last. You have called me here now yet you are hiring me for a task that will only be completed next spring. This means that I will need to be here for an entire year and possibly longer. Am I correct in my understanding?'

He gave a quick smile.

'Everything has been taken into consideration. The winter will offer you the perfect time to reflect and draw. When the family returns to Milan you can enjoy a bit of the city with us, if you like, as I hope you will, while we wait for the pleasant weather to return. I am keen for you to be able to experience these subjects in all their states: life, dying, death and resurrection. It's quite crucial to really understand what you will be portraying. Time is secondary. Don't you agree?'

'I see,' she said, nodding. She had never before been so far from the house she had grown up in for such a long period of time. But the place she had once called home no longer belonged to her.

He jotted down a sum on a piece of paper and handed it to her. The figure was so incredibly high that she could not refuse it. A year it would be.

And so she stood up and shook his hand. It was the right moment, before either of them was at a loss for words, before the silence between the two strangers became as deep as a well. Bianca didn't want to find herself in any complicated situations. All she wanted was to be at ease in the house. If she encountered Don Titta in the garden again, with his long beard and dirty shirt, she would once more pretend not to see him. She would imagine it was his restless twin, a harmless creature, a village madman. This estate was almost a village, was it not? She would ignore him, like everyone else did, either out of respect or because he was the lord of the house and a poet. And, Bianca thought as she left his study, everyone knows that poets are unlike ordinary men.

※ ※

'It's a simple task. You're smart and you'll do it well. Of course, there's the chance that you might get bored with the environment and the people. It's a test of patience for you. A form of discipline. It will do you good. Accept the offer.'

Bianca is thinking back to her final conversation with her father, many months prior, after she received the letter. It was a long yet concise missive; the penmanship was pointed and oblique, the paper ruled and heavy. There was a wax seal on the verso of the envelope, which she kept touching with the tip of her finger.

'Why me, Father?' she asked him.

'Because there's no one like you. Not here. Because you're unique, darling.'

'But to be so far away for so long . . .'

'It was bound to happen sooner or later. It's what you've chosen to do. You didn't think you'd be here your whole life, did you? I didn't raise you that way. You are perfectly able to take care of yourself. You have seen some of the world. My only concern is that you might bury yourself in the countryside. Personally, I would prefer that you went to the city. But on the other hand, you need to be where your subjects are. Follow them. This is an important commission. It could mark the beginning of a career . . .'

She did as he bade. She was already buried in the countryside after all; the difference would be the company.

The letter proposed a commissioned project in a tone that Bianca couldn't define. It was both serious and vague. Or perhaps it was just the unfamiliar nature of the idea itself and what it implied that confused her. The sender of the letter had seen and appreciated some of her watercolours of landscapes and botanical subjects, it seemed – the ones she had sold on the insistence of her neighbour and long-time friend Count Rizzardi to an illustrious guest.

The intended project was to depict every flower and plant on a specific estate in Lombardy.

'I would like to bequeath to posterity not only my compositions in verse and prose, as is my craft, but also my flowers and my plants, which are no less significant to me. I am inclined to spend much of my time with them and desire to capture their perfection in order to have them forever with me, even in winter, even if they might never flower or bloom again. A large part of my culture is experiment, chance, failed attempts. As an amateur, the pleasure is as great as the risk.'

He's a gambler, Bianca thought. She liked the idea. She wrote back herself. Perhaps the sender was expecting a letter from her father; at the time she was no more than eighteen years old. But the letter was addressed to her, was it not? Don Titta was clearly a man of liberal ideals with a modern point of view. He was widely seen as a worldly man too. But it was also known that he had chosen a sober and secluded existence for himself.

'You will live within our family,' he specified in the letter. 'Ours is a simple life, far from everyday distractions.'

'Sounds like an interesting fellow,' her father added. 'It seems as though he understands what he needs and despite his profession has managed to free himself from the lures of fame. It's admirable, I'd say. See it as a great adventure, Bianca. And I will be here, waiting for you, if you don't take a different path along the way. Though, of course, I will be happy either way.'

'What other paths?' she protested. 'The only right path is the one that will bring me back here.'

'Anything can happen,' he said solemnly.

And like that, they made up their minds.

☙ ❧

Anything can happen.

His disease arrived swiftly. They had been out on one of their favourite walks, at La Rocca. As always, the lake looked different from so high up. She wished she could fly over it and see their little white house, the details of their garden, and the winding, rocky path that disappeared into the shadows of the parkland.

'Look at the lake, Papa,' she had said. 'It looks like it's made of turquoise.'

She turned back and saw him bent over, speechless with pain, deathly pale. Bianca knelt down beside him, overcome with fear. And yet, amazingly, she managed to contain it. They waited together for the pain to subside a little and then set out homewards. He leaned on her out of caution. She was his walking stick in flesh and blood.

'It's nothing,' he said reassuringly at the dinner table that night, still quite pale but stronger now. 'It's just a sign that I'm growing old, Bianca. I'm not made for La Rocca any more.'

'Then we will simply have to take our walks at the Cavalla,' she answered, relieved. 'There's a nest of baby geese near Villa Canossa. I will show it to you tomorrow. The goslings are about to hatch.'

Instead, she went alone. He chose to stay at home and rest. The baby geese had just been born and were grey, damp and snug. The mother's beak was red, ready to cut into something. Bianca kept her distance and sketched them on the pad she always carried with her. On her return trip, she saw the doctor's carriage from a distance. Her father died two days later, seized by another attack, this time fatal.

Everything had been decided far in advance: the property was entrusted to Bartolomeo, some of the money went to Zeno to finance his military career, and some went to Bianca, who was granted lifetime occupancy of her own little quarter of the household. Thank heavens Bianca still had somewhere of her own. Bartolomeo, who had filled out after his successful nuptials, and his pregnant wife quickly started eyeing the home and the garden with the cynicism of new proprietors. To watch them wander about the beloved rooms talking about carpets and decorations made her unbearably sad. They had agreed that Bianca's rooms would remain locked and intact until her return, but it was still torture for her to say goodbye to her collection of silhouettes and miniatures, her small rosewood desk, and her balcony that looked out onto the lake. It had been torture but also a relief, because it was evident that the spirit of the home had departed with their father. Her leaving had come at the right moment.

Her neighbour Count Rizzardi was, as ever, a gentleman.

'Remember,' he said, 'there will always be a room for you in my home.'

But all of a sudden he had seemed so old to her, as if her father's death had forced him, too, closer to that threshold.

Zeno had his own opinion about work and women.

'You're a girl, for heaven's sake.'

'So what?'

'So it isn't right that you go prancing off alone, waving that letter around. It's a passport to trouble, I'm telling you.'

'What should I do then, according to you?'

'You could get married. Girls tend to do that, you know.'

'Not all of us.'

'But you're pretty.'

'And I have no dowry. My only asset is this,' she said, waving her fingers in his face. He took hold of her hand, pretended to bite it, and then hugged her tightly.

'You're going to get yourself into a sticky situation, Bianca.

You could always live with me, you know. You could be my manservant.'

'Oh, sure,' laughed Bianca. 'I could cut my hair, wear boy's clothing and sleep on a cot outside your room.'

'When you were younger you could easily have passed for a boy. And you bossed us both around.'

They smiled in recollection.

Bartolomeo, on the other hand, seemed relieved at the prospect of her departure. Until then, he had been living in discomfort in his wife's home and waiting for his inheritance. It was evident that he now wanted to enjoy his new circumstances to the full, without any obstacles.

'Come home whenever you want,' he said, because he had to, because a brother should say that. She pursed her lips into a smile, trying to remember the boy with stars in his eyes, the boy he was, before becoming the rotund dandy now standing in front of her.

※ ※

'There's something I'd like to show you, if you'll follow me?'

Bianca wipes her hands on a rag. Donna Clara leads the way. She uses a highly varnished black cane, but is incredibly quick for a woman of her small stature. She crosses the lawn, goes into the house, up the stairs, and down a hall that Bianca has not yet explored. As she moves, Donna Clara's starched clothes crackle and whine. Bianca wonders whether she still wears a whalebone corset, as was the vogue in her youth, and if so, who tightens it for her each morning.

She stops in front of a small painting, near a row of nymph statuettes. It is a portrait of a mother and child. Positioned right in front of a window, it soaks up all the natural light. Bianca studies the work with the eye of a professional. The dark

background allows the [...]
One has curly brown [...]
blond. The mother has a[...]
perhaps due to her curls [...]
a resemblance between th[...]
outside: the same curve in [...]
She understands.

'I was pretty, wasn't I?' [...]
pomegranate-shaped handle[...]
boy . . . he was five years old th[...]
school and left for Paris with n[...]
a long time. An eternity, it seen[...] [...]tta grew older,
our paths crossed again. He can[...] to Paris when he was twenty
and we've never been apart since.'

And then, as though fearing she has revealed too much,
she wraps her shawl around her, turns around and walks away,
leaving Bianca to contemplate the painting on her own. She
notices other details now: the boy's gaze seems restrained
and distracted, as if there is a dog somewhere beyond the picture frame, barking and inviting him to play. She notices his
mother's sharp expression, like that of a fox, with her slight, coy
smile. The pair are positioned closely within the frame, but it is
clear that each one anxiously wants to be elsewhere.

᙮ ᙮

Bianca starts her work. Following the generous instructions of
her master – it makes her smile to think of him as her master,
and yet that is his role – she takes all the time she needs. Each
morning she carries out her box and easel and a large, somewhat frayed, straw hat. Soon, hampered by all the trappings,
she decides to leave the more bulky props behind. Feeling light
and reckless, she goes off to where domesticated nature ends

Wild is perhaps an exaggeration, for in ... – who follows her like a shadow – are ... one. There is always some gardener snipping, ... ecting and carrying away dry branches. The men ... up from their work, nor do they speak to the ladies. ... a constantly gets the feeling that she is being watched. But ... ch time she turns around, the man nearby will be looking elsewhere and seems interested only in his pruning tool, his axe, or the clutch of weeds he holds in his clenched fist, raising them to examine the naked roots. It feels like wandering in a forest full of Indians: eyes and blades everywhere. But this is the only fear that the women allow themselves. Though, in fact, Minna is also afraid of insects, which is strange for a girl who has grown up in the countryside. She runs away from bumblebees, horseflies and praying mantises.

'They won't harm you,' Bianca says, picking up an insect in the palm of her hand to examine its big eyes before placing it back on a leaf, which it grips like a castaway at sea. But the girl keeps far away, and stares in admiration at Miss, who isn't afraid of anything. Maybe it is because she is English. *The English are strange*, Minna thinks.

Insects, children, flowers: how limited Bianca's new world is and yet, at the same time, how incredibly full of potential ideas. Insects and children: Pietro has the malicious insistence of a hornet. Enrico, on the other hand, has the feeble blandness of a caterpillar that knows only its own mouth. The girls are like grasshoppers, green, lilac, baby blue, all eyes, never at a standstill. Minna looks like a young beetle: the tiny, iridescent kind that never knows where to perch, and is capable only of short flights.

Bianca sketches and captures specific moments, sensations, gestures and movements. She speaks the plants' names out loud. She is drawn to the plants and flowers whose names she doesn't know. The estate at Brusuglio offers an unlimited variety of new species. There is the *Liquidambar*, rooted into the earth, and pointing to the sky as if it is an arrow. There is the little green cloud, a *Sophora*. There is *Sassafras albidum* with leaves that look like gloved hands. There is the *Catalpa* tree, known as 'the hippopotamus' because it is so large. And then there are the shrubs: the *Genista*, the *Coronilla*, the *Hamamelis*, with its dishevelled and fading flowers, and the *Mahonia*, which smells like honey. And then the plants with modern names like *Benthamia* or *Phlomis*, names which often sound too lofty in comparison to their humble appearance.

It doesn't feel like work. It isn't that different from her ardent childhood and adolescent pastime, except for the absence of the person dearest to her. A gracious but inadequate group of strangers has taken his place. As a unit, they only make her long for her own family even more.

※ ※

Everyone in the household is very devout. A small parish church has been built near the estate by Carlo, Donna Clara's deceased lover and the previous master of the house. The pungent smell of its recent construction blends with the overpowering scent of incense. The priest, a burly old man with a kind face, entrusts the censer to a young altar boy. Bianca lets herself become distracted by the trails of light blue smoke. She contemplates the Good Shepherd, who gazes out at everyone, one by one, from beside the apse. She feels surrounded by lambs. The children sit in the second row with their governess. Pietro takes something out of his pocket and shows it to Enrico, covering it with his other hand like a shield, so his sisters cannot glimpse it. Of course, they stretch out their necks to see and, in so doing, miss echoing the psalm. Their grandmother turns around from the front row with a threatening scowl. The girls fall back into line and the object disappears into Pietro's pocket once more. Enrico sighs. The children's mother and father are two composed backs of solid mass.

Bianca's gaze wanders. Several old women sit in another row. Not many country folk could allow themselves the luxury of attending two services a day, morning and evening. Since Bianca is not a believer, she wonders how she would cope with these rituals.

It is Don Dionisio, the elderly priest, who surprises her. She is wandering in the park one day when he approaches with a timid bow. He holds out his arms towards hers.

'Come with me,' he says, opening his hands to her and taking a few steps backwards. She raises her arms and makes to move forward. He stops and drops his hands by his side, as if he has asked too much of her too soon; hers are left hanging in air. She doesn't really know how to behave with Catholic priests, or with priests in general, but she senses that obedience is appreciated so she hurries to catch up to him. They walk on, both lifting their skirts from the ground in strange unison. He stops in front of a small door to the side of the church, which has, it seems, been built for a dwarf. 'Here we are.' He pushes it open, bends forward, blocks the passageway for a moment, and then disappears inside. She follows him in, head bowed. She finds herself inside a simple, bare vestry, where a crucifix hangs between two tall, narrow windows of light brown glass, which create an amber light. 'That door is always open,' he says. 'Prayer doesn't always happen on a schedule. It's not a postal carriage. God comes to us when we least expect him. And you can do the same.'

From that moment on, Bianca doesn't enter the realm of the

kingdom of God on a twice-daily schedule. She doesn't have to explain herself to anyone and no one asks her a thing about it. Donna Clara seems perplexed but not altogether amazed.

The governess whispers to her in confidence and with a hint of envy, 'Innes doesn't come to service either, you know.'

But prayer occurs within the home, too, and without any forewarning. Donna Clara keeps a jet rosary on her at all times, wrapped around her wrist like a bracelet, a Christ figurine dangling from it like a strange sort of charm. Whenever the conversation turns into an appeal to the saints and Mary, she slips it off and clings to those beads that reconcile the heavens and earth. Donna Julie follows her example. The children mumble their Hail Marys in a distracted singsong. Don Titta, on the other hand, doesn't pray. When he is present, he simply lowers his head and folds his hands together, as if prayer is just another opportunity to leave this world and get lost in another. Bianca takes advantage of those moments to study them all. She is the only one to keep her eyes open.

≈ ≈

Innes, the English tutor who doesn't attend Mass, returns from his salubrious holiday. The little girls, who have been anxiously awaiting his arrival since morning, dash towards him as soon as he descends from the carriage, screaming with glee. The boys look up silently from their game – a complex construction made up of small pieces of wood – but only when their governess tells them to, do they stand to greet their tutor, taking their time to brush away the sawdust from their trousers. Innes sweeps Giulietta up while the other girls hug him tightly around his knees. He is very tall, Bianca thinks, enormous, even for an Englishman. She is sitting in the shade of the portico with a book in her lap. Innes laughs and stumbles forward,

35

the little girls still clinging to him. When Donna Clara comes out, everything resumes its order. The sisters let go and line up. The boys join the group so that the family formation is complete. Bianca stands with the others while the servants, Berto and Barba, unload a worn suitcase and an incongruous carpet bag embroidered with purple flowers. When the carriage departs, the governess runs to shut the gates, too excited to leave it to the valet, before taking her place at the end of the line and staring intently at the new arrival.

'Dear, dear, dear Innes!' Donna Clara exclaims, opening her arms to him and clutching him briefly. Her face only reaches to his chest. 'I trust you are well rested and fortified. You must tell me everything about the Paduan spas. I, too, would like to take the waters there one day . . . when I find time to leave the family!'

As always, Donna Clara has placed herself in the precise middle of the circle that is her whole world. Her gaze is its radius and it is as though everything that happens has to be connected to her in some way, to make her shine – if only from reflected light. Such is her arrogance, and it is supported by rank and habit. Innes doesn't pay it the least attention, or perhaps he is just used to it.

'Donna Clara, you have no use for miracle waters. Here at Brusuglio lies the fountain of youth. I am certain it's somewhere here on the estate and you're keeping it secret while I wander high and low to find it!'

Innes speaks Italian with no trace of an English accent. Bianca finds out later that his mother is Italian, too. He switches immediately to his paternal language when talking to the children and when Donna Clara introduces Bianca to him.

'And here is Miss Bianca, with whom you will have a lot in common, I'm sure. But you must speak our language together from time to time. We don't want any conspirators in the house!'

And with this, the children take hold of him and drag him away to see a brood of ducklings. They are halfway down the path when the master of the house leans out the top-floor window.

'Innes! Finally!'

The Englishman turns around with a smile, unable to free himself from the grasp of the little ones.

'My friend, I've just returned and already I'm being held captive!'

'I can see that,' replies Don Titta. 'As soon as you manage to escape from that tribe of savages, you will find me in my study.'

Innes smiles in agreement before letting himself be dragged off once more.

༝ ༝

His full name is Stuart Aaron James Innes. He studied at Oxford before the collapse of his family business – shipping and trade in the Indies – forced him into another, truer, profession. His natural passion for travel and a strong desire to avoid ridicule from his peers led him to leave England. This is his third appointment as tutor. He has already been to Paris and the Savoy region before being stranded – his words – in the Milanese countryside. He tells her all this in their common language, standing together beneath the portico, waiting for dinner to be announced. Darkness falls sluggishly, little by little, first swallowing up the forest in the distance and then the confines of the great lawn. His hair is curly and somewhat long. He constantly brushes it away from his face in an unintentional, almost feminine, gesture. His eyes are of a piercing blue, strong yet distant. He wears a thin, precise moustache and has a hint of a beard that gives him a medieval air. His elegance is sober and neat. His frock coat, though on its last legs, is impeccably pressed and beautifully cut. After telling her his story Innes is quiet for a long moment, taking in the view of the estate, which is so beautiful in this, its bluest hour.

'I am pleased that you are here,' he says. 'I feel like your presence will make my exile more tolerable.'

Bianca thinks this comment rather dramatic and somewhat forward, and hides herself behind a silence that he interprets as shyness. And perhaps this is for the best.

At the dinner table that evening, he and Don Titta are the only ones to talk. They speak of another poet, an Englishman and old acquaintance of Innes's, who lives somewhere between Venice and the countryside. The man in question keeps his horses at the Lido so that he can ride along the beach, where sea meets sky. They speak, too, of a mutual friend, Jacopo, who died in uncertain and mysterious circumstances.

At one point, Donna Clara throws her napkin down on the table in irritation.

'Can't we talk about something that is of interest to us, too?'

Her son glances over at her with calculated slowness.

'I am surprised you do not find any of this interesting. It concerns all of us.'

Bianca would like to know what he means and struggles to find the way to phrase her question, but stops when Donna Julie places a delicate hand on her husband's arm.

'Your absence has been a burden to your mother. Don't be surprised if she seeks your full attention at one of the rare times you are at dinner with us.'

There is an exchange of glances between Titta and Innes that reveals a certain tacit understanding.

'I apologize, Mother dear,' he says. 'Sometimes I forget that time passes differently for me than it does for you.'

Satisfied, Donna Clara replies, 'It's because we're women and without you men we're nothing and we know nothing.'

'Only if you want it to be so,' he retorts.

She lets the matter drop and changes the subject, moving on to a discussion of silkworms and the experiments Ruffini is conducting in Magenta.

'Perhaps, we can go and visit. What do you think?'

❧ ❧

And just like that, the whole family is back together, and life in the villa regains its pleasant routines. The poet joins them more frequently for dinner since Innes has returned; it is clear that he appreciates regular male company. Unlike the governess (whom Bianca starts calling Nanny, quickly followed by everyone else), who is encouraged to disappear after meals with the children, both Innes and Bianca remain seated at the table. Their opinions, it seems, are both desired and appreciated. They speak about everything, from the astronomical cost of seeds from Holland to the washerwoman's marriage and the secret societies of illuminati in Milan.

Innes, who goes to the city twice a week to attend gatherings of a group of fellow countrymen living abroad, always returns with news that excites something more than a polite curiosity in the poet. And just like that, the two of them will begin a discussion that often uses the word 'fatherland'. The term explodes like a firecracker in the centre of the table. Mother and daughter-in-law will look at each other worriedly. Donna Clara will abruptly interrupt with some mindless topic of discussion: Enrico's latest stomach ache, the umpteenth doctor's visit on account of Giulietta's fever, or the pestilence of rabbits. Bianca, who has seen and heard more than would generally have been allowed for a woman of her age and status, and who has also learned a great deal from her father, is still not quite the free and complete creature that she desires to be. So she remains silent, hushed by good sense, and yet impatient and eager to say something bold and intelligent that will make these two men look at her in admiration and realize that women have minds too. But no, she says nothing. She doesn't have a legacy of ideas; her best tutor left her too soon. Bianca is like a half-finished marionette, a prisoner carved out of wood. But she may not fully know it. *If you could see me now, Father,* she thinks, *how I take in every new word, every modern sentence in an attempt to understand how the world is changing, just as you wanted me to . . .* If he could see her, he would surely be troubled.

※ ※

She overhears voices while walking past an open French window.

'She's beautiful but glacial too. Her name suits her. White is a frigid colour. She's like snow and ice and wind and storm. And hail.'

Someone chuckles.

'She doesn't show off, she keeps to herself. You can't expect her to mingle with us servants. She's an artist, she is.'

'Sure, an artist,' another voice speaks sarcastically. 'She's a servant, but one that gets a nice big bag of coins. All we get is soup, these rags on our back, a cot up in the attic and a kick in the arse!'

This brings laughter all round.

She wants to walk away but stays there, needing to hear more. She tries to shrug the comments off, but finds she can't. She just feels angry and upset. What irritates her most though is their accent, how they stretch out their 'e' sounds, as if they are made of rubber. And at the same time, behind her back, the servants laugh at the way she pronounces her own 'e' – quick and closed – and at her clenched double consonants. Deep down she knows they aren't malicious, though. They are just suspicious of anything new, like all country folk.

On another day a further snippet of conversation comes from another window, painting another portrait of Bianca.

'She's not talkative, and as far as conversation goes, she's as bristly as a porcupine, but she does draw like an angel. Or a devil! Anyway, it's the same difference,' Donna Clara says to a mysterious listener. And then she presses a finger to her lips and shushes herself, snickering slightly.

Bianca cannot see the gestures that soften the maliciousness of the words, though. She can only hear the pair's laughter. She walks away, vexed. She wanted to find out what they thought of her and now she knows.

※ ※

Since the return of Innes, evenings unfurl predictably. The men talk among themselves. The women sit in silent disapproval, eyeing them, and desperately seeking to change the subject. Bianca listens, watching Innes's demeanour and her master's fervour.

'Do you really think that things can go back to the way they were? I'm sorry, Don Titta, but I think you're dreaming. The memory of that Italian officer being killed by the mob just because he wore an Austrian uniform is still fresh in their minds.'

'It was not as if we wanted to kill him! It was an accident. You know how these mobs can be.'

'Of course. I can't imagine you, of all people, stabbing a poor disarmed man with an umbrella. But other people have other predilections. Need I remind you of the chef who was roasted at the Tuileries? Or Simon the executioner with blood up to his ankles? Listen to me, thanks to the death of that poor devil, the Austrians will have an easy time slamming their iron fist down on the table. There will be no lenience, not even towards you patricians.'

'It's too late to go back to tyranny. The people are tired. Populations are no longer indistinct masses; they want to claim their own identity. And we – we who know, we who understand – must try to act as new men or at least attempt to renew ourselves. Even if this means risking our world.'

'You should hear yourself, using words like "too late" and "no longer". You are so absolute, so excessive, my friend. When people have bread for dipping into their soup, calm will return. And we shall stick to fighting our princely battles in the safety of our salons.'

'What you say is terrible, Innes. Offensive, even. You make me feel guilty for how things are being played out. Though I suppose you are right. If I stay here, I am hiding behind a screen.'

Donna Clara looks up from her embroidery and interrupts the conversation with measured amusement.

'Ah, the new one *is* charming, isn't it? The chinoiserie is exquisite. Donna Crivelli saw it and ordered the exact same one . . .'

It is strange to hear the men speak so openly in front of the women. Usually their more serious discussions – complete with whispers and sudden outbursts – are reserved for the other drawing room and paired with cigars and alcoholic beverages. Bianca follows this exchange attentively but achieves only a vague understanding of it. She knows there is unease in Milan following recent violent acts. Even her journey here, to Brusuglio, risked being postponed. But the waters calmed and she took her uncomfortable carriage ride.

The last time she heard about world events directly was from her father. She no longer has anyone who will explain things to her. Zeno, in his letters, writes only about parties, hunting scores, or young ladies named after flowers.

Now Don Titta frowns at his mother as if he is surprised to see her sitting there, like she is a fly on a glazed cream puff.

'You know, the Oriental screen, the one we put in the boudoir up in the gallery,' Donna Clara insists.

'Indeed, it's incredibly useful,' her son observes drily. 'You never know when a gust of wind will blow in and hurl you across the room like a balloon.'

'Speaking of that, you know, I read in the *Gazzetta* that you can take a day trip by hot-air balloon from Morimondo now. You just need to book in advance.'

'It's not for me,' Donna Julie chimes in. 'I'm not going all the way up there. I'm too scared. If man were born to fly, our Lord would have designed us with wings like birds.'

'And a beak to peck with,' little Pietro interjects. Out of place and largely ignored, he chuckles to himself.

'To fly . . . what a dream,' Innes adds. 'We have no idea what feats man is capable of. This is the mystery and the miracle of science, is it not?'

'I prefer poetry,' observes Donna Clara. 'And not just because it provides us with food on our plates and a roof over our head. I've always admired it.' Placing a hand on her heart, she starts to recite:

> *Je serai sous la terre, et, fantôme sans os,*
> *Par les ombres myrteux je prendrai mon repos.*

'How lovely, Mother dear,' Don Titta says with a sigh, tossing his napkin onto the table in an act of surrender. 'Balls, screens and musty rhymes . . . I can't take this any longer.'

'Well, taste is taste. Poetry doesn't have to make us laugh, now, does it?' objects Donna Clara.

'Ask our Tommaso what he thinks of poetry when he arrives.'

Donna Clara can't resist the urge to get in the last word.

'Wonderful idea, my dear son. I will ask our Tommaso. That boy needs to have his head examined. You know, you are setting a terrible example for young people who aspire to an artistic life. *You* were good enough to succeed, but art is not meant for all. Let's just say that not all buns come out perfect.'

'Interesting. First I am told I am an artist and now I'm a pastry chef.'

'Well, what difference does it make? You knead with words, you knead with flour. People are as greedy for verses as they are for cream puffs. Luckily!'

Titta and Innes laugh heartily. Donna Clara looks around proudly, to see the impact of her witty remark. Donna Julie and Bianca only smile weakly. To Bianca, the thought of poetry being bought and sold like pastries – verses on a platter to be picked up with two fingers and eaten – disturbs her profoundly. It seems out of place and hateful, and she wonders why Don Titta is laughing.

'Our Tommaso' arrives to stay. Tommaso Reda is also a poet. His family wanted him to read law, but he was against the idea and felt summoned to a higher calling. Somewhat of a dreamer, he had even been locked up in prison for several nights on account of his erratic behaviour. Finally, Don Titta offered the boy help – and shelter too – something which angered Tommaso's father. Donna Clara explains all of this to Bianca without hiding her disapproval.

'It's not like his poems are as good as my son's. In my opinion, he doesn't even have a voice,' she says, stressing her words. 'He's just a figurine, a *gros garçon* used to having anything and everything. And Titta, God bless him, took him in like a stray cat only because he pities him. But this isn't a hotel. Not at all.'

Why the younger poet evokes such compassion in the master escapes Bianca. He is a young man of medium height, elegant and intense, with a worried look in his deep, dark eyes that contrasts with a cockiness stemming from the privileged status into which he has been born. He wanders indifferently about the home in which he is a guest. He has been coming here ever since he was a child, knows the estate inside and out, and everyone knows him. He eats little and drinks a great deal. He sleeps until late and his candle is the last to go out at night. This moderately excessive lifestyle blesses him with a feverish air and a pallor suited to the role he has chosen for himself. Bianca cannot decide if she likes him or not.

'Nature really does provide us with the most delicious things,' comments Donna Clara at the table one day. Her son nods in agreement as he enjoys the last glossy grains of rice from his plate.

'And the most beautiful,' adds Bianca impulsively.

'You are absolutely right,' Donna Julie agrees, looking over at her children all seated in a row.

But Bianca meant something else. She looks out of the French window again and admires the imperfect contours of the poplar trees, their tips like brushes painting the deep blue sky.

Don Titta leans forward.

'Yes,' he says, 'and art is the attempt to imitate the inimitable. There's something frustrating about that, isn't there? I obviously speak for myself, Miss Bianca. Perhaps it comes easily to you?'

'Oh, I don't know,' she answers, her mind returning to the table. 'My aim is more one of interpretation.'

'Which inevitably means transformation,' he remarks.

Bianca purses her lips into a smile.

'Perhaps. But that doesn't worry me. Mine is purely an attempt.'

'The advantage is that no poppy or anemone will complain about their portrait not looking like them. Or rather, I should say that *I've* never heard them complain,' Tommaso intervenes, smiling coyly. Bianca ignores him. 'But, who knows? Maybe they do complain,' he says, pursuing the fantasy.

'What? You think flowers can speak?' intervenes Giulietta, the only child to have followed the conversation, with all the attention possessed of a nine-year-old.

Enrico and Pietro chuckle.

'And you can hear them,' Enrico says, making a circular gesture with his index finger near his temple.

'I'm not crazy,' retorts Giulietta, offended, 'but I do listen!'

'And you're right to do so. Of course flowers can speak,' intervenes Bianca. 'But they have such tiny, soft voices that all the other noises drown them out. They are born, they live, and they die; why shouldn't they be able to speak?'

'This conversation is nonsense,' says Donna Clara, who has a fondness for eccentricities but only those she champions. 'Have you ever considered painting children's portraits rather than likenesses of flowers? There's a business in that.'

'Yes, indeed,' intervenes Tommaso, 'given that everyone is convinced that their child is the most beautiful in the world.

Surely you would find clients in Milan. Rich men who marry beautiful women in order to breed well. Men who don't always get it right the first time, but try and try again . . .'

'We can help you, if you'd like,' Donna Clara adds, not picking up the irony of Tommaso's comment. 'We know people, I mean.'

'No, that is not my profession,' Bianca says firmly.

'But you are so talented,' Donna Julie adds.

'And, anyway, Miss Bianca,' says Donna Clara with a laugh, 'if, in the end, you find that painting a convincing, realistic portrait of a child is impossible, you can always create one of your own instead.'

Her son and daughter-in-law laugh. Bianca blushes. She hates being the centre of attention but smiles nonetheless. Sly old lady. She certainly knows how to lead a conversation. It is an art that Bianca still has not mastered, and perhaps never will. It is easy to imagine Donna Clara perfectly at ease in a Paris salon, surrounded by beautiful minds, an elegant and respectable man at her side listening to her playful quips complacently. What sort of man was Conte Carlo, her lover? Why is there not even one portrait of him in the entire home? After all, the house was originally his. The older woman inherited it when he died. Perhaps they are hidden away like relics in the secrecy of her private chambers, or inside the locket around her neck, shut away like prisoners within her bosom . . .

'Miss Bianca? Miss Bianca? Where did you disappear to?' It is Innes. 'Our little dreamer,' he jokes.

'I wasn't dreaming. I was just thinking. Is it not allowed?' she answers, thrown by his intimate manner.

'If it takes you away from us, then no, my dear, it isn't. You must remain here. Propriety imposes this on us.'

Bianca looks at Innes in confusion. It's something Donna

Clara would say. She wonders whether Innes is mocking the mistress.

Don Titta intervenes.

'Personally, I don't mind. You are free to go where your heart and mind take you, on the condition that you will come back and join us here on earth occasionally. I understand.'

'Of course you do! You love to visit that secret place that Miss Bianca disappears to, isn't that right?' laughs Donna Julie. 'Far away from here, from us, from our incessant voices, the buzzing disturbance that we are.'

'But I love my crazy bees, too, and you know it,' he says, smiling. 'And love has the right to disturb me whenever it feels like it.'

※ ※

He said, 'Whenever *it* feels like it.' He should have said, 'Whenever *I* feel like it.' If she hadn't heard him with her own ears and seen how pleasant and serene he is, Bianca would never have identified this as the man who walks indifferently past his children while they call out for his attention, eager to show him their recently finished drawings. At other times, he shuts himself in his studio for days, refusing trays of food placed at the door. He won't even open the window of his study. Donna Clara paces beneath it, looking up, waiting for a nod, for some sign of life. Sometimes the poet has nightmares and calls out during his sleep. She has heard him. It isn't a dog or a local drunk, Minna tells her. It is him.

'He does that sometimes when he is writing,' she says.

Bianca begins to understand why the children are always so insecure in front of him. They are stuck between shyness and the urge to reclaim his other, kinder side, the side that sends the gardener to plough the grounds at the confines of the estate into five parcels so that each child can have their own garden. Each area is labelled with a wooden tag and the children have their own set of miniature hoes and spades and tiny bags of seeds to plant. Don Titta is a complicated man, this much is certain. One moment he is there and the next he is gone. He isolates himself for weeks so that he can pursue, capture and tame his muses. And then, all of a sudden, he resurfaces: a pale and serene convalescent. He becomes that other self then, the man who joyfully goes out on a limb for everyone. The man who kneels down next to Pietro and Enrico, fascinated, as they watch a watermill churn over the brook. Who admires the girls as they dance to the rhythm of Pia's drum, smiling so sweetly he looks almost foolish.

If their father is either fully present or fully absent, their mother, delicate and devout Donna Julie, is a constant source of love. It bubbles up from deep inside her. Precisely because of her uninterrupted presence, though, she runs the risk of going unnoticed. It is her daily devotion that watches over the children's health and their metamorphoses, providing woolly sweaters, poultices, decoctions or mush as needed. She offers them all the nurturing that they require. But the children, observes Bianca, are no longer so young that they need such doting attention. They are at a point when they desire something else: games, friendships, stories and laughter. Kisses and hugs are excessive. They reciprocate with swift pecks on the cheek and then wriggle free, the same way they do from unwanted scarves and sweaters. Although when Donna Clara offers herself to them, they greedily take everything they can get their hands on. They adore Innes too, like little puppies. He is the only one who can get respect from the two boys, and the girls love him unconditionally – maybe because he is as tall as their father but not as distant; maybe because he swings them around him as if on a wonderful carousel ride.

ঌ ঌ

One day, through an open window, Bianca hears Nanny complaining.

'Oh, that Miss Bianca . . . she's going to take him from me. I know it. And she doesn't even speak French!'

Bianca is astounded: Nanny is revealing her feelings to a maid! And probably a smart one like Pia. She wonders what would happen if she were to make a dramatic entrance, draw back the curtains, as in a Goldoni comedy, and say, 'You're wrong, mademoiselle. Innes is all yours. I'm looking elsewhere.' The foolish girl would be at peace but it might also kindle the fires of her hope, which is a mere illusion. She ought to realize on her own that Innes is unattainable. Maybe she wants to delude herself. Maybe it makes this house, her prison, more tolerable. But the children will grow up, Nanny will have to find another home, and by then Innes will surely be far away. He doesn't strike Bianca as the type to stay fixed in one spot for very long. Not here, anyway. He is a dreamer. And the dreams will ultimately carry him away.

She stands very still, thinking and listening. Pia, surprisingly, comes to Bianca's defence.

'What are you talking about? Miss Bianca isn't a bad person . . .'

Bianca wishes that she could transform herself into a beautiful statuette. No one would notice her; she would simply be an ornament, an ornament preferable to the one she feels she already is. Words would simply slide off her smooth skin. She recalls a French story her father used to tell, the one about an ancient statue, a Venus in a garden somewhere, that fell in love with a young man. Every night the statue would visit him, leaving mysterious traces of dirt in the hallways of the villa. To prevent him from marrying his flesh-and-blood fiancée, she held him so tightly that she killed him. Even statues have a soul. The advantage is that no one knows it, and they can conceal or reveal them as they please.

As she turns the corner of the house, Innes comes towards her, as though he has been waiting for her behind the bushes.

'And where are you off to, Miss Bianca? To explore the wild moors?'

Bianca turns to look behind her. If she has seen this exchange, Nanny will have fainted, her suspicions all but confirmed.

'I was just going to walk down to the fields, where it is a bit less wild,' she says with a smile.

They start walking together. He has to slow down and she has to quicken her pace. Once their initial differences are dealt with and the doses of irony are measured out and understood, Bianca realizes that not only does she enjoy Innes's company, but she also doesn't care what Nanny thinks.

'Were you referring earlier, perhaps, to our employer's wild habits?' he says. They exchange a smile of understanding, but he then becomes serious. 'He is a great man, you know. I feel fortunate to work for him. And so should you. The bourgeoisie of the Po Valley, the landed gentry, the aristocrats who inhabit these spaces that exist somewhere between land and sky, are rarely so enlightened. More often than not they are simply satisfied with conforming to the landscape.' And then Innes changes both the subject and his expression. 'I have something for you. It has just come from London, where it seems to be a great hit. It's a romance novel and I am sure you will appreciate it.'

'Don't you want to read it first?' Bianca asks, trying to suppress her curiosity.

'I've already read it. My nights are inhabited by books. It's the only benefit of having insomnia: one has more time to dedicate to passions. I also sleep a little during the day, when it's nap time for the children.'

She notices his paleness. His eyes are more deeply set than usual. In the vivid daylight, barely screened by the leafy tree-tops, she notices, too, a vertical line that runs from the corner of his eye down his cheek. It looks like a scar from a duel but is merely a crease of age, perhaps a distinctive sign, a message saying this is the spirit at work. Bianca has begun to suspect – and in this she is correct – that Innes is a revolutionary. Merely thinking of this word sends chills running down her spine. It evokes torture, chains, prisons, heads rolling in pools of blood. His frequent visits to the city surely serve a duplicitous purpose. And the role of tutor in a noble and respectable family is a wonderful cover.

Bianca senses that even the master of the house is involved. Their partnership in these matters explains many things: Don Titta's secrecy and his frequent trips to the city residence (which she imagines as being dusty and decaying, in ruins, given the fact that none of the women ever want to go) with the excuse of researching the novel he has been writing for the past ten years. The risk of course is even greater for Don Titta than for Innes. He is the poet, loved and pampered by all for the person he appears to be: an elegant, charming seeker of words. Bianca, who is familiar with his work, finds his poems pleasing but wan. She doesn't see great passion in his verses but rather delicate sentiment, idylls, still-life depictions of an illuminated life, a life which does not truly exist.

Perhaps at heart he is a collector – that would explain why he is driven to commission portraits of his flowers and plants as though they are people. But what if, under that Arcimboldo of petals, strange herbs, exotic fruits and foliage, there is a different man, a man filled with strong ideas, waiting for the right moment to reveal his true identity to the rest of the world?

His novel. The revolution. Perhaps he is writing a novel *about* the revolution. Bianca feels only a detached curiosity about these matters. She is aware that they are important, that it is an issue of rights being denied, and that the insurgents operate through contempt, secrecy and violence. Apparently, there is no other way to protest and change the direction of things. There will be blood. It is inevitable.

Bianca, though, feels engaged in her own transformation. It has turned her world upside down and set her apart from everyone else. She tries to imagine the new and daring map of the world to come. She feels like a seamstress working on a corner of an enormous tablecloth: she has her portion to bring to completion and she simply fills it with stitches and then unstitches them, little understanding how that same motif will multiply and echo across the cloth.

The book that Innes lends her takes her breath away. It keeps her awake at night; it steals away her common sense, and creates a confused knot of sensations inside her. It is entitled *Ponden Kirk* and focuses on a desperate and impossible love story, on injustice, and on ghosts that inhabit a desolate moor near the sea. She can imagine Tamsin's small hand, white against the black of night, scratching at the windowpane. Or perhaps it is only a branch. That hand, the description of those curls and amber eyes, eyes that are common here but rare in the north, takes hold of Bianca's heart. She feels the darkness that surrounds the beloved character of Aidan and feels for him with her innermost soul. It is completely different from *Udolpho*; Emily is a silly goose in comparison and not worthy of holding Tamsin's umbrella. Tamsin would hate umbrellas, anyway. Bianca is certain of this. If she ever did own one, she would have snapped it in two in a burst of rage or forgotten it under a hedge, torn it with carelessness or allowed it to be swept away by the wind. All of a sudden, everything Bianca has read that year is discarded in favour of this novel.

Innes smiles and tries to answer Bianca's insistent questions about the writer.

'The author's name is D. Lyly, with a "y". That's all I know.'

'No first name?'

'No first name. I think it must be a pseudonym. It has to be a woman.'

'Another Ann Radcliffe?'

'Why not, my dear?'

'I tremble for her.'

'You tremble?'

'Out of repressed envy.'

D. Lyly, Delilah, Dalila: a woman of deceit. Deceit in order to exist. To write. In comparison, Bianca's pencils, charcoals, all the accoutrements of her drawing, seem as bland as the oatmeal that her mother served her at breakfast while her brothers enjoyed pumpernickel bread and sausages. Her flowers are mawkish in their light green and gold frames. The leaves in her sketches have been dead for an age. Everything she does is so graciously finished – and so useless. Life looks so much better alive than when it is drawn on paper. When it is written about, on the other hand, life becomes stronger, colourful, more vital. And what is more, writing comes to life each time you read it. A leaf drawn on a piece of paper does not. When a leaf dies, you have to wait for spring to be able to see it again, and it will never be the same leaf it once was.

Bianca is curious. She wants to find out more about this mysterious Lyly, who is very possibly a woman. Who knows what depths and peaks of passion she has experienced in order to be able to render them so miraculously well on paper? Maybe she is like her character Tamsin, both impulsive and obstinate, reaching out for everything she wants against all obstacles. She is never defeated, only by death. But no, not even that can stop her . . .

'The author is most likely a middle-aged man with gout,' observes Innes playfully. 'He spends every day at the club and has never travelled further than Hampstead.'

'You like teasing me,' Bianca protests.

'You should write, if you think you might enjoy it,' says Innes, both indulgently and in all seriousness. They are walking together in the rain as if they are in England. They cross paths with servants and peasants who look at them askance. It is one thing to *have* to get wet, but another to do it on purpose, dragging one's skirt through the high grass in a strange pique. 'Write. Try it out. No one is stopping you. I know that your true talent is drawing, but it needs to find its right course. Don't tell me you're only interested in herbals. That's just the surface.'

And so, with that challenge, Bianca gives writing a go. On a stormy night, illuminated by candlelight, she starts a fictitious diary. It doesn't come easily to her. She gives herself a false name, rolling it around in her mouth as though it is a strange sweet, unsure whether to keep sucking on it or spit it out. She writes out the false name three, five, ten times, tilting her flourishes here and there. Finally, she recounts her experience travelling from Calais to Dover. She leaves out the more distressing details, the jumbling of innards, and favours a more romantic sketch: two mysterious characters in wind-swept capes, the moon peeking out from behind the clouds . . . She rereads it. It has all been said before. She gives it another go, adding the innards and their by-products. The effect makes her shiver. There is action and atmosphere, but it all feels shallow. She cannot find the right words. She ends up with blackened fingers and torn-up pages. It is better to read than to write, she thinks. And what's more, it's easier.

She gets into bed to read the novel, and is immediately reunited with Aidan; she locks that silly Tamsin in the storeroom, ignores her small fists pounding on the door, steals her cape and effortlessly clambers up on a horse behind her hero. Together they ride off bareback, the beast trembling beneath her thighs, her arms gripping his waist tightly. He, too, trembles with the fury of the gallop. It is pouring with rain, and the moon is shining . . .

The moon is always present, she reflects as she closes the book, thunder sounding far off in the distance. She looks out at her own moon through the distorting glass pane of her window, and thinks it looks like a fried egg. *It is always with us,* she thinks, *even when we don't see it. And we need it like we need the sun. It's the other side of the coin, the splinter of darkness we carry with us, wedged into our hearts.* She sighs and picks up a pencil and begins to draw. She draws the fried egg in the sky, the profile of a sycamore, a star like a tiny kiss of light. This much she can do. And this she will continue to do.

❧ ❧

The feast day of San Giovanni is a small but important tradition in the household. Friends from the city visit on the way to their own summer retreats in the countryside in a kind of farewell until October. It is an opportunity to show off the estate and prove that some things never change. Bianca learns about the feast only during the commotion of the preparations, from the servants' incomprehensible, fractured sentences; from the contrasting expressions of Don Titta and his mother, who is reassured by the agitation and shouts orders left and right like a captain from the bridge. Don Titta confirms his own place by retreating into his chambers. When his opinion is needed about the menu, the flowers or the music, he raises his eyes to the sky and purses his lips as though to hold back any impertinence.

St John's Wort is in bloom during the period of the feast. Bianca has an idea, voices it, and it is approved. Her role is to prepare dozens of *boutonnières*: a cluster of the little yellow flowers bound in ivy shoots. She sends out troops of children to search for the smallest ivy – *only the ends of the branches, about this long, no more than that, be careful not to cut yourselves, don't run with scissors in your hand*, and so on. Despite Nanny's worrying and the devastating pruning job, the mission is completed. When the ladies and gentlemen arrive, the children present them with these *boutonnières*, sprayed with water to appear fresh, from two trays in the foyer. The guests, of course, remark on the children's growth before pinning the gifts to their chests.

'Oh, how big you've got, Giulietta. You look like a young lady.'

'And is this Enrico? He looks like his grandmother. What a beautiful boy.'

Nanny watches the children from behind a pillar, ready to sweep up her prey as soon as the last guests make their entrance. The gates close, keeping out the local peasants, who are travelling to their own festival in the village piazza, and who stop to watch the arrivals. They hang onto the gate and spy for a while on the gentlefolk and their painted carriages, neatly assembled along the gravel drive like a collection of exotic insects.

'See that one? That means Berlingieri is here, too. That light blue and black carriage is from Poma. Can you see the family crest on its door?'

Bianca watches the townspeople and listens to their voices, the rise and fall of their strange dialect, so difficult to understand. Once the soirée here is over, Pia and Minna will head to the festival in town. They have been talking about it for days. They will let their hair down and dance like lunatics, they say. Whether it is her wild streak or simply her impetuousness, Bianca knows that eventually her feet will lead her there too. The urge is irresistible. But not yet. The evening is about to commence. She greets the guests and leads them towards the refreshments, illuminated by a fringe of lanterns.

꙳ ꙳

La Farfalla is Don Titta's most recent and well-known literary work. It is so popular that even Bianca has heard of it. The master of the house recites some appropriate verses, even as moths flit about them rather than the butterfly of the title. When he concludes, he bows and basks in the applause.

'You've given us all a little flutter of excitement, Titta!' says a beautiful lady in pale rose, causing her friends to laugh.

'You must have swallowed a Lepidoptera,' he answers back.

'Oh, how horrid! You're a Lepidoptera.' More laughter follows.

'Unfortunately, dear Adele, the butterfly is a female.'

'Well, next time write about dogs then,' says Young Count Bernocchi, strutting like a peacock to the front of the room.

The women in the kitchen, poets by association, have put Bianca on her guard when it comes to the young count, with a memorable verse:

> *An occhio [eye] of regard to Bernocchio,*
> *his pockets are full of pidocchio [lice],*
> *he has a very long occhio and even longer hands.*

With this introduction preceding him, Bianca is instinctively cautious. Young Count Bernocchi is definitely not handsome. He is short with an enormous belly. He wears a horrible, outdated white wig that makes his forehead look excessively broad. And the socially inexpert Bianca suddenly finds herself standing next to him. As the guests begin to move off in different directions, he corners her in the room, with the intention of keeping her there for some time.

'So, Miss Bianca, have you grown accustomed to the wilderness? You're surely used to big cities: London, Paris . . .'

'Yes, I have been there,' Bianca replies curtly and almost impolitely. Her short response doesn't offer him anything to build on. She isn't trying to be rude, though, she simply lacks confidence. They have just been introduced to each other but he already seems to know a lot about her. Of course, the opposite is also true, but at least Bianca has sense enough not to show it. The diminutive that precedes his name is a joke: despite his advanced age, he still has not inherited his father's position as count. This father, the servants have told her, clings to dear life with his teeth. So even though he is past forty, Young Count Bernocchi seems frozen in eternal adolescence.

He inspects her through an eyeglass that is so out of fashion it is deeply comical. It surely isn't often that someone cuts him short. He furrows his brow and continues, as though nothing has happened.

'Vienna, Turin, Rome . . . In my opinion, the Grand Tour is nothing more than a grandiose invention. It allows for European *fainéants* to continue to practise the activities they enjoy most. It prevents them from getting involved in the fields of humanities and economics, which they should leave to people summoned to that duty – and the true engine of the world – and it gives them the opportunity to dissolve a giant portion of their assets into travel, hotels, rent and thoughtless purchases of mediocre works of art . . . Actually, this healthy circulation of money does quite a bit of good.'

'Didn't you travel, too, in your youth?' Tommaso suddenly appears at her side.

Bianca senses a slight tension in his tone, held in check by politeness. The phrase 'your youth' is actually a slight. Clearly Bernocchi cares a great deal about his appearance, but his excessive regard for it only highlights the defects of his age. His over-enjoyment of food and wine has led to puffy features and skin coloured by a reddish network of veins.

'But of course,' he answers calmly. 'And, rightly so; I include myself in the category of drones of which I speak. Let's just say that I have always had the good sense not to consider myself destined for great accomplishments and have been deaf to the callings of the Muses, who can do great harm if summoned forth by the wrong person.'

If this offhand comment is intended for Tommaso, he doesn't seem to notice. Instead, he offers Bianca his arm and they move off. Disgruntled, Bernocchi follows the couple to the centre of the sitting room. There everyone is seated, attentive, and ready to resume the show. Donna Julie seems lost in one of her daydreams. Innes's long fingers fiddle impatiently with the hems of his trousers. He provides silent company to the old priest, who appears either intimidated or profusely bored, or maybe a bit of both, thinks Bianca. His big white head droops forward over his threadbare tunic as though he is inspecting a strange landscape.

When Pia enters the room with a tray of refreshments, the old priest is shaken out of his stupor. A beautiful smile, affectionate and warm, spreads across his worn face. A grandfatherly expression, Bianca thinks. Pia is silent. After depositing her

tray on a small table, she takes a step back to make room for
Minna, then responds to the priest's gaze with a kind smile. At
times she seems to go back to being a child, the way she likely
was before her work aroused an endless guile within her. Right
now she looks like an infant who wants to take her old guardian's hand and let herself be guided. But of course she cannot.
The moment passes. Pia bows, turns around and disappears. A
smile lingers for a few more seconds on the old man's face until
a glass is forced into his hand and he comes back to his senses.

Bianca is not the only one to have noticed the exchange.
Donna Clara, for whom Innes has given up his seat, turns to
the pious man.

'Did you see how grown up your student has become?'

'Yes,' Don Dionisio says, sipping his drink.

'There's not a holy dove story there, is there, Father?' Young
Count Bernocchi asks, stifling a yawn. 'Charity is best when we
practise it on ourselves, Donna Clara. At least that way we don't
risk delusions.'

Donna Julie shoots him a glance.

'Do you know that Pia reads stories to the girls? She plays
with them and cares for them too. She's so precious to us, our
Pia.'

'Do you mean to say that she even knows how to read? How
is this possible?' Bernocchi asks, raising an eyebrow.

'And why not?' Don Dionisio says, putting his glass down
on the tray excitedly and with a dangerous rattle. 'Pia is a girl
just like any other. And she's quick to learn.'

'Don't tell me she knows Greek and Latin, too,' Bernocchi
says with a smile.

'A bit, actually,' retorts Don Dionisio, before withdrawing
into a hostile silence.

'Ah, how generous and enlightened contemporary Milan is!

Not only does it take in, raise and feed orphaned children, it also follows them step by step down the road of life, providing them with a higher education which will certainly come in handy when they are milking cows, raking hay and waxing the floors! Even the great Rousseau entrusted his bastard children to public care. And who better than he, with his illustrious work to prove it, to know the best way to raise a child?'

'Oh, you . . . you speak nonsense. And anyway, Rousseau was wrong.' Donna Julie speaks quickly, animatedly, as if a flame of thought has been lit from deep inside. She casts a feverish look at Bernocchi. She is no longer the poised, invisible creature she usually is. 'Rousseau was a monster to force poor Thérèse to give up her children. They ought to remain with their parents. They ought to live with them, enjoy their affection, receive kisses and spankings alike . . . only in this way will they learn to love: by example. Isn't this true, my dear husband?'

Don Titta bows his head in agreement. Bianca watches Donna Julie attentively as she recomposes herself, the colour in her cheeks fading. Never has she spoken with such vehemence.

'I know you have your ideas, Donna Julie,' Bernocchi retorts. 'You even nursed your children yourself, isn't that true? Or at least, that's what people said. I must say that I never saw you do it, but I would have liked to . . . you, the most spiritual of women, engaged in such an animalistic act. What a strange spectacle that must have been.'

'It wasn't for the public,' says Don Titta, frowning.

'Come, come,' Donna Clara interrupts, throwing her hands in the air. 'We don't want to start a fight on account of that boring man, Rousseau.'

She laughs her full-bodied laugh, throaty and frivolous.

'Donna Clara, you will never change,' Bernocchi speaks gallantly. 'You always were the queen of the salon.' As soon as he says this, though, he bites his lip, aware of the involuntary offence that does not go unnoticed.

'Oh, yes, dear Bernocchi. Those were good times. Now vanished forever.' She sighs and puffs out her taffeta chest, and with another gesture – her hands are never still – she shoos away a thought. 'But we are all much simpler and happier now. A little wild, but happy. Isn't that right, Julie? Isn't that right, my son?'

'Really, you are very special,' says Annina Maffei, a dark-haired lady in an intricate dress. 'You've created your own entourage. You pride yourself on being simple and rustic, but deep down you are very unique. You have a governess for the children, whom you refer to as Nanny even though she's French. You have dear Stuart for English, which, if you don't mind my saying, is an incomprehensible and violent language, worse than German. You even have a domestic painter and a poet in residence. Everyone in Milan gossips about you. And here you all are, hiding out. What I would do to bring you to a show at La Scala!'

Donna Clara seizes on this comment.

'Have you seen the most recent performance by Signorina Galli? How is she?'

'Signorina Brignani is far better, in my modest opinion,' replies Bernocchi. 'Signorina Galli is always the same. Exquisite and angelic, a little too much so. Signorina Brignani is small, exotic and spicy . . . if you know what I mean,' he adds, looking for signs of understanding from the men. 'But anything's better than the sylph-like doldrums of Signorina Pallarini.'

Tommaso nods with an all-too brief smile. Innes contemplates a corolla of tulips in a vase on a table behind him. Don

Titta assumes that distanced stare which is his usual defence against the world. Don Dionisio, the old priest, is immersed in his own private meditations, which look dangerously similar to sleep. And Bernocchi is vexed: he hates it when his quips fall flat. So he stares at Bianca, cocking his head slightly to one side and wetting his lips lasciviously. Despite herself, she blushes. A second later, his gaze drifts over to Pia, who ought to have been dismissed by now but who stands staring at Contessa Maffei's too ornate but nonetheless extremely enchanting gown. Pia neither notices Bernocchi nor feels his gaze on her, which even from a distance lingers a little too long.

≈ ≈

Bianca dismisses herself with a curtsey, which always works for a person of her status – somewhere between hired help and guest. But when she realizes that she has left her mother's ivory fan downstairs, rather than wait until the next day to retrieve it and risk finding it broken, she returns. Shrewdly, she stops at the threshold. Young Count Bernocchi is talking about her.

'It seems as though that awful Albion has given us the gift of an authentic gem. A coarse gem, of course, as brusque as she is pleasant. She needs only to be cleaned and polished with patience. Do you really think she will stay and draw all your flowers? You, my friend, are an eccentric man. It is you that everyone talks about in the city. Our poet peasant.'

'It's a shame she has freckles. She looks like a quail's egg,' Donna Annina says.

'And what about a man? Will you find her a husband? Or is she one of those modern girls who want to be "independent"?'

≈ ≈

'We must marry her off.'

This had been declared at every dinner with both insistence and some menace. Bartolo used to announce it to their father without even looking at her, as if she were merely one of the furnishings.

'By all means, we must not,' her father would reply, steadfast and unwavering. 'Bianca doesn't need to be married. We have given her the independence she needs to choose what she wants, even a husband if she so desires. But only if she desires.'

'But, Father, really. She is in her prime. Who will want her in five years? She will end up being an independent old maid with ink on her fingers and too much pride.' Bartolo spoke with sarcasm.

'Bartolomeo, I don't want to discuss this any further. Your sister will do what she pleases.'

Bartolo's face would redden and Zeno would slump down in his chair, raise his glass towards his brother and gulp down its contents mockingly. She would have given anything to disappear when she was at the centre of an argument or the cause of one. Her father would look at her with a kind smile but really she didn't know *what* to do with all her freedom. She wished she could have chosen to stay in that dining room with its walls of fading colours forever.

❧ ❧

She has heard enough. Bianca walks into the room with neither a smile nor a greeting, picks up her fan and leaves again, annoyed. She ignores their surprised gazes. Even Donna Annina blushes.

She looks at her reflection in the candlelit mirrors in the hallway and sees a delicate face with light freckles and high cheekbones. Wisps of hair fall out of her chignon. *Perhaps I am odd but so what?* she thinks. *I am me. J'ai quelquechose que les autres n'ont point*, she tells herself snobbishly. Too bad that the mirror in her room, aged by the modest white candle in its holder, shows only a blurry image of a half-formed woman.

Why should she stay in the house on her own? The night is young and there is another celebration going on, not too far away. All she needs to do is go down the servants' stairs, sneak through the small gate, and venture down the dark road with its strange shadows created by strange houses.

The street lamps are illuminated and cast a yellow glare on things, softening their contours. She follows the pounding of a drum and soon finds herself in the piazza, in front of the old church. A stage has been built and people are jumping about in a kind of dance, offering an enthusiastic, disorderly accompaniment to the violin. Giant torches at the corners of the stage shed light on the dancers. The musician, who stands on his own platform, has a large nose that looks even larger in the shadows. He has a slender face and wears dirty leggings that lend him an air of scruffy elegance. He is talented in his own right, even if his instrument screeches savagely. Bianca leans up against a wall in the darkness and watches. The torches reflect the people's red, straining faces. It is a revel of witches and wizards, united by the beating of the drum to celebrate Walpurgis Night. It is innocuous but not innocent. Bianca watches a girl jump down from the stage, laugh, and run, only to be followed by a young man who catches up with her, grabs her, turns her around, and kisses her on the neck and mouth with violent rapture. The girl tries to wriggle free but that only incites her partner further. He presses her up against the wall with kisses. A tug on Bianca's sleeve distracts her from the show.

'Miss Bianca! You sneaked out too?' Pia laughs excitedly and looks at her in complicit understanding. She follows

Bianca's gaze to the couple and shrugs. 'Our Luciana, she never can get enough.' She laughs again and takes Bianca by the arm. 'Come with me. Want to dance? Let's dance.'

She drags Bianca onto the stage, where the dense crowd shifts to make room for them. Bianca knows nothing about this kind of movement. It is some sort of noisy square dancing where couples shift from side to side, hooked by the arm. Pia guides her expertly, though, and it only takes a few seconds for her to understand the configuration of steps. There is the smell of camphor, leather, warm bodies and dust; of best outfits and shawls taken out of trunks; of jerkins tarred with sweat and pulled with twisting gestures. The smells mix with the sweet aroma of hay and flowers and the warm night. Pia laughs. Bianca laughs too, and they dance until they are tired. Pia leads Bianca to a stand resting on two barrels where Ruggiero and Tonio are busy filling mugs with red wine, young and tart. It doesn't quench their thirst and it leaves a tinny aftertaste. Pia gulps hers down and slams her mug back on the wood with wilful, masculine violence.

'We are all equal on the night of San Giovanni,' she says. Bianca doesn't understand what she means by this: men and women? Noblemen and country folk? Pia and Bianca? She doesn't ask because it isn't important. Pia takes her by the hand and then leads her down an alley. They turn a corner and continue along the side of a house. Bianca is silent, bewitched by the young girl's initiative. She has the feeling that they are being followed but when she turns around there is no one.

They continue on, through the wild undergrowth, where it becomes increasingly dark. Bianca calculates that this path must lead towards the fields. And precisely where the shrubbery ends and the great stretch of cultivated land opens up, a wonder lies waiting for them. Fireflies. There are hundreds, thousands, millions of them, suspended between sky and land, busily flying to and fro. They are dancing, too, guided by the instinct to draw circles, arcs, vaults and volutes in a breathtaking spectacle. It doesn't matter if there is no music here. The delicate singing of the crickets is all they need, the perfect accompaniment for the procession of tiny floating candles.

The shadow, if it is a shadow, leans upon a tree trunk and sighs.

❦ ❦

The following day, in the kitchen, all the talk is about Saint Peter's ship. The ship sits in a bottle, slightly chipped at the top. It has, as every year, been set up on the high windowsill so that people can parade beneath it. It has sails made of egg whites, and inside the bottle are thousands of bubbles. It is a ghost ship that has been caught in the fury of the northern seas, and has survived thanks to a miracle. Tradition has it that the family and staff consign their wishes to this small boat before it ferries the wishes off somewhere secret where they will be kept safe.

It is always this way and in the morning everything is as it should be; the servants have cleared away the remains of the party but something still lingers, something unfinished, which the fresh morning air cannot dissipate. Life goes on. Real life, not shiny or flashy, but a life that nonetheless emits its own pale radiance. It is like a replica of a precious jewel worn by a lady who keeps the original locked up in a safe for special occasions.

'I wish I could travel,' whispers Minna, contemplating the egg-white ship on the windowsill.

'You're not supposed to say what you wish for, silly, otherwise it won't come true,' Pia says, berating her with the wisdom of a thirteen-year-old.

'It won't come true, anyway,' Minna mumbles, before heading down to the laundry and the mountain of tablecloths that need washing.

'I don't care. *I'm* not going to say my wish out loud anyway,' Pia insists, looking for Bianca's approval.

But Bianca only smiles. What can she say to these girls? They have essentially been born prisoners. How can she console them when their future is already laid out? It is written in the stars. It cannot be any other way.

Bianca hovers there for a bit and considers. *Each and every one of us makes our own destiny. But this is only really true for men. Am I different?* she thinks. It is a pity that the great equality they experienced the night before disappears with the light of day. It is a pity it isn't contagious, that it cannot be gifted, a little bit at a time, like a mother yeast that is passed from home to home, making different doughs rise in the same way. Whoever has the power to transform things, or to transform themselves, doesn't share it. *Come dawn, we were all Cinderellas,* Bianca says to herself. *We had to slip back into our grey rags, pick up our brooms, and clean up the shards of our dreams before we stepped on them and wounded ourselves.*

The thought makes her furious. She storms outside, forgetting a hat, swooping the rest of her things up along the way. The gardeners mumble veiled greetings and then watch her lewdly. She notices nothing, just keeps on walking, up and down the hills and then beyond the ditches. Despite the water and mud, it isn't hard to find what she is looking for: those strange, small, wild orchids – the sweet peas. They crawl up and around the big bushes of lavender and across the elastic slouch of lespedeza, which in its current flowerless state looks mute but is still beautiful. The jasmine, likely not happy with the fact that the sweet peas have bloomed, proposes its own new reddish shoots like fumbling hands moving towards new adventures. She stops and sighs.

On closer inspection, she discovers new details. The garden is so big and variable that the poet's experiments overlap and get confused. Even those left unfinished – and there are many of them – reveal their own kind of harsh and rebellious grace, the secret charm of possibility. Bianca begins to draw and soon everything is restored to its place, at least for now.

༄ ༄

Some days are simply not long enough for all the life that runs through them; the climate is perfect, shifting miraculously from cool to warm, from shade to sunshine and back again to the shade. For the days are not always clear – at times the clouds pass rapidly overhead and stain the ground below. On those days, every natural thing seems to have just been born and at the same time seems to be a hundred years old, every natural thing looks back at you in challenge: you inconsequential crumb, you miserable, minuscule mortal. You understand that everything of significance has already happened and will continue to happen long after you're gone. And instead of feeling frustrated, you feel a profound happiness because you realize that this is how it is supposed to be, it's the course of non-human life, things that need to be contemplated but not understood, for this kind of comprehension is simply too vast for brains the size of a fist. Whatever you do on those days, you come away feeling both satisfied and incomplete: nothing will ever compare with so much glory and yet you have wasted all this time on banalities. You should have just sat still and reflected on what was happening: both everything and nothing. That would have been better. And instead you busied yourself like an ant, filling your hours with mindless tasks:

eating, sleeping, talking. And when the day disappears into the velvet blue there's nothing left to do but pray that tomorrow will be identical, but it won't be, because perfect days are always different, one from the next; no one can ever recall two being alike.

※ ※

Some days begin badly for Bianca but get better as the dissatisfaction, anger and capriciousness that force her to hate everyone – first and foremost herself – melt like frost in the sunlight. It takes so little, sometimes just an excuse, to laugh or even smile. Since she cannot fly as she might wish, she chooses to walk very slowly, thankful for her two feet.

She thinks of the time she went to the kitchen to ask for some clean rags and found Donna Clara seated there on a high altar, like a gargantuan queen, intent on teaching the cook something new. She read recipes out loud from Agnoletti's *Nuova cucina economica*, some in perfect Italian and other parts translated into dialect, naming ingredients, directions and measurements. The cook wanted to know what was wrong with her gnocchi, and why they weren't good enough any more.

'Listen,' Donna Clara said. 'Here it says to add two eggs to the mixture to make it more compact, do you understand? Do you usually do that? No? Well then, don't complain if your gnocchi are too soft.'

They are a strange family: at times snobbish and then practical and down to earth. Sometimes they mix with the peasants and moments later they give off airs of superiority. First they laugh and then they are serious. Even Donna Clara's ailments have something comical about them.

'I've got an awful headache. It's as if a beast with large hands were squeezing the back of my head . . .'; 'Today I have a stomach ache. It's as if a beast with large hands were taking hold of my intestines and shaking them . . .'; 'If you only knew what a backache I have today. It's as if a beast with large hands were punching me here, here and over here . . .'

Old Pina, maid and Cerberus to Donna Clara, is the only one who pays any attention to her complaints. She cocks her white head to the side like a perplexed chicken and spews out suggestions of herbal remedies in no particular order: aniseed for the belly; bittersweet to rid her of phlegm; fava plants, but just a little, for her headache. The other maids listen, containing their smiles with bowed heads. And when Donna Clara drags herself to the living room awaiting the treatment most suited to this day's ailment, the giggling begins.

'Be careful the beast doesn't put his big hands up your skirt! Because that'll definitely make you feel better.'

'But how big is he?' snickers another maid.

'This big!'

Bianca doesn't engage with them but can easily imagine the vulgar gestures that accompany the exchange. She pictures a mythological animal, some sort of Minotaur, slipping into bed with Donna Clara and massaging her white shoulders with his giant hands in a prelude to providing her with the kinds of pleasures that are now only memories for the lady of the house. Bianca wonders about those memories. She herself does not yet possess any.

⁂

'What kind of name is Minna?' Bianca asks. It sounds almost Nordic to her but she cannot imagine how the girl's parents – two peasants with red, rugged faces – came to choose that name from the Litany of the Saints or a list of relatives.

Minna, who has been folding shirts, drops what she is

doing, sits down on a stool, crosses her legs, rests her elbows on her knees, and looks Bianca up and down.

'It's a long story.'

'I'm listening,' Bianca says, brushing her hair.

Minna begins to tell her story. It is clear from the start that it is one she enjoys recounting.

'Minna is the name that they copied by mistake from the document that the parish issued. They already had a Mirta, Carlo, Battista and Luigina. There was no room for me in the house, and since I was born at harvest, in May, and Mamma had to go and work in the fields and couldn't even breastfeed me, they left me at the group home in Milan.'

'What do you mean?' Bianca says, putting down the brush and facing the girl. It seems the story will indeed be long and complicated.

'The group home was where they brought us abandoned babies,' Minna explains.

'An orphanage,' says Bianca, convinced now of having understood.

'Oh, no, Miss Bianca.' Minna laughs, covering her mouth with her hand. 'I had a mamma and a papa, I told you. I still have them. Not only orphans get abandoned, you know. Poor children are abandoned too. Sometimes just temporarily. They came back for me when I was five.'

'And until then you lived in the institution?'

Minna raises her eyebrows. 'Institution?'

'Yes, the place where they keep abandoned children – the home, as you call it.' She has seen one in Paris. It was a big building, white and elegant. Her father told her about this custom of entrusting newborns to the public institution so that they could grow strong and educated, as was their right.

'Oh, no, Miss Bianca, you don't understand,' Minna says. 'In this place in Milan, there's a kind of big wooden drawer that slides in and out of the front door. Babies are placed in it and they are pushed through into the building. But the babies don't stay there. They only remain when they're newborns. They are taken in, inspected to make sure that they're healthy, and then given to a wet nurse in some village. The real parents provide clothes, a blanket and some money now and then if they can. The new families are either farmers, they herd geese or they work in the fields. They take good care of the babies. Every so often someone goes to check on them. If a baby dies, the money stops coming and it's all over. When the mothers and fathers – the real ones – want their babies back, they go and get them. If they want them. If and when they can afford them. They came to get me when I was five,' she says again, proudly. 'But my name was wrong. My document said Erminia but either the priest was old and deaf, or the man who copied the name into the book wrote it wrong, or the priest read my name wrong to the people of Cusago who took me in, because he said Arminna, or something that wasn't even a Christian name, so they had to give me the name of a normal saint. Anyway, they changed Arminna to Minna. When I finally came home, the name stuck. Now I'm used to it. It's like dogs and cats: if you start calling them something else, they don't understand.'

So that is Minna's story, Bianca thinks. Not at all Nordic. Bianca wonders if Minna has any memories from those five years she spent with strangers; if they cared for her well; if they treated her like their own child or like a servant. Maybe she won't be able to answer. Probably she has forgotten everything; or perhaps she doesn't want to talk about it. Bianca looks at her with newfound respect. That little girl with the face of a kitten has dealt with her own trials and tribulations, and yet, here she is, alive and whole. That is not insignificant. That is the stolid force of one who takes life as it is, because nothing can be done about it.

Bianca turns to the mirror and looks at Minna's face in the reflection behind her. 'Would you like to finish my hair?' She sees the child smile from ear to ear. Minna is finally being considered more than just a maid – a lady in waiting. Bianca doesn't mind if Minna pulls her hair; it is only because she is excited. It is all right if she doesn't fix the tiny bone pins tightly enough in her bun, even if it means she can hardly move her head throughout dinner. Later Bianca sees Minna's reflection again in the mirror in the dining room, when she peeks in to check on the public effect of her hairdressing.

No one notices her hair except Tommaso, who hurries to sit next to Bianca after dinner.

'You have the neck of a nymph,' he whispers while others are chatting amongst themselves.

Bianca frowns. She doesn't know how to take compliments. She has never learned, never having had the time or the occasion to do so. Instead of blushing or looking down, as is customary, she stares at him fiercely. *What nerve.* Her neck flares with anger. She feels it transforming into a scarlet map of an archipelago, and she places her hand to her throat and coughs.

'Have you caught a cold, Miss Bianca? You ought to take care of yourself and wear a scarf,' Donna Clara says, unwittingly dissipating all embarrassment with her prickly thoughtfulness.

Tommaso turns away, resting his elbow on the table and leaning his chin in his hand. He changes the topic.

'Titta,' he says, 'if it's no burden, I'd like to talk with you about something that is dear to my heart . . .'

The two men get up, bow and take their leave. Bianca's flush of colour slowly fades under Innes's severe gaze.

❧ ❧

Perhaps encouraged by a new sense of trust – and not quite ready to accept that what has occurred between them is a one-off – Minna never leaves Bianca's side even though she doesn't need an assistant and has already told her so. But Donna Clara thinks a domestic painter should have an assistant and Bianca fears that by turning Minna down she will offend the older lady. So, in addition to letting her care for her hair, Bianca allows Minna to carry her paintbox and easel. And when the drawing session is over, she lets the girl clean her brushes, but always under close observation for those little hands can also be rough. Minna follows her wherever she goes, as loyal as a puppy, curious to the point of appearing insolent. She is a domestic servant who has barely been domesticated herself. Initially, Bianca suspects that Minna follows her so that she can watch her paint and tell the others about it later. But then she understands the loyalty of servitude.

'I don't tell people about our conversations. I swear to you, may I die as a spy,' Minna tells her, crossing her fingers in an X and kissing them.

'Cross my heart, hope to die,' Bianca says, in English.

'What?' Minna asks.

Bianca explains the rhyme and has Minna repeat it. Later Minna goes to the girls in the courtyard and tells them that she knows English. And she does know a little: several rhymes, deformed and mumbled, *yessir, yesmadam*, things that she has picked up in Innes's lessons. Bianca enjoys correcting the child's pronunciation and has her repeat Mother Goose rhymes like 'Mary had a little lamb'. She chooses rhymes about animals so it is easier for Minna to separate the words from the rhythm and connect them to the inhabitants of their own courtyard: the geese, the baby lamb, the cats, dogs and ducks. Each time she learns a new word, Minna's face brightens, amazed by these tiny discoveries. It occurs to Bianca that because the pleasure of learning isn't being imposed on Minna, but rather gleaned with the eagerness of someone who is not privy to it, she absorbs everything. The other children, meanwhile, sit at their desks in the nursery and repeats dull phrases in French that echo all the way down into the garden. The maids in the kitchen giggle and repeat their own lessons: *mossieu a un shevall, madame a un paraplooie, bonshoo, bonswa, addieww.*

Pia joins Minna and Bianca as often as she can. Her presence has a strange effect on Minna. At first the younger girl seems annoyed, but then she calms down and almost seems relieved not to have to take on assignments that are too complicated for her. With Pia around, Minna plays happily on the sidelines. She will take a little dolly out of her apron, give Pia her seat, and still manage to keep herself under control. As Bianca retreats into her world of drawing, Pia also disappears into a secret world. She doesn't carry toys or dollies in her apron. She has a book. The first time Bianca realizes this, her surprise is evident.

'I'm allowed, you know,' Pia says defensively. 'The books come from the library – I don't steal them! Don Titta said I could borrow them. All I have to do is show him which book I want so he can see if it's right for me.'

From then on, Bianca looks with amusement at the books the maid chooses. She sees *Breve storia della rosa*, *Il Castello di Otranto* and *I fioretti di San Francesco*. She understands now why Pia's vocabulary is a mix of popular dialect and more polished words.

The three girls keep each other company, each in their own silent world.

Pia too, though, is only a child. And sometimes she is overcome with excitement. Once they reach their selected location, she will set down Bianca's box of colours which she happily carries for Minna, and run off, like a little horse, until she reaches the limits of the woodlands. Then she'll come back laughing, worn out but calmer, breathlessly justifying herself.

'That feels good!'

Once, upon her return from a galloping excursion, her bonnet slips off and reveals light blue satin ribbons braided through her glossy brown hair.

'The ribbons come from the young misses,' Pia explains quickly. 'But they're mine now. They were a bit spoilt, and they weren't wearing them any more, and so they gave them to me. This too, look.' She lifts up her dark red skirt to show off a white lacy underskirt. 'Even my knickers,' she says, laughing and twirling. 'But they belonged to Donna Julie.' She looks at Bianca for signs of understanding. 'I'm more comfortable in these.' She pulls up the skirt to reveal a pair of white knickers with bows at the ankles. Donna Julie is very petite and not much bigger than the girl. It occurs to Bianca that this passing down of used clothing must raise some dissent in the kitchen.

In fact, Minna is staring at her friend as if she wants to hit her, but then she bursts into a smile that is too genuine to be false. Pia understands.

'The maids don't want me around. They say I'm the misses' darling. But I am always alone with the cook and with Minna, or with the girls, so it's all right. And now,' she adds, with sincere glee, 'you're here too.'

Sometimes Pia sings.

'Sing the one about the fire,' Minna says, clapping her hands. And so she begins.

> *Brusuu, brusà*
> *Chissà chi l'è staa?*
> *Sarà staa quei de Bress*
> *Che i fa tutt a roess;*
> *Sarà staa quei de Cusan*
> *Che i è svelti de la man.*
> *Brusuu, brusà*
> *Chissà chi l'è staa?*

> Burn, burn
> Who made it burn?
> Maybe it was the folk from Bress
> Just like they do all the rest;
> Maybe it was the folk from Cusan
> Who are fast with their hands.
> Burn, burn
> Who made it burn?

Bianca doesn't like this song. It is shapeless, like a sweater that has lost its form following too many washings. Her favourite is far softer, sweeter.

> *Ninna delle oche*
> *Tante, medie o poche*
> *Bianche con le piume*
> *Ninna delle brume*
> *Che vengono drumeumee*
> *Che vengono e vanno*
> *Sommesse, senza danno*
> *Che celano nel manto*
> *Un cavallino bianco*

Cavallo e cavaliere
Li voglio rivedere
Mi porteranno via
Lontano a casa mia
Ma casa mia dov'è
È dove sono re
Son re e son regina
Ninna della bambina.

Lullaby of the geese
Many, some, or just a few
White feathers
And foggy song
They come in autumn
They come and go
Soft and no trouble
In their capes
Hides a white horse
Horse and rider
I want to see them
They'll carry me away
Back to my home
But where's my home
It's where I am king
I am king and I am queen
Lullaby of the little girl.

'That's pretty,' Bianca says the first time she hears it. 'Sing it again.'

And Pia, in her strong, clear voice, obeys.

'Don Titta wrote it for his daughters,' she offers, without anyone asking her. 'I wonder what it's like to have a father like

him. Sometimes he plays with them, too. I've never seen a
father like that on this earth.'

'Well, they don't get to see him very often. He's very busy
and often travels to the city . . .' Bianca stops herself mid-
sentence.

'Yes, but it's better than nothing, isn't it?' Pia pushes away
one thought with another. 'Antonia, my friend from the piazza,
gets beaten by her father every night. He drinks too much and
then strikes her and her mother. Sometimes her arms are black
and blue; they look like plums from the garden. And Minna's
father doesn't even look at her.'

She says it without malice and Minna nods, never taking
her eyes off her faceless dolly.

Pia laughs bitterly. 'I wonder what my own father was like.'

'Maybe he's still alive,' says Bianca.

'No,' Pia says. 'He died for sure. Otherwise he would
have come back to get me. But let's pretend that he didn't die.
We're allowed to dream. Yes, let's pretend he went to the other
side of the world in search of his fortune and that one day he
will come back for me and he will be a lord and I will become
a lady and he will be happy that I studied and am not ignorant
like the others. I know how to behave in society; I even know
English, and we would go to live in a palace. First, though, we
would visit my mother's grave. He knows where it is. I'm sure
he does.'

Quiet falls over the little group. Bianca doesn't know what
to say. Finally Pia breaks the silence and continues.

'She's dead, you know. She passed away giving life to me.
She flew into the arms of the Lord, up there, where it's more
comfortable. Don Dionisio told me, so it must be true.'

Ribbons, second-hand knickers, books on loan. There are other manifestations of Donna Clara's favouritism for Pia too, and sometimes it seems excessive to Bianca. Pia is just a maid after all and Donna Clara is the lady of the house. Sometimes, in the evenings, Donna Clara makes Pia get up on a stool and recite poetry for whoever is there. A circle of tired but curious listeners will form and Pia always has a handful of new verses ready. She'll blush slightly, close her eyes for inspiration and begin, her hands folded in front of her to prevent herself from fidgeting.

> *Pensoso, inconsolabile, l'accorta ninfa*
> *Il ritiene e con soavi e molli*
> *Parolette, carezzalo se mai*
> *Potesse Itaca sua trargli dal petto;*
> *Ma ei non brama che veder dai tetti*
> *Sbalzar della sua dolce Itaca il fumo,*
> *E poi chiuder per sempre al giorno i lumi.*
> *Nè commuovere, Olimpio, il cuor ti senti?*

> Distressed and inconsolable, the clever nymph
> Held him and with soft and gentle
> Words, caressed and tried
> To remove beloved Ithaca from his chest;
> If only he could see the smoke rise above his sweet Ithaca
> And then forever close his eyes to the light of day.
> Does this move you, Olympian, can you feel your heart?

The maids comment on her performance.
'I didn't understand one word of it, but she's good.'
'Those little words sound just like caresses.'
'She follows her lessons well.'
Judging from the comments, it sounds like Pia really is

everyone's daughter. She bows, hops off the stool, picks it up, and nods to Nanny, who then pushes the two boys forward, dressed up in sheets. Enrico is Telemachus and Pietro is all of the suitors. They recite their parts timidly, their eyes fixed on Tommaso, who has taken it upon himself to teach them the verse and who whispers along with them, sending nods of encouragement. They conclude with a happy brawl with small wooden swords, round shields and leather armbands made by Ruggiero. No one can stop them. The duel goes on – it lasts an age; the verses of Homer are forgotten and all that is left is brotherly rancour mixed with joy, jab after jab.

⁂

'Pia trusts you. She sees you as a mentor. I have never seen her so content. And I am pleased with the way you treat her,' Donna Clara says one day to Bianca, taking her aside in an imperious yet intimate manner.

'I can tell that she is very dear to you,' observes Bianca, trying to appear nonchalant but taking advantage of Donna Clara's conversational mood.

'Yes, you're right. It's not just our Christian duty that pushes us to treat her favourably. Pia is truly a special girl. She's so alive. My granddaughters are such delicate daisies; they take entirely after their mother, poor dears. Even my darling Giulietta: she cries over nothing and is always ill. I love them because they are my flesh and blood, and it's the law of nature. But it is nice to let oneself, every so often, choose whom to love. And Pia is my choice. When she is older, I will be sure to give her a real dowry, not like the Ospedale Maggiore, with their horse blankets and two cents. We will help her find a good husband who will respect her – a shopkeeper, a merchant, or a small property owner.'

Bianca falls silent, irked by this compunction. *You treat her as if she were your doll,* she thinks. *You grant her certain privileges that other servants only dream of. It's all fine now, while she's young, but when she's grown up she will have to fend off jealousy. You are using her.* Bianca would like to voice some of these things but the words stay bottled up inside. She has no right to speak her mind to Donna Clara. She has the feeling too that there are other things at work in the background, blurring the focus of this painting whose only distinguishable feature is Pia's face. She has been told that the girl's father has disappeared and her mother is dead. But if Pia truly is a foundling, how do they know all these things? Who told them? And what if her story is the same one told to many lost girls, the details sewn together like a quilt? Do they simply feed the girls' fantasies?

Pia will end up heartbroken, Bianca says to herself. The thought pains her and she silently promises to watch out for the girl as long as she can.

※ ※

Bianca needs to focus on her work. She decides that she will make all the preliminary sketches in the summer and then, during the winter, when her subjects are temporarily away, she will begin painting. Without the liveliness of colour before her, though, it will be difficult. She therefore compiles a selection of different colour swatches. She takes large pieces of paper and draws rows and rows of the same-sized rectangles, and fills them with the colours she knows she will need: innumerable shades of green and brown; creamy whites; whites with hints of pink, orange or yellow; the powerful vermilion of the upside-down fuchsias and the fresh bougainvillea from Brazil; the lilac blues of plumbago and rosemary. She positions the mixtures in front of their originals to verify their intensity, force and sweetness. What she discovers is a palette of harmonious colours, shading from the palest to the most intense. It is beautiful to see. Pia is fascinated by the chart; she devours it with her eyes and speaks the names of the colours out loud, savouring them as though they are flavours. Burnt sienna. Scarlet. Viridian. Lapis lazuli. Carmine.

Bianca's work does not end there. Next, along the border of each rectangle, she jots down in pencil the proportions of pigment that she has used in each mixture, hoping to catch the exact hue. How much is science and how much is enthusiasm, she doesn't know. Painting, though not a science, takes precision. It requires methodology and application, two predispositions that are not natural to Bianca, but which she has nonetheless mastered, as one does an exacting yet healthy sport that reinforces both muscles and posture.

She also has lovely calligraphy. One day Don Titta calls her to his study to ask her to copy out, in alphabetical order, all the names of the flowers, plants, shrubs and vegetables that grow in Brusuglio, or at least the ones that grow within the confines of the walled garden.

'It's part of a bigger task that I need your help with,' he explains, showing her the ledgers he has prepared precisely for this purpose. One lined column takes up a third of the page and the rest is filled with small squares. It is for accounting. He plans to fill it with the dates of the plants' arrival, their costs, the origin of the grafts, and comments on their outcome: if they wither in two months, resist, die, are struck by scale insects or powdery mildew, and so on.

'I need to catalogue. In these kinds of things I am consistent,' he says. 'I would like to do it myself, but I would have to dedicate all my time and mental energy to it. And now my mind is possessed by other thoughts . . .' He draws a small vortex in mid-air with his index finger. 'I'm like a coil: infinite. One thought attached to another attached to another . . .'

Bianca wonders if that's how poetry comes into being. Does it start with a chain of thoughts, and then – either suddenly or with premeditation – a flow of words fills out the chain the way a hand fills out a glove? She doesn't dare ask. She has not reached that level of confidence with him yet. She fears that he might be thrown by the question and she understands that for the general well-being of the family it is best for him to be calm. When he is absent, cooped up in his study for days on end, or out on his long walks, he does not talk about his plants, the harvest or the possibility of a drought. It is as if the persona of poet is too fastidious and demanding to be able to live with that other self, the one that drags him literally back to earth – towards the land, flowers, plants, vines and grain. But it is also evident that Don Titta feels nostalgia for the part of him that he has to neglect at times.

'If only one could keep ledgers of sentiments as well,' Bianca blurts out. She brings a hand to her mouth in shock. What has she said? Why did she say it? The master looks at her in surprise and then smiles.

'Even a man as highly unrealistic as myself could tell you that this would be useless. So, when will you begin the task?'

Tomorrow. There is always a tomorrow for postponing things. The days are long and slow and she is already busy. But despite the large undertaking, she decides to add a miniature drawing to each of the entries, as well as copying out the names. It will make the ledger even more precise and complete, with its old papers, documents, accompanying letters, receipts in French and English, and accounts of seeds purchased from afar.

From these master books, Bianca discovers more about the grand ambitions of the garden project than by visiting the greenhouses and fields in person. She learns how atypical shoots are planted and if the climate is conducive to them. She gets a sense of which seeds prosper and which wither. Every so often, though, she has to get away from her desk and get more precise information from Leopoldo Maderna, the head gardener.

At first Maderna looks into Bianca's eyes and answers every one of her questions in an irritated tone, as if he disapproves strongly and does not understand the hasty need for results from such a project. But then he contradicts himself, becoming excited.

'The black locust trees are rooting well. Actually, the roots are propagating and are shooting up from the ground in places you'd least expect them. It's exhausting to rip them out because they're formed like an upside down T, like this.' He holds out his left palm horizontally, the middle finger pointing up, to explain the shape. 'To pull them out you need to get really deep down. There they are – over there, and there.' And he points all around, along the horizon, at some green splotches. 'They're tall now. And they make up a wonderful dividing hedge, a flexible wall, but they prick worse than brambles.'

Bianca thinks about the green tangle that surrounded the home of Sleeping Beauty. Was it planted with *Robinia pseudoacacia*, with those small, seemingly innocent, bright green, oval leaves that never seemed to age?

There are trees everywhere: *Acer negundo* and *platanoides*, a grove of *Salix babylonica*, and the *Liriodendron*, with its aspiration for height and yellow flowers as big as fists. There is *Ailanthus*, as beautiful as it is fetid; *Gleditsia*, a thorny locust even crueller than the black variety. And there is *Inermis*, constrained to a sapling. Leopoldo tells her too about *Andromeda arborea* with its beautiful star name, which looks like a blazing fire in autumn. And the *Clematis* from Lake Como, which

Bianca has always found overly dramatic, but she doesn't say so because Como is Maderna's home town and she doesn't want him to stop talking now that he has started. Anyway, it is no use, he says, the *Clematis* won't take. He points to these plants, struggling to climb the taut lines along a south-facing wall that ought to supply them with the necessary shade and instead puts them to shame. Maybe they prefer the north. There are the *armandii* and the *cirrhosa* varieties, with their three, pointy, garnet-coloured flowers. They are lovely, yes, but too sparse to make an impression. The *intricata* is all leaves and might remain as such, and the *pagoda*, with its exquisite name, hints at sophisticated chinoiserie. Passing from the delightful to the useful, there are vines from Burgundy and Bordeaux, but they aren't faring too well.

'The issue here is the land; it's only good for *Bersamino*, that fussy grape that comes from young Don Tommaso's parts. To find really beautiful vines, one needs to take the Via Francesca, or go beyond the Po River to the foothills of the mountains,' Leopoldo explains, as he guides her through the estate. 'These are grown in the French manner, as dwarves.' Together they skirt the neat bush-trained vines from which hang miniature bunches of acid-green grapes. 'You'll see how good these grapes are, but a few is all that Don Titta's table needs. Let's hope that powdery mildew doesn't take hold of them first.'

After conversations like these, Bianca goes back to the study, rereads her notes, compares them with the organized shopping lists written by Don Titta, verifies the spelling and checks them against guides and dictionaries. She discovers that out there, though she does not know where exactly, there really is everything: cherry, apple, pear, apricot and plum trees, in millions of varieties. If the world were to end, everyone in town could live for weeks off these fruits.

Bianca finds she doesn't want to know a thing about the repugnant art of silkworms. The mulberry trees, on which they feed, are numerous.

'You mustn't plant them too close together,' Leopoldo tells her. 'In the first year you breed only three branches, and keep them clean cut. We planted eight hundred and then another eight hundred. If we have too many leaves, we can always sell them.'

In fact, she has seen many young boys coming and going with baskets full of fresh leaves to give to the silkworms that live in the peasants' homes. They take care of them day and night like guests of honour. If you get close enough, you can hear the incessant gnashing of their jaws.

'They are a Japanese green breed,' Leopoldo explains with pride. Bianca, who does not want to see them, not even from afar, imagines them as being fat, bound in tiny flowered pieces of fabric, and wrapped in silk string. She knows they work hard, but she doesn't want to even try to appreciate them. Leopoldo, who clearly feels more comfortable with her now, takes a dark pleasure in inviting Bianca to see where they blanch the worms.

She saves the best for last, like a child before a plate of sweets. The flowers. Obviously, she focuses on the ones with which she is less familiar. She knows a fair amount from her studies, from her books and from visits to the most important botanical gardens in Europe. She has already come across hydrangeas and their exaggerated richness in Kew Gardens, but she learns that they are almost unknown in Italy. To get there, they come from France by sea and then wagon, like enslaved princesses. Bianca fantasizes about the shrubs in their jute sacks and the young mahogany-coloured servants who bring them fresh water every day, water that the servants want to drink themselves but cannot. She pictures the ship sailing on and on. What if there was a storm and the boat was wrecked – where would those plants end up? At the bottom of the sea? Would they breed with algae and decorate the hair of mermaids? Or would they drift along the surface, helped by the current, until reaching some desert beach, forming a grove in a new corner of the earth that has previously been known only to monkeys? No, the hydrangeas that Leopoldo Maderna is so proud of are merely the outposts of a whimsical invasion commanded by a French friend of Don Titta's, named Dupont. In the ledger, Dupont is nicknamed 'the flower correspondent'. He has sent plants from Paris at regular intervals with several folio sheets from the *Almanach du bon jardinier*. Plants also come from the offices of Longone Constantino da Dugnano, a great cello of a man, big-boned and rather slow, who carries his last name proudly and who has the tendency to blush every time he sees a woman. He brings shoots that need to be transplanted in a hurry.

Almost all the flowers are Parisian by birth. This explains, perhaps, their reluctance to take root in these rustic lands. The *Lathyrus*, for example, is something of a failure in all its forms. The *Bignonia* fare better, and actually are so invasive that their orange flowers are overwhelming. The *Digitalis*, with its poisonous qualities, has been planted in the far reaches of the gardens, where no child would think of feeding their dolls with those colourful tube-like flowers. The light blue and lilac *Lobelia* create colourful stains along the border of the great valley, light and dark hues depending on the tyranny of shade and soil. The *Achillea, Aquilegia canadensis* and *Rudbeckia*, with their ordinary gay colours, grow semi-wild and are planted at the far ends of the garden. Pink sachets of *Silene*, as light as silk, stand shivering along the confines of the field. This is neither an Italian nor a French country garden; it is different from everything, a bastard child, whose mother is beauty and father is experimentation. It lacks the charm of the English garden, where rare flowers look like dishevelled weeds, where roses rest against tree trunks like weary girls, and where emerald-green grasses are compact and lovely with moisture. It is a garden of contradictions, like its owner. It is high and low at the same time, plebeian and haughty.

To learn the names of things makes Bianca feel somewhat omnipotent. To learn the history of a seed, its timing, and its ways gives her a strange sense of self-possession. Copying down all that information in the correct order – and adding her personal touch of a tiny ink drawing of a leaf, flower or fruit in the column she has created herself – is Bianca's own way of making sense of the world. She expects to receive compliments from the entire family once her work is finished: the poet's sincere gratitude, an evening of oohs and aahs, the little girls being allowed to turn the pages so they can recognize the flowers and fruits they have seen thousands of times, and learn to spell out their Latin and common names. They will ask if they can copy the drawings, and Bianca, with enthusiasm, will promise them a colouring book with the best drawings on a larger scale for their small hands. She will enjoy a small triumph and ignore envious glances or sly comments – the honey on the rim of the cup that holds a bitter drink.

❧ ❧

One day, Bianca walks into the library in search of *Traité des arbres fruitiers*. She saw it in the hands of the master a few days ago. It is a beautiful edition with hand-coloured tables. Don Titta purchased it in Paris, he told her once at dinner, when he decided to dedicate himself – 'ignorant as a newborn' – to the land. Instead of taking the book and leaving, however, Bianca cannot resist the urge to leaf through it immediately. She stares at the drawings of the dappled skin of a pear, and then at the rust-coloured network of some strange apple, its name sweeter than its actual flavour. Behind her, Don Titta approaches in silence.

'Are you interested in apples, Miss Bianca?'

She jumps, then, regaining her composure, turns around and takes a step back. He is so close to her she can smell his clothes: a scent of verbena, somewhat feminine.

'I was curious to see how Monceau managed with fruits,' she says. 'In the drawings from a century ago they always look so small. Not to mention the branches – so spindly they're frightening.'

'A little, but that is their natural structure – they look like the hands of old men. But as far as the fruits themselves go, it is because you have ours in mind. Brusuglio is a rediscovered paradise, or better, an Eden where we have been happily forgotten.' He speaks without a hint of irony. 'Our apples, do not fear, do not bring damnation. There are no prohibited fruits here or sick ones. You can bite them to your heart's content. You know the unwritten rule: nothing halfway. We have magnificent plants, or nothing,' he finishes with a smile.

Bianca returns the gesture. She knows about Don Titta's attempts to plant white cotton and the Nanking cherry. The former caught on at first, for in one of the ledgers there is a triumphant message detailing a bountiful crop: five kilos of raw cotton transformed into eighty aune of precious percale through octane spinning. But it was only a one-time miracle. The cold, frost, rain and hail brought it to a bitter end. Too many enemies for a small plant that wants only heat.

Even now they are going through a strange season. It rains

like there will never be sun again. The children, confined to the house, are bursting with suppressed energy. A faint green mist presses against the trees, concealing the edges of the world.

'Shall we send out a dove?' Innes suggests. Both Donna Clara and Donna Julie look at him with disapproving glances. 'Or a dog?' he corrects himself. Bianca lets out a little chuckle.

'Dogs don't like to go out in the rain,' Pietro replies. 'That's why they end up pooing in the house and stinking it up.'

Shocked laughter follows from the little girls and from Enrico.

'Stinky poo, stinky poo,' Enrico sings.

'Children!' Their mother tries to call them back to order. Nanny covers her mouth in shock. Innes, master of deflection, distracts them.

'Do you know how many days the Great Flood lasted? Seven? Five? One hundred? Twenty?'

Satisfied looks come from both mother and grandmother. It is always a good time to review the sacred scriptures.

❧ ❧

In the space of only two days, all three girls fall ill. Hiding her own cough, Donna Julie shuttles back and forth between nursery and ground floor, carrying either insipid food or smelly herbal concoctions. The poet, as always in such family crises, shuts himself in his study. Tommaso, afraid of being left alone with the boys, does the same. Donna Clara spends her time worrying. Innes is left to entertain the boys, turning down Nanny's offer of help. Bianca passes the days in the extremely humid greenhouse, watching drips of water run down the panes of glass from her place on the iron bench, identical to the kind she sat on in the Condorcet gardens. Bianca feels good in the rain, and in water, generally. It has always been that way. It is her element – if not by nature, then by choice. Being there, surrounded by it, she daydreams the way she did while swimming in her slow, precise manner across the dark lake at her home. It is as though she is in a light green bubble. The aromas of the greenhouse, accentuated by the prevailing moisture, daze her. Memories take her away from this world, which clutches her like a tight corset even though it has all the elements of comfort – freedom, independence, and a certain amount of fun. She doesn't know quite what to make of this nostalgia. It isn't a feeling that she enjoys. She thinks it useless, a wasted exercise, to want things that are no longer attainable. She doesn't really miss the lake because she knows it is still there. Its quiet, mineral existence carries on without her. She knows she can get to it in two days by carriage. When you know something is there, when you can reach out and touch it, it exists. It's there, even if you *don't* touch it. Really, the sole person she misses terribly is inside her, ready to answer when she calls, present the way that spirits are always present, their company perceived only when you listen hard enough. And yet, Bianca feels, something is missing.

⁂

'Who was it?' Don Titta storms into the nursery, dripping with rain, his frock coat steaming before the fire. He looks like a ghost, a slight mist blurring his contours. His hair, long and darker on account of the water, sticks to his pale cheeks, and his eyes flash. The little girls whisper, then Franceschina runs to seek shelter in Nanny's arms. Even the boys huddle together instinctively.

'Who was it?' he repeats, holding out the *Traité* before him, its cover blackened and soaking wet.

Bianca feels a pain shoot through her. Without speaking,

she comes closer, takes the book from his hands and places it on the rug in front of the fire. Kneeling down before the book, she opens the pages carefully, separating those that are already buckling together.

'You know my books mustn't leave the library,' Don Titta says sternly. 'You children used it to copy out the fruits, isn't that right?' No one answers. 'Isn't that right?' he repeats more loudly.

Five silent heads nod yes.

'But we stayed inside. We didn't take it out there,' Enrico objects, as if the book is a rare animal to be kept in a cage.

'I would like to know who brought it up to the rotunda, and above all, who left it there.'

Silence.

'I saw Miss Bianca carrying it under her arm. She was going that way with a box of coloured pencils.'

It is Pietro.

'It's true,' says Bianca. 'I took it with me. But I also brought it back, of course, before it started to rain.'

'Well, I'm only saying that I saw her with the book,' Pietro repeats, staring at his feet. Bianca does not lower herself to reply. *Imagine that*, she thinks, *being accused by a child*.

Don Titta walks out, leaving them alone.

'This is serious,' Bianca says, looking at them all, one by one. 'You all know that this is a precious book and that your father is very fond of it.'

Pietro is silent.

'It wasn't Miss Bianca,' Francesca says to Pietro. 'I saw her coming back.'

'What if we hang it up to dry?' Giulietta proposes and the others laugh a little too loudly, needing to release some of the tension in the room.

'That's not a bad idea,' Bianca says. 'But not now. First let's finish what we were doing.'

Their game, however, has lost its momentum. Dinnertime is slow in arriving. Later, Bianca unstitches the book's binding and hangs up the pages, a quarto at a time, in the room where they hang the bed sheets to dry. Pia helps her, pronouncing the Latin names of trees as they pin the pages to the lines with wooden clips. As the forest of paper grows denser, shaming the masses of socks, underwear and leggings, Bianca almost forgets her anger towards Pietro, his lie, and the prank that she is almost certain hides behind it all.

❧ ❧

'Signorina, Miss Bianca! Signorina!'

Bianca is sewing the dried and ironed pages back into their binding and sighs in resignation. The job takes the kind of patience that she doesn't have: her thimble is too big and her finger keeps falling out of it, causing her to prick herself repeatedly. In the end she just gives in. The *Traité* will be decorated with a patchwork of pinpricks of blood, the silent witness to a sinister pact. Who would ever need the image of a Saint-Germain pear? A fruit vendor, perhaps? And what does Tommaso want from her now? Bianca puts down the needle and thread in irritation and reluctantly lifts her head.

'Yes?'

'I'm sorry about the book. I told Titta that I saw you bring it back to the library.'

'Were you spying on me, perchance?'

Tommaso's face reddens. 'I would never, Miss Bianca. I was only in the right place at the right time, as they say.'

'Thank you, but I don't need a lawyer in training to defend me from the accusations of a spoiled and deceitful child. Or are you practising for when you get your life back together?' Bianca isn't sure where all this malice has come from but she doesn't feel like holding back. Her index finger burns with piercings. She puts the tip in her mouth and sucks on it.

'Oh, wonderful. Now you, too. You're like my sister: a portrait of wisdom. In reality she's so hideous that no one wants her.'

'If my brother said that about me, I'd spear him with a paintbrush.'

'I see you also know how to tease . . . No, but seriously, you should know how important it is for me to be here. I live in Don Titta's shadow. He is my mentor, master and model.' Tommaso speaks with fervour.

Bianca wonders why he is telling her all this. What is going on? A second earlier they were teasing each other.

'I will never become as important as him,' he continues. 'I've decided to have my plebeian muse speak in the manner most appropriate to her. In dialect. Would you like to hear something? I need to reveal her to the public, my simple muse, to see what kind of effect she has on people.'

Bianca does not know whether she should be annoyed or pleased by Tommaso's attempt at winning her trust. She hasn't asked for it. The language of the town bothers her too; it is different from the rugged singsong dialect that she heard as a little girl. But she realizes that it is just a matter of familiarity, that each one of us finds beauty in that which we are most familiar with.

Tommaso falls silent, waiting for encouragement. He smiles, blushes, rakes his hand through his hair, and all of a sudden the pale-faced dandy is taken over by a young boy with dishevelled wisps of hair across his forehead and a vein of cheerfulness. Bianca understands only about half of the words he recites: a confused story about nuns in love, it seems. She smiles despite herself, so great is the passion which ignites him. One strange verse catches her attention:

> *Mì t'hoo semper denanz de la mia vista,*
> *Mì non pensi mai olter che de tì,*
> *In di sogn no te perdi mai de pista,*
> *Appena me dessedi, te see lì,*
> *Mi gh'hoo semper in bocca el mè Battista,*
> *Semper Battista tutt el santo dì . . .*

> You are always before my eyes,
> I can't think of anything but you,
> In my dreams I never lose sight of you,
> As soon as I lie down you are there,
> The name of Battista is always on my lips,
> Always Battista, all the blessed day . . .

The performance ends.

'Miss Bianca?'

'Yes?' Bianca comes back to earth and applauds, as deserved. 'Bravo.'

Tommaso composes himself. 'Really, you liked it?'

'Well, I must admit that it wasn't all very clear to me . . . maybe I liked it because I didn't know what you were saying. But it has a melody to it. Isn't that important in poetry? That it has a melody?'

'Oh yes, as long as it's a tune and not a toot!'

He has gone back to his wisecracks. This improper side of Tommaso is much more fun. Bianca looks at him in fake shock and they both burst out laughing.

૱ ૱

'I've noticed that you're becoming more intimate with our junior poet,' observes Innes coldly, a few days later.

'Are you jealous?' Bianca asks, a hint of a smile on her lips.

Innes ignores the insinuation.

'Tommaso definitely has some artistic feeling inside him but he's just wasting his time,' he tells her.

'At least he's not a drone, like Bernocchi.'

'Don't be so quick to judge, Bianca. Drones are not bad insects.'

'If you like Tommaso so much, why does it bother you that I talk to him?'

'I didn't say I liked him. I said that I see something in him, but I can't stand watching him waste his energy. I think that for his own good he should leave. Everything that is holding him back, including certain gracious maidens who are willing to indulge him, harms him. As long as he lingers in the shade of the oak tree, he will remain as fragile as an offshoot.'

'You're accusing me of exerting too much influence over him, Innes. He's here because of his master, mentor and model. But wait,' Bianca says with a little shrug, 'maybe that's not the right order.'

'Right. But now that the cuckoo has made his nest here in Brusuglio, it's going to be difficult to get him to leave.'

'I think a nest is exactly what he needs.'

'Don't deceive yourself, Bianca. He's your age: neither a babe nor an orphan. He's a man. This "nest", as you call it, allows him to prolong his boyhood at the expense of others, avoiding confrontation with hardship. If he truly wishes to live as a poet, he should tend to his own matters, make his own decisions and sever ties.'

'But he won't get a penny from his family if he gives up, the poor thing.'

'Poor thing? He could be a handyman by day and write at night, if he really cared so much about it. He could rent a room at an inn and sort out his thoughts. But here he finds warmth or a breeze depending on the season. He drinks and dines well. He is cared for. Sooner or later his clothes will wear out and I don't think Don Titta will want to buy him a new wardrobe.'

'You are quite vicious. You sound like me.'

'Perhaps I do only feel envy, Miss Bianca. He is so young; everything is still possible for him and it irks me to see him throwing away such an opportunity by fooling around with the ideas he has of himself.'

'And what are you, old? Come on. At thirty, a woman is old and a man is in his prime. Soon, I will surpass you in this gloomy race. I will be in mourning for my withered years of youth while you will still be a promising shoot.'

'That's what disturbs me.' Innes grows solemn and melancholy. He becomes reflective, as though Bianca isn't there. And she, who has failed in her attempts to amuse him, is annoyed with herself.

᪣ ᪣

'The ghost is back!' Pietro lunges into the room, bringing a gust of cool air with him that remains even after Nanny has shut the French window. He removes the cap that his grandmother and mother force him to wear even during the summer, on account of his earaches, and drops it on the floor. Nanny retrieves it swiftly. The boy's colouring is vivid and his hair dishevelled, making him more attractive than usual, livelier. He stomps his feet in excitement: 'I saw it! She was on top of the rotunda, and when I got near, she disappeared inside! She's in the rotunda!'

The girls cover their mouths and hold their breath. Donna Julie sighs and looks away, as if to erase the sight of her son looking so wild. She detests these sorts of displays.

'You could have taken me with you!' Enrico whines.

'I like doing things on my own.'

Donna Clara takes Pietro's hands in hers and warms them while speaking to him both reassuringly and with reproach, a combination she often uses when talking to the boys, as though forcing them to reason is a vain effort.

'Oh my, you're so cold! Now you're bound to get sick and drive your poor mother crazy. You know you're not allowed to go out at night-time. You know nobody likes this story about a ghost. And you mustn't tell lies – we have told you thousands of times. What were you doing outside at this hour anyway?'

She casts a surly glance at Nanny.

'I was busy with the girls, signora,' Nanny says in her own defence.

Pietro, triumphant – and happy to take both blame and merit – realizes that for once they are one and the same, and clarifies his story.

'Nanny has nothing to do with it. She was in the nursery and I was very quiet. I slipped out. You can't expect to keep us prisoners like girls or workers.'

Donna Julie ignores the offensive juxtaposition and tightly presses her hands together in prayer, imploring the saint who is supposed to protect children from the evils of the world, even when they are good.

'But Pietro—'

'She wore a veil,' the boy continues, throwing his cape back over his shoulders. 'She was walking above the ground. She was frightening, but she didn't scare *me*. I got so close, I almost grabbed her, but then . . . well, she ran off. It was dark up there, so I decided to come back. To tell all of you,' he concludes, transforming his cowardice into bravery.

Enrico watches him with clenched fists and repressed anger. The girls take sides. Matilde and Franceschina stare at him, spellbound, while Giulietta remains sceptical. Bianca sides with Giulietta: Pietro does not have the makings of a hero. And most likely he has made up half of what he has said. However, this particular ghost is clearly nothing new.

Donna Julie lowers her head.

'Ghosts do not exist,' Donna Clara insists.

'I'm telling you, it was a ghost,' retorts Pietro. 'It was the same one, Nonna, the black one with the veil in front of its face, the one you saw in the fields that time, the one that terrified you.'

'I was only spooked,' Donna Clara replies. 'But since ghosts do not exist, they don't really spook anyone. Now go upstairs and get changed. And don't bother coming down for dinner: liars are not welcome at our table.'

Donna Julie is clearly tempted to intervene but refrains with difficulty. She has a hard time challenging authority. Bianca thinks it unfair that Donna Clara exerts control whenever she wants. Pietro isn't her son. But on the other hand, the child isn't being pleasant either and to see his embarrassment brings Bianca a brief but sharp sense of joy, which goes hand in hand with Enrico's sour glare. Pietro shifts his weight from one foot to the other in anticipation of a reprieve, until he realizes that his mother's indulgence won't cancel his grandmother's punishment. And so he goes up the stairs, his eyes downcast.

Donna Clara inhales as deeply as her silk corset permits and then shakes her head.

'Too much imagination. They listen to too many stories, these children. I'm always telling you that, Julie.'

'Actually, I saw the ghost once, too,' Matilde says, surprising everyone. Matilde, who never speaks unless spoken to, has bright red cheeks. Her sisters stare at her, flabbergasted.

'Enough of this chat,' her grandmother says. The child hushes.

Soon it is dinnertime. Enrico shoots a suspicious glance at his brother's empty seat, uncertain whether to envy him or to appreciate that his absence allows him for once to be the only boy. As he lays eyes on the meal, he explodes with joy: stuffed veal sweetbreads are one of his favourites and now he can have twice as much. It is as if not being found guilty of anything this time makes him innocent forever. Bianca watches with poorly concealed horror as the child devours his plate of offal. She will never eat, nor has she ever eaten, anything of the sort. It feels like savagery to put something so holy and at the same time so intimate in one's mouth, stripped from the body of a once-living being. Enrico passes his days with animals – dogs, cats, rabbits and lambs – doling out snuggles and violence in equal amounts. He obeys all his impulses and he follows his cravings. Bianca looks down at her own plate of pale lettuce and then over at Donna Clara. She relishes her food with the same joyful ardour as her grandson.

'If I am not being indiscreet, can you tell me more about the ghost?' Bianca says.

Donna Clara looks up from her meal, her fork in mid-air, and then waves her free hand as if to shoo away a pesky fly, gesturing at the boy, and shaking her head quickly. Bianca gives up; she will keep her curiosity to herself. But at dessert, after the children have said goodnight and followed Nanny upstairs, Donna Clara continues.

'In the presence of the little one I wanted to avoid talking about it,' she says. 'Children are so impressionable.'

Bianca wants to counter the comment but keeps her thoughts to herself. This isn't the time to interrupt or distract her. Soon, mollified by *une petite crème*, the older lady gives in.

'You, of all people, should know that any ancient dwelling, or even merely an old one, has phantoms. We have the Pink Lady. I don't know whether you have ventured out north of the fields, but there is a dilapidated turret out there. It is said that those are the ruins of what was once the castle of the Pink Lady, who lost her soon-to-be husband in battle just before being married. Romantic stuff, you know.' She shakes her head slowly back and forth in an expression of disapproval. 'Like those novels that are in vogue now. Anyway, the widow-to-be closed herself in the castle and never came out, dead or alive. It's a story that everyone around here knows. And you understand how children can be: they listen and they repeat. They invent. They must have overheard it from the help. Some fool in an apron shrieks and sees what they want to see.'

'That's too bad. I would have liked to paint its portrait. The phantom's, I mean,' jokes Bianca.

Donna Clara smoothly changes the course of the conversation.

'This Chantilly *crème* is excellent. It seems as though the cook has finally learned that in order to make it you need to have a delicate touch.'

'I made it,' Donna Julie says with a smile.

'Oh no!' Donna Clara exclaims. 'You mustn't tire yourself out, you know that.'

'Tire myself over whipped eggs and cream?' laughs Donna Julie.

'What will they think when they see the lady of the house

amidst the pots and pans,' objects Donna Clara, forgetting about the time she herself spends in the kitchen. Although in truth she never lays a finger on a pot.

'I like it. It's fun for me,' insists Donna Julie. 'You never let me do anything.'

'Oh well, if you want to get sick again . . .' Donna Clara says, scraping her bowl with a spoon. Bianca eats in silence, savouring the cream's airy texture, its softness and the contrasting tartness of the fruit.

'My mother taught me how to make cakes,' Bianca says. 'Would you like the recipe?'

Donna Julie lights up.

'I'd love to try it but only if you help me.'

'Of course! With all the children,' Bianca says, smiling.

Donna Clara scowls and asks for another helping.

'I don't understand you two. The idea of getting your hands dirty with dough, bringing the children into the kitchen . . . it will only confuse the help and people will lose their sense of place.'

'The children are always sneaking into the kitchen, anyway, and I don't see anything wrong with it. Perhaps they will enjoy themselves more than they do with Nanny. They will certainly learn more. And with my hands, I can't be a lady. Look,' Donna Julie says calmly, holding out her small white hands marked by imperfections; they are swollen, rugged, even, to look at.

'I always say you work too much. It isn't proper. You should wear gloves.'

'I'm tired of doing what I should.'

'You're making a mistake.' Donna Clara speaks without even looking at her.

'You, of all people . . .'

The sentence hovers over the table in mid-air, powerful

enough to cause the old signora to finally look up from her plate and into the eyes of her daughter-in-law.

'I what?' Donna Clara replies disdainfully.

'You . . . you, at least, have lived,' mumbles Donna Julie. And then it is as if a sudden gust of wind extinguishes her tiny flame. She lowers her head and is silent.

❧ ❧

Later, while she is unbraiding Bianca's hair, Minna, who as usual has heard every word, cannot resist the urge to speak her mind.

'Don't listen to Donna Clara. She doesn't want to talk about it because she says it distracts us. The Pink Lady is an old story and is over. No one believes it. The ghost, however, does exist. She's real. She comes to evening vespers every Monday.'

'If she's always so punctual, she must be English,' Bianca jokes. 'With a pocket watch hanging from a long chain.'

'Oh, that I cannot say. What I do know is that she appears out of nowhere and disappears into thin air.'

Minna stares at her in the mirror.

'Seriously, Miss Bianca. Open your eyes and you will see.'

Bianca knows that in order for ghosts to exist, someone has to believe in them. She lets herself be lured into imagining the phantasmagorical creature as though she is a gullible child.

❧ ❧

The rains end, the ground dries out, the sun returns and summer makes its way back – one last time before the winter decline. It is hot and the world, invigorated by the hydration, is green with life, blooming, exultant. On Monday, when the church bells chime for evening Mass and a handful of old ladies hobble towards prayer, Bianca makes her way towards the northern gate. She takes a basket, her gardening gloves and a pair of shears. Her apparent goal is to find some unusual roses that grow in the beds farthest from the house. There she kneels among the bushes that flower far from anyone's sight. Roses have an air about them that is too uncertain for her taste, and yet they are beautiful. Their heads hang close together and their smell is faint. Bianca slips on her gloves and chooses several stems, but not the longest ones. She wants to use a specific crystal vase that she has spotted in the bottom of a cupboard. When she looks up from her basket, she is startled by what she has really come to see. Far off in the distance stands not a phantom, but a woman. She is dressed in dark clothes and wears a veil that drapes down beyond her shoulders like a short cape, giving her a monastic look. This trend hasn't yet arrived in these parts but Bianca recognizes it from certain foreign magazines. Maybe the woman is a traveller. Maybe Bianca is jumping to conclusions; perhaps she simply chooses that apparel because she does not want to reveal anything about herself. Even without a veil, though, the uncertain light of early dusk will hide her facial features. Because of the tall grass, she looks like a silhouette on a theatrical stage.

In the time it takes Bianca to gather her skirts and quicken her step towards the gate, the veiled woman has disappeared. Bianca tries to see where she went but the gate is closed, and she cannot follow the shadow any further.

※ ※

'What nice roses,' Donna Clara says to her later, as she arranges the trimmed flowers in the glass vase. 'Your hunt was successful, I see.'

Bianca is silent. Her real prey has escaped her. At least she will have her portraits of the roses, which will last far longer than the flowers themselves. She imagines everyone admiring the dark tangle of thorny stems beneath the surface of the water.

❧ ❧

A good hunter is dedicated. He returns time and again to the place where he first catches sight of his prey. In order to make the hunt his own, the hunter must be patient and methodical. The following day Bianca seeks out a point in the garden where she remembers the wall is slightly lower. She climbs over it without too much difficulty in an old grey pinstriped skirt that has seen some wear and tear, and retraces the woman's steps across the flattened grass, searching for clues. She isn't sure what she is looking for. If there are traces, she will never be able to find them. She isn't a dog that can follow its sense of smell. But she is lucky. Right there on the ground where the path gives way to the tall grass, she finds something. Bianca kneels down and picks up the strange object. It is a small pillow of striped pink and green velvet, sewn in a delicate golden whipstitch. In the middle, on a pink background, is an embroidered lamb with a real bell hanging from its neck. Bianca shakes the pillow and the bell jingles softly. It looks like it has been made for a tiny bed in a doll's house or like an elaborate sachet to be placed among one's linens. Bianca brings it to her nose: it has no scent.

❧ ❧

The following Monday brings steady rain. But on Tuesday the sun shines once more. Bianca climbs over the wall again and into the fields. She doesn't come across any surprising finds this time but does meet someone, just not the person she was hoping for.

'Well, look who's here: our painter! Out and about, and

disguised as a servant, no less. A delectable Colombina. What are you doing, Miss Bianca? Are you dressed up for charades? Or are you simply strolling incognito in search of new and original subject matter? Are you a fan of the people, dedicated to marrying their filthy cause? Listen to me, forget about them: flowers like you thrive in closed gardens. Or come with me to the city and I will show you how beautiful life can be . . .'

It is Bernocchi. He is dressed in a light blue spencer designed for another kind of figure. His trousers and white socks amplify his more than robust thighs and calves. He removes his hat and plunges into a deep bow, showing off a florid and sweaty neck. It is a most unpleasant spectacle and encounter for Bianca, who would give anything not to be subjected to the prying gaze of this man. She tries to defend herself with indifference.

'Conte Bernocchi . . . well, this is the last place I'd imagine to find you.'

'Indeed. I arrived early and asked to be let out right here. I wanted to take a stroll in the open country . . . like you. I hoped to find out if here, among the tall grasses, lay the font of your inspiration. But of course, the fields are filled with interesting little creatures like yourself. Ah,' he says, looking off into the distance with a malicious air. 'Now I understand . . .'

Innes is crossing the field towards them, approaching from the house with long strides. When he arrives, he rests his hands on the wall from within.

'Who is luckier, the people inside or the people outside?' Innes says with a smile. Bianca's sombre expression does not escape him, nor does her plain outfit. He reaches across the barrier wall. 'I beg of you, come back to us. We simply will not let you run off,' he speaks light-heartedly, as he helps her climb back over the obstacle. Count Bernocchi peers at her naked calves, made visible by her movement, looking away only when Innes glares at him.

'Do not expect me to do the same,' he jokes. 'I am not a born gymnast like you English folk. I'm taking the long way round. A healthy stroll will do me good. Please tell them to prepare refreshments, as I will certainly need them upon my arrival. And let them know that I will bring an armful of roses with me, like a damsel. Like our Miss Bianca.'

Bernocchi walks off down the path, swinging his walking stick.

'Then be not coy . . .' mumbles Innes quietly in English, but Bernocchi either does not hear him or fails to understand because he doesn't turn around.

Innes and Bianca share a laugh. There are moments, and this is one of them, when it is right to suspend the rules of the salon: forget the plaster mouldings, ignore the delicate crystal and china, and walk past the family portraits. This is the joy of conspiracy. How nice to discover that Innes doesn't care for Bernocchi either.

Half an hour later they see him on the great lawn, stretched out on a chaise longue, his belly in full view, admiring the girls as they play with Pia. Each time Pia runs off to catch the ball, the count's head follows her.

> *Nella pozza c'è un lombrico*
> *Molle interrogativo*
> *S'inanella sotto l'acqua*
> *Non sai dir se è morto o vivo.*
> *Rosagrigio grigiorosa*
> *Dentro il fango cerca sposa.*
> *Se nessuno troverà*
> *con se stesso a nozze andrà.*

In the puddle there is a worm
A wet question
Twisting under water
You can't tell if he's alive or dead.
Pinkish grey, greyish pink
He seeks a bride in the mud.
And if he finds no one to bed
He will have himself to wed.

'Hurray, Papa!'

The children clap their hands and laugh, especially Pietro and Enrico, who has a particular fondness for worms. Over the years they have chopped up thousands for play soups or just for fun, watching them writhe in silent pain.

'How do you do that?' Giulietta asks. 'I want to write poems like you.'

Don Titta caresses the little girl's cheek and she snuggles up to him as if she is a kitten. Enrico crushes the sweetness of the moment.

'I know where to find lots of caterpillar moths! We can make homes for them!'

The children run off, even the little ones, followed by Nanny and her pleas.

'Don't touch them, they're dirty!'

The adults remain seated, awaiting their coffee.

'All children are poets by nature,' Don Titta declares. 'It's in the way they look at things.'

'Yes, but really, Titta, to speak of worms like that when we've just finished eating.'

The reproach comes from Donna Clara while the others have all smiled indulgently.

Bianca looks around at them, trying to understand them.

Innes exudes a certain detachment but a minuscule contraction of his mouth reveals a smirk held back with difficulty. Everyone else ignores the exchange, inclined in the name of peace to accept the vagaries of their host. Donna Julie nods and picks up on the bit of the conversation that interests her.

'They are our angels,' she says.

Bernocchi looks up at the sky and then down at his pudding, driving a spoonful into his mouth.

Children as poets and angels? Children are complicated, difficult, often sick, a source of anxiety, frequently whiny, and usually incomprehensible. At least *these* children are. They have been confused by rules that have often been contradicted with exceptions and turned into new rules. They are different from others and aware of the privilege that is bestowed upon them as their grandmother's pets, their mother's stars, and their father's arrows of hope. They are never simply children. Innes is the only person who approaches them from a different angle: he teases without humiliating; he reignites dormant interests; he knows how to engage and challenge them. He is a natural-born father. Maybe it's easier to educate other people's children than it is your own, Bianca thinks to herself, in the same way that it is easy for her to play with children, too. Playing is one thing she can do with ease.

One time Bianca lures them into the kitchen, taking advantage of Donna Clara's absence, to make a batch of fairy cakes.

'Sweets for fairies? Really?' Matilde asks, her face revealing incredulous conviction.

'They're called that because they are tiny and delicious and because they are the same ones that fairies have with their tea.'

'But fairies don't really exist . . .'

'You bet they exist; they are this tall' – Bianca makes a C

shape in mid-air with her thumb and index finger – 'and they have wings.'

'And they drink tea every day like the English,' Pietro intervenes drily.

'Every day,' Bianca repeats solemnly. 'But now, enough chitchat. If you used your tongue to mix your dough, it would be perfect.'

'My tongue? Yuck!'

'Yes, exactly. Hush and get to work.'

The twenty minutes in the oven feel like an eternity. While waiting, the children listen to her story about how a fairy is born each time a child laughs.

'So if we laugh they will come?'

'They will come and will never want to leave.'

'Never ever ever?'

'I don't believe it,' Pietro says. 'It's all horse feathers.'

'If you don't believe in fairies, you won't see them.'

'That's right, Matilde! That's exactly how things work.'

The scent of the sweet dough rising makes the girls clap their hands. Finally, there they are: the fairy cakes, perfectly golden on top.

'They're too beautiful to be eaten,' Matilde says.

'Now I understand why fairies love them so,' Giulietta adds.

'What are you talking about?' Pietro says greedily. 'I am going to have mine now.' He snatches two and runs away, followed by his brother, who grabs two in each hand. The girls look at Bianca, who, in turn, smiles at them.

'And now we will get the tea ready.'

She offers a cup to Innes when he peers in from the threshold, while the girls, who have been patiently waiting and couldn't care less about the drink, savour the strange cakes with their eyes closed. They have made these treats with their own hands, and as such they have to be exquisite.

'They are the best cakes in the whole world,' Francesca says with her mouth full, every so often peering at the window to check for the fairies. Bianca reminds her that they need to save a few for them. Innes smiles and raises his teacup in a toast. Bianca does the same. A cup of tea really is the best thing in the whole world. It is the taste of certainty in the face of uncertainty; it's like coming home.

'You're a rotten liar,' Innes says later on, as they walk together through the open countryside.

'Me? Why?'

'You've always said you don't like children.'

'I don't. Not all children. But these interest me.'

'If only mothers and fathers thought the way you do, they would make their children quite content. But I have another theory.'

'Let's hear it, Signor Know-it-all.'

'Perhaps you're not lying. But it could very well be true, so let's take it as the truth: you do not like children. The fact is,' and Innes pauses to look her in the eye, forcing her to reciprocate, 'that you, too, are still a child. And that is why they like to be in your presence.'

'I see. And what should I do now? Pretend to be offended? Slap you?'

'Do what you see fit, as long as you don't act like a prim young lady. There must be some benefit to the candour of the wilderness. Can't you see? It invites us to resemble it. It asks us to be what we truly are. What harm is there if every so often you allow yourself to be young?'

Right, what harm is there? Bianca gets up on the tips of her toes and snatches Innes's hat from his head. She then hurls it like a disk, sending it flying through the trees before it lands in the middle of a small clearing. Innes smiles and walks off slowly to retrieve it, watched by two surprised gardeners.

☙ ☙

At some point, Minna falls ill with a cough that won't go away. Perhaps it is due to the changing weather or from wearing clogs with no socks. She is not allowed to go outside. Even house-maids have the right to not be well. Consequently, the duties of assisting Bianca are passed on to Pia, who is pleased to do it. She gossips, she organizes, and if Bianca asked her, the girl would crush stones and boil tinctures like a true studio apprentice. Bianca watches her eager and precise hands at work, amused and inspired. She is not at all like Minna, who is clumsy in her youth and inexperience, and who only does things to follow orders, because it is expected of her. Minna completes tasks for Bianca in the same distracted way that she plucks a duck in the kitchen or washes clothes at the well. When Bianca later asks to keep Pia as her maid, she doesn't realize the storm that will be unleashed. In all good faith, she has imagined that for Minna one task is the same as another, a notion that, once she is better, the servant girl hastens to clarify. At first she doesn't say any-thing; her silence is downright hostile. She brushes Bianca's hair jerkily, and pulls at it like she did when she first arrived. She is so ill at ease that one clumsy gesture sends a porcelain vase of dried flowers crashing to the floor.

'Pardon me, I'm so very sorry. I didn't mean to.'

She bends down to pick up the shards but then drops every-thing again in a rage.

'It's all her fault I'm so worked up. It's her fault if I break things,' she says, crouched to the floor, her tiny face looking up.

'Whose fault?' Bianca asks, knowing the answer.

'That witch. Mamma says that she tricks everyone, even ladies like you. That . . . Pia.' She spits out her name as if it is a cuss word.

'Oh, come now, Minna, what an awful thing to say. I thought you two were friends.'

'Friends? I turn my back for a second and she steals my place.' Minna is silent for a moment. She forces herself to take command of her insolence, bites her lip, takes a deep breath, but still can't hold back. 'She always gets what she wants. Who does she think she is? She's no one's daughter; she was placed in the home just like I was, but no one came back for her. She should just be quiet, that's what my mamma says. She's lucky she ended up in a respectable house like ours, instead of having to keep the bed warm for some bum up in Brianza.' The venom seeps out, unstoppable. At this point Bianca is too curious to change the course of conversation. 'Oh no, but we aren't good enough for her. She always has to be different. Hasn't she told you about her "lamb" and the rest of it?' She pronounces the word 'lamb' with a grimace and in a strange voice, imitating her new enemy. Bianca is lost now. Minna sees that she has confused her listener. 'Do you not know about the "lamb"?'

And from that point forward Bianca becomes truly perplexed. Minna incoherently blurts out details, complicating the picture she has already tried to paint before: the world of children given up as newborns so that parents can save money, children who are sometimes taken back and restored to their regretful parents, but not always. The story has become so contorted and complicated with technical details now that Bianca has difficulty understanding.

'She says that when they left her at the orphanage she was wearing beautiful swaddling clothes. That's what she says. And when Don Dionisio went to get her with his sister, who weaned her so that she would be able to serve in his household and be like a daughter to her, she who had no children, he said that there was a tiny piece of paper pinned to her that said she was the daughter of a woman who had died in childbirth. He said that she was dressed in the clothes of a wealthy little girl, and that inside her bassinet she had a pledge token with a lamb on it that was embroidered in gold and silver. Of course, she couldn't have been a poor girl like the rest of us. She had to be a princess in the orphanage, too.'

'Wait a second. You're going too fast, I can't follow you. This lamb—'

'Me, I didn't see my pledge token, and even if I had seen it, I was too little – three days old – and I wouldn't have remembered it. But anyway I didn't have one. And I didn't say I had one either. My parents were poor folk, and the poor folk don't give pledges to children who would lose them, of course. They keep the pledges there, at the orphanage,' Minna continues with an air of impatience. 'They keep them safe alongside all the belongings of the other abandoned children from Milan. Pia's pledge is a little square, about this big,' and Minna draws an imaginary square with her tiny thumbs and index fingers. 'The mothers put the pledges in the swaddling when they know they will come back for their children one day. Then, when they do come back, say after three years or so, they can tell the people at the orphanage: I left my baby here on such and such a day and she had a pledge that looked like this or that, and the people at the orphanage look in their books to check so that they don't give the parents the wrong child, and if it's all true they go and find the child, who in the meantime has gone to live in the countryside with some farmers – the fake parents, I mean. And if the child is still alive they give him back to his real parents and together they live happily ever after. Pia had a pledge with a lamb on it, but poor parents leave half a playing card, half a San Rocco devotional card, half a medallion, something that poor people have. And they hold onto the other half so that when you unite the two parts, it makes up the whole, and that means you get the right baby. Your baby. Do you understand?' Minna is silent now. She is out of breath and her face is flushed. She stands up, the shards of the porcelain vase crackling under her clogs, but she doesn't notice. 'Anyway, the truth is, no one wanted her back, so it's about time that she stopped showing off and learned her place, and that's that. And with that, I pay my respects and wish you a good night.' Minna stomps off with tiny, angry steps, leaving behind a cloud of confusion.

Bianca feels disconcerted. What is all this nonsense about abandonment and recovery, beautiful swaddling lambs and pledges? Aren't two abandoned girls under one roof too many? Or is it normal around here to just dispose of your burdensome children? What does Don Dionisio have to do with anything? Perhaps Minna is just stringing together bits of gossip she has overheard in the kitchen, embellishing them with spite and fantasy. It is surely just childish confusion, a joke born of jealousy, something that happens downstairs in every large household. Minna is a good girl really. She will get over it. She'll probably even feel sorry about what she's said. But Bianca also realizes that Minna knows how to find the right words, even complicated ones, despite being red with rage. She has been under the impression that the girl is accustomed to getting distracted and lost in thought, but not this time. The little girl has spoken and heard this speech many times and it clearly always leaves a bad taste in her mouth.

❦ ❦

Bianca tries to think about other things but in vain. She feels irritated with herself for not being able to soothe Minna's spite. She replays the girl's monologue inside her head, trying to make sense of all that scattered information. And then, all of a sudden, she remembers the little pillow she found. She opens the drawer of her nightstand and, pulling out that odd square she'd found on her walk in the woods, she thinks back to Minna's words.

Pia's pledge is a little square, about this big . . . The mothers put the pledges in the swaddling when they know they will come back for their children one day.

Bianca isn't sure if this is a pledge because she has never seen one. Neither has Minna really, so she can't ask her. But if it is, what was it doing lying in the grass without a child? Or maybe – could it be that somebody has abandoned a newborn in the woods and left the token behind? No, it cannot be. She would have heard rumours about it, and the child most likely would have been torn to pieces by wolves. *Don't be foolish*, Bianca tells herself, trying to repress the absurd thoughts that crowd her head. And yet she continues to rack her brain, unsettled and intrigued. This is better than a novel. This is real. That odd pillow embroidered with so much care actually exists – and it has to mean something. Bianca decides she will take it upon herself to discover what that meaning is.

❧ ❧

The rivalry continues. Pia and Minna don't talk to each other. The little one is steadfast, obstinate, and convinced that she has been subjected to an unforgivable wrong. Pia shrugs and calls the other girl crazy, but Bianca can see how sorry she is, how she torments herself to make the situation right again. Bianca, who feels guilty for having unleashed the dispute, finally finds a remedy after explaining the situation to Donna Clara.

'A conflict, you say? Why on earth, when we treat them so well?'

Yes, Bianca thinks to herself, *like little animals in a cage.*

'You know how young people are: they have their tantrums, their little fights.'

She thinks minimizing the situation is the best way to achieve her goal. She makes an offer. At first Donna Clara seems a little uneasy and looks at her with suspicion: is Bianca, a stranger, trying to lay down the law in her own home? Who cares about the housemaids' bickering? And yet, it is clear that she feels a special kind of love for those girls and wants justice and harmony on her land. Bianca understands all of this.

'Very well. Just keep me informed. What little scoundrels they are! We give them everything: clothes and shoes, warmth and food.'

Bianca cannot help but comment.

'I suppose you're right. Once man's primary needs are met, other aspirations are awakened. It is inevitable.'

Donna Clara looks at her with a scowl. She won't let herself be taken for a fool.

'You are a true intellectual, Miss Bianca. Ah, women with brains . . .'

And with that, the rotating shifts begin. One day it is Minna's turn, the next Pia's. Sometimes both of them divide the tasks: the one who brushes Bianca's hair doesn't accompany her, and vice versa. When Bianca tells them of her new plan, they listen to her in silence. Minna is stubborn, retaining her identity as the violated one. Pia, on the other hand, is pleased. And it is she who holds her hand out to the other.

'Can we make peace?'

Minna glances at Pia with her outstretched hand, and stares at a point in the sky in front of her. Then she giggles, shrugs her shoulders, and lets herself be hugged. Bianca gazes from one girl to the other, amazed at how different they are despite being raised under the same roof. The little one is contentious and a trickster, with a sharp tongue and a sly mind. The older one is generous, willing to give up some ground for the love of peace. It is useless for Bianca to play favourites. But perhaps Minna will change, if guided appropriately. She hopes that Pia, on the other hand, will never change: she is beautiful and sincere, somewhat vulnerable perhaps, but only inasmuch as the other is armed, and nonetheless strong in her simplicity, keeping her one step ahead of the game.

❧ ❧

The following Monday it rains again but this time Bianca can no longer resist. She takes down a rain cloak from the coat rack outside the kitchen and walks out. It takes only three steps for her to regret making the decision: all kinds of smells linger on the oilcloth fabric – dog, gravy from a roast, ash. An overall film of dirt that has come to life, thanks to the humidity in the air. It isn't very pleasant being enveloped by such intense smells; they suffocate the wonderful scents of the wet park. But it is too late to go back now and besides, Ruggiero's cloak does the job: the drops of rain roll right off it.

Her sixth sense has been right. The ghost is there. But this time she has pinned her veil up to her hat. She moves forward through the tall grass slowly, holding her skirt with both her hands. She stares into the distance. Even from far away, Bianca can see her large eyes and pale skin. Her pace is long and elegant. Bianca is ready to approach her. She isn't far. She will find out for certain who she is. But then she freezes suddenly, overcome by a wave of dread as well as respect. The lady stops, lowers her head, and stands as still as a statue. A sudden gust of wind blows the veil over her face. Now she is frightening, and truly ghoulish. Bianca turns around and darts back to the gate, which she has left ajar. She closes it behind her, turns the key in the lock, and takes it. And then runs as fast as she can.

She sketches her vision that same night so as not to forget any details. That veil, embroidered with small droplets, is like a bride's, fit for a fairy-tale princess. The woman's eyes are large and deep, even behind the grey material. She has a generous mouth, a determined nose and an imperious chin. Bianca is certain that she will be back.

▪ ▪

But, in fact, she never returns. She isn't there at the vespers hour the following Monday, Tuesday or Thursday. Her absence does not go unnoticed. Even the help gossip about it.

'She's not coming back.'

'Her soul must have finally found peace, poor thing.'

'Maybe she died of the flu.'

When Bianca asks around for more information, the women hush, look at one another, and change the topic. Apparently, since she has stopped coming, she no longer exists. Soon there will be another curiosity to serve as the topic of discussion while plucking quails. Like old Angelina's son, for example, who won't stop growing: he is twenty and looks and eats like an ogre. Or the button seller, who has the eyes of a gypsy: they say he robs virgins of their souls, or something easier to come by.

Bianca is bothered by the chatter and anxious about the disappearance of the ghost, who has shown her art by vanishing. But she is done with thinking about it. She feels silly pondering such a futile curiosity. And in any case, there are other things that need to be done: in the kitchen, the nursery and the study. The children wail, the guests wine and dine, the help swear and complain, the owners give orders, and then they all sit down to tea. Flowers blossom and wither. She needs to pick them while she can.

> *Manina béla, con to soréla,*
> *'ndo sito sta'?*
> *Dalla mama, dal papà.*
> *Cossa t'hai dato?*
> *Pane, late,*
> *Gategategategate . . .*

> Little hand,
> With your sister,
> Where did you go?
> To Mama and to Papa.
> What did they give you?
> Bread and milk and
> Tickle tickle tickle . . .

'Me too, me too.'

'Do it to me, too.'

The children stretch out their arms so she can tickle their palms. The house seems full of them, a centipede of little hands. All the children are desperate to be distracted from the boring rain.

'What does it mean though, Miss Bianca? We don't understand.'

She speaks in rhymes from her 'recent childhood', as Innes calls it.

'Will you do it to me, too?'

Silly Tommaso, he always makes his way into the nursery

hoping for an escape. He gets down on his knees, and then onto all fours like an animal, making the children laugh. Bianca giggles but then shoos him away.

'We are busy learning,' she says.

'I don't see Nanny. Did you lock her inside a trunk?' he asks.

It is a tempting hypothesis and brings titters all round. Tommaso, still on all fours, moves backwards out of the room, swinging his head like a loyal dog.

'Now we're going to play dressing up,' she says.

'That's for girls,' the boys complain.

'Fine. You may be excused. Should I ask Tommaso to accompany you?'

'Nooo, we'll stay.'

'Miss Bianca, Miss Bianca, what should we do? Who should we be?'

Bianca considers.

'You should dress up as the person you most want to be.'

They all have good ideas and run off to prepare. Pietro and Enrico grab two old capes – whether they are uniforms or costumes it is hard to say – and twirl them around themselves like toreadors. The girls laugh.

'I'm ready!' Pia announces from her hiding place. Minna incites her to come out by clapping her hands and cheering her on. Bianca looks at Pia's creation. She cannot believe that the girl can have made it herself. She wears a headdress of dress swords that looks almost dangerous. She is like a peasant girl from another era, ready for a country wedding.

'What do you mean, another era?' mumbles Minna when Bianca says this. 'What peasant girl? She's a spinner, can't you tell? That's a party outfit that the ladies who work with silk wear. My mother comes from those parts. I took it out of my hope chest, but don't tell anyone. And be careful it doesn't get ruined, Pia – I'm going to wear it on my wedding day.'

'If anyone ever wants you,' Pia says, teasing.

Minna frowns seriously. Then she bursts out laughing and everyone laughs with her. Meanwhile Pia, dressed as the bride, looks down and smiles to herself. This is a performance and she is every bit the young actress.

Minna disappears behind the Chinese screen while the smaller girls fumble through a chest of hats, scarves, vests and old corsets. In between oohs and aahs and a couple of sneezes, they transform into other characters, and run to look at themselves in the mirror. They laugh with the complicit goodness of sisters when they get along.

'Have you really never played this game?' Bianca asks in surprise. 'We used to play dressing up all the time.'

She was the first one to explore the attic, probing the wide, damp space, with its tall, narrow windows that open out onto the world like eyes. She went back there a second time, with more ease. In the dresser she chose, among other things, this armful of clothes. When she asked permission to use them, Donna Clara only shrugged. 'I know nothing. I have never been up there. You're free to take whatever you want.'

Her accomplices, Minna and Pia, help her choose the strangest and most attractive items; they beat the dust out of them with broomsticks, lay them out in the sun, then hide them from the little girls to ensure they are a surprise. The scheme has worked.

Minna keeps chatting in that little voice she uses when she is excited.

'And who will the groom be, Pia? Shall we hand you over to Pietro or to Enrico? Or would you prefer Luigi, the bell ringer?'

This is followed by much laughter. Luigi is a scrawny teenage boy who gets pulled upwards every time he rings the church bell. Pia pointed him out to Bianca once, as she was guiding her to an alcove inside the sacristy.

Finally, Minna appears from behind the screen, standing with her arms crossed and a smug expression across her face. The breeches and lace shirt transform her into a charming young man.

'It is I who want you to be my wife, my damsel! Will you accept my offer?'

She falls to her knees at the feet of the bride, who clenches her shawl tightly around her, feigning reluctance. Everyone begins to laugh, and then suddenly the laughter fades and the bride falls silent. Pia stares at the doorway.

'What happened?' Minna asks.

When Pia doesn't answer, they turn around one by one. The girl looks down. Bianca first sees his reflection in the mirror, the rest of his dark clothes blending into the gloom of the hallway behind him. She turns to face him, ready to defend the children.

'We were only playing,' she says but her tone comes out more apologetic than she would like. They aren't doing anything wrong; this is the playroom, and it is raining outside.

Don Titta doesn't say a thing. It is as though he is hypnotized by Pia. The girl looks at her master with a serenity that could be mistaken for arrogance. Bianca wants to interrupt the exchange. She is afraid Pia will be punished for her impudence. But the master continues to stare at her, his head tipped to the side like a painter studying his model, thoughtful and detached.

Matilde interrupts the silence and hugs her father.

'You see how pretty I am?'

Don Titta finally snaps out of his daze and holds out his arms to pick up the little one, who pushes her curls back with both her hands to make herself more attractive.

'I'm dressed as a valet, can you tell?' She wiggles her feet in their blue silk slippers. 'I also have a feathered cap . . .'

She pulls away from his grasp to go and get her hat. In all the playing, it has rolled under the sofa.

Still, Don Titta is silent. Bianca doesn't know what to say. She wants him to leave and take the awkwardness with him. And finally that is what he does, without even a goodbye.

Liberated from his presence, the playroom seems more spacious, almost luminous. It looks like the sky beyond the glass window is finally lifting too. Minna holds out her hands to the other girls.

'Let's play Ring-a-Ring o' Roses.'

And whilst they sing the song, a little out of tune, Bianca remembers how they played on that first day, when she had just arrived, before Pia had entered the picture and everything had seemed so innocent, so pure. It's not Pia's fault, of course. She sings loudly in ignorant bliss, her cheeks as pink as a bride's. Then she leans towards Francesca, and then to Matilde, and whispers something in their ears, obtaining muffled laughter in return. She frees her hands from her playmates' and places them on her hips. And in an instant, she returns to a country girl, her feet moving in a complicated dance. She is talented. Everyone slows and then stops to watch her in awe. The swords in her hair tremble with every jump, capturing the soft light of the candles. She dances as though she has no memories, as if she is alone under the dark summer sky, listening only to the music inside her head, happy and free.

※ ※

'Will you also include their meanings?'

Bianca hates being watched while she is working. She could shoo away the children or Nanny but not Donna Clara. So she pretends not to hear, hoping that the lady will change the topic or wander off. But she remains.

'You should. A yellow rose for jealousy, a red rose for passion, a white rose for innocence, a lilac rose for excitement. I'm quite good, aren't I? Like mother, like son.'

The children laugh with their grandmother without fully understanding the conversation, giggling only because she does. Enrico reaches for a piece of charcoal, Giulietta smacks his fingers, he growls like a dog, and Nanny clucks her tongue in disapproval. Bianca ignores them and keeps on drawing. Donna Clara continues.

'The secret messages in colours. What was it? Mallow for understanding, tuberose for delight, myrtle for infidelity?'

'What about daisies?' Matilde asks, holding out a bunch of wilted daisies in her clenched fist.

'Innocence, little one. It's your very own flower.'

Bianca puts the finishing touches on the fuchsia (for frugality) and then gives up, letting go of her pastel somewhat brusquely. It rolls to the edge of the table, wavers a little, and stops. Francesca holds out her hand but there is nothing to rescue.

'No, I don't believe those things,' Bianca says. 'I can't. Flowers, the poor creatures, are faithful because they depend on our care. But they are also traitors, because so little is needed to take them away from us: frost, wind, a worm. They do not have a brain. They only have their costume. It is we who must learn to be better: constant, patient and helpful. We mustn't expect anything in return, only the gift of their beauty when it comes.'

A shadow appears in the doorway of the greenhouse.

'Well said, Miss Bianca.'

The voice of Don Titta makes her jump. The children turn to swarm around him. Bianca makes an effort to clean her fingers with a rag. The poet crosses his arms and leans against the door. Innes stands just a couple of steps behind.

'At ease,' he continues. He studies her. 'Look at what an interesting colouring this work gives you: sky blue and crimson hands, as if you have been catching butterflies. Something I advise against doing, Pietro, or,' he adds, 'I will get very angry. Do you understand?'

Although Pietro hasn't considered the idea beforehand, he is now smirking, and runs off to prepare for the cruelty to come. Bianca wipes an indigo stain from her palm; it doesn't want to go away, she will need to use soap. Donna Clara interrupts.

'Surely the lists of plants are much lovelier now, in any case? Before they were only black, or black with red ink for the French grafts. They reminded me of police rosters.' She frowns. Her son ignores her and continues speaking to Bianca.

'You are right to do as you do. He who soils his hands is the true gardener; anyone else is just a hobbyist.' Bianca hides her fingers behind her back, aware of the dirt under her fingernails from where she sunk her fingers into the earth at the foot of the path in order to feel how warm and grainy and alive it was. Innes notices and smiles. Don Titta continues. 'I will never be at your level. I am only a mere horticulturalist, a theoretician who ponders questions from behind a desk. We are in need of a modern-day Linnaeus to decide the names for all things green, so that they can be fixed forever, for everyone. I could seriously dedicate myself to that cause. What do you think, Innes? I suppose it, too, could be considered a form of unification.'

'Well, if you ask me,' Donna Clara interrupts, 'when they're on my plate and well cooked they're one and the same. It's the flavour that counts; do your treatises speak about this?'

Innes rolls his eyes a little at Bianca, who would laugh but coughs instead.

'Are you perhaps allergic to the leaves? That would be too bad, given your vocation. In any case, we have pickled snow peas for dinner tonight, not green beans. We have already finished those,' Donna Clara concludes and begins to leave the greenhouse with the children.

'Are you coming too, Papa?' Francesca tugs on her father's hand and he surrenders willingly, closing in on the procession with the little girl by his side, who is just happy to have him to herself.

Bianca is left feeling unsettled. She wouldn't mind continuing what she had set out to do but now she is distracted. Innes steps forward, leafs through the nearly complete master copy and nods.

'This is a small masterpiece, Bianca. You truly are the lady of the flowers. You know them like you own them.'

'I'd say the opposite is true: that they own me. Beginning with the fact that they take up all my time, all my enjoyment and, essentially, everything else. But let's not talk about me. It's boring. What about you? What are you master of? Tell me.'

Innes sits on the elegant and uncomfortable chaise. He looks out of place; he is far more comfortable in a worn leather armchair, book in hand.

'I don't know, Bianca. I don't know. I want what is not for me.'

'Even philanthropists deserve to be happy,' she jokes.

'Oh, come now, don't be naive,' he says seriously. 'One

doesn't deserve happiness; one takes hold of it when it comes along, if it comes along, out of pure luck. One takes a bite out of it like an unexpected fruit, knowing that it will never fill us up.' His voice softens. 'Don't pay attention to me, please. Life will explain itself to you in due time, provided that you listen.'

'I don't like you when you're serious.'

'In the end,' Innes continues, as if he hasn't heard her, 'no one said that happiness was the way out. I, for example, am happy with a far less resplendent gift – generosity.'

'Giving or receiving?'

'Bianca, Bianca, this is your biggest flaw. You couldn't be light-hearted if you tried. Or maybe it's a virtue. Your question is an important one but I am not going to give you an answer. Not now. It's a beautiful afternoon. Will you come with me?'

'What will that answer?' Bianca asks, confused.

'Your question, obviously.'

They laugh together. She stands and they walk out, arm in arm, from the warm shelter to the perfect briskness of early evening.

Bianca walks in the garden. She marvels over the shapes and colours of the vegetables poking out like jewels among the shrubs: the horns of the late courgette flowers, the red-faced cheeks of the tomatoes, the cardinal-vested aubergines. Without even thinking, she picks some of these fruits of the earth and puts them in the pocket of her apron. As she walks back towards Innes, she inhales the holy aroma of the rosemary that grows along the path and caresses it with her free hand.

It is the scent, more than the gesture itself, that reawakens a vivid memory. She remembers strolling with her father in the Botanical Garden of Padua. They gave a few *scudi* to a monk so they could wander about, but he stood nearby and kept an eye on them.

'I could walk away with a cutting in my parasol,' joked Bianca.

Her father, using his body as a guard, picked a little rosemary branch from a bush and placed it in the parasol's folds, making her giggle.

'Who is simpler, the herbs or the people who grow them?' she asked in all seriousness. She was only fifteen and they had just begun their trip. She had never had her father's full attention before. It was a privilege that never tired her, and in exchange she offered her unconditional attention, like a student in the presence of a revered tutor, overflowing with love.

'A good question,' he replied. 'I believe the two things go together: if you aren't pure at heart, you will contaminate the plants that you care for. If you aren't simple, you cannot possibly be pure at heart. Simple herbs are those that cure ailments and restore health. The monk is surely a simple person or else he wouldn't be standing there in his sandals. He would be in a hall full of frescos, in a crimson robe, or on his way to Rome. But I am certain that he is a happy man even without all of those other colours.' He added, 'Your name is Bianca because we wanted you to be simple, essential and pure. Because we wanted you to choose your own colours.'

The gravel crunched underfoot. Gusts of wind made purple petals rain down from a tree, like a child throwing confetti into the air.

'Do you want me to become a painter?' Bianca asked, pausing and turning to face her father. 'What if I am not capable?'

'Don't be so literal, Bianca. I mean you should be something different, something greater.'

She blushed and felt simple-minded, but then understood.

'You mean like choosing the colours of a flag or a banner?'

'Precisely. Warriors of certain tribes in North America paint their faces before going into combat to show everyone the colours of their courage. There's no need to paint your cheeks with your own colours. The important thing is to recognize that you have them.'

On that same visit she saw a sycamore tree. When she asked the monk about it, he bragged as if it was his very own baby.

'It's over one hundred and thirty years old.'

Bianca wondered how he could possibly know this. Maybe someone in the seventeenth century had taken it upon himself to record the date in the register. '*Planted a shoot of* Platanus orientalis L. *It looks promising; we will make it the Methuselah of our domestic forest.*'

The monk kept on speaking in a pedantic tone.

'As you can see, the trunk is hollow. This is due to a bolt of lightning that struck the tree when it was a hundred years old, but did not kill it. Indeed, it still bears leaves and fruits and seeds every year.'

'So it's a plant without a soul?' Bianca asked her father, wanting to make the monk feel uncomfortable. He did, in fact, blush and tried to come up with an explanation.

'The spirit is in the leaves, flowers and fruits. The spirit is not the heart of the tree, I mean. The tree has no heart.'

Returning to her studio with vegetables inside her apron after her walk with Innes, Bianca reflects that she still doesn't really know her own true colours. She places the vegetables in a basket, but it looks too much like a Baschenis still life. Resting in an almost random fashion on the rough table, however, they are perfect. She draws them and then colours them in. She is not sure who would find this little bit of garden pleasing, but it is beautiful. It is life. When she finishes, she picks up a tomato with her hands, which are still dirtied with colours, and bites into it. She eats it greedily, sucking down both the juices and the colour. Red is also a taste.

🌺 🌺

At times, Bianca thinks, children – and especially boys – really are unbearable. Pietro needs total attention. He is greedy and manipulative. He always wants to be right, and as the firstborn he enjoys certain privileges that the other children are denied. These defects accentuate his propensity towards tyranny. Enrico follows him around and imitates his every move, as best as he can, since he is more fragile and inclined to cry. Taken together, the boys are pernicious. One day, Bianca finds Pietro throwing a spider into another spider's web. From a distance she can't understand what he is doing. She sees him lying on the ground next to his brother, tossing something and then looking into a void. She walks up to them, curious, just in time to see the spider envelop the stranger in an excited frenzy. The victim is moving and then it stops. Pietro glances up at Bianca. She has stood in his light. He looks her up and down with daring eyes, his lips pursed in a smile.

'You're cruel,' Bianca says.

'Even Papa does it,' he replies. He looks around for another little insect and finds an ant to condemn. Bianca turns and walks away without saying a word. She never knows quite what to say to Pietro.

The next day he comes up to her with his younger brother as if by chance while she is strolling in the gardens. He has his hands behind his back as if he is a miniature adult. He stands in her way, like a bandit.

'I have written a poem, like Papa. Would you like to hear it?'

Bianca nods, without letting herself be deceived by his innocent tone. He takes the piece of paper that he has been hiding in his hand, unravels it like a messenger, and reads aloud:

> *I ossi dei morti*
> *son lunghi, son corti*
> *son bianchi, son morti*
> *Ti fanno stremir.*
> *Sta' attento alle spalle*
> *se vengono piano*
> *se hai tanta paura*
> *ti fanno stecchir.*

> The bones of the dead
> Are long, short,
> White and dead
> They worry you
> Watch your back,
> They sneak up on you slowly
> If you're too scared
> They will even kill you.

'Did you like it?' he asks, waiting for the usual overindulgent praise.

'There's a missing rhyme and a word that's not in Italian that I do not understand. Also, "ossi" are animals' bones, you should use "ossa" for human bones. That's another mistake. Principally, though, poems about bones are no longer the fashion.'

'Maybe they're not popular any more, but they certainly are spooky. If you saw bones, you'd scream so loud you'd shatter glass. Be careful, because this place is full of bones. Aren't I right, Enrico? They grow like your dear little flowers.'

Enrico, playing the part of a good sidekick, nods. Pietro walks away with his hands behind his back, gripping the piece of paper like an offended dignitary. Enrico follows him.

❧ ❧

'Minna, what's this story about bones in the garden?'

'Who told you about the bones, Miss Bianca?' Minna says, eyes open wide in alarm.

'I overheard the boys talking . . .'

'Oh, those two troublemakers. It's an ugly story. Do you really want to hear it?'

'Go on.'

'Well, they say the bones belong to Don Carlo.' She sniffles a bit, and then tells the story rather too quickly, as if she feels guilty. She looks off into space, frowning as she speaks. 'Don Carlo owned this house. My grandfather says that he was a good man, for a count. When he died, he left everything to Donna Clara, and then everyone else came, like grasshoppers. And the bones, well . . . at first the old lady did everything she could to make Don Carlo's tomb beautiful. Masons came, even a master mason from Bergamo. And then, well, they moved the tomb. There was a party . . . well, not really a party, more like a second funeral, with a priest and everything. Even Frenchmen came from France and they gave speeches about how great a man he was. I never saw him myself. I was tiny, but they told me. They sealed the coffin in the tomb. At first Donna Clara went there every day, praying and making daisy crowns, as though she was a saint. Then I suppose she got tired of it. Or maybe her son wanted her to stop when he moved in. Anyway, they tore down the tomb. It took two days. I remember because by then I was older. And they used the stones to build the rotunda up there on the hill. The coffin disappeared. They say that the bones are still here, that they wander around. It makes me frightened to think of dead people's bones.'

'Who are *they*?' Bianca dares to ask, trying to make sense of the girl's words.

'People. Everyone,' Minna concludes, wringing her hands beneath her apron. 'Why do you want to hear these ugly stories, Miss Bianca? You wouldn't want the ghost of Don Carlo to get angry and come and tug on your feet at night, would you?'

Bianca laughs.

'Ghosts don't exist, Minna,'

Not until we conjure them. That's when they begin to take shape, when we imagine them. Once we summon them forth, for whatever reason, there's the chance that they will never want to leave. They become so tightly wrapped up in us that they blind us with regret, guilt, and the sting of renewed grief.

❧ ❧

There are moments when Bianca thinks of Pia as a friend. She is not *really* her friend but she wishes she could be. Theirs is a relationship that needs no words but feeds only on glances, gestures and trust. It is an understanding that concentrates on things of small importance, transforming what little they have into things infinitely more precious. Pia gives Bianca gifts of flowers that she picks and arranges herself with an innate tenderness, mixing the high with the low – wild snapdragons, buttercups, a nosegay of miniature roses – as if she has always been doing it. She will put them in a teacup – with black and gold decorations – and suddenly the flowers are fit for the gods. Bianca gives Pia ribbons – not old, used ones but new and crisp – a lace collar, and three handkerchiefs with decorated borders.

'Do you ever daydream, Pia?' Bianca once asks her impulsively.

They are lying on the grass, looking at the sky, hands behind their heads, feet close together.

'Yes, I like the ones I have where I am in charge,' Pia answers coolly. 'I like to invent a life as it will never be.'

'But you don't know what your future will bring.'

'Oh, yes – if I've already imagined it, then it cannot be. For this reason I invent things that are impossible. That way I can have fun and not waste my time.'

Hers is a practical economy of self-satisfaction.

'So what do you daydream of, then?'

'I cannot tell you, Miss Bianca. You'd laugh at me.'

'Me? Never.'

'What about you? What do you daydream of, Miss Bianca?'

'I only dream at night. And I never remember anything afterwards, except for the fact that it happened. No . . . once my father came to visit me. He was dressed in a long white shirt, like the Christ of the lambs, and he wanted to hug me but he was too far away.'

'What about your mother?'

'She never laughed. And then she died,' Bianca says, grateful that they are not facing each other.

'Maybe she knew. That she was going to die, I mean. But even Donna Julie . . . she only laughs rarely.'

What about your mother? Bianca wants to ask. *The pretty swaddling and all the rest?* But she holds back. She doesn't want to risk losing what they have. They can say anything to each other and know that there won't be any consequences; neither will either repeat what the other has said, and they don't need to be ashamed of anything.

'Do you think Tommaso is good-looking?'

'Oh, come on, Pia. He's only a boy.'

'I know. But his hair is as smooth as silk. I'd like to run my fingers through it, mess it up a little.'

'It's messy already!'

Laughter, and then silence.

'Anyway, *I* think he's good-looking,' Pia continues. 'Even Luigi will turn out to be good-looking. His father wants to send him to become a servant at Crippa of Lampugnano. We will never see each other again.'

'It isn't that far away. He can always come back to visit.'

'A maid is like a prisoner. And anyway, I only like to look at him. I don't want to marry him or anything. It's better to be alone. I'm used to it.'

'But one day it will happen.' Bianca turns onto her side, propping herself up on her elbow. The child is still on her back with her eyes closed.

'Do you feel the same way, Miss Bianca?'

Sometimes silence is the best answer.

❧ ❧

'So, you finally decided to paint portraits. I told you it was more worthwhile.'

Bianca is startled to discover Donna Clara standing behind her, and this time in the space she has carved out in the study. She has no place just for herself downstairs, and so when she does work there, these interruptions happen often. Even so, she needs to get out of her room. Donna Clara pulls out the portrait of the mysterious woman that Bianca has composed quickly and then never touched again. She fixes her lorgnette on her nose in a nest of flesh and wrinkles.

'Beautiful. It reminds me of someone . . . Was it done from memory?'

'No, actually it wasn't. It's a woman I met.'

'Tell me, who? I know, I know . . . but no, it can't be. There's no way you could know her. My mind is deceiving me, my age, my imagination, and all the rest of it.' Donna Clara strides around the room as she speaks, bobbing her head from side to side like a bird. And then she discards the idea. 'Anyway, it's a good job. Very good. My compliments.'

Bianca is silent: what can she possibly say in return? The old woman puts the composition back down on the desk.

'When will you do my portrait? Although, thinking about it, I don't really want a painting of myself. My mirror is good enough. It's a sad day, my dear, when you don't recognize the person in the reflection and she's staring you straight in the eye. You'd like to make her disappear with a wave of the hand – shoo, you ugly beast! – and instead see the person you once were. But that other woman is gone. She's lost, never coming back. Time is no gentleman, not one bit. So unless you can be kinder than the mirror . . . but I know you. You are fixated on the truth and you'd make me into a monster, into the monster I am.'

She chuckles, turns around, and walks away.

There is nothing to laugh about later, however, when Bianca comes across her sketch of the mysterious woman torn in half, and deliberately placed on top of a pile of her other drawings. Just two days have passed; she hasn't shown it to anyone else, nor has she reworked it. She has only put it aside, as one does with ideas when they are still unclear. Whoever wished to slight her clearly looked for that specific drawing.

Bianca lifts the two pieces of torn paper and fits them together, her hands trembling. The woman stares out at her, her eyes slightly off-kilter and her mouth folding into a smile. She is beautiful, achingly beautiful, aching *but* beautiful. And she no longer exists.

The sabotage is unexpected and fills her with anger.

The children's mother and grandmother are not around; they have gone to the city to run some errands. Although it is late summer, it is still incredibly hot, as hot as July. Even Donna Clara admitted yesterday, after three lemon sorbets failed to restore her energy, 'It's as hot as hell here in Brusuglio. Summer is scorching. And then in winter we freeze. No matter how you look at it, we lose. Although, the sky is so beautiful when it's clear, it's heavenly. I always tell my son, not even in my beloved Paris did I see such skies.'

Bianca is shocked that someone would actually tear her drawing. She decides that she will have to deal with it in her own way, and in the meantime do something that makes *her* happy, for once. Nanny is taking her nap now and she sleeps heavily. The boys have gone with Ruggiero to see the foals in the Bassona stables and won't be back until nightfall. The cool water of the brook is inviting and far enough away that no one will hear them splashing about. Minna is Bianca's accomplice.

'I'll help you, Miss Bianca. But will the girls be quiet?'

Bianca doesn't know and doesn't care. She wants to have some fun. If someone finds out, she can always count on the master's support. Hasn't he applauded the English form of education some time ago at dinner? And so, off they go, one after the other, Minna leading the procession with a basket of delicious snacks hanging from one arm.

The girls are perplexed.

'Where are we going?' Giulietta speaks for everyone. She understands that this isn't going to be just like any other picnic.

Usually they go up to the clearing or to the meadows with the birches, but no further than that.

'It's a secret,' Bianca tells them, as she guides the girls along the trail that brings them to the far reaches of the estate, where the brook divides the cultivated land from the wilderness.

'Are we allowed to do this?' whispers Francesca, intelligent enough to realize that secrets can also often be trouble.

'Yes, we are,' Bianca reassures her. 'Just because you have never done it, doesn't mean it's not allowed.'

They are all pleasantly surprised to find Pia already there, sitting on the ground and leaning against a tree trunk, braiding a garland of different kinds of white wildflowers.

'What are you doing here?'

'I overheard you speaking to Minna, Miss Bianca. But I know how to keep secrets. May I stay?'

There is an absolute calm to her manner. She already knows that Bianca's answer will be yes. Actually, Bianca almost feels bad for not having asked her earlier or sending someone to seek her out. But Pia is already standing, joyful and incapable of bitterness.

'And now what?' Francesca asks. She still does not understand exactly what they are doing there.

'Now we will take a dip,' Bianca explains.

'In the brook?' Giulietta asks with a smile.

'In the brook,' Bianca echoes. 'It's cool and clean. You'll see how nice it feels.'

Being obedient, the girls don't react, but it is clear that they would prefer to be somewhere else, even in the nursery, although it is the hottest room in the house, with their dolls, the tired wooden pony, and the wooden blocks. They stand there, transfixed, arms hanging by their sides, staring at the water. It has never looked so frightening. Pia begins to undress

Francesca, Minna helps Giulietta, and Bianca takes care of Matilde. It is she, the youngest one, who screams first.

'I'm not taking off my clothes! It's embarrassing!'

Bianca picks the child up and carries her behind a tree that is wide enough to hide her.

'No one will see you here,' she says, continuing to undress her with a calm firmness. Matilde's little body is round and pale and her tummy juts out. Bianca would love to draw her now. The other girls, undergoing the same treatment, don't say a word. And then finally Giulietta shrieks, her voice suffused with excitement.

'Can we learn how to swim like Pietro and Enrico?'

'Better than Pietro and Enrico!' answers Bianca, coming out from behind the tree holding Matilde by the hand.

Bianca quickly steps out of her own clothes and stands in her undershirt and slip. If she was alone, she would also remove those items but she suspects that none of the girls have ever seen an adult fully undressed. She is sure that Pia and Minna wouldn't mind, but the other three might.

Giulietta looks at Bianca closely.

'Miss Bianca, you have freckles on your arms, too!'

Bianca smiles. 'I've always had them. What can I do, erase them?'

Giulietta laughs at the idea, and then gets distracted by Pia, who looks so different without her bonnet. Pia slips down the smooth bank of tall grass and splashes into the water, laughing.

'Is it cold?' Giulietta asks.

'It's delightful,' answers Pia, moving through the water like a dog.

'Look, she's floating!' Francesca says.

'Everyone can float. All you need to do is move around a bit,' explains Bianca, entering the water slowly. The water in the brook is not deep. It comes up to her waist, and is stingingly fresh. She feels sand and grass beneath her feet. The ground is firm.

'So who's coming in first?' she says, holding her arms up high, ready to embrace the most fearless one. Surprisingly, Matilde makes her way forward. She only needs to be in someone's arms. When her tiny feet touch the water, she lets out a little shriek but doesn't cry. Bianca holds her tightly as the water swirls around her undershirt.

Francesca is more courageous. She takes a seat on the grassy bank and lets herself slide into the brook as Pia has done. In an instant she is standing with the water up to her chest and laughing in excitement.

Minna and Giulietta hold hands and enter the water together cautiously, shrieking when the stream takes hold of them. Everyone is finally in. Pia has swum off and now turns back towards them, creating ripples in the water. They all hold hands and make a sort of ring, Bianca with Matilde in her arms. The game ends when Minna does some sort of dive, throwing herself forward, disappearing and then reappearing again, her hair dripping in front of her face. They all laugh. Minna raises her arms victoriously.

'It feels so good.'

'Can I go underwater too?' Giulietta asks.

'Yes, but remember to blow your air out, otherwise you might drown,' Pia explains and shows her how, by going underwater herself and emitting a whirlpool of bubbles.

'What should I do with my eyes?'

'Do as you please. Keep them open and you'll see green. Keep them closed, and you won't see a thing.'

Giulietta goes down and then comes right back up, coughing and rubbing her eyelids.

'I have water in my nose!' she complains.

'Pinch it closed,' Pia says and again shows her how.

The little girl makes another attempt, this time with her nose pinched. When she resurfaces she is smiling.

'I saw green, I saw green!'

Matilde, still in Bianca's arms, moves her tiny feet back and forth in excitement, splashing rhythmically.

Francesca copies her older sister.

'I saw a fish!' she exclaims as she resurfaces.

Everyone laughs. Above them, the sun toys with the leaves. Splashes of light pass through the branches, rest on the surface of the brook, and then disappear. There is no noise, only the humming of cicadas and the slow swishing of water. They enjoy the moment silently. Bianca looks at all her companions' faces, one by one, and their differing expressions of pleasure. Giulietta wears a concentrated smile, trying hard not to forget a thing. Francesca, though, smiles widely and holds tightly to Minna's hand. Minna gazes up at the sky, now a light blue above the leaves. Matilde looks serious, her eyes large, dilated by wonder.

And then, just like that, the quiet moment ends. Pia, who Bianca now notices is actually quite curvaceous and not so little, pulls herself up the bank, takes the garland she has left there, and crowns herself with it. She laughs and goes under the water again, kicking her feet and splashing the other girls, who shield themselves with their hands.

Pia stands up in the brook, combing back her hair with her fingers, pulling it away from her face in an elegant motion. The little ones copy her. It is then that Bianca notices the resemblance. It is in the shape of her head and her facial structure, and it is shockingly apparent.

The perplexity on Bianca's face must be evident.

'What's wrong, Miss Bianca? You've gone all white,' Pia says, then giggles. She laughs cheerfully, and so do the others, and then suddenly none of them can stop.

After their outing, the only trace of the crime is a few white shirts and knickers hung out to dry on the clothes line behind the kitchens, bottoms up, like ghosts dangling from the trees. Nanny, who has no idea what has happened, is surprised by the girls' fatigue, and she comes down to chat to Bianca after having put them to bed.

'They were dead tired and went to sleep immediately. If only they were always so cooperative. Ah, I see Ilide did some laundry? But, it's not laundry day today . . .'

Bianca and Minna look at each other conspiratorially. Pia is not there. She must have gone on one of her walks. The evening is mild and quiet. The half-moon hangs in the air, as bright as a lantern.

⁂

The afternoon dip hasn't been enough to satisfy Bianca. And so she retraces her steps back down the path that she, the girls and the maids took, but this time alone. The leaves shield the moonlight now and make it hard to see, but she knows the way. It is as if the smell of the water guides her – a green, pleasant, familiar and natural scent. Like her very own, within the folds of her sheets.

This time, given that she is alone and darkness hides her, she removes all her clothes the way she used to do at home in the small swimming hole near the manor, which belonged to a *conte* who only left the house to go to church. It is dark and deserted. The water feels more daring, though, and it caresses every bit of her body, even the most hidden parts.

The moon is high and the trees along the bank form a straight corridor, fringed only by some light branches. The moonlight casts parallel shapes on the black water. Bianca leans back, her feet anchored to the soft muddy ground, and looks up but doesn't let herself go. It is as if she doesn't want to lose control, abandon herself. She breathes in the perfume of the wet country night mixed with the velvet smell of the water. She feels good.

Her hand brushes up against something. Tangled in a branch is Pia's crown of flowers, still intact. Bianca frees the wreath and lets it float off. She follows it, moving her arms and legs gently, only enough to keep afloat. She allows herself to think about what she hasn't had time to before, but which presses on her mind like a migraine. Is it conceivable? How can it be? But . . . the shape of her face. It certainly is possible. Everything about Pia's history leads Bianca to believe that it is possible. It is strange, though, that the girl lives there, so close to him. Maybe it is chance. Or maybe it is a bolder way of challenging fate, displaying the fruit of the crime right under everyone's noses. But whose fault is it, after all? Certainly not Don Titta's. It is never a man's fault. It must be the mother's fault. But who is the mother? Is she still around, somewhere, or has she been forgotten like a minor historical figure? And when did it all happen? *He came to Paris when he was twenty*, Donna Clara said. Something must have happened at some point between the era of the curious child in the portrait and the twenty-year-old man going to meet his mother in Paris.

No, it cannot be. It is too much like a romance novel, Bianca tries to reason. But . . . the likeness. If the others notice it, if they know . . . She has to make sure that Pia never removes her bonnet. No one can find out, no one can suspect a thing.

Or maybe – the thought shoots across her brain in all

clarity – everyone knows already. *Yes, that's it*, Bianca thinks. It explains Donna Clara's inexplicable surges of affection towards Pia, Minna's hangdog gaze and cruel tongue, and the women's gossip in the kitchen. What about the ghost, though? And the priest? Is he an accomplice, too? Is it possible?

No, it cannot be. Perhaps she alone sees a resemblance because she has an outsider's eye and is able to identify the invisible ties that connect different people, like a spider's web. The others may never have noticed.

Or maybe Bianca is imagining it all. It is just the excitement, the intense heat. It is her eagerness to put order into all the coincidences and mishaps she comes across, to frame them on the same canvas. As if classifying and understanding are one and the same.

There is the sound of twigs snapping and then footsteps on leaves.

'Who's there?' whispers Bianca. In the silence her voice is as loud as a scream.

Nothing. It is a hare, or maybe one of those ferocious wild animals that besiege Minna's dreams. Bianca lets herself go then, falling backwards, water filling her ears. She hears nothing more except for the far-away rumble of a much greater and deeper body of water, like the echo of the ocean. Even her body remembers her own lake. It is a different kind of memory from all others and it is reawakened by her every movement in the brook. The green water is cold against her skin. Algae move around at the bottom like the hair of the dead. She feels that good sort of melancholy that takes hold of her every time she remembers her home.

There is another rustle, this time louder and closer. But Bianca doesn't hear it. She floats on the water and stares at the moon. She doesn't notice the shadow crouching among the bushes, watching her drift in the current. His gaze takes in her small breasts, the way her hair swirls around her head like a cloud, and her knees and feet poking out of the water.

Part Two

And then comes winter. Or rather, autumn arrives but it feels like winter. After a mild and colourful October, the skies become tinted with grey and vary only slightly in hue: pewter, stormy with a streak of blue, deep blue with leaden edges, steel, silver, iron and platinum. The temperature plunges. One morning, on waking, Bianca sees that the great lawn has turned completely white. It reflects the pale sky and promises only cold, not the joyful feeling of snow. Chilblains appear on Minna's delicate fingers. Bianca takes it upon herself to cure them with a white paste she brought with her in a ceramic jar that has the consistency of artists' *gesso*.

'This is Serafina's magic paste. Trust me, they will go away. You just need to be patient enough for your skin to absorb it.'

Minna, at first suspicious, soon realizes her luck. She can think of nothing nicer than sitting in one of the pink pinstriped armchairs in the nursery and waving her hands in the air while the cream dries, without having to do a thing more. She doesn't even have to bring the girls tea. Actually, the girls take it upon themselves to serve *her* tea, with all the clamour and ceremony and dangerous clinking of porcelain cups at risk.

Minna's miraculous healing from her chilblains and the teatime ritual are amongst the final events of their serene country life that year. The ladies decide, in a flash, that the change of seasons, though inevitable, is entirely unwelcome, and in response they want to close up the house and move back to the city. The poet seems unhappy with the decision and for some time he resists. Eventually, though, he surrenders to the fact that it is expensive to warm the entire household, worn down by the endless complaining of how they will be better off in the city, with the good fireplaces, fewer windows, and so on. Don Titta stays on a little longer after their departure with his faithful Tommaso, with the excuse of having to finish a commissioned ode that will pay many of the bills. He lets the caravan of women, children and luggage set off without him. Bianca suspects that the Big Bear only wants a bit of solitude; no one will deny him that. She has started calling him this in her head recently and in the fragmented letters she mentally writes to her father, a habit she hasn't quite lost. Only common sense prevents her from taking up a quill and transforming everything into a real missive:

Imagine a bear after hibernation, dearest Father, one of those bears you showed me when I was a little girl in that book of Russian fables, with dirty and rugged fur, a thin body, pinched muzzle, and drooping shoulders. This is the master of the house. He looks uncomfortable in his clothes, which seem to be cut for a man of another size. He will never become a bear of formidable stature and will always remain the thin being he became after his long sleep. He is always in search of something, with a great disquiet about him, so much so that it almost inspires compassion. You can see him wandering through the woods in search of honeycombs and fruit, and if he turns around, you will see the beast in those deep, dark eyes. You will be afraid of him, and fear and respect will linger on even when you see him play with his cubs on a sunny summer day. But it's never really summer for him; it is always the beginning of spring. He has just awoken and he doesn't understand or remember what sense there is in the world around him. Even when he is full, his eyes are hungry.

Whatever reasons he has to stay on, the Big Bear proves shrewd in sparing himself the total chaos of their arrival in Milan. Although the domestic staff have been on alert for several days – the personal maids have gone on ahead to prepare – it feels as though they have reached a lodging that has not been lived in for a long time. The trip has been short, but it is next to impossible to gaze out at the road along the way because the children are so rowdy. They do nothing but scream and bicker, and Nanny soon gives up scolding them, leaving Bianca the duty of entertaining them with new games. It is foggy and there is little to see in the wide stretches of cold, open countryside. The streets of the city soon make themselves heard, though, through the sounds of hooves on cobblestones, bells, and the calling of tradesmen. The facade of their town house is dark and closed. It looks out onto a cobbled piazza and is surrounded by other homes in a similar style.

The bleakness Bianca feels when she first sets eyes on the house is briefly interrupted by the grandness of the foyer and its red-carpeted staircase. But that soon fades as they make their way to the bedrooms, which are melancholy and look uninhabited. It is all so sadly chaste. Only the living room, with its frescos in pastel colours, has the guise of magnificence. The other ceilings are all dark, with solemn miniature decorations lost in the shadows. Not even the children's cries of joy when they come across forgotten old toys and the shadows of their younger selves enliven the bleak atmosphere. The bedrooms that have been closed off for some time feel cold, as cold as the living rooms in the villa in Brusuglio, pierced by its numerous windows.

And then, slowly but surely, things get better. The light becomes denser, enveloping the house. There is a milky glow on grey mornings and an uncertain light on clear ones. The rooms surrender and begin to welcome the intruders, to the point of finally allowing them to be lived in. The house is much smaller than the family's country home and feels less mysterious. An opaque glass skylight situated above the staircase promises – and yet shuts off – the sky above. It makes the sky look small and square, especially when there isn't a cloud in sight. The garden is lush and quite remarkable: palms, banana trees and oriental sweet-gum trees create an exotic backdrop. Two struggling grapevines recall the countryside, and a pair of very young magnolias, situated closer to the house, stand tall. Donna Clara's bedroom is the most beautiful. It is on the second floor and looks out onto the garden, which, seen from above, winds between the other houses like an escape route towards nature. Her walls are adorned with a delicate motif of pink and pale scarlet rhombi and the furniture is exquisite. She cannot resist pulling Bianca in and dragging her over to a very small picture which might otherwise go unnoticed. It is of a *putto*, a child embroidered in *petit point* and protected by a glass cover.

'Queen Marie Antoinette made that in prison, before they chopped her head off, poor thing,' Donna Clara explains. 'She gave it to one of her guardians as a gift and she in turn sold it to a friend of mine in Paris, who then gave it to me. Doesn't it just give you the chills?'

Yes, it is somewhat eerie to think of a gloomy jail cell where time can never move slowly enough, counting down to death. What a bizarre gift to give to a friend. Who knows what it means. There are no other macabre relics in that bedroom, only graceful watercolours depicting non-existent landscapes, crystal bottles on the older woman's bureau, and the vague scent from open drawers.

The servants' quarters are at the narrow top of the house. It is as if that section of the building has nothing to do with the frilly bedrooms and elegant salons below. Bianca happens to walk into one of the rooms while she is exploring but leaves hastily, disturbed by the low ceilings, iron beds, rough wooden floors and damp. Her own bedroom is downstairs, near the others. It is a small beige room that has the bland feeling of a guest room. Tommaso and Innes sleep at the end of the dark corridor, far from the clamour of the others. Nanny has her own bedroom near the nursery that is furnished with salvaged furniture, but she doesn't complain. She never complains.

The room that attracts Bianca the most is Don Titta's study. And even though it is completely out of bounds at all times, one day she sees the poet passing through the French window of his study into the garden, and decides to linger. It is dark inside, despite being morning. Rows of books line every surface. The bookshelves are protected by doors of mesh that absorb the meagre light. There is a sharp smell of old paper. The chimney is both dark and damp; a cylindrical heater of recent manufacture allows for modern heating, but in the absence of a legitimate inhabitant even this looks cumbersome and gloomy. On the desk of peeling Moroccan leather there are large ink spills, creating geographical maps of imaginary countries, and a pile of dark blue notebooks that Bianca recognizes from Brusuglio. On a tray rests a row of quills, ready for use. The inkpot is full. Instinctively she leans forward to smell its bitter aroma, which she has always liked. She looks for other clues about the poet, but the fragment of free wall space bears no paintings or images, just a crucifix engulfed by shadows and grief. Footsteps on the parquet floor in the hallway outside force her to leave quickly, and she pauses only when she arrives at the square of grass in the courtyard, which is still green but for the areas where dead leaves have now fallen.

❧ ❧

There are no large windows from which to throw all domestic tensions, but there is a great deal of coming and going, and doors opening onto other doors. It takes Bianca some time to realize how this concentric house works. It is a maze, a puzzle. Soon she finds her way, though, and is able to move around lightly and silently, making the most of the play of doorways and using them to her advantage. She listens and overhears, and absolves herself by telling herself that although these exchanges aren't meant for her ears, only chance has led her there.

'Everyone knows that she was a whore when she was young.'

'But she is so sanctimonious now. All she does is talk about her grandchildren, as if they were the stars in her sky.'

'Well, anyone can feel regret. The beauty of religion is that there's always a shortcut to forgiveness, even in the most extreme cases. She has carried herself forward, and has done things right. It's not as if she waited for her deathbed to bury her past. She even had to take in that burden of a son. Luckily, her daughter-in-law brought in a dowry of sanctity and money in equal parts . . . I imagine the old lady will end up in Purgatory because she sure as hell won't be singing psalms with the angels.'

'And what makes you think you'll end up in heaven to hear the singing?'

'Me? I wasn't talking about me. I wouldn't mind a little atonement, actually: virtue is so boring . . .'

In the city, the family receive more guests, and in addition to the usual ones there is a whole host of new characters. Tommaso, surrounded by these people, retreats into his shell like an irritated hermit crab, although he remains kind to Bianca, to the point of irritation. Once, he stopped to admire a drawing she had done of the girls – the one she started on her first day in Brusuglio, and which she then finished upon Donna Clara's insistence.

'You have style and personality, Miss Bianca. But be careful not to lose yourself in fashion.'

Bianca actually wishes she could spend some of her money on clothes, but she is set on increasing her savings, which are growing ever so slowly, month after month. Soon she comes to the realization, though, that it is one thing to be in the country, where her somewhat outdated but nonetheless refined outfits give a decent impression, and another to be in the city where ladies are elegant and proud. *We are avant-garde. We might look to Paris, but Paris looks to us, too*, their clothes seem to say.

Even Donna Clara and Donna Julie, who are so at ease in the country in their uniforms of ordinance – black for one and a lighter colour for the other – are more worried about their appearance in Milan. They correct – or perhaps pollute – their usual sobriety with certain bold touches that make them stick out. All they need to do is put on a turban wrapped in a complicated way or wear a waterfall of frills on their sleeves to set the children off in giggles. They stare at the two women, puzzled, and then make their inevitable remarks.

'Where's the rest of the bird?' Enrico asks when his grandmother comes down to dinner in a feathered headdress.

All the credit goes to Gandini, the seamstress, who has been summoned to the confused household and put to work. Bianca is unable to hide her dismay when the ladies appear wearing the craftswoman's most recent creations. It seems as though elephant sleeves are the latest trend, puffy at the top and narrow at the wrist, like a trunk, in the Kalmuk style. On the delicate arms of Donna Julie the styles derived from the Russian steppes look graciously frivolous, but on Donna Clara they look comical, though no one smiles when they see her. And in fact, her guests' compliments are futile. It is clear that neither of the two ladies are emblems of avant-garde fashion. They let themselves be convinced by the skill of the seamstress and are only vaguely aware that her adaptations of French fashion aren't perhaps all that successful.

When Carola Visconti makes an entrance into the living room one day wearing a light green spencer with egg-yellow braided decorations, a long, fitted, dark green dress, and a nocked bow and heron on her head, Donna Clara suddenly looks like grey wattle. And Donna Julie, wearing a fichu over the square neckline of an old emperor-style dress, appears no more than a provincial girl who has just left the convent in her dead mother's clothes.

⁂

Bianca discovers with a mix of delight and chagrin that the city is full of things to buy. Many of the generous guests to the house offer her gifts with a joy that appears authentic. She receives a small crystal phial containing the essence of fraghe by Giuseppe Hagy – three drops to be sprinkled inside the folds of one's handkerchief, like the three distilled droplets of the queen's blood. She accepts many *boutonnières* of greenhouse violets too to decorate her jackets. She enjoys the desserts of the Galli – dates sliced vertically and filled with bits of pink and green marzipan, and pralines from Marchesi wrapped in brown paper and entirely delectable. And finally, she receives four brand-new outfits sewn by Signora Gandini. These come as a complete surprise. They are carried into the house for a fitting and then taken in accordingly. Bianca's face lights up when she sees them arrive.

When the time comes for the fitting, the smell of the new fabric is intoxicating and their rustling sounds are music to her ears. As she looks at her reflection, she discovers details about herself that she didn't even know existed. Her *décolletage* and her tiny waist are prominent in the two evening gowns. The seamstress has to fold and take in the fabric.

'You know, my dear, that your hourglass figure is most esteemed,' she says.

She also has a round and svelte *derrière*. It is strange how the French language can make any word sound pretty. A charcoal-blue outfit in 'a colour made for you' wraps around her waist and draws attention to her curves, thanks to a short blazer that ends just above her lower back. Naturally, Donna Clara and Donna Julie are privy to the entire fitting – front-row audience members – muttering comments under their breath that Bianca chooses to ignore.

A few days later, in addition to the new outfits, she also finds three complete sets of undergarments from Ghidoli, everything from long underwear *à l'anglaise*, which combines modesty and elegance, to exquisite lace undershirts. Bianca puts her pride aside and is overcome by vanity and pure joy. She thanks the ladies with her heart, her eyes, and with words, too.

'Go and get changed. Seeing you well dressed will be the greatest thanks of all,' Donna Clara says.

That evening, she comes down to dinner in her favourite outfit: a pinstriped dress of white and light green silk that reminds her of daffodil stems and makes her feel just as delicate. In the large and somewhat cavernous living room it feels cold, despite the lit fireplace, and Donna Julie runs upstairs to fetch her a white cashmere shawl. At times, the house still feels like an invaded fortress, leading Bianca to think that it was happier before they arrived – sealed, empty, and alone.

Bianca's room has a floor made from irregular red tiles. She often trips over them, and it feels as if the whole floor is waiting for her to fall. The pale wallpaper with a pattern of rhombi does nothing to brighten the room, and even with the tall window, the light that seeps in is always greyish and dirty. Pigeons coo on the windowsill, which Bianca does not like. They look like rats with wings, stolid and insistent. They are everywhere here, she soon finds out.

The city is revealing itself to her little by little, like a bashful and discreet lady batting her eyelashes and playing coyly with her fan. At first she finds it hostile. It is too silent or too noisy or just strange. She doesn't know many other large cities. Verona, compared to this, is a village, with its semicircle of coloured *palazzi* surrounding the arena. London, as seen from numerous carriages, is large and grey, white or red. There is nothing mysterious about it, nothing scary or miraculous. Not like this place, which reveals itself slowly, like the closed hand of a child holding a secret, being pried open finger by finger.

When she applies herself, Bianca sees things she has never imagined. Everything is bigger here. The markets are more market-like. In Verziere, the green stalls are set up at the feet of the statue of the tortured Christ. Apparently it is also the place where witches have been burned at the stake. When Bianca takes walks there, she observes the vendors as they hawk their goods with full-blown obscenities, trying to detect traces of evil on their dishevelled faces. The streets are more street-like, with cracks engraved in the manure and the incessant traffic of public and private carriages. They rumble by like a stormy sea, so loud they bring on headaches. Even the churches are more church-like. Guided more by instinct than piety, she discovers that there is an infinite variety of them. The Duomo, with its lacy facade, reminds her of the evanescent play of sand when it seeps through her fingers. Santa Maria delle Grazie, with its firm, erect cupola and mystical silence, relays the cold numbness of the monks – God's dogs, as her father used to call them. She watches the monks there walking on the flagstones under which other monks sleep in eternal rest, smiling remotely, their hands hidden under their elegant black-and-cream-coloured tunics. In the cloisters, bronze frogs spit streams of water onto the emerald stone of the fountain. San Lorenzo, with its indoor and outdoor columns, reminds her of a peeling set design. It is like the travel writer, Lady Morgan, said: Milan is a city of bricks transformed into a city of marble. And yet the cement and mud reappear so rapidly, just by turning a corner or crossing a piazza. It makes her think that the city's transformation has been hasty, or interrupted.

Bianca wanders alone, relying on her shrewd independence where she can, knowing full well that her behaviour is at the limits of respectability and delighting in the thrill this gives her. She keeps several coins inside the small green velvet purse that came with her new clothes and relies on these to get her out of sticky situations, such as when she gets lost and needs a carriage. She'll hail one, stare straight back at the suspicious driver and show him the coins in her palm. Bianca gets lost often because she daydreams as she walks. She looks at things without really seeing them, and when she shakes off her daydreams, she no longer has a reference point, no street corner, palazzo or bell tower that she can refer back to. She is like Theseus without his string, reawakened from a nap. She likes it that way. It reminds her of the adventures she had with her father, on foot in London, and the thrill of wandering into neighbourhoods like Soho or Bethnal Green, knowing that, with her arm in his, she could go anywhere. Although now things are different; there is the thrill, but there is awareness too. The open road tempts her with the ambiguous lure of adventure.

⁂

In the beginning, the family encourage her to go out for strolls, but when she starts venturing out more frequently, they begin to get suspicious.

'Where has she gone to this time?'

'To look for trouble, that's what I say.'

This is the gossip from the kitchen. Donna Clara limits herself to open curiosity.

'What wonderful things have you seen today, Miss Bianca?'

And when Bianca answers vaguely or simply describes a façade or street corner in her own approximate, particular and distracted way, the older lady just shakes her head and sighs.

'My dear girl, are you sure? I don't think I've ever encountered anything like that.'

Of course you haven't, Bianca wants to answer, *because you only travel in coaches*. Milan has surely changed a lot in the previous ten, twenty, even thirty years too, and Donna Clara no doubt knows Paris better. It was the city of her second youth and the home of her most recent love, and it has a way of always insinuating itself into her conversations. Her tired litany includes references to Carlo, Claude, Sophie, the *maisonnette*, and then Carlo once more, although any mention of them is quickly brushed away.

Bianca feels that she is on a mission. She wants to fully understand the city on foot, as a woman of the people. This goes hand in hand with her approach to drawing, as it has evolved over time in the countryside and at the end of the autumn. The mission is made possible by their move to the city. She doesn't speak of it to anyone, not even Innes, who in any case seems to be preoccupied with his own activities.

'Is he writing a novel as well?' Donna Clara teases on many occasions, making Donna Julie giggle.

'What are you saying, Mother? His novel is his life. He's not writing it, he's living it.'

The thought of Innes competing against the poet makes even Bianca smile. She has noticed a tacit understanding between the two men that she cannot quite fathom. Is it a simple masculine alliance or some other serious passion that they hide under their waistcoats and living-room banter? She never dares ask, even if Innes does treat her with the sort of gentle familiarity that makes him feel like her accomplice in the household that welcomes them with open arms. Arms that grip a little too tightly at times.

While Bianca is slowly learning about the city, several other fundamental insights come to her, thanks to the family itself. One night, the three ladies, accompanied by Innes, go to see a performance by La Sallé at La Scala. Bianca is not as impressed by the gold and velvet decor as Donna Clara expects her to be. Actually Bianca watches the audience more than the dancers themselves, observing their expressions and reactions. She has already been to La Fenice, Covent Garden and the Opéra, and has told them so, trying not to sound presumptuous. This theatre definitely has a particular charm, but she enjoys spying on people, trying to understand their intentions and conversations – about couples, love and other scandals. Bianca wears her new light blue velvet dress and the diamond necklace that her father gave her mother, which became hers after the inheritance was divided, despite predatory glances from her sister-in-law.

A splendid snowflake rests in the hollow of her neck and pulses with her every breath.

'You look delightful,' Innes whispers into the camellias in her hair. The show begins before her embarrassment can set in. Since the women are seated in a box facing the stage, Innes chooses to stand in order to see clearly. She feels his gaze on her neck and shoulders, delicate and constant. What is there to contemplate, aside from the performance? Certainly not the armoured back of Donna Clara, traversed vertically by a row of tiny buttons, ready to burst off like lethal bullets. Nor the white wool and silk that covers Donna Julie's own petite form. Distracted a bit by her own self-conscious vanity, Bianca nonetheless enjoys the performance to the very end. She doesn't know much about dancing, but she has always watched and appreciated opera. The new fashion of wearing ballet slippers that La Sallé seems to have invented gives the star a lightness in her step and allows her to flutter above everything else. Her veils don't entirely conceal her slim and handsome arms, but it is a happy kind of indecency that makes one question why arms cannot be revealed in all their glory. Her long tutu, as it swirls around her, intensifies her inconsistent character. The dancer is not just a sharply dressed woman gifted with acrobatic talent; she is something else, too. She is an image, a yearning, and a desire for a life where sylphs truly exist – spirits without a body. During the intermission, Donna Clara comments on the character.

'Everybody wants a lover like that. Maybe because she's attractive. But beauty doesn't last; it's a moment and then it's over.'

Bianca imagines the older woman is thinking of herself, and thinks it unfair to assume that ballerinas need to be as light in their everyday existence as they are onstage.

Innes offers all the women rose-flavoured sweets, small crystals filled with faint colours. Donna Julie consumes them with a childlike delight but Donna Clara refuses, asking for the more mundane pumpkin seeds, toasted and lightly salted.

Bianca peers out at the theatre's other boxes in search of the beauties that are so often talked about: Signorina Bongi, Signorina Barbesino, Signorina Carrara Stampa. She wonders if there is a Milanese form of beauty and thinks she identifies it in ladies with light olive-coloured skin, dark eyebrows, large eyes, and rosebud mouths that are full of promise. She wants to sketch these ladies, one beside the next like a bouquet of flowers in season. But then she thinks of the boredom, the complaining, the empty silence of interminable poses, and realizes she is happy to have more docile and yielding subjects.

At the end of the performance they linger for a while in the foyer, so that all their lady friends can welcome back Clara and Julie 'from the wild'. Their friends have white curls and surprisingly slim frames, notwithstanding their age. They wear dark grey, almost black, velvet dresses.

'And this is your Miss Bianca, is it not? Why, how precious . . . she doesn't even look foreign.'

Bianca doesn't like being talked about in the third person, but she hides her impatience under a slight smile, which pleases Donna Julie.

'You did well, Bianca,' she tells her later. 'Those monkeys can really wear you down.'

'Come now, Julie,' Donna Clara intervenes. 'We shouldn't speak of our friends like that.'

'Your friends, maybe,' Julie whispers snidely as they climb into the carriage.

Again, Bianca is amazed by Julie's sharpness. If only she would unsheathe it more often. With her sense of irony, she would make an exceptional rival to Donna Clara during their living-room skirmishes. But she never engages in them. Perhaps her role of model mother is a front to avoid the boredom of society.

'Now that you've been to La Scala, it is safe to say that you're an official Milanese lady,' jokes Donna Clara the following day during lunch, which is actually their breakfast, since they've all slept late. Bianca smiles patiently. She doesn't want to be Milanese any more than she wishes to be Turkish or barbarian. She belongs to her own world and doesn't need to borrow someone else's. But she has learned to keep her mouth shut, remembering with a smirk that silence is one of the virtues that best suits young ladies. Her tendency to speak her mind, which at first was considered a curiosity, is now the target of reproach. As adventurous as Donna Clara's previous life might have been, she is – in public and at home – tremendously conventional. Bianca has learned it is worth adjusting to this situation, even if it means keeping her mouth shut.

Sometimes Bianca wonders whether all this repressed behaviour, hesitation, and silence actually hides a duality that is far from noble. When, in the name of decency, is one supposed to stop being sincere? To what extent are silence and consent a form of courtesy and not grim opportunism? Bianca thinks about these things over and over. The more she considers, the more her thoughts darken. She has no one to confess them to and so they get tangled up inside her.

❧ ❧

Everyone rejoices when Pia finally joins them in Milan from Brusuglio. She has travelled alone in a carriage. When it arrives in the courtyard and the valet opens the door, Pia holds out her hand like a lady, but her eyes are full of laughter. The children, who have been waiting for her since morning, run towards her like marbles strewn across the floor. They hang from her arms and neck, all of them, even the boys. Pia looks charming in her austere jacket, which surely came from someone else's closet. She is composed and behaves like a proper young lady. She emanates a sweet haughtiness that she may have picked up from the ladies who visit the villa, serious but not without a trace of affectation. Bianca waits her turn to embrace the girl, and in so doing discovers that Pia had grown so much that their eyes almost meet at the same level now. Pia reveals her brown-heeled shoes, the tips of which are slightly scuffed and which fasten with a velvet bow.

'From the young lady,' she whispers.

During Pia's absence Bianca has thought a lot about the different pieces of her puzzle. She has moved them here and there until an image became clear. Of course, there are still many dark areas: things unsaid and unknown. But there are too many coincidences to ignore it entirely. There are also many fragments. Bianca has the eagerness and spirit of an amateur; she feels an immense, inexhaustible pleasure in classifying others' inclinations and passions. It is hard to say if this comes from her habit of considering the genealogical life of plants, which provides reassurance with its familial divisions and sub-divisions and makes everything understandable to the eye, or whether it is a passing fancy of her age, an affectation of a young lady who thinks she knows everything there is to know about the world, but who cannot truly recognize herself in the mirror. The truth is that the botany of affections is an inexact science, but it is the dearest thing to her at this time. One day it will pass. One day she will be overcome by her own first-hand passions. But for now, it gives her days both rhythm and meaning. She could have worried about consequences, but Bianca does not understand herself well enough to worry.

Now Bianca smiles complacently, folds up her imagined composition and puts it away, pleased. She could try to reconstruct it for someone to see how much of it is clear. But whom? Everybody is already too caught up in the web. Bianca fears, rightly, that her taciturn nature might tangle the threads even further. There is always a third option: delve deeper, continue her investigation outside of the family, alone. To what end? Just to know. To be certain. Then she will be able to decide what to do. What will it take, really? The courage to ask a couple of questions and trust the answers. The guests that come to the house are interesting, intelligent and honest people – they will surely be pleased to satisfy the curiosity of such a pleasant and alert young lady. All she needs to do is guide her conversations with the lawyer, the official, or the full-breasted benefactress in the right direction. Bianca applies herself to this puzzle with the zeal of a young scholar who wants to achieve excellent marks. She makes witty remarks here and there. She prepares her terrain. If she hesitates, it is only because the timing has to be just right. She knows how to do it and she enjoys the wait. Also because, whether she likes it or not, she has to roll up her sleeves and work.

❧ ❧

Away from the envious eyes of Minna and the silly kitchen maids, Pia blossoms and prospers. It is as if, all of a sudden, she has taken a step forward, detached herself from the shadows of domestic help and reclaimed her place at the front of the stage in a key role. No one scolds her if she reads or lounges about because that's what everyone does during that endless winter. And she doesn't really lounge about that often. She spends most of her time with the children. She is more joyful than Nanny and more creative at inventing games for them to play, keeping them happily distracted. The children don't venture out in the city. Both mother and grandmother are against it. There are vapours from the sewers, they say. There is the danger of whooping cough. And there are the other kinds of children, hordes of them, ready to attack.

'But they would have such fun. They could ice skate on the frozen lake,' Bianca insists, but in vain.

And so the tiny prisoners are kept within their confines. They don't suffer that much because they don't realize what they are missing and therefore don't even desire it. And Pia does everything she can to make their captivity more enjoyable. Christmas comes. There is the scent of honey from the forced hyacinths that grow along the windowsill and colourful wooden toys from Germany. There is the medicinal scent of tangerines that lingers so long in the air it becomes bothersome.

A new year comes but nothing changes: the city is still frozen, closed under skies that appear to have forgotten they too once possessed a colour. Everyone remains happily at home. The chimneys and the fireplaces burn at full force, but Donna Clara doesn't complain about the bills from the wood and coal suppliers, even if they deliver enough fuel to power a steamboat.

Bianca works hard, like a madwoman, she thinks to herself. It is a happy damnation, because it makes her feel at one with the world, worthy of her place, which belongs to no one but her. Her work brings her money, too, cash in velvet and damask pouches.

To think that only a couple of months earlier, when winter descended on them all of a sudden, she suffered and thought she wouldn't make it. She became obsessed with flowers during the one season that denied her them. For several long weeks she did nothing but colour in corollas, like a child. *Here, do this, good, fill in the empty spots, don't go over the lines.* Without the true colours in front of her, though, and because her ruled blocks of paper now seemed pathetic, she got frustrated. What would she do until spring returned? And what if it never returned, as the lugubrious, short, grey days suggested?

'If winter comes, can spring be far behind?' Innes quoted to her, in an attempt to console her as she traced the streaks of rain on the window with her finger.

'Nice. What's that?'

'A verse by a friend.'

'No. Spring, what's that?' she replied, depressed, without even looking at him.

A slow, thick melancholy had settled inside her, a profound dullness that could not be dissipated even by the vivacity of the children. *You should go out*, she told herself, as she ripped out pages from her sketchbook – more images of dead leaves. But where would she go? With her empty pockets and four outfits? The thought only made her angrier, and it was followed by bitterness and unease. *My dear father, what am I to do now? If I cannot even do this, what place shall I have in this world?* She would have preferred to have an entire army of human models, male or female, chubby boys or bored ladies, to draw. It would be better than her vain efforts.

One morning though, Pia brought her a vase full of bare branches. Not one leaf on them. Empty and yet full at the same time.

'What . . . ?' Bianca stuttered. Then she was silent and looked more closely. She looked harder still and then that was enough. She saw. The tall white vase was simple and lacked adornment, not even a touch of gold; it had probably been fished out from under some staircase. The branches, in all their bony grace, pushed upwards, reaching out arthritically towards something – towards the idea of leaves, the leaves that betrayed them, left without warning (as is their habit), at the beginning of autumn.

And just like that, Bianca made up her mind: *I will draw you, poor dead hands. And we shall see where it takes us.*

Surprisingly, she produced one of her better works. Actually, it was more than better. It marked the beginning of a new era, a fresh way of looking at the world that excluded colours and instead opened her eyes to new shapes. Flicking through some of her old sketchbooks, Bianca smiled. It took her but a moment to reject an entire army of colourful corollas made with complicated patinas and to embrace this new direction, composed of straight, curvy and broken lines, light and dark silhouettes. Leaves and flowers were reduced – no, elevated – to their essence. The intricate bare branches had been collected from the Milanese garden. They turned out to be an ideal subject for her new artistic calling. Her marks were clean and neat. The branches were bones of black ink, freed of one meaning and prepared to take on another.

Her audience was uncertain when they saw the new work.

'Miss Bianca, did you run out of colours? I can lend you mine, if you'd like,' Giulietta offered, perplexed.

'I liked your roses better,' added Matilde, nodding her little head to stress her statement.

'These are so . . . strange,' Donna Clara said.

'It's true. I have never seen such modern botanical drawings,' Donna Julie interrupted, surprising all of them.

And her husband, so frugal with displays of affection, took Donna Julie's hand and kissed it.

'Well done, dear wife. You have caught the essence of her work, just as our Bianca has done with her neo-botany.'

Donna Julie blushed but did not pull back her hand, delighting in both her husband's tenderness and Donna Clara's uncomprehending gaze.

Even Innes complimented her work.

'Brave is she who sails unknown waters,' he said, winking at her to soften his words.

And so, released from other obligations, and indeed encouraged, Bianca closed her box of watercolours and expanded her collection of pencils and charcoals. She spent an entire morning in Brera at the dimly lit Barba Conti shop. It was an odorous cavern where paints and powders were crowded together on high shelves, and filled with gleeful and impoverished students from the Accademia. While she waited her turn, she took her time to explore the place.

That afternoon a shop boy in a dark apron delivered a package of four reams of fresh, heavy paper and an entire set of charcoals. Against all logic, the much despised and feared winter became her season of renewal, a spring of experimentation and new endeavours. Oh, what pleasure she found getting her fingers dirty and extending her thought process down to the charcoal stick itself, her dowsing rod, foreseeing and extracting life from dead things. It was pure joy not to think and just to act, to trust in instinct. Technique gave her confidence, but it was the spontaneous movement of her hand that made invention possible. But there really was nothing to invent. Leaves and flowers existed already. They weren't the little faces of false young mistresses, trapped inside senseless poses within miniature ovals. Nor were they landscapes depicting orderly ruins and roaming shepherd boys and musicians. Leaves and flowers had their own unmistakable traits. It was the way one presented these – overlooking colours in favour of texture, getting to the basics – which continued to transform the working habits of this young artist. Because that was what she was. An artist. She had finally found her calling.

> *Dear Father, if you could see me now you would approve.*
> *You always appreciated the new over the old. You would be*
> *the first to receive a collection of my very own alive/dead*
> *leaves, or dead/alive, if you prefer. Truthfully they are more*
> *alive than ever, first when they flow from my fingers, and then*
> *when they are framed under glass . . . they are my natural*
> *preserves, delectable to the eye. I feel a deep pleasure in*
> *distilling them: it's my own way of removing them from the*
> *corruption of the world. Just as Daphne transformed herself*
> *into branches and fronds in order to escape Apollo's grasp,*
> *I, too, seem to be able to transform into that which I draw.*
> *I feel those veins and the sap that runs through them mixing*
> *with my blood . . . I know what I am fleeing: triviality*
> *frightens me most of all.*

Like any artist, Bianca knew that she had to confront her public. Friends and family were called upon to express their opinion. Her first series of four branches in black and white had been carefully framed by Signor Grassi and hung above an antique table in the house's main entrance. The opinion was divided.

'She's got an odd little noggin,' Bernocchi exclaimed, looking more and more like a large frog in his dark coat. 'I'd be curious to know what goes on inside it . . .'

The women were unpredictably enthusiastic. There was a moment of suspense as they awaited the decisive opinion of Signorina Caravatti. Then, after a long pause of intent silence, the lady tipped her bountiful white head of hair to the side.

'I could never imagine a branch and a few leaves to be so *expressive*. I want my own series. Of course, if and when your time permits,' she added, alluding politely to the binding contract which tied Bianca to the family, of which no one spoke explicitly because, after all, Bianca wasn't a servant. What was she? It was hard to say. A dependant? In order to survive she was dependent on the commissions of others. But truthfully, she was also the owner of her own time and her own hands.

'I am certain my husband will have nothing against it,' Donna Julie said immediately.

Bianca felt like she was floating. To work for others as well as for the family would allow her to boost her savings. This was her first true step towards independence. Only now could she fully understand her past occupation: she had been, essentially, a masked governess. But no longer. Now she had a profession. She started to fantasize as the other women, following Signorina Caravatti's comments, devoted themselves to paying compliments and giving her comical directions.

'Perhaps a bouquet of roses, you know, the ummm . . . what are they called again? Well, you certainly know better than I.'

'Or the modest jasmine.'

'I do love jonquils so . . .'

Please, let them be, Bianca was about to say, but refrained. She recalled the enchantment of the English fields in springtime, the bicoloured daffodils blowing in the wind and the clouds chasing the sun. She remained silent. After all, she was a businesswoman now and the flowers belonged to those who bought them.

She thus welcomes the silent joy of habit into her day. Her desire to feel a struggle is once again renewed. She wants to carry through: to prepare, work hard and bask in the result. All of this in order, with order. Bianca's ambitions thrive on planning her personal black-and-white garden. Her funds grow inside her armoire and she counts and recounts the money with a passion that borders on greed. If it weren't for her sense of irony, she would be like a greedy princess from an eastern fable.

As her secondary obligations to the external world increase, she reminds herself that she needs to maintain her primary ones. She can dedicate herself to the art of commerce only in her free time and still has to take part in the family's mundane events, obligatory visits, and the occasional, unavoidable Mass.

Being a perfectionist, Bianca devotes herself entirely to her activities, disdaining any shortcuts of repetition. Each and every drawing has to be unique, or at least quite different from the others. Once she has exhausted the possibilities of the household garden, which has given her twisted branches of every shape and size, she starts to look elsewhere. Donna Clara, her accomplice, is able to secure for her an off-season visit to the botanical gardens. The numb, vegetal architecture of late winter there serves as inspiration for one of her more happy works: the sleeping hawthorn.

She finds inspiration everywhere. One day, a piece of a leaf slips out from the pages of her red morocco leather-bound Bible. It is as fragile as a relic, the colour of tired hay, only barely more than dust. It brings back memories.

Dear Father, how bizarre was your ability to find four-leaved clovers in any corner of wild grass. You used to say that all you needed to do was read the anomaly in a repeated schema of threes, and the four would appear out of nowhere. It was obvious to you. I remember how, when we were out for a walk, you would suddenly kneel down with an air of understanding.

I knew in that moment that you would stand up with a four-leaf clover in your hand, for me.

Remember the time we stayed out all afternoon when I was only a little girl, and you were able to come across an entire bouquet of them? You tied them together with a strand of grass and gave them to Mother as a gift. She looked at you with delight and clapped her hands as if you had offered her a precious stone. Remember? Remember?

She doesn't know if he can remember from where he is now or even if she remembers correctly herself. And yet, it is precisely this random recollection that inspires one of her more successful series. She draws long and wide meadows of clovers in which is hidden one single, isolated, four-leafed clover. Everyone wants one; it is a game: they scrutinize the picture with their naked eye or with a magnifying glass, and have the utmost fun. And that's when it stops being pleasurable for her, and when she begins to understand Tommaso's advice about art that is also fashion – which this has definitely become.

᳇ ᳇

'I can never thank you enough, Pia.'

'For what, Miss Bianca?'

'For your idea. For . . .'

Bianca points to the objects scattered on the table: leaves, her English pencils, charcoals, sketches, and the branches in their vases.

'For everything.'

'It was just a moment's whim, Miss Bianca. Nothing more.'

'But in order to be inspired one needs to have both a heart and a brain.'

'I don't know about that but I definitely do things better when the heart is involved.'

Pia is clumsy. This awkward speech, which comes out hesitatingly, is not her style. Bianca's eyes mist over.

'I'd like so much to . . .'

But she is unable to complete her sentence because Pia curtseys quickly, turns and leaves the room, avoiding the embarrassment of gratitude. Bianca shakes her head, amazed once again at the young maid's mild manners. *It doesn't matter; there will be all the time in the world for me to repay you*, she thinks to herself. *And you'll see . . . you'll see what a surprise is in store for you.*

❦ ❦

The market offers its own marvellous displays of cut flowers and bouquets. They arrive twice a week on trucks from the Ligurian coast and are as colourful as they are odourless, as if somewhere along the journey a toll collector has demanded their perfume as tax. It doesn't matter to Bianca, though. She only needs their shapes, lines, positives and negatives. She becomes friendly with one vendor, a small, heavy man with piercing grey eyes whose name is Berto. He saves her his choice cuts of the first blooms from the greenhouse: carnations with ruffled heads, noble and pale calla lilies, and a certain kind of rose that climbs incredibly high and that seems cold despite its warm colour. Bianca has many preferences but only one aversion. She detests gladioli, with their off-tone colours, the primitiveness of their green fleshy stalks, their swollen tongue-like buds, and their flaccid bells. She pushes them away as though just the sight of them is painful. Berto doesn't even try with these any more. Instead, being a polite and astute businessman, he offers her the best of a small private creation:

miniature narcissus flowers with white bells that seem to capture the purity of snow, clusters of tiny white muscari firmly connected to their bulbs, their home and source of food. Bianca takes the trays and keeps them far from the fire and close to the windows so that they can at least taste the cold air through the cracks and live longer. After they have bloomed, she places the wrinkled, potato-like bulbs back into their jute sacks as she has been instructed to do, confident that they will bloom again, although she barely has the patience to wait an entire year.

Her heart, though, belongs to hellebores. Until now she has only known the kind that grow in English gardens, clouded with frost, candid and simple, with a few striations of green and pink. The ones that Berto brings her have double and triple blossoms; they are opulent, of an intense violet and blue, and in stark contrast with the cream-coloured stamens. Sometimes they are fringed with purple, reminding her of the veils of frivolous widows. Often they are green, almost an acid shade, and veined with crimson. There are some that are speckled like wild beasts, dotted with lavender on pale pink.

'They are strong but delicate. Just like you,' Berto tells her after they have been working together for some time. 'They must be planted in the ground. They will die in pots.'

They agree that he will bring her several of these plants when they are ready to return to the country. She is sure the poet will be happy to add them to his list of experiments. Meanwhile she is content to place pots of them on the balcony on the first floor of the great hall. As far as shade is concerned, the garden, though barren, provides enough because it is walled in. Hellebores love darkness and it is winter after all. She waits until their blooms reach their peak and then despondently cuts back the stems, hurrying to wash her hands afterwards because the flowers are full of poison. She places the cuttings in a tall, narrow vase, their heads tilting as if they are looking around perplexed at their new arrangement. And then she begins to draw them. She uses an infinite range of hues for the pinks, violets and crimsons; the minuteness of the pistils, which vary from kind to kind, like small eyes; the webbed veins on the petals, rosy-cheeked children who have played too long outdoors.

The drawings are a great success. All the ladies want to have one of Bianca's hellebores, maybe even two or three, to hang above their nightstands or in their studies, to look at while they write love letters.

'And to think that in nature they seem so very modest, almost invisible,' one of them says when she comes to retrieve her very own portrait of the flower.

'There never was a flower more suited to you, Signorina,' Bernocchi says to the guest. She turns, smiles lightly, and walks away, convinced that this is a coded compliment.

'Do you know, Bianca,' he continues, winking, 'what hellebore means in the language of flowers? It means scandal.'

Innes frowns and tries to catch Bianca's eye, but she is not in the mood and simply sighs. Bernocchi has become a coat rack, a tea cosy, an embroidered fireguard; he is a household object of communal use, ready to come alive when one least expects it. Fortunately, no one pays any attention to him. Unfortunately, he is always around.

⁂

If only she could just let go of those thoughts about Pia. If only she could let herself enjoy the present. Every so often doubts like these brush through her. She knows she is doing the right thing by acting on Pia's behalf, though, so she stops questioning, and focuses on confirming her suspicions. Pia will gain her fair advantage, her rights will be restored, and she will have a future. But what about Bianca? She'll have to be content with the shadows.

Now that she is, in one form or another, a young and successful portraitist, Bianca can interrupt her work temporarily and pursue her hunt. She devises a plan as she is drawing, her hand moving spontaneously across the paper, and it seems perfect in its simplicity. Naturally, if she could confide in someone she would feel more certain, but she has her own certainties to rely on. She doesn't worry that the picture is missing either details or precision. She owes this to Pia, her young benefactress who has inspired the path of black and white. At first she has simply been curious, but now her courage is kindled by gratitude. And anyway, what will it take? She has only to make a visit, knock on a front door, ask some questions. The worst thing that could happen will be that the front door will be locked, or there will be no answer. She needs to prepare.

She chooses to wear a grey dress with silk trimming, which conveniently ages her, and a flimsy hat that ties with a big bow under her chin. She slips on her grey kid gloves and fastens their rows of tiny buttons. She places the precious token she discovered and a couple of coins in her green purse. She leaves the house, careful not to run into anyone so she won't have to lie about where she is going, and hails a coach on the street by the gardens. She reasons that a lady being chauffeured is more credible than a lady on foot, even if the journey isn't very far.

She descends from the carriage in front of Santa Caterina alla Ruota, the driver not hiding his vague disapproval at the choice of destination. From a distance she sees the pass-through wooden drawer in the church's door that Minna has told her about. Her curiosity becomes mixed with a feeling of unease. Up close it doesn't look so strange, though. It is a kind of rough wooden cradle. She has imagined it differently, more like an object of torture. She knocks on the door and waits. Behind the grated peephole an old woman's face appears. She wears a kerchief on her head like a peasant.

'What do you want?' the woman asks.

'I am here because I need some information about a girl,' Bianca replies.

'We can't give out information to just anyone. Are you family?'

'No, but I have her pledge token.' She opens her purse and shows a corner of the small pillow.

The peephole closes and the door opens with a clamour of locks and bolts. The old woman lets her in, closes the door, and walks away without saying a word. Bianca hesitates for a moment and then follows her down a long hallway illuminated by tall, barred windows. Seen from up close, her guide isn't all that old, and her manners reveal a certain genteelness. Her outdated black dress contains a trace of elegance in the tubular sleeves, and her kerchief is neatly folded and tied behind her head, not under her chin like the townsfolk. Walking swiftly, she pauses and turns around for a moment to inspect Bianca, who clutches her own fashionable hat with an intent expression. Bianca hopes that she doesn't seem too frivolous and that she has chosen the right dress for the occasion. Instinctively, she lowers her head and folds her hands together as if she were in church.

They walk together through an area of the cloisters that is sleepy with cold. The woman appears both clumsy and cautious in her movements, like someone with bone problems, but her feet move rapidly and silently. Bianca glances to her side and sees a wall of headstones, the graves of men and women, with phrases engraved into the stone in Latin. Her guide stops in front of a small, low doorway. She ducks into it. Bianca goes to follow, but is stopped halfway.

'You wait here.'

The small door shuts firmly. Bianca looks around. She stamps her feet to keep warm. The chill grows more intense. Maybe the humidity of past centuries held within these thick walls is designed to mercilessly ward off intruders. There are no voices, though, no crying. The door creaks and the woman reappears.

'The Signora will see you now,' she says, holding the door open for Bianca, then closing it behind her after she's passed through.

The room is small with a high ceiling and a remote window – part cell, part study. There, a heavy woman dressed in black sits at a monk's table. Her hair is a shiny white. It neatly frames her severe, though almost youthful face. The contrast between her white hair and smooth skin is surprising.

The woman does not stand. She inspects Bianca and then points to the straight-backed chair in front of her.

'Biagina informed me of your request. Can I ask who you are, why you are here, and what is your intention, if I may be so bold?' She speaks in an authoritative tone. 'And how did you come to be in possession of the pledge token?'

Bianca bears the scrutiny of those serene brown eyes and, as clearly as possible, explains the whole story. Her version of it, at least. She pieces the tale together, relying on gossip, real events and conjecture. Saying it out loud makes it feel even more concrete. If it isn't really the truth, she is close at least. An abandoned child was entrusted to an elderly couple. The wife was the sister of the town priest. The married couple lived with the priest. The little girl brought sunlight into the home of the elderly couple. She was bright and alert. Unlike her peers, who were condemned to forced labour by families who earned from them, this girl was raised with all possible comforts, given her situation. She had pretty clothes, good food, toys and affection. The priest, her uncle, taught her how to read and write. Her adopted parents passed away when the girl was too young to take care of the priest but old enough for it to cause rumour and gossip if she did. So she was sent to work in the household of the local lord, enjoying a privilege or two above the rest of the maids due to her vivacious intelligence and the priest's protection. Bianca mentions that all of this should appear in legal documents.

The old woman takes notes, scratching away at a piece of paper. At the end of Bianca's speech, she puts down her quill and sighs.

'Convincing, indeed,' she comments. 'But this could be the story of tens of hundreds of abandoned girls over the last two centuries. You certainly have not gone out of your way to come here and tell me a fairy tale, though. You must have good reasons. Let's be frank, young lady.' And here it seems to Bianca as though the woman is stressing the words '*young* lady'. 'Are you the mother?'

'Oh, no. No, no, no,' Bianca replies hastily. She hasn't considered the possibility of being so grossly misinterpreted. 'I am . . . too young. I'm just a friend.'

'Whose friend?'

'A friend of the child. Of the girl. Of the daughter, I mean.' Bianca catches her breath. 'And to confirm everything that I have so far said, I have brought this.'

This is her *coup de théâtre*. She puts her hand inside her purse and pulls out the small velvet pillow, which she has wrapped in a white cloth. She uncovers it and places it on the table, between herself and the woman, who takes it, turns it over in her fingers, lightly palpates it, and then smells it. She returns it to the table and looks at Bianca.

'It was found on the border of the property where the girl lives,' Bianca explains. It isn't a lie. It is the truth, only somewhat modified. 'I have reason to believe that a woman left this with you, a woman who every so often makes an appearance there. Someone who deserves, more than any other woman, the right to know the fate of this girl. I believe that this woman is her mother.'

Bianca lets the sentence fade out. They both sit in silence. The older lady picks up her quill and then puts it down again.

'We shall see,' she says. She excuses herself and stands, leaving Bianca alone in the room. She is definitely a lady. One can tell from the shape of her hands, from the way she walks, by the elegant cut of her dress. It is difficult to know what she is doing here, why she is here and not outside, riding through the city in a carriage. Perhaps she is freshly widowed. This, more than her position, would explain the black dress. Perhaps she is one of those generous souls who, unsatisfied with living their own life, take up the causes of others. Donna Clara would know, but Bianca cannot ask her. And nor does Bianca know how she can drop Donna Clara's name into the conversation without putting the whole endeavour at risk.

The woman re-enters the room through a side door, holding in both hands a large green book stuffed with papers and objects.

'It ought to be in here.'

She places the book on the desk, opens it and traces her finger down the pages. Bianca tries to read upside down but in vain: the handwriting is too small, oblique and somewhat faded; a damp stain extends across one page, eating away at many of the sentences.

'Here.'

The woman takes the token again, turning it over in her hand.

'The description matches. "A pink and green pledge with the image of a lamb embroidered in gold and silver thread. A thin linen shirt with the initials cut out. Fine linen swaddling with initials cut out. The baby girl, in good health, one month old, was received and given to the custody of Berenice A. on such and such a date. The child was passed on to the care of family M. in such and such year, with the following belongings, etc., etc."'

She turns the page. This time the *coup de théâtre* is all hers. There is the pledge. It is the twin of the one that Bianca has brought, only less aged. It has the same pink and green embroidery and small embroidered roses. Bianca reaches out a hand but the woman shuts the book quickly. The volume is full of irregular lumps. It surely contains more of those awkward and strange relics.

'And so?' asks Bianca, after a brief moment of silence.

'And so what?' The gaze of the woman is precise and penetrating.

'The two tokens are identical. This proves that my story is true.' Bianca ends her sentence by placing both hands on the table, one next to the other.

'It only proves that there are two identical tokens in existence,' objects the woman. 'The story which you so compassionately shared with me could be true just as it could be false. Try to understand: I have no reason to doubt your good nature. You seem like an honest young lady, prompted by the desire to help and perhaps driven too by a certain, natural curiosity – which in itself is not bad, but could lead to harm. I do not know what secrets people have told you to make you come here today. But in any case, there are rules to this game. The fact that you have the token does not give you any more rights than if you had come here empty-handed.'

The woman glares at Bianca pointedly, as though trying to convey a warning. Bianca decides to ignore the insinuation nestled within the speech – that somebody has sent her. She isn't there to buy the truth, and the idea that it could be for sale hasn't even crossed her mind.

'You cannot tell me anything else?' she says instead. 'My young friend has reached an age where she would like to know more about herself, about where she comes from . . . And I am here of my own free will.'

'Ah, my dear, you will have time to discover that free will is a strange beast.' The woman seems to want to continue but stops, biting her lip, as if she has already ventured too much. 'Your young friend,' she continues, 'has no right to know anything about her past. These are the rules. Weren't you aware of them?'

'Actually, no, I wasn't,' Bianca says, straightening up in anger. Why is there such reticence here, such resistance?

'Legitimate parents or legal guardians have full liberty to reconnect with the children they have entrusted to this precious institution, as is the case with your friend about whom I have already generously shared information. But the children have no right to find out who their parents are, if the parents don't explicitly ask. Just think of the harm it could bring. We need to remember that there must have been a good reason for these parents to separate themselves from their children. Even if,' she says, lowering her voice and adding in a whisper, 'often the reasons are simply not good enough. In any case, whether it was destitution or fear of scandal, whether our children came from high-profile families or from the most wretched ones, for us they are all equal once they arrive here. We cannot allow ourselves to make distinctions. Please understand,' she added. 'I am not required to tell you this but I will: from the swaddling and the token, your girl seems to have been born into a good family, which complicates things. Perhaps the mother bore this child out of wedlock. Or she was married but produced this child with a man who wasn't her legitimate husband.'

The woman ticks off both hypotheses on her fingers.

You forgot one, Bianca thinks to herself. *A young man might have run away.*

'It is risky for us to dig further,' the lady continues. 'We might crack open a hornets' nest. This is all I can share with you, young lady. If you are guided by good intentions, as I believe you are, the best you can do for your girl is assist her in her physical and spiritual growth and make sure that she is good and devout. When the time comes, if you have the authority to do so, help her marry in the most opportune way.'

'But . . .' Bianca's objection lingers in mid-air. The woman has already stood up and motions for Bianca to do the same.

'I will walk you out.'

Bianca picks up the token, places it back inside her bag and follows the lady from the room. They walk back down the hallway, more slowly this time. Bianca wants to find an excuse to ask more, to think of another way to seem more convincing, the way a generous protectress occupied with a legitimate investigation should be. Instead she is shown the door.

'May God be with you and with your protected one,' the lady says in farewell. The woman who guards the door stands up to open it. 'Entrust yourself to the lamb, which rids the world of sin, or at least, in immense clemency, ignores it,' she concludes.

Bianca can do nothing but curtsey and exit, pushed out by that calm, heavy gaze. The door closes firmly behind her.

Outside on the street the jumble of coaches, carriages, and shouting tradesmen is deafening and in stark contrast to the silence of the place she has just left. Bianca feels defeated. But resolutely she straightens herself up and heads back towards the house, as Donna Julie has taught her.

In the city you must always look like you are going somewhere.

She is so lost in her thoughts – replaying the last scenes in her head, the details, seeing again the large water stain on the paper, the piercing gaze of the woman – that she doesn't notice someone blocking her way. She has to stop suddenly to avoid bumping into the figure. Her eyes take in a pair of scuffed shoes, then two legs splattered with mud, followed by a layer of coats, a dirty neck, and a splotch of fresh mud on a boy's cheek. A flimsy, faded cap completes the portrait of a young street urchin.

'Go away,' Bianca says nervously as she attempts to walk around him. But he steps in front of her again and flashes a hint of a smile.

'Miss, do you need help?'

'Of course not,' answers Bianca.

'But yes, you do. Didn't you just come from the orphanage? And didn't you want to know certain things that they didn't tell you?'

Of course, she thinks. The coming and going of people like herself who seek buried information is certainly not new around here. There is bound to be someone who will try to profit from it. The young boy – he must be thirteen or fourteen – continues walking beside her.

'I have a friend who works in there. She can find out what you're looking for.'

'They already told me everything,' Bianca says, slowing down reluctantly. The boy continues in a confident tone.

'Oh, no. There's the public registry and there's the secret registry, which they don't show to outsiders. In the secret one they write other things, like names. The real names. And when someone comes to ask about a child, and who that person was, the when and why . . . well, my friend is good at finding out these things. Trust me,' he says with a wink. 'Only two *scudi*. One for me, one for her.'

Bianca hesitates. How embarrassing it would be to buy secrets. Then, on impulse, she decides that she likes this boy, that two *scudi* isn't that much and anyway, she would have spent them sooner or later.

'Can you read?' she asks.

'No, Miss, I can't, but my friend can. And anyway my memory is good. I keep everything up here,' the boy taps his temple.

The transaction is quickly concluded. She gives her name, they set a date to meet again and she pays half of the compensation. She will pay the other half once the information is retrieved, in precisely two weeks, in the same place, at noon.

What do I have to lose but money? Bianca asks herself, placing the coin on the child's curiously clean palm. If only Pia's happiness could cost so little.

'What is your name?' she asks.

'Girolamo,' he says, taking off his hat. 'Here to serve you, Miss.'

He runs off before Bianca has the chance to question him further. Instead she follows him with her eyes and watches him disappear down a dark alley that swallows him up as if he was made of the same matter. She leaves reluctantly then, feeling the weight of things unfinished.

Her feet move her forward while her mind retraces the encounter. She lingers on a phrase, embroiders a detail, and doesn't notice where she is going. As if waking from a trance, she finds herself seated on a stone bench by a big brick church. She has no idea how she has got there. She regains her senses, feels the cold seeping in under her clothes, and around her the heavy stares of men. No, these aren't men; they are dirty delivery boys bringing rolls of hides to the leather artisans in the area. The air is swampy; she is near the canal, and it gives off a diabolical stench.

I need to get out of here, Bianca thinks. She stands up with resolve, ties her hat ribbons under her chin, jumps over some puddles of dark liquid, and then looks up and around for the golden Madonna statue, a beacon for people navigating the streets of the city.

Miss Bianca, where on earth did you ruin your skirt like that? In the Naviglio? one of the maids will probably ask her later. Carlina, Titina, Annina . . . they lead their lives in the shadows, give themselves up to some dolt, and then become forgettable like all the others. She won't answer their questions if they ask. And she doesn't answer the question that she suddenly hears behind her, making her jump.

'Miss Bianca! You aren't lost, are you? Miss Bianca?'

She is just about to turn around but he is faster and steps in front of her. It is Tommaso. He greets her, taking off his hat and offering her his cheek. How different he is outside; no longer a shy extra, so much surer of himself. Bianca hesitates.

'I understand the cloudy allure of our shadows,' he continues. 'And I understand what drives you here: boredom is stronger than a machine.'

Bianca is silent but then regains control of herself.

'Ah, but I am never bored. Maybe you were bored – is that why you ran away? Or did your muse allow you to leave?'

She finds that this is the right sort of tone for him, the affectionate banter of siblings.

'My muse, my muse,' he replies, guiding her quickly across a wide field beyond which stands a row of luminous Greek-style columns. 'My muse is a tyrant, that's for sure. But my muse is also my only faithful partner. I can't be with her, and I can't be without her. I won't ask what you were doing in that sewer in full daylight,' he adds, meaning the opposite.

Bianca decides to take him at face value and remains silent.

'You are indeed mysterious, Miss Bianca.'

'Me? I'm like a piece of white paper,' she replies teasingly.

'An appropriate comparison. Anything can sprout from it. Perhaps it was already written but in the ink of conspirators, revealing itself only to the astute eye . . .'

'Oh, be quiet. Don't we have enough conspirators around the house already?'

A skilful move: Tommaso's attention is diverted.

'Don't be like Donna Clara, I beg you. She sees shadows everywhere,' he says.

'That's because she is afraid for all of you,' replies Bianca immediately.

'And for herself. She couldn't bear to lose what she has built with such tenacity. Her little citadel of ease and respectability would topple down if her most intimate guests and her very own son insisted on playing politics.'

'And isn't she right to worry? She's a woman: she defends what she has. Her horizon is the house and the garden.'

'Exactly. And she can't see beyond the front door. But the day will come when women will stand by our sides instead of lagging one step behind.'

'Like in a dance?' Bianca tries to joke.

'Certainly. At the great ball of the new world.'

Without realizing it, Tommaso has quickened his pace, and Bianca is forced to almost run to keep up.

'Slow down,' she protests.

'I apologize but these discussions touch me deeply,' he says, amending his gait.

'More than poetry?'

'Much more. We should all have the courage to hang our harps from the willow tree; the heart cannot sing if it isn't free.'

Bianca is silent. She is touched. This Tommaso is completely different from the one she knows. He is so intense and alive.

As they walk silently towards the house, a house that belongs to neither of them but which they have both made their own, united in their search for a calling, she almost forgets what happened earlier.

❧ ❧

'If you suspected something, Innes . . . something good, that could do a person dear to you some good, that could change her life, what would you do?'

'If it was only a suspicion? Nothing, my dear. I would keep it to myself, and I'd try to make it a certainty.' Precisely. Even Innes would do as she has done. So why not confide in him? Could he be her ally, her accomplice? He is so capable and in control. 'But to change someone's life is presumptuous, Bianca. If I were you, I'd take care.' He is also so inflexible. As straight as a cypress tree. A man of only logic. 'I know you, Bianca. You are plotting something. I can see it, and I don't like it.'

They are alone in the living room, waiting to be called to lunch. The long, dull moments in a large household.

'Oh, come now, don't be so serious. I was just wondering.'
She thinks it best to be light-hearted to distract him. She will
only tell him when it is necessary. Only when every bit of evidence is clear. In the meantime she defends herself. 'You are
always plotting, too. You and Don Titta. I see you. Sometimes
I can even hear you. No, don't worry, I can hear but I don't
listen. But I do sense something even from behind closed doors.'

'What you do not know will not harm you, Bianca.'

He is so serious he is almost frightening. And yet he is, too,
a man to whom gravity is becoming, perhaps because he is then
especially handsome when laughing or smiling. Like now: his
whole face is lit up with a smile, distracting her.

'I'm happy to be a source of laughter for you,' Bianca says
condescendingly.

But she is just teasing and he knows it. In fact, he takes her
arm and grips it firmly before letting it go.

'I, too, would like to be entertaining to you but I fear that
I don't have such an amusing personality.'

'If I wanted to be entertained, I'd go to the theatre, where
everything is pretend, even passion. It's real passion that interests me. Your passion,' she says.

He misunderstands, perhaps on purpose.

'Mine? There's little passion here. Horses, maybe, but I
cannot afford my own. Literature, yes, because it costs less. Life,
with all that it sets aside: surprises and trapdoors, twists and
turns.'

'In one word, revolution.' Bianca indulges herself but he
doesn't react.

'I like *you* because you never give up, Bianca.'

Since when does he know her so well? The idea that he
thinks he knows her deeply makes her wonder. Or is it something else, this strange and growing intimacy? Bianca isn't sure,

so she keeps quiet. The pair exchange glances. Bianca feels confused, light-headed and naive. Their exchange has been far from innocent.

❧ ❧

'It's not right, Titta. It's not right at all.' It is evident that Donna Clara is in a bad mood as soon as she starts complaining about the wrinkles in the tablecloth. There is only one, Bianca notes, and it is almost imperceptible and for the most part covered by the pewter centrepiece overflowing with tulips. Then Donna Clara complains about the tepid and flavourless consommé. And the soft bread. When the food is not to her liking, there is usually something else she isn't happy about. It doesn't take long before she explains. 'They say that the Austrian gendarmes visited the Viganò family and it wasn't as a simple courtesy.'

'Yes, I heard about it, too,' Don Titta says calmly.

'They say that Count Eugenio had quite a shock. They say,' she continues, lifting up a letter that has been resting on her lap, 'that they might come by here. I am going to put my foot down and say no, Titta. These indulgences have got to stop. They say' – her tone goes up a notch as she waves the letter about – 'that you refused to write an ode for the new general whose name I can't even pronounce. They asked you to write it but you said no, so they asked Monti, and he agreed and got a hefty compensation, as well as praise from the governor. Is this true?'

'Yes, Mother, it's true. How can you doubt your informers?'

'Don't play with me, Titta. You didn't say anything.' In the frenzy of this discussion, her son is reduced to a rebellious child. 'May I remind you that money is necessary to survive? May I also remind you that in order to live there must be peace? And peace must be cultivated.'

'That which you call peace, Mother, I call collusion. Complicity.'

'Ah, I see. I wonder why we never attribute the same meaning to some words. But fine, let's pretend to be a gang of rebels. We'll all end up with our heads chopped off, like the queen.'

'Mother, let's not get ahead of ourselves. Aren't the Austrians notorious for being intelligent governors?'

Donna Clara misses the irony or perhaps chooses to ignore it.

'What do you think – that the era of Theresa is over? They're not standing there just for fun. But anyway, I don't want to have a *political* discussion.' She pronounces the word with a grimace. 'I just want to say that your rekindling of patriotic love might take the bread away from the mouths of your children.'

Donna Clara looks around the room to see the effect of her words on the others. Bianca stares at Tommaso, who in turn stares at the pale turnips on the dinner table. He has no intention of intervening. Innes watches a blackbird hopping on the windowsill. Outside it is drizzling.

'I would rather starve than eat from a foreigner's hand,' Don Titta says calmly. 'My children won't die of hunger: we always have the countryside and its fruits.'

'Right, and what about the creditors lined up outside our door?'

'Can we please stop discussing these things in front of everyone?' Donna Julie interrupts, blushing, a sour note in her voice.

'Everyone?' Donna Clara blurts out, making Bianca feel like a decorative object. 'It's not like we're going to get through this by hiding facts behind good manners. I have nothing left to give you, nothing. I've sold my most precious joys . . .'

Bianca looks at Donna Clara's hands, heavy as ever with diamond rings and other valuable stones. Clearly, she thinks to herself, those are less precious joys.

'No one asked you for a thing, Mother dear,' Don Titta says. 'You've given us a home and your affection, and this is the greatest gift. Don't worry. We will manage. The novel—'

'The novel, the novel! You've been working on it for ten years. Ten! And what about those beautiful poems that brought you bread and fame at the same time? I don't mean the ones for the Austrians – God no, let us not soil our hands if we really want to play at being heroes. But at least the others. The innocent ones. What went wrong?'

'They were useless, Mother. Useless word games for useless people who sit in their living rooms drinking rose-water and concealing their laughter. I'm tired of creating useless things. Just have faith, and you'll see.'

'I do have faith, but in the dear Lord, not in your soiled paper . . .'

'Signora, may I serve you some soufflé?'

In his many years of service, Ruggiero has learned how to clear the air over the dining-room table. And, as suddenly as it arrives, the storm dissipates. Bianca, who would have voluntarily collapsed onto the floor a moment before to create a distraction, now exchanges furtive glances with Innes and sinks her fork into the golden mound on her plate. Donna Julie's face is pale. She has deep, crocus-coloured shadows beneath her eyes. It is another small, pathetic family brawl, no more important just because it is about money and pride. Incriminations are launched without tactic and accusations swell out of proportion. These aren't battles. They are just card games in which everyone is bluffing. At least the soufflé holds up. And, thankfully, lunch ends soon after.

Later, in the living room, Bianca opens the French window to feel the cold air outside. The winter garden appears to have shrunk. Those trees, which will never be part of a forest but which try so hard to grow nonetheless, give her a sense of refuge and relief. City life is complicated. It is onerous to be so intimate with a family that is not one's own, and to be part of the burden. The simplicity of nature would restore her, she thinks, even if she were a prisoner.

She slips into the darkness, breathing in the dank smell of dead leaves and wrapping her shawl tightly around her. The cold clears her mind. Who is right – the women of the house with their small concerns, or the poet? He is brave, yes, but perhaps he is also thoughtless. Is it more important to protect the nest and defend it from turbulence and change or journey untethered towards the unknown? *What manly questions*, she tells herself with a hint of irony. She is proud of having thought of them, even though she doesn't know the answers. She has no connections to tie her down, no big ideas to carry her away. She only has some intelligence, talent and a spark of imagination that is enough to nurture both.

'Noisy as always, no?'

It is Innes.

'You scared me,' she says.

'I don't believe you. You didn't even blink before Donna Clara's wrath.'

'Because they weren't talking to me. But I felt oppressed nonetheless. No, rather, I felt like a bird in a cage being clawed at by a cat.'

'I understand. You will get used to it. As you know, Italians are always a bit theatrical. But it's a tempest in a teapot. He always does what he pleases.'

'You admire him.'

'At times. I care about him, and therefore I forgive him some things.'

Bianca finds it difficult to decipher Innes's facial expression in the darkness.

'And I care about you too, don't get me wrong. But everything passes, even words as heavy as stone. Only art is destined to last. Only that counts.'

❦ ❦

She receives a package. It is wrapped in damask printed with tiny flowers on a pale background. It is heavy in her palm and tied with a bright green silk ribbon. Bianca sits on her bed and pulls the ribbon impatiently. The fabric falls away and a smooth, round, white rock appears. It is almost too smooth to be natural. She turns it over in her hands and notices a pale vein where the stone is slightly hollow. Only time could have done that. There is a note that says in small capital letters, *NIVEA LAPIS*. White stone. Her name set in stone. Bianca Pietra smiles. She weighs the stone in her hand again and caresses it with the tip of her index finger, testing its dense yet porous consistency. She wonders who sent it, but puts the thought aside. It won't get her anywhere. Oh, to be a stone once in a while, impenetrable, impermeable.

Her father once gave her a coat of arms with the motto *Semper Firma* underneath it. The insignia was of a white stone resting on a horse-chestnut leaf on a blue background. The mysterious gift-giver must know about her father's present. But no, she thinks, that is impossible; no-one knows about this, it happened years ago, and the coat of arms disappeared long ago too. Could it be that someone simply had the same thought as her father? She asks herself if this is a gift or a warning. But it is somehow nice not to know. The stone is not an egg. It can never be cracked open. It will forever hold its mystery and this makes it both dangerous and beautiful.

❧ ❧

One night Bianca cannot sleep. Having finished all her books, she leaves her bedroom, intent on choosing one or two new ones from the library, which Bianca is sure will be empty at this hour – the men have gone out. From the staircase where she is standing, the house appears murky grey. A sliver of moon, visible through the skylight, lights her path. But after two or three steps, Bianca realizes she is not alone. Tall twin shadows are standing in the entrance. And although they are dressed in heavy overcoats, she recognizes them and is instantly curious. Should she go back to her room, pretend not to have seen anything? No. She goes down the stairs. She isn't doing anything wrong. The pair look at her briefly, and nod. Innes speaks first.

'Would you like to come with us?'

'Where?'

He puts a finger to his lips.

'Come.'

Don Titta walks back and forth impatiently. His cape dances around him, falling and swishing with his movement. Innes disappears into the closet and comes back with a third cape. He holds it out for her. It feels like a yoke on her shoulders. He responds to her quizzical look with a flash in his eyes that she has never seen before and which makes her even more curious. Her hesitation lasts only a second. She will not say no. Innes hooks the cape under her throat, the way a father would, and takes her by the hand. The intimacy of the gesture makes her flinch.

There is a sound at the door – the signal. They go outside. The cold February night air is as clean as glass. The cobblestones in the piazza are covered with a thin film of ice that shines under the street lamps. She has just enough time to hop into the carriage before it starts on its way. She smells the damp fabric inside and sees small clouds of her breath in the momentary light. Don Titta looks out at the shadowy city. It is deserted. Innes, seated next to her, tries to speak to her with his eyes. But what is he trying to say?

Bianca feels agitation building up inside her. Something she hasn't felt before. She isn't dressed appropriately; her cape isn't heavy enough; she is wearing the wrong shoes, no gloves, no vest. It is winter after all. Where are they going, on a winter's night, all dressed in black, two men and a woman, and no chaperone? She imagines them talking about her later: *No, Miss Bianca stayed home tonight. Actually, she followed them for a bit until they pushed her out of the carriage and then they left her on the pavement. She was not needed. No one wanted her there. Adieu, go home, go back to bed with your books; can't you see we're busy living?* The other Bianca, the one who *is* invited to come along on the adventure, sits up straight.

He is sitting so close to her. To touch him, all she needs to do is reach out her arm. What an idea! Why should she touch him? Why indeed. Innes's warmth emanates from under his clothing. Bianca no longer feels cold, maybe she has a fever. It has to be a fever, this kind of fire inside her, a little below her heart.

The carriage slows down and then comes to a full stop. They have arrived. Don Titta steps out without offering to help her. Innes does, though. But he doesn't lower the stairs. He just picks her up by the waist and lifts her down. She smells tobacco and spices, and then the frigid cold takes her breath away. The street is empty. Via a small stone bridge, they pass over the canal. There, two churches stand side by side like old friends.

The silence is interrupted by the sound of footsteps. Another caped figure arrives, this one with messy curls and the flash of a familiar smile. It is Tommaso.

'So you've come, too,' Innes says, with some disapproval.

'How could I miss out on this madness?' His grin, growing wider, turns into a smirk. 'What about her?'

Her? Me? What am I, a parcel, an object? Bianca thinks, taking a step forward to stand her ground.

'Why not?' Innes says. 'Come on, there's no time to waste.'

The driver has already lowered a trunk, placed it on the ground and opened it up.

'The light?'

'Here it is.'

Sparks fly, the fuse catches, and light is cast on Ruggiero's round face. Bianca sees now that he bites his lip and looks around furtively. What sort of game is this?

The cold has all but disappeared. Innes and Don Titta take turns fishing out fragile wooden and canvas objects from the trunk. Lanterns. They light them, stuff them with small scrolls of paper and toss them up in the air, giving an extra push to the more fickle ones, which fall back down. Once she gets a clear picture of what is going on, Bianca helps, passing the lanterns – which are fragile in her hands – to the person who is ready to light them. Over and over. Several drift down towards the water and go out with a brief sizzle. But a small horde swarms into the sky above, their light reflecting off the black waters. A few catch fire – a brief flame and then nothing. Many endure and take flight.

There are more pieces of paper than lanterns, so once she has finished assisting, Bianca takes one out and unravels it.

'People of Milan, friends, and strangers: now, when we have most to fear, is the time for us to be courageous . . .'

Tommaso reads out loud over her shoulder, almost too close to her, painfully present.

'Well put, Titta. Now it's my turn. I have my own system and it might be more efficient than yours.'

Innes shakes his head while Tommaso takes a handful of papers, goes down to the canal, pulls out a few small boats made of waxed canvas from his sack, and launches them into the water.

'I should have used bottles, like the castaways that we are.'

Don Titta, who has been silently contemplating his flying messages, leans out over the bridge and mutters some words, indistinctly at first, as if weighing them, then more loudly.

> *Giochi dolceamaro, bimbo mio:*
> *affidi le tue barche alla corrente*
> *ignaro e sorridente*
> *pago del loro navigar di stella*
> *nel piccolo mare dei tuoi occhi . . .*
>
> *Bittersweet games, my child:*
> *Entrust your boats to the current unknowing*
> *And smiling, repaid for their*
> *Journey under the stars*
> *In the small sea of your eyes . . .*

'Titta, Titta, our private wandering minstrel,' Tommaso teases from below. 'You have a rhyme for every occasion. As usual, I'm envious.'

The cold is even more acute now, the flickering lights growing distant in the night sky and on the water; the trunk is empty, the wick has died out, and Ruggiero is back at his place in the driver's seat of the carriage.

'Are you going home?' Innes asks Tommaso in an effort to be polite.

'You know I have no place to live. There's a party at the Crivellis'. I might stop by. He has invited some French girls.' He smacks his lips.

Innes frowns.

'Don Titta's right. Everything is just a big game for you.'

'And what's wrong with that, my friend? It is night-time; we have engaged in a most civil and noble folly – a nice, reckless gesture that will not amount to anything. I tell you, we could just as well have risked more.'

He bows mockingly to Bianca and blows her a kiss. Then he turns around, raises his arm in a goodbye, and walks back along the shoreline to join his friends.

Don Titta doesn't say a word. He still contemplates the vanishing lights.

'He's right. Our message will only end up educating the washerwomen. We weren't daring enough, Innes. It's the heart of this city that needs to be reawakened. The higher the risk, the greater the reward.'

'This is only the start, Titta. Our first time. We are mere beginners, schoolchildren. We will learn to do better. There's the lake, the sea, and as much sky as we'd like. Now let's head back.'

Bianca is startled for a moment when Innes says 'lake'. A fleet of wooden ships on her lake? Please, no rebellion, only poetry. Now the tutor turns to face her, making her visible again, real.

'Come on, it's late for you.'

He takes her gently by the elbow and leads her towards the carriage. She trips, her legs frozen with cold. He swiftly picks her up, as though they are dancing, and places her inside the carriage. He then clambers in himself, followed by Don Titta. Ruggiero flicks the reins and the horses set out for home.

❧ ❧

Everything looks much smaller from the carriage on the return trip. Don Titta slumps back against the seat, his long legs in their tight-fitting trousers stretched out before him, his hand resting palm up on top of his knee, as if asking for something. She dreams of putting her hand in his, a kind of silent gift. Surprise, an awkward press of skin against skin, a reverse hand-shake. Innes, seated close to his friend, cannot take his eyes off her. Three is plainly one too many.

They arrive home and shuffle up the stairs, each to his own room. No 'goodnights' are exchanged; the night will not be a good one, it will only bring wide-eyed reflection.

The next morning, her shoes look like papier mâché. The soles have peeled off and the upper part is damp and hard. She ends up hiding them at the bottom of the cloakroom, so that no one will find them, not even the maids, who always have something to say. But Alcina finds them anyway and dangles them in front of the others in the kitchen.

'If Miss Bianca wants to go out and run free at night, she should at least wear her overshoes or a nice pair of boots. Am I right?'

'Yes, you are. But you know that young ladies have their heart in their feet. They're head over heels, I tell you!'

'As long as someone doesn't come knocking . . . and knock her up!' Raucous laughter ensues. Bianca walks in, snatches the shoes from Alcina and walks away. Fortunately, because of their strange dialect, she hasn't understood a thing.

❧ ❧

The long, harsh winter seems never to end. Perhaps it is the ailments that afflict the children, but a grey patina shrouds the windows of the house on Via Morone. No one goes out, for fear of infection. And they don't receive any guests for the same reason. It is the horrible boredom of February. Everywhere it is the same. What is the point of going to visit friends only to hear them talk about mucus and phlegm?

It has even happened in the famous salon of Signora Trivulzio. What an odd place that is, Bianca thinks. It is as if the salon exists in a bubble: its four rooms of yellow damask, those candles laid out on great big trays of silver instead of in the usual candelabras, the waiters in yellow, blending in with the tapestry. Bianca imagines it as if it were a theatre set – a house without kitchens, bedrooms or closets. She thinks of a stage, and behind the curtain, the props: Signora Trivulzio's costumes hanging on a rack, her shoes lined up on a strip of carpet, and an elegant toilette replete with little bottles ready for her *maquillage*.

Bianca wishes she could share these thoughts with someone. Innes has gone to Magenta to discuss some new academic theories with Pellico, his oft-mentioned but never-seen colleague. Maybe, like Signora Trivulzio's house, Pellico doesn't really exist either.

Don Titta has authorized Innes's leave and actually encourages him to go; he plans on joining them and his own friend, the host, Count Porro Lambertenghi. Bianca tries to imagine the four of them together, the ranks mixed in the way these liberal patricians enjoy and Donna Clara does not. But in her present situation, the older lady cannot oppose resistance.

Donna Clara is tired and grey, like everything around her. For the first time she looks weak. She is curiously compliant and more considerate with others, a behaviour that only a short while ago she abhorred. With her son gone and her daughter-in-law banished to her own quarters due to a bout of her secret illness that everyone knows about and nobody speaks of, she does nothing. Bianca is reluctantly made witness to the sad display of this weak and vulnerable Donna Clara.

'Things change, the world changes. And when you don't like it any more, they say you simply no longer understand it. That you're ageing. I don't understand all these polemics based on good government and the rest of it. Who are we to say that one man is good and another is not? Kings, believe me, are all the same. And the people without a king is like a chicken with its head cut off.'

'But you aren't the people. *We* are the people,' Bianca ventures.

They are sitting in the boudoir next to Donna Clara's bedroom, a small room, usually well lit but gloomy now, like the rest of the house. They are having coffee, a speciality blend purchased from 'the Turk', who isn't really Turkish, but who has a shop at the end of Corsia dei Servi. Neither the aroma nor the heat of the beverage, sweetened with pillows of whipped cream, is able to lift the old woman's spirits.

'No, we aren't the people. We are women. We float somewhere between here and there, tied down by ropes, like great balloons.'

Bianca holds back a smile as she imagines a fleet of women floating ten feet above ground, tied down by the ankles, bobbing lightly in the breeze.

'It's as if they've created a limbo just for us,' Donna Clara continues. 'When we are useful – for love, children, looking after the house – they pull us down. Otherwise they just leave us there, in the air, so we don't cause too much disturbance, with the excuse that we are light and can't possibly understand.

Thirty years ago it was the same thing. Nothing has changed. Heads still roll, blood is spilled, everything seems as though it's about to change, but then we are right back where we started. A woman's only power is her beauty, and then it fades. If I had a choice, I'd be the girl who could still fit into that corset over there.' She motions towards a half-dressed mannequin covered in a delicate architecture of sticks, lace and silk. 'I used to laugh, drink champagne and chat with the most refined intellectuals in the world, in Paris. Look at me now; look at what I've turned into. I can't even glance at myself in the mirror for fear of seeing the other me. I've turned into a peasant woman, sanctimoniously sent to the country for eight months of the year and the rest of the time a prisoner of this city, surrounded by the blood and urine of children.'

Bianca shudders, as she always does when Donna Clara shifts from formal to personal with her. She never knows whether to consider it a concession of intimacy or a gesture of slight disdain. The old woman keeps talking. Bianca realizes it makes no difference how she responds.

'She won't last, that one,' Donna Clara continues in dialect.

'What, beauty?' Bianca asks, trying to understand.

'No, no,' Donna Clara replies. 'My daughter-in-law, she's too delicate for this world. She's like this piece of china.'

She holds up a cup. It is almost transparent in its delicacy. With the flames from the fireplace flickering behind it, it really does look like a shell. She puts it down.

'When she dies, what will we do?'

Bianca feels obliged to alleviate such pessimism.

'What are you talking about? It's just the winter. It's been hard on us all. When the nice weather comes, signora will regain her strength, you'll see.'

Bianca doesn't really believe her own words. Why is the

poet away with other men discussing things that are only important to him instead of being here, alongside the woman he has married, who is suffering? How can he not know that any day could be her last? Is he a monster? Has he simply given up? Or does he know something that no one else does? Bianca has seen Donna Julie run to her room, racked with coughing. The children have thrown all sorts of tantrums to hide their fear. Anxiety is everywhere: in the eyes of the help, in the presence of the doctor's coach in the courtyard, and in the red-splotched handkerchiefs that the washerwoman sluice again and again, trying to restore them to their original whiteness. Too many children, too much life.

In spite of this, Donna Julie always appears so serene, wrapped in a peacefulness that softens the effects of grief and transforms them into a sweet, deaf, anticipatory nostalgia. It is as if she has already gone far away and will return only for brief visits. The world is too much for her. Her absence is felt more than that of her husband; the children ask about her unrelentingly and are allowed only brief visits, one at a time. They sit in line outside her door. Bianca sees them waiting patiently and silently, their feet dangling from the sofa, their eyes fixed on the door handle, eager to see it open. If the old woman is right, there won't be much time before they will be left only with the bitter tears of loss.

❧ ❧

Two weeks pass. Bianca finishes a new series of drawings, divides them into their separate folders, and gives orders for them to be picked up. She feels liberated. Instead of putting on her smock after her morning tea, she pulls on her gloves, hat and redingote.

'I'm going out,' she announces to no one in particular, and

runs downstairs with the frenzy of a child who has been freed from her tutor.

'She's as mad as a horse, but I suppose that's why we like her,' Donna Clara says before devouring her *oeuf au vin*, which she has requested for additional sustenance at breakfast. She, too, is trying to combat the recent weakness she has been feeling. She has said it must be due to the change in the weather.

Donna Julie's health has, in the meantime, improved. A miraculous recovery brings her back to the centre of her world – her home and children. The unsettled climate of the past few days is suddenly replaced by mannerist optimism.

Bianca doesn't hear Donna Clara's comment as she leaves and it wouldn't have mattered to her anyway. She is already in the courtyard, admiring the intense blue rectangle of sky above their house. She smiles at Rossetti, the doorman, and gives him her final instructions: the folders should not get bent and the servant who picks them up should treat them with great care.

Via Morone is as bleak and grey as always but that turquoise strip of sky hangs like a path that needs to be followed. She heads towards the open spaces of the Corsia del Giardino, with its coming and going of carriages. On her left she sees La Scala poking out into the piazza like the great chair of a giant. Bianca crosses the street and heads towards the arches where it is said that a maiden with an unforgiving name died of a forbidden love. She passes under them as if they are the entrance to a new world, and walks on through the gardens of Acqualunga, watching the ducks and thinking of her own lake at her father's house. She isn't concerned with botany today so doesn't even notice the young fan-like leaves of the ginkgo tree, which blow in the wind like small flags. She has a destination.

She walks around the pond, passing well-behaved children and their governesses who are busily launching wooden boats that have waited all winter to come out. Girls jump skipping ropes and play with hoops. Two men on horseback look over the scene benevolently. A young lady in light blue stands in an arc of sunlight. It is a perfect *tableau vivant* for this first day of sunshine. It is not yet spring but it feels like it.

Bianca suddenly notices that an old woman in rags has approached the young lady in blue. She speaks to her, gestures, and holds out her hand. The lady in blue takes a step back, freezes, then turns around, fumbling for something in her bag and handing it to the woman. Then she leaves in a hurry. The tableau is ruined, but the occurrence is interesting. What had the old woman wanted? And why was she so insistent? Maybe she had a secret to sell, a secret like the one Bianca is about to buy herself.

The sunlight disappears into a cloud of haze, as if it has been siphoned out of the picture. It is now only a sour, cold March morning. The chill makes Bianca quicken her step. As she walks she looks at her reflection in the windows and likes what she sees. A young, independent woman taking great strides in the world, on her own. It had been easy. No, that wasn't true. But it hadn't been all that hard either. Mainly, it just happened. Could it have taken place any other way? Was there another way to be content and at ease in the world? Bianca sighs and then smiles to answer her own question. A gentleman, passing her, tips his hat, as if to return her greeting. Bianca smiles again at the misunderstanding, and then turns back. The gentleman slows and turns, too, flashing her a grin. Bianca hastens her step. He was a stranger – how embarrassing! Part of her, though, almost wishes that he *would* follow her. After a while she turns back again, but he is now far away.

Now there is nothing to smile about. The city grows darker and uglier with every step. The boulevards narrow into alleyways and houses lean against each other carelessly as if drunk. A beastly stench comes from a dark rivulet that passes through the middle of the street. *What am I doing here?* She reminds herself: *I'm seeking the solution to a mystery.* This neighbourhood is like an entirely different city; gone is the airy vastness of the great tree-lined boulevards; there are no piazzas with ornate churches here. Are secrets always so crooked? Perhaps it is their nature, she tells herself, trying to ignore a woman in rags squatting on the steps in a doorway, surrounded by barefoot, naked children playing in the mud. A rusty sign for an inn squeaks in the breeze, the only music around.

She isn't scared. She has no fear. Dozens of heroines before her have ventured to even darker depths, with only their courage and sincerity to shield them. Many have revealed lies in order to see the true and just triumph. She is not frightened, but she is cold. The returning sun shines crookedly down these alleys, and only meagrely at this time of day. Foul, fetid smells emanate from the cracks in the walls. Cellar windows leak frigid bursts of air that snake around her ankles. She wouldn't be surprised to see claws emerging from a grate. She walks faster; the alleyway is long and she has to travel its full length. Finally, the houses separate, the sky becomes visible again in all its vastness, and a young boy stands waiting, leaning against a fountain, his arms crossed, clogs mired in dirt. He has a smirk on his face – no, it is more of a smile.

❧ ❧

Afterwards, Bianca looks around and notices the hackberry trees. Their roots are so strong that they crack open rocks. Their Italian name, *bagolari*, is too plain for a tree that is so true, so beautiful, vertical, sensitive and strong. They have the arms of day labourers with veins and muscles, and a delicate grey bark filled with sap. The air is filled with pollen that makes her eyes red and itchy, and it is hard to breathe. Springtime cannot be rubbed away; it is an assertive and capricious child that likes to step on people's feet. The skies have never been this way – and yet memory tells her that they always were. Springtime always brings first times. She suddenly senses the countryside beneath the paved roads. She feels the streets ready to be freed of their winter coats. Daisies poke out of cracks between the cobblestones. Life is coming back, blessed and expected. Men's eyes are flirtatious, insolent and possessive. She needs to laugh – laughter is good, and it makes her feel safe. The air is like a cool wine that burns and freezes simultaneously. You could drink it from your skin, from your hair, from everything.

The expedition has been a success and the day is splendid. Bianca returns on foot, the road made shorter with so much to think about. She has her drawings, her projects, and what's more, this magnificent season that pulsates inside and out. Now that she knows, everything is possible.

❧ ❧

'Come, my little one. Let me look at you. May I hug you?'

'May I call you Mother?'

Bianca imagines that beautiful word falling silently from Pia's lips, erasing all hesitation and boundaries, confusing everything into an embrace. It will be so simple, and each of them will reclaim their rightful place in the order of things. Pia will step forward uncertainly, her head bare, her hair as shiny as chestnuts. It will be wonderful to see her self-assuredly show herself the way she truly is, tender and pure. Pale, almost translucent. She will be reduced – or rather elevated – to the essence of herself in this most precious of moments. And the woman – the mother, who will now have the right to call herself this – will be made youthful again through her repressed joy. Shadows under her eyes still speak of countless nights of torment but the light that will radiate forth will smooth out all wrinkles. Her lips will utter that serious and perfect word 'daughter'. Hands will seek hands, hands will reach for arms, the pair will embrace, and this hug will dissolve all doubt.

At that point in time, in her imagination, Bianca will leave them. It is hard for her to see more than this. She is certain it will happen. Perhaps it won't happen in that exact way, but it will happen.

It will be so lovely to see them together.

※ ※

She has to make it happen. But how? Who could act as her accomplice, if not Innes? The moment has come for her to speak to him without reticence or deception. It is simple, really. She practises her speech in her head:

I understand everything now. It's all clear. You knew all along, didn't you? You could have told me. But no, of course not, I understand. Loyalty, your sense of honour, duty, et cetera. Save yourself the sermon. Now that I know, and now that you know that I know, I need your help. We must do something. That poor girl has the right . . . what right, you say? You, of all people? Of course, in front of the poet you bow down to all noble principles. Or is there something else I should know? You need time?

I solved the puzzle myself. What, it's not a puzzle? Well, you are correct. There is no mystery. It's the same old story. No, I can't, I won't ignore the situation. It is for her own good, you understand? Don't you want to give her even the smallest glimmer of hope? She's been nailed to a fate that she didn't ask or wish for. She could have so many possibilities in life; she needs so little, and could reclaim everything. What's that? Like me? You flatter me, really, you do.

But I am a poor role model. Trust me. I have had everything all along, and I did nothing to deserve that which she has been denied. Talent, you say? You really believe that my talent makes a difference? It doesn't count a whit more than fortune, or fate, or whatever you call it. And how do you know that she doesn't possess unspoken talents? She is still only a child . . .

Bianca's imagined Innes is complacent in his silence, the best confidant for the situation. If only she had the courage. But she is scared. She doesn't know how to give herself courage. She is also frightened that he might stop her for any number of excellent reasons. So she contradicts him in her head. But it is only a matter of time and patience. A fourteen-year-old secret can wait another couple of weeks. So she waits, convinced that eventually she will be able to move the chess pieces across the table. She doesn't understand that the game is not hers to play, and that she has no power really, not even over the poorest pawn.

※ ※

Bianca's drawing needs full outlines before she can fill in the shadows, and several details are still missing. She needs to imagine the poet before he became a poet, back when he was just a reckless boy, a city boy with a long name and an empty brain, before the muses kidnapped him, before the desire for domestic piety pushed him to seek his perfect bride. She needs to find out more by teasing it out of Donna Clara.

Bianca is like a cat with a ball of yarn. She almost feels bad about having to trick Donna Clara, but she has to find out.

It is a pity that the poet's mother is so cautious. She ignores the inappropriate parts of the story and sheds light only on her preferred ones, the parts that illustrate her in all the glory of filial love. The rest of it might not have even occurred. Don

Titta was born when he decided it was the right time, which is to say when he was twenty years old. But Bianca keeps her ears open for clues as the story progresses.

'I remember it well. He arrived in Paris on the tenth of April. Before that, you know, the season wasn't right and the road not safe, so he waited for the first safe journey. He waited because he knew I would be worried about him crossing the Alps, up there in the snow among the wolves and avalanches.' Bianca smiles sympathetically as Donna Clara takes advantage of the occasion to bask in her memories. 'They got along from the very start, my Carlo and my Titta. Father and son in spirit, I used to say. Ah, I recall those first strolls in Parc Monceau, our garden of delights . . . We needed to get to know each other again, he and I. We recognized ourselves in each other, you know? Between mother and child there can be no other way.' Bianca nods but has stopped listening. She subtly counts on her fingers. Pia was born in the December of the same year the poet arrived in Paris. Therefore, it is plausible and possible. All she needs is proof, some kind of confirmation.

Donna Clara cannot stop talking. 'It was the most beautiful time. Today everyone is fixated on their children. But I sent my boy to a boarding school with the priests because that was the right thing to do and his father wanted it. And then, when things unravelled as they did, and his father left us for the Lord, I went to Paris with my Carlo, and the boy stayed here in order to finish school. The good Lord wanted us to be reunited, but as adults, as equals. I don't know if children really need their mothers when they are young. They don't know a thing; they barely even know they are alive, and, as I see it, the more a mother worries, the more a child is spoiled. And then we forget . . .'

It is almost as if she is trying to justify herself. By comparing her own behaviour with that of her daughter-in-law, she wants to come to some absolute conclusion, prove she hasn't made a mistake, that she has done the right thing. It is true that the times have changed. But it is also a fact that conventions make life comfortable and easy. They help us to avoid confronting complicated and risky sentiments.

Bianca thinks of her friend Fanny, who lost her heart to Zeno, only to be informed by her family that she would instead be married to Cavalier Gazzoli, a man twenty years older who owned an immense property near the rice fields of La Bassa and whom she had never met. She cried for two weeks. She cried even harder when she met her husband-to-be: pudgy, wearing a wig, his nose a network of veins. Then she visited his home, Villa Salamandra, and came back amazed by the number of rooms. 'You could play hide-and-seek there,' she said. 'And the vast gardens!' Her tears dried up. Everything became quite lovely, mosquitos included. Which was all well and good as Zeno, with his good looks, never even looked at Fanny.

'I was everything for my Carlo,' the older lady continues. 'I was his confidante, a sister, a mother, a true-life companion. And I knew I was lucky that I had found my soulmate. Then when Titta came back to me, I had the both of them.'

As Donna Clara lists the glories and joys of her life, it occurs to Bianca that she truly has been fortunate. She's had everything, and what she didn't have, she acquired. First a solid husband. Then a rich, intellectual lover. Then, once her youth faded, she had her son, a fashionable poet whose fame reflected back onto her. Bianca doesn't need to exert herself to piece together the joyful past of the proprietress. Everyone knows that Carlo, whom she followed to Paris when her husband was still warm in his coffin, was her lover long before her marriage. Everyone also knows that Titta and Carlo (who could well have been his father although this was never officially stated) never got along. It is known too, that when Carlo died, Donna Clara was somewhat relieved. She was tired of being a mediator between the two men, ready to bring her French romance to a conclusion, eager to continue her life of comfort with her lover's money in his countryside villa that she'd inherited, and happy to indulge Titta's desire to leave Paris. And yet she insists that she would have gladly stayed on in the city and become the next queen of a new salon; that she'd go back tomorrow if she could.

Donna Clara is astute and accustomed to worldly things; she knows that her story has unfolded in the most elegant way, far more than the predictable, banal debaucheries of Parisian life could ever have permitted. As her beauty fades, familial piety becomes more important. In other words, it is all for the best. It is a shame, though, that she can only talk about Carlo when Titta is not around. All traces of that other man and his rural domain – his drawings, writings, collections – are in the attic of the country house, inside a long row of chests covered by old rugs that a maid has once shown to Bianca.

At this point, having obtained the information she wants and from a primary source no less, she takes her leave with the excuse of having a drawing to finish, while the old woman continues to recite her litany to herself.

The drawing isn't an excuse, actually. Outside the viburnums have flowered and Bianca wants to draw their white flowers before they fade. Viburnum: the word rolls off her tongue like a plump berry. She picks up a pencil and asks herself which is more beautiful, the word or the flower. Perhaps poetry *is* a superior art, she thinks. It summons things with a sound and on paper with a symbol, while her art is mute and rallies only one of the senses, never producing echoes. She wishes she could share her complex thoughts with someone to see if they are absurd or actually make sense. She might surprise them.

Should she have run away from Donna Clara? There is nobody else in the house to keep the lady company. No, she is better off being quiet and drawing, she thinks. It's what she knows how to do best.

Be quiet and draw, be quiet and take a walk, but most importantly, be quiet. The house is a cocoon of enforced peace. The three men disappear once again, this time to discover more about silkworms, it seems. When Bianca raises an eyebrow at Innes, he shrugs without even trying to answer her silent question. Traitor.

Donna Julie gets her much-needed rest. She is always resting these days, with Donna Clara watching over her, dealing with a silence that must be unbearable for her. The children have been instructed to behave. Pia is absorbed and pensive; she minds her own business, as if she feels something stirring in the air, the distant arrival of a storm. Bianca leaves her alone.

Sometimes Bianca gets the feeling that her own voice no longer works, she uses it so seldom. It is fine only for 'good morning,' 'goodnight' and 'a little more soup, thank you, but no dessert'. Bianca's interior monologues remind her of the watery spirals of bindweed, which she tries to draw. By evening, though, she can no longer stand the peace and runs out to the garden.

Thanks to the insistent rains and mild weather, the city garden has reached its most luxuriant state and has become a neglected realm of delight. She enjoys this weather. She likes to watch the earthworms, how they contort their bodies to smell the air with their nose, only to return underground, ready to eat up the world. And then there is the moving loyalty of the bulbs. They are the ever-faithful dogs of the flower world, ready to bloom in the same place, year after year. But in that small swatch of green between the high walls of the buildings, their generous little hands close too quickly. No one takes the time to look at them, and then suddenly, they are gone.

What a waste, Bianca thinks as she caresses the tips of the palmetto leaves and the corners of the banana plant, burning with green. *What a waste*, she thinks again, the thought itself like a sharp splinter of glass that one picks up so that someone else does not step on it and bleed. *When does spring end? Is summer really more beautiful, when everything has happened, when everything has already been decided, when imagination is useless?* For the first time, Bianca has the feeling that what was will not always be; that any kind of flowering is merely a delicate deceit. There is no grand design. There is no room for the unexpected. It is all anticipated, predictable, and therefore as if it has already happened. *Where will I be when this tree is laden with fruits? What will I be like? Will something have changed, or will I still be here, leafing through pages?* Bianca delights in these thoughts. She lets herself be transported by a melancholy that makes her feel both serious and adult. She doesn't realize, however, that she had spoken out loud.

'I've never heard someone summon forth autumn with such grace.'

The man's voice catches her by surprise and makes her jump.

'Is that you?' she asks the shadow with some discomfort, although she is unsure why.

'I've returned alone. Silkworms aren't for me. They require too much patience. I was scared when I saw the house so dark and silent. The servants are too quiet. It's as if they have a secret. Is something happening that I don't know about?'

'Only the same old dramas.'

Bianca tries to sound light-hearted, but the phrase comes across as brazen, or perhaps just overly sincere. In any case, it is true. What is more normal than Donna Julie's perpetual discomfort? Tommaso completes her thought.

'If it had been severe, we would have received word and, in any case, I am certain that tomorrow morning at breakfast I will be given an abundance of details. I can wait. But you, so alone in this damp garden . . . you'll catch cold. Or are you demanding your share of attention?'

Bianca is stupefied. What did she say or do, now or even prior to that, for him to know her so well? Has he guessed? Or is this just another innocent skirmish? Tommaso often says things only for the sake of saying them. He conquers boredom through provocation. How long has he been spying on her, listening to her strange rant? She isn't quick enough to answer so he presses on.

'Don't be afraid. If you are so eager to taste the fruit, inevitably it will be attracted to you.'

There is so much intimacy in that sentence. It is the sort of intimacy that is not permitted but is often stolen without consideration. Bianca wraps herself up tightly in her shawl, trying to avoid those burning eyes, which, even in darkness, see her clearly.

'Come on, Miss Bianca,' he jokes. 'It's almost dark and we're alone. It's not right for a well-mannered lady like you. But what do we care about conventions? And do you really want to be afraid of me? Look at me: I am only a half-poet bound to a great oak tree that ignores me, an insignificant lichen stuck to the bark on which it feeds. And you, on the other hand, are so intrepid, free, a working woman . . .'

Bianca collects her thoughts and pride. She doesn't like the carelessness in Tommaso's concealed, offhand manner. She finds it offensive.

'You know nothing about me.'

'You're right. And that seems only fair after all the effort you have put into hiding your cards. From me, at least. Anyway, we know nothing of anyone, especially when one has the arrogance to believe he knows everything. Perhaps you are mistaken about me, too though.'

'How could I be, when you define yourself with such precision? I abide by your own self-portrait. And anyway, I'm not judging you. I don't have the impulse or the desire to do so.'

Tommaso is silent. He sighs.

'I've erred again. Miss Bianca, you have the power to confuse me. Please use it sparingly; be generous and kind. My poor heart cannot bear such torment.'

'Now you're teasing me.'

'Me? Never. I, I . . .'

'It's getting chilly. Goodnight.'

And with that, Bianca leaves the garden, passing through the open French window without waiting for a reply. Well played, she thinks. She has left him speechless. But she is left exasperated and tired and moreover she doesn't quite know what their exchange has signified.

She feels too the burning sensation of wasted opportunity. They have been in the garden. It is night. She could have spoken out.

I don't like him, I don't like him, she repeats to herself as she climbs the stairs. She goes into her bedroom, but her half-closed window summons her. She cannot help but lean out on such a beautiful night and ask the darkness for confirmation. Tommaso is still down there. She sees the embers of his lit cigar. It looks as though he is coughing. *No, he's laughing. Or crying.* Is he crying? Bianca has the feeling that he knows she is watching him, so she stands up but lingers at the curtain still. Is he crying?

☙ ❧

Bianca isn't stupid. She is rash, impulsive, equipped with a ferocious imagination, tumultuous and passionate. She is also timid, contemptuous and arrogant in convenient doses. But she is anything but stupid.

So why, now that everything is clear with Pia, is she still protecting Don Titta? He is guilty and will soon be charged with a crime that is terrible in its very banality.

Maybe he doesn't know about it, she thinks. Or more likely, maybe he didn't know at the time. Maybe he found out later and is still coming to terms with it. She thinks back to his bewilderment that afternoon in the nursery, when, perhaps for the first time, the truth had become apparent to him. Why should he have known? He has been away from Milan for so long. It is one of those things and life moves on. Maybe the woman has kept quiet; her family, if they even knew, remain silent and act as if nothing has happened, as one does in this world of scandals. Only others know.

As sly as a detective, she realizes she needs a perfect stranger with a clear-headed gaze to help her put events in the right perspective. How happy the poet will be when he realizes the precious role that Bianca has played in unveiling the mystery. A spirit as righteous as his will surely be content to fix his mistakes. How grateful he will be to her for having finally created an opportunity for sincerity. Bianca likes to imagine it this way. She does not understand that certain truths are not meant to be paraded around like banners, but need to remain carefully folded up in the bottom of trunks. This ignorance of hers is forgivable. It stems from her youth, naivety, and tendency to see and draw the world only in black in white.

❧ ❧

But things do not happen quite the way she had planned.

'Titta, Titta . . .'

Donna Clara mumbles her son's name and looks around the crowded room for him. Donna Julie stands next to Bianca and smiles with great effort. Her eyes are glassy and she wears two splotches of artificial pink on her cheekbones as a kind of mask. It takes her a long time to become aware of Bianca's presence, and when she does, she turns to look at her as if to explain.

'This is one of the most luxurious salons in Milan, you know. Things happen here.'

Bianca follows the gaze of her companion until it rests on Don Titta, surrounded by a cluster of people. He is facing away from them. Bernocchi hangs off him as if he is a beggar. Even from far away, she can tell that the count is speaking quickly and animatedly. Then she sees him go silent and stare at Titta, as though listening to his reply. Bernocchi takes his hands off the poet's arm and makes to walk away, but Titta detains him by placing a hand on his shoulder. Their positions change: they face one another directly. The discussion continues. Don Titta glances away and then back at Bernocchi without stopping the conversation. He looks away again, but this time slowly and deliberately. Bianca follows the direction of his gaze: it is focused on the entrance. The lady of the house is welcoming someone now, her shoulders largely concealing the guest. Bianca catches sight of a long, shiny, smoky grey skirt. Donna Clara and Donna Julie look in that direction too, the expression on their faces darkening. Donna Clara seems excited, while Donna Julie's face simply clouds over. Another couple stand behind the woman who has just arrived. Bianca turns back to Don Titta and Bernocchi; they seem stunned, as if hypnotized. Their eyes are fixed not on the hostess but on this newly arrived guest. Bianca looks at the woman again. She is dumbfounded. It is *her*: the ghost, more real now than ever. As the woman moves into the room, she looks around in search of a cluster of people to join. She freezes for a second and her forced smile cracks. Then she continues forward towards two elderly ladies dressed in black.

Don Titta and Bernocchi say goodbye by gripping each other's forearms, like a move in a wrestling match. Bianca cannot see their faces any more, just that strange gesture uniting them. Who is about to leave? And where is he going? Who is stopping whom? And why? Donna Clara, who has been mute until now, chirps to interrupt the silence.

'Isn't there anything to drink here?'

Her voice comes out hoarse. She coughs to clear her throat.

'I'll get something for you,' Donna Julie replies and walks away in a rustle of clothing.

As soon as she is gone, the lady of the house takes Bianca's arm and directs her firmly towards a group of women who want to meet her. They speak of flowers, naturally. Of flowers and commissions. Bianca has to concentrate and act complacently, receive compliments, make promises, and book appointments. Viola Visconti follows the conversation with a triumphant smile, as though Bianca has been her creation. Bianca smiles back generously in return.

When she is finally set free, she sees Don Titta cornered by his mother and wife in a screen of flesh and fabric. Bernocchi has vanished. The ghost, too. But that comes as no surprise. Perhaps Bianca has only imagined her. Or it could merely have been someone who looks like her. She walks towards the back room where she has been told there is a Luini painting of rare beauty. But she never gets there. The back of a figure in grey, with tiny buttons dotting her spine, blocks her way. The lady is leaning out over a balcony railing and looking down at the dark street below, from which comes the sound of a departing carriage. As the sound retreats, the lady straightens. She turns around, shocked to see Bianca standing in front of her. Bianca feels herself blush but doesn't know why. She has nothing to be ashamed of.

The two women fall silent and study each other for as long as they can, without conversing. With one penetrating look, Bianca takes note of the woman's amber skin – it is beginning to slacken along her jawline. Her chestnut-brown locks of hair are so dark they look, and perhaps are, artificial. She wears too much colour on her cheeks and a large, oval brooch speckled with small seed-like pearls at the centre of her neckline. Bianca stares at her in silence, unabashed.

The other woman responds with an uneasy smile and then flutters her fan aimlessly.

'Nice evening, isn't it?'

'Yes, it is a nice evening indeed,' replies Bianca, who has no desire to speak about the weather.

'Do . . . we know each other?' the woman asks.

'No. But that's just because no one has introduced us yet.'

'Yes, of course. Let's not pretend. What good would that do?'

'Exactly. It would be useless.'

If Bianca could see herself from a distance, she would say that the two of them face each other like insects at battle. One advances and the other recedes in barely perceptible movements; it could be an exchange of pleasantries or the defence of one's territory. But beneath the surface there is so much more. Both of them are accustomed enough to the rules of society to know better than to go for the eyes.

'Shall we see each other tomorrow, at the fountain in the gardens? We will be able to talk there,' Bianca says, beginning to feel nauseous from this stealthy game. 'Goodnight.' Then, without even waiting for a response, she walks away. Her heart is racing. Her improvised rashness has given her a sense of vertigo. She isn't at all certain that the other woman will agree to the meeting.

Donna Clara walks up to her now, brandishing a tiny glass.

'I see you made a friend. What do you think of her?'

She looks Bianca up and down slowly.

'Are you talking about the woman in grey? I thought she was someone else. Salons aren't the best place to get to know new people,' Bianca observes, trying to sound offhand.

'Oh, and why not? In places like these, witticisms shine. When there *is* wit, of course,' Donna Clara says drily.

'Of course,' echoes Bianca indifferently, following the older woman's piercing gaze back to the woman in grey. Their trajectory is diverted by Donna Julie.

She is panting, rosy-cheeked and speaks in a rush.

'Here you are. Nice evening, isn't it? I can't remember the last time I had such a lovely time. Signora Visconti really knows how to throw a party. And you? Are you having a good time too, Miss Bianca?'

She is confused and excited, when she is usually so quiet and calm. Her eyes burn feverishly, flickering here and there as if she wants to stop everything and take it all in. Then Donna Julie freezes and her face goes pale. Bianca looks over to see what she is looking at: Don Titta is speaking with the ghost.

The pair are wan and unsuitably serious. They look intently at one another, staring in silence. At this distance it is impossible to comprehend the meaning of their exchange. But Bianca has her proof now. She has received her confirmation.

❧ ❧

The report from her young informant, Girolamo, was extremely clear. Bianca was not expecting much, just a couple of confusing words hissed into her ear. Instead the boy has maintained his promise and given her a name and a history, written in dark penmanship on a piece of heavy paper smudged with dirt.

> *Costanza A., unemployed, moneyed, single, twenty years of age, entrusts her daughter to the care of the hospital and the services of Alberta Tonolli, midwife. Her daughter, one month in age and in good health, still needs nursing. The child has been baptized in the name of Luce but will receive the new name of Devota Colombo. The child does not cry. She is clothed in a batiste white camisole stitched with ringlets, she is swaddled in plain white cotton, she wears white leather shoes tied with a pink lace ribbon, and a bonnet with the same ringlet embroidery as her camisole. She is resting in a French-style carriage cushioned with strips of fine linen and has three other camisoles and three less precious bonnets. She is wrapped in a white woollen blanket with bunting. Her pledge token is a pink and green velvet pillow embroidered with a golden lamb with a silver bell. The mother has declared that she is intent on reclaiming her child as soon as circumstances allow her to do so.*

The child who was given up is vividly described, Bianca thinks as she rereads the note, piecing together the details, making the fragments fit with care, like trying to mend a broken teacup. That dry farewell must have agonized the mother. Bianca sees in her mind the authority figure that interrogated and the other figure that surely wept. She tries to imagine the scepticism of the official in charge. Perhaps they let women handle these things because they are gentler and can feel that unspeakable grief across the table. *The child does not cry.* But somebody else did. Fourteen years ago, a baby girl by the name of Luce, then renamed Devota, was brought to Santa Caterina alla Ruota and abandoned there. The age corresponds. The rest is evident. Devota's Christian name is changed to Pia: the same name in a simplified form, an ugly orphan name so that she will never forget her poor beginnings. The identifying token of the lamb pillow is unique, though, an unclassifiable luxury in that cold hospital.

Everything is so clear, so obvious. *Costanza A., unemployed* . . . If she was twenty then, she'd be thirty-four now. How could Bianca ever have searched all of Milan and its surroundings, all of its 150,000 inhabitants, for a thirty-four-year-old woman who is well-off enough to have entrusted her child with an exquisite set of goods, but so alone that she had to give up her newborn to public charity? A woman who wanted to return for the child when in fact the girl was adopted by a country priest? Bianca never dreamed that she would meet the target of her own investigation at a social event. It is clear that the woman is discomfited, but she is not grieving. Bianca wonders whether time really does heal all wounds, as people say when they want to appear wise. But if that woman really is Pia's mother, and has been so rash as to go out searching for her daughter, why has she stopped behind the gates? What has kept her from tearing down all the obstacles in her way? And if everyone knows about it, as it is beginning to seem to Bianca, then why hasn't anyone

taken a step forward? Why perform that strange dance of confrontation and retreat? Questions, so many.

❦ ❦

Bianca doesn't really expect Costanza A. to show up at their
rendezvous. She disguises the sortie so that she will not feel too
silly when she is disappointed. The season is so mild that the
children are able to brush aside the hesitations of both mother
and grandmother and go outside. Of course, they are over-
dressed, bundled up in their stuffed jackets. But Nanny has the
good judgement, for once, to allow them to remove some of their
clothing as soon as they turn the corner. She quickly becomes a
porter, lagging behind with her bundles. Bianca leads the group
and holds the two smallest girls by the hand. The other three
children follow, Enrico and Giulietta arm in arm, Pietro with
his hands in his pockets and his cap to one side, like a ruffian.
The route isn't long but they travel slowly. There are so many
things to stop and look at: an old woman selling bunches of wild
flowers, three identical boys dressed in light blue who are playing with hoops, and a stray dog with a thin snout like a ferret
who runs off after some delicious smell. And then there are the
palazzi, carriages, and small shops. This is a game of discovering
a city that has, until then, been a mystery to them.

They finally reach the green swells of the park and the wild
smell of grass that makes them want to run freely. There are
other children sailing boats in the big pond, and some mallard
ducks floating there too.

'Why is one colourful and one not?'

'The one without colour is female. The male is dressed as
if he were a soldier at a grand ball. But she looks as though
she had to rush out of the house and didn't have much time to
prepare.'

The children laugh.

'That's because we men are better,' says Enrico, stealing a glance at Pietro in search of approval. For once the older brother disagrees.

'I don't like soldiers. Papa says they are persecutors.'

Nanny smirks but Bianca ignores them. She looks around, pretending to focus on the landscape. She feels sure the lady in grey will not come.

But there she is. Bianca recognizes her from her bearing. She wears grey again, a spent grey this time, almost penitential. Bianca whispers something to Nanny above the heads of the children, who are busy watching the launch of cutter ships, and wanders off. In a sign of understanding, the woman in grey follows her. They stand beneath a row of linden trees pruned into boxes and planted so close to one another that the foliage meshes together in a geometric tunnel. If someone were to observe them, they would see only shadows.

'I decided to come,' the woman says, as if she herself is unable to believe it.

'Indeed.'

Bianca sighs and hesitates for a moment. Then she recites the speech that she has so often rehearsed at her window, to the fire, to the mirror, to no one. The words slip out of her easily and in a long and weighty chain. Words connect, affronted and accusing. Instinctively, the woman takes a step back, as if Bianca might strike her. She fumbles with her hands and blushes, red splotches surfacing on her neck and cheeks: the ugly signs of shame. When Bianca finishes, the lady in grey looks down at the ground.

Almost to herself, she says, 'It's all true. But it's all in the past now. I do not want to think about it any more.'

'But not even a year ago you were playing the part of ghost for all of Brusuglio! Do you remember?' Bianca asks, convinced that the woman must be mad, and that maybe it is for the best.

'Yes, I do remember. And I am sorry.' The woman speaks in a low whisper. 'But you see, things have changed. I . . . I am about to be married. You will laugh at me,' she says, but it is she who laughs a dry, low, bitter laugh. 'I'm a withered old maid, but I might have found an arrangement. My parents did everything for me. I did not ask them to. I do not have the right to ask for anything. Who am I to say no?'

She seeks Bianca's eyes and then looks down again and shakes her head.

'What do you want to know? You are young and beautiful and independent. Your name is on everyone's lips here in Milan. You're the rising star of illustrated botany.' She recites the words as if she is reading the headlines of a newspaper. 'You have everything. You can manage on your own. I have always done what others expected of me. Always. Up until . . . after I gave the child away. I spent my days berating myself for my mistakes. I didn't know any better.'

Bianca feels neither compassion nor pity.

'The child, as you called her, is a girl now. Or did you perhaps forget that, too? I don't understand you.' Bianca tries to keep her calm, but disdain has got the better of her and her words become sharper. 'How could you possibly deny her like this? You bury the past, and that's that? It seems as though she is dear to you. You look like you are desperate to see her. And now I can help you.'

Bianca adds this impulsively, without really meaning to say it. It isn't entirely true. She will help Pia for Pia's sake, not for the sake of this woman who has abandoned and avoided her child. But ultimately, won't it have the same outcome?

The woman looks at Bianca as though she hasn't heard a word. She continues her train of thought.

'People are right: what good is there in rummaging in the past? It's like turning over a stone and watching the insects and worms wriggle in the sunlight. I could only do her harm at this point.'

Haven't you done enough harm already? Bianca thinks to herself. *You and your stupid apparitions, the artfully abandoned token, and all the rest of it?*

'I didn't know better,' the woman says and gazes off into the distance.

If she could, Bianca would hit her, right there and then. But what is stopping her? Nothing. So she slaps her, just once, and only the kind of slap a small hand can give, but it's piercing. It leaves her palm burning. The woman brings her fingers to her cheek, perplexed, and as Bianca takes her hand away, she looks at it in horror, as if she is expecting to see it stained with blood. Despite their position, a little girl playing with a hoop nearby has witnessed it all. She freezes in place and lets go of her toy, which keeps on rolling and then, finally, falls into the grass. Bianca turns to stare at the child until she runs off. What is a tiny slap compared to the kicks, punches and torn-out hair that this woman really deserves in order to bring some justice to the world? But what sort of justice would that be?

The mistake is made, though, and the outcome is immense. In front of Bianca now stands a contrite little lady, a poor woman searching for another chance, a woman who has turned her back on the past. She is ashamed. And Bianca is ashamed, seeing her own reflection in this lady, seeing her own silly passions laid bare before the dark conspiracies, mysteries, plot twists, and imagined happy endings. She feels foolish. Her actions are like those in a cheap novella printed on inferior paper, paper that is good only for wrapping vegetables. Costanza A. will marry a rich old man. Maybe she will be blessed with a child at a late age to replace the shadow of her little girl. Or perhaps she will lead an isolated, second-hand life. The only thing real in all of this is Bianca's illusion that Pia's life will change. The mistake lies in having nurtured this illusion as if it is something precious. It is living one kind of life whilst reasoning that one is entitled to another.

Bianca cannot think straight. She stands face to face with the ghost that she has been chasing, who is nothing more than a pale woman with three red stripes along her cheek and great, hollow eyes. Eyes that now avoid her own. She is a woman who probably dislikes herself but who has learned to absolve herself; a woman who cannot wait to leave and to forget. Bianca only comes to her senses after Costanza A. has turned around and walked away without a goodbye. There is nothing left to say.

Bianca looks for a bench. There, she sits down and reflects. She tries to calm her heartbeat. Enough is enough. She throws her head back and looks up at the light blue sky above, in all its obtuse honesty. The little girl comes back to reclaim her hoop, regards her warily, and runs off again. It is time to leave.

Bianca can hear the other children, her children. She follows their voices and finds them in the middle of a big field doing cartwheels and tumbling about, their clothes horribly soiled with green striations, evidence that will be impossible to conceal and which will raise loud complaints in the laundry room. But it has been worth it. They wanted to play horseback, to roll in the carpet of grass, and smell its sweet murkiness. Bianca claps her hands and organizes an impromptu game of horsemen and princesses. She plays the part of a horseman.

Nanny, as usual, does nothing. The rest of them laugh, trip, gallop and fall about. By the evening, Giulietta has a fever.

※ ※

Once she has calmed down, Bianca thinks things over. She has been a presumptuous fool. She is a more provincial, faded copy of Emma Woodhouse, far less witty and with fewer accomplishments, who has tried to organize a mixed-up world and then recompose it to fit her own design. She doesn't possess a vision of a final version; really she is sustained by nothing at all. She can only busy herself with flowers, examine them through a lens up close. It is right for her to limit herself to this.

What had the ghost said in the park? *Your name is on everyone's lips.* Thank heavens her name isn't on everybody's lips for her demented attempt to repair the lives of others. No one – or almost no one – is aware of her theories; only a handful of strangers who have no interest in sharing them, people who have been paid to talk only once and who will therefore now remain silent. The comfort of knowing this, though, does not make her feel any less embarrassed. She has learned her lesson. Or at least, that's what she believes. She doesn't realize that she still has many lessons to learn, things that cannot be taught, things that one only picks up a little at a time, through living. How can she know? Her life has been lived in a glass box, like the ones she keeps her most precious subjects in, sealed and yet still vulnerable. She has viewed the world only from inside this glass, as though waiting for a storm to break it open. There is no defending herself, no escaping. She can only hope that the clouds will rain down somewhere else. But that is a lame hope: it will be better to stop and run for shelter, or dash out into the open and feel the cold rain on her body. She will risk it to feel alive. She wants to feel alive.

It doesn't take much to console a young woman who doesn't like herself. Bianca only needs to know that someone else likes her. And, after the white stone, Bianca soon receives other gifts. She finds them in unusual places: at the door to her bedroom, under her breakfast teacup, resting impudently on her empty desk. A green and white shawl made of lightweight cashmere, and as warm as an embrace, has been wrapped in a piece of flowered fabric. A few lines of writing, perhaps the beginning of an unfinished poem, or maybe the end of one – *It is here that my heart rests* – have been folded around a small silver box full of seeds and other symbolic items. A false pomegranate that looks incredibly real, its peel speckled with brown flecks. It is evident that someone is courting her in a discreet and ingenious manner. Someone who knows her well but doesn't want to scare her. Someone who wants to remain in the shadows, at least for now, and so sends her messages from there. Whoever it is knows that it will be pointless to give her flowers and so focuses on objects instead. Bianca loves the fact that she doesn't know who the sender is. It doesn't force her to make decisions or to react. At this point in time, choosing a witty remark or expressing a common courtesy would be difficult for her.

That is how she is: resolute to the point of being reckless where it concerns other people, and as uncertain as a child when her own feelings are tangled and confused. It is easy for her to recognize these sentiments in others and classify them with the detachment of an academic. But she doesn't even try to decipher herself. Perhaps her admirer has understood this and is taking advantage of it in his own elegant and malicious way. This option shouldn't be excluded. But Bianca doesn't even dig that deep. She is satisfied with the surface and with the portrait it gives her in return; she is a Narcissus who leans over to enjoy the best possible reflection.

She is tired of her own conjectures and imagined fantasies. They haven't led anywhere. She needs to work; she has many commissions, and she ought to bring them to a conclusion before returning to Brusuglio, where she will have to dedicate all her energies to her main project. Her contract lasts until autumn. Everything has to be completed and handed in by then. She is expecting intense months ahead and is prepared for them; work doesn't scare her. If there is something she fears, it is herself. The self that she doesn't know and that she doesn't understand. But she will never admit it, and in fact ignores it. She keeps her eyes on the ground and stumbles forward, as if she is playing blind man's buff. Be careful not to fall, Bianca.

❧ ❧

But still there are things that Bianca cannot let go of. She is like a dog tugging on a glove or shoe. She doesn't fully understand that the game is over. And because the dream of a happy ending – with its round of applause and smiles and gratitude – has dissipated, she feels spite. She feels anger at the poet and his indifference. Here is a man who has lived two lives with ease. First, the immoral life of a young libertine and then the inspired life of an artist. Now he is satisfied with his current family, with the compassion they inspire in him, and with their boring, comforting, shared rituals. She wants to stop him in the hallway, grab him by the shoulders, and shake the truth out of him.

How can you, Don Titta, you, the model of paternal love – strange in your ways and as bizarre as you please, but so damned good – how can you ignore your own daughter? She is an outcast who moves and breathes just one step away from those who have the privilege of bearing your name. She has nothing, only a licence stating she is an orphan and the future prospects of a maid. How can you be two people? Is it because of the customs of the era or because of your breeding? Or does the combination of the two, a topic so dear to you, foster this conflict? Are they really just words? Simple living-room banter?

If only she could speak these words, as honestly and as angrily as she feels like saying them. She wants to see his expression change, to see him laid bare, unarmed, stripped of his high rank, and suddenly sincere. In his sincerity, he will be humble, thankful and magnificent. She wants to be the one to tear the veil from the mirror and show him his true face. *Don Titta, one can always change,* she will say. *One can always make right that which went wrong.* He will be so committed to her afterwards for giving him the courage of truth. She wants to be the inspiration for his renewal. It is an arrogant thought, at first just fleeting, and then cultivated in a myriad of variations. She is just one step away from understanding what she truly feels – but it is the one step that she doesn't take. At the age of twenty it is difficult to be honest with oneself. And then her anger will cease. She will turn on her heels and make her way back to the house in the heat of scorn.

Her anger never lasts long though. It explodes like a storm and then dissipates into mitigating rivulets. She fumes and then is quiet in tumultuous succession. And she loves in silence, too, so secretly that even she isn't aware of it. Hers is a love like water, that takes the shape and colour of that which holds it.

※ ※

She loves, and because of this, she forgives. In the end, since she forgives herself, she can extend the privilege to whomever she desires. It happens quickly. All she needs is a spark of intuition, a notion that she can hang on to. She finds it on the balcony overlooking the garden: there Don Titta and Pia are standing under the shelter of the catalpa tree. She draws back but remains nearby, in the shadows of the corridor. Even if they turn around, they won't be able to see her. But they don't turn. They are too involved in their conversation. Bianca is a little far away to read the words on their lips.

She should feel her usual anger, the usual repertoire of venom: *You are her father but you act like her master.* But the sweetness of their exchange – hands moving in mid-air, nods of understanding, conversational gestures – everything about those two bodies reflects a closeness that isn't there merely by chance. They aren't speaking about that evening's dinner menu or about Enrico's tantrums or the umpteenth book on loan. Something else unites them, Bianca is certain of it. She leans back against the wall, relieved, and full of unexpected joy.

What if she can actually bring together these two people who have been so cruelly separated, and thereby obtain a semblance of justice? If all that is needed to fix things is desire, can't she just desire it for them and imagine it a million times over? Won't that bring about some tiny result, even if it is infinitesimal? It will still be the right and natural one that she has imagined. All won't be for naught, Bianca tells herself. Although, she suddenly thinks, if these two are speaking to each other like this already, something must have happened.

All of her rage, suspicion and acrimony suddenly vanish. How strange, Bianca thinks. There's so much grace and intimacy in their exchange. As she continues to watch from afar, she feels like a spy, even if it has happened by accident. She can't help staring at them. She can't avoid it. Perhaps Don Titta is actually doing what he can for the girl, given the circumstances. And perhaps he does this every day, lightening his conscience and eliminating his guilt. No, the evidence is always there in front of him, the vibrant memory of his mistake. Maybe he actually holds on to it, nurtures it, wants it close by. Bianca acquits him in a rapid verdict.

Now that she has her target centred, she can finally walk away from it. She smiles to herself and goes to her bedroom, leaving the pair to say whatever they need to say to each other, whatever their hearts tell them. They are alone in the world, like two lovers who have finally found the courage to be themselves.

❧ ❧

In the days following, nothing much happens; there are no announcements, revelations, or clarifications. There is only a quiet normality, as if each of them has returned to their ranks and is pleased to be where they are. Bianca grows agitated. She draws and scribbles, and then tosses everything away. She breaks her charcoal and gets her hands and arms dirty. She goes downstairs, intent on finishing her drawings, but is left speechless when the poet walks out of the room in a hurry, without even taking his hat. He casts a glance at Innes but the latter does not respond. She slips away from Tommaso, who has in the meantime handed her a tiny glass of cordial or rosewater, and goes back upstairs, opening the window and looking for answers in the treetops outside.

When she goes back downstairs she is intercepted by Donna Clara, who needs a confidante for some of her gossipy affairs. She spends half an hour nodding like a mindless doll. She ignores the little girls, who wave to her as she walks by. She ignores Nanny's look of silent reproach. She sends for Pia, but in front of her smiling innocence she falls silent. She cannot make up her mind about anything. In the end she asks only for a cup of tea.

※ ※

Love and war. Love is war. It's a careless occupation by a foreign territory within you — daytime, night-time, in everything you do. One is invaded, one resists, one surrenders. And surrender is productive. If one could measure the benefits by placing a piece of oneself on a scale and on the other side what is produced, lost, and what remains, the only certainty would be that something is consumed. If you fantasize about what you want, do you lose it? Or does it become ruined? There's always an abyss between the desired and the achieved; the abyss attracts and summons like a wall that needs to be climbed over or jumped from.

Should I come forward and take what's mine? Should I take what's not yet mine? Should I move towards what I want but do not know, or should I wait for it to be placed into my hands? To take or to give? To give in? Should one do this?

Should I sit on the sofa with my hands in my lap and a smile on my face? Should I peer out of the window into the night to see who is in the shadows?

We give some things and we want some things. In the end, what counts is what we can give. I can give something. But can I, a lone female in this world, only desire, hope, and then finally say yes? Can I also say no? Yes, the arrow points to the future. No, the stone drags you to the bottom with the algae, dazed as though dead. Father, how many things you neglected to teach me. You left me too soon. By your side, I could have learned how to distinguish and evaluate, how to listen to myself, how to understand. No, that's not true. I would only have been able to interpret your eager and curious signs. I would have carried myself towards an easy place and given up on thinking and deciding. I would have been happy that way. That, too, would have been a kind of love. But I don't know it now. Or perhaps you would have helped me understand myself. With infinite patience, you would have helped me to understand an unknown language. You had already decided to let me go before everything else happened, before this torment. And now I know nothing. I do not know myself.

❧ ❧

It happens. The living room is empty of unwanted presences. She stands in front of him. For just a moment she sweeps away all conventions: he is her equal. She has to do it; she can do it.

'I must speak with you.'

'I, too, need to speak with you. But it's so difficult to be alone in this house. Even talking is difficult.'

'I know. I wanted to tell you that I understand. You have a position . . . you choose to ignore the legitimate rights of someone less fortunate . . . I understand, but I do not accept it. A man like you, so open, so progressive. It can't be . . .'

Everything is said without hesitation. Followed by the just reply, the beautiful humility of an admitted fault. A shadow hides his face; he leans in towards her, their eyes lock, for once. A sigh.

'You are right. I take full responsibility for my mistakes. But the day will come when finally everything will be clear, everything will be able to be said in the light of day. Miss Bianca, this day is not far off. I imagine it in my darkest moments when I feel there isn't anything left to hope for, when oppressive fetters bind me to my role, as you point out. That's when everything will change. Only then will we be allowed to be ourselves.'

'So then . . . you . . .' She trembles, encouraged. Yes, yes. It is about to happen. Yes.

'I want to say that the moment is close, the moment when things will change forever, there will be no going back, and we will no longer hide. Do you understand?'

He takes her hands in his and squeezes them. Bianca doesn't know what she is supposed to understand. She is confused. Has she understood, or not? And then, as if in a farce, there is a distraction. A sound close by. They let go of each other's hands. It is Tommaso.

'Ah, here you are. I was looking for you, Titta. Our friend has arrived.'

Don Titta turns around sharply.

'Yes, certainly. I'm coming.'

A bow, and he is gone. Tommaso casts a bewildered look at Bianca before closing the study door, where apparently someone is waiting for them. Has he heard everything? Has he seen them holding each other's hands? No, the poet's back faced the door.

Bianca stands alone. Their conversation has been left hanging. In that other room, voices rise and fall in excitement; there is an invasion of arrogant strangers. Here, things have been said that cannot be undone, like a flood consuming everything in its path. He has said that he will no longer hide. He has said it. What else is there? Bianca, swept up by the current, floats on its dark waters, a blessed Ophelia in her innocent, though not harmless, folly.

❦ ❦

Later, Bianca shudders when Bernocchi's eyes seek her out in the sitting room. She calms a little when he lowers them back to the curled pages of his *London Review*, which he has clearly brought with him to show off, and which he attempts to translate aloud from English into Italian as he reads.

"'She knows far too well that the man she loves can never be hers unless extraordinary circumstances take place, a situation which she desires but which she doesn't dare hope for. And yet she continues to love . . ." Let me say this, Innes. Your friend, the writer, is the first and last of the romantics. What a delightful portrait of female innocence he has put together. To think of enjoying such pure love – and pure because it is impossible. What an honour, what privilege, and what relief! And listen to this here: "They hide their advanced age by speaking without hesitation of their youth . . . or they show off their frenzy of virtue in manifesting a passionate indignation for the same . . ."'

'Might I interest you in an English lesson or two?' Innes interrupts, poking fun at Bernocchi. 'At a moderate price, of course.'

'Why don't you read it, then?' Bernocchi says, irritated, and hands him the paper. 'It is quite difficult to translate on the spot. Go on, read, right there, the part that talks about love. It will be instructive to all of us.'

Bianca feels averse to all of this but tries not to show it. They are so mistaken. Everyone is wrong. Love is not *always* impossible. But she mustn't and won't say anything. She looks up, surprised to see Tommaso staring right at her gravely.

Innes leafs through the pile of papers. The Italian language in his mouth sounds lovely and exotic, precise, though slightly blurry.

'As you wish. "Love is no longer a cunning rascal, laughing in his heart while he pretends to cry, nor is love a small curly-haired boy . . . Today love bears the expression and the grave posture of an old sage. Do not imagine him running around naked like a cherub, as he once did. Today love is dressed from head to toe in the clothes of a lawyer."' Tommaso chuckles and stamps his feet on the ground. Innes continues. "'Love's quiver has turned into a blue postal bag, and his arrows into documents and contracts, his most powerful tools, for both men and women." Is that enough for you?'

'Oh, more than enough. For once, your Foscolo was right. "Listen to me; love no longer exists." How did he phrase it? Didn't he compare love to a child that had grown up and become a serious businessman? And thank goodness. Everything that can be bought can also be measured.'

'Indeed,' intervenes Donna Julie, who has been silent until now. Her boiling point is slow to reach, but once she achieves it, her lid bursts off. 'How rotten this world is when we make a business out of sentiments,' she exclaims, more desolate than disdainful.

Bianca shoots her a perplexed look.

'Ah, but I didn't say that. You misunderstand,' Bernocchi retorts. 'Sentiments, unfortunately, are utterly unreasonable and difficult to tame. All of us, sooner or later, will fall prey. The important thing is to know how much damage they can cause and to try, as reasonable beings, to control them.'

'I continue to abhor the world you describe,' Donna Julie insists.

'Or perhaps it is me whom you don't like very much? Poor, wretched me,' Bernocchi says.

Everyone's eyes are on the count, judging him, nailing him to the armchair from which he tries to rise, ready to flee. But the depth of the chair combines with his own feebleness and the weight of those stares keeps him fixed in his place.

᚛ ᚜

'To hear Bernocchi speak of love is an outrage. What could he possibly know, that toad who I doubt has ever been kissed? How can he claim to lay down the law? And everyone just sat there listening to him, nodding their heads like asses. Don't you find it horrible?'

Bianca, enraged, looks at Innes leaning against the doorway, his hands behind his back. They are alone. The others have gone to get ready for dinner. The count has finally left.

'Bianca, Bianca, brazen and contemptuous Bianca. Come along, they were just words, thrown like harmless darts.'

'Harmless, perhaps, but not innocent.'

'You have the right not to like them, but also the right to ignore them.' He pauses, then says more seriously, 'Be wary.'

Bianca throws back her shoulders and faces him with an air of challenge. She paces up and down nervously, marking the carpet with her feet.

'What are you trying to say?' she says, finally.

'You're playing with fire,' he answers elusively. 'I wouldn't want to see you burn your feathers.'

'Is that how you see me: as a chicken? Or better, a wild goose with her feathers clipped? Rummaging in the yard among the rest of the fowl?'

'If you're fishing for compliments, then I actually see you more as a young heron with its claws stuck in the mud: elegant in flight, clumsy on the ground.'

'Of course. And soon they will pluck me for dinner. Is that what I should be careful of?'

'I'm telling you to watch out for yourself,' answers Innes solemnly.

He must have understood. Yes, of course, he has known all along. But what Bianca wants is a friendly shoulder to lean on, not an authoritative guardian. She cannot accept seeing everything reduced to dry accounting, to hear someone tell her not to run risks.

Donna Julie was right in her argument but then suddenly she had fizzled out. She is too inconsistent, barely worth considering, at least not until she made that comment. Consequently, Bianca has simply propped Donna Julie and her counter-argument up against the wall and forgotten about her as though she is transparent. It embarrasses Bianca to think of taking away from Donna Julie something that is legitimately hers. It is like pricking blood from a vein. She of all people, who is so innocent; she'll hold her wrist out for a phlebotomy with a smile on her face, convinced it is for her own good . . . how embarrassing. What confusion. What folly.

'Are you all right, Bianca? You've changed colour.'

Innes is attentive. Suddenly he is next to her; he takes her hands and squeezes them. He seems sincerely worried. He bends over her, so close that Bianca can smell the Indian scent of his cologne, and just barely below that, the warm current of his skin. Bianca realizes that Innes is not just a friend. He is also a man.

He is too close. Bianca slips out of his grip, turns, and flees. Innes's gaze follows her as she runs up the staircase in a hurry, anxious to be alone with her thoughts.

᚜ ᚜

Dinner is torture. Innes seems angry and doesn't say a word to her or to anyone. The absence of his conversational grace, which usually fills the pauses and dissipates the conflicts, weighs over the entire table. Bianca cannot even look at Donna Julie. Don Titta is distracted. Tommaso hasn't come down, apparently unwell. Donna Clara begins a soliloquy based on the preaching of Don Dionisio, the only merit of which is that it fills the silence, interrupted on occasion by the clink of china and crystal. It is sad to eat in divided company.

⚜ ⚜

They disband in a hurry after dinner. Before disappearing upstairs, Innes looks at her in pained anger. She ignores him and immediately forgets it. The women disappear to the sitting room. Bianca starts to follow them but then returns to the library to recover her personal copy of Shakespeare that she has left on a side table. Don Titta is there, leafing through one of his magazines. She takes the book and holds it tightly, as if it carries her salvation. This is where she wants to be. She needs to try again, to be clearer this time. She has feared and desired a situation like this for so long. Instead of leaving, she looks over at him. He, provoked by the power of her eyes, puts down the newspaper and returns her stare. It isn't the right time for words to muddle the situation. How different this silence feels compared to the one in the dining room. How much purer and more profound; it is a kind of water that provokes thirst, then appeases and renews her. Bianca stands there for a long time, hanging onto that gaze that tells her everything she needs to understand, perhaps even more.

But in a large house one is never alone. There are shutters that need closing and curtains to draw, and almost invisible beings appear to complete these duties. The order of each day depends on them. They enter rooms, ignoring the glances that extend like taut strings between the other people, the people who have a place in the world. The beings tread over these strings or skirt around them, but don't trip on them since they don't really see them. Their duties break the tension.

More than a minute has passed – a long, yet fleeting minute – and then it is over. Bianca walks away without saying a word.

She is sure that she has said in silence everything that she has wanted to verbalize. She is sure she has received the correct answer too, the only possible and acceptable one. It is the misunderstanding of silence.

She climbs the stairs in a hurry, clutching her book like a buoy. Once in her room she leans against the wall and lets herself drop down to the floor. The book slips out of her hands and falls open. Bianca picks it up. In the dim candlelight that one of those invisible beings has lit, she searches for a message in the words on the page. *Tolle et lege.* If only, if only there is a little note, a letter, something.

Nothing. The open page merely says things that she isn't willing to understand:

> Now is the winter of our discontent
> Made glorious summer by this son of York;
> And all the clouds that low'r'd upon our house
> In the deep bosom of the ocean buried.

No, wait, something *is* there. A piece of paper pokes out like a bookmark. Cautiously, Bianca picks it out with two fingers. It is what she least expected to find: a portrait of her mother at the age of twenty. Beautiful and remote, this is how she needs to be remembered. Her father used to use these commemorative portraits on sepia-coloured paper as bookmarks; he took notes on their backs, and caressed them secretly with the tips of his fingers. It isn't surprising to find one inside this book. *Would you, Mother, whom I did not know well enough, would you understand? If you were still here, perhaps I wouldn't be searching for other people's mothers. Would you judge me harshly? Are you judging me now, your paper eyes piercing me from afar? Are you condemning my passion because it is insulting, illegitimate, and useless? Or perhaps you're just holding me in your arms without saying a thing?*

The face stares back at her, unperturbed. Bianca remembers her mother just like that, as a woman who didn't smile. Or was that a mask? She closes the book on her mother's face. *Enough. You're a stranger. You have no right to scold me like that. You aren't here.* And meanwhile the moment has been ruined. The night of discontent will be a long one.

❧ ❧

The days pass and nothing happens. The steady stream of secret gifts ends. Don Titta leaves again and takes Innes with him. The house full of children and women feels like a prison. Bianca forces herself to catch up on her work and make up for the time she has spent fantasizing. Work is good for her. It numbs her and rids her of thoughts; it leaves her feeling exhausted and empty, while her folders fill up and the money rolls in. *Will I end up like this: rich and unhappy?* She fastens her purse strings without even counting her money. She is far from being either rich or happy – what she feels is physical exhaustion.

'It is springtime and we need something to invigorate us,' Donna Clara announces, convinced that there is no bodily or spiritual discomfort that does not have a chemical solution. She sends one of her most trusted maids to the herbalist for an infallible recipe. Bianca and Donna Julie, both under her care, are forced to surrender. In the end, it is just a concoction of boiled herbs to be drunk once a day. The table is set with nutritious food and Donna Clara makes sure that the two young girls, as she calls them, eat everything on their plates, the same way that Nanny oversees the children. There is something comforting in feeling looked after. Bianca gives in to the concoction, feeling just a tiny bit of residual guilt towards her companion, who is far more feeble and sick than she. But she puts her guilt aside. In the end, she hasn't acted on things, she has only *imagined* them, and dreams never harm anyone except those who invent, cultivate and nurture them.

One thing still bothers her, though, and after it is resolved, she promises herself that she will behave. She will fold her wishes up like a handkerchief and put them away in her pocket, and that will be the end of it all. She has to clear the air with Pia. She feels the need to tell her. It all began by trying to do what was best for her. She needs to talk to her, to explain herself. She needs to find the right time and just do it, get it over with. She has to absolve herself sincerely. Bianca has not confronted Pia because it is the simplest thing to do; she does it now because she knows she won't be able to escape the trap of the young maid's gentle lamb-like eyes. She has failed with everyone else but with Pia she cannot afford to.

※ ※

Pia stares at her for a long time and seems not to understand. For once, she has taken a seat on the sofa and she fumbles with her hands on her lap and kicks her feet, as if she cannot wait to get up and leave. She looks so dazed that Bianca feels like shaking her. *On the other hand*, she thinks, *what was I expecting from a person who all of a sudden has found out who her real mother and father are?* It is as if she has been struck by lightning. Bianca smiles encouragingly and gives the girl a gentle pat on the shoulder, waiting.

'And when you finally understand the situation, we will decide what to do,' she hears herself say, not knowing how exactly she can help.

The moment couldn't be more perfect. A cool evening breeze flutters in from the open window in a pale blue wash of light. Pia, bewildered, her lips pursed into an adorable smile, has the inanimate grace of a Flemish portrait. Bianca observes her promising beauty like an indulgent older sister, with a vague air of consolation. When she finally looks up, Pia does not cry, her voice does not tremble; she is submissive and serene.

'You . . . you are confusing me,' she starts to say, her hands fluttering from her lap into the air, in a childlike gesture.

How strange the words sound to Bianca, as though they have been stolen from one of the books Pia reads in secret, as if the character is speaking to someone she is fond of. But the maid continues in a different tone.

'You speak of things that I am owed. You tell me that you are thinking of my well-being. But I do not understand. I am happy like this. What do you expect, Miss Bianca? This is my destiny. Don Dionisio says that it is the duty of a good Christian to accept what the heavens have laid out for them, and that I should thank heaven for what I have. I look around and see so many people who have a lot less than I do: young girls, beaten, ignorant and alone. I not only have a bellyful of food, clothes on my back and a roof under which to sleep, but a lot of other things, too.'

Pia brings her hands down to her lap again and secures one in the other, as if to keep them from flying away.

Bianca is speechless. Is the child ungrateful, after she has spent so much pity on her? The correct answer comes to her slowly. Pia hasn't asked her to do this. No one has. She has done it all on her own. And then come waves of anger, a river of fury, because the young girl, as stupid as she sounds at that moment, really and truly does deserve better.

'Pia, Pia, Pia,' mutters Bianca finally, unable to contain herself. 'Are you telling me you don't care to know?'

Pia doesn't speak. She just presses her lips shut, raises her eyebrows, and then looks down in apology. But she doesn't say sorry.

'Really,' Bianca insists, 'are you satisfied with hand-me-down skirts and ribbons and with having to ask for permission to put a book in your pocket now and then? Are you satisfied with so little in order to be happy?'

'I don't know any other kind of happiness apart from the happiness I feel now,' replies Pia simply. She shrugs, opens her hands in a gesture of surrender, and repeats herself. 'I am happy just the way I am.' She crosses her arms in front of her and stares back at Bianca. It is as if her look is saying, *You're the one who doesn't have what you want; you don't know what you want. You're the orphan. Don't unleash your anxieties onto me.* 'May I be excused, Miss Bianca?'

Pia doesn't wait for a reply. She gets up and leaves, without even turning around. Bianca lowers her head and bites her lip. Pia's look has said so much, and it hurts Bianca to admit that the girl has been right.

Part Three

❧ ❧

The joy of returning to Brusuglio in nice weather cancels out her last memory of the estate in autumn, when an oppressive sky and a thick layer of fog had smothered everything. She is now able to substitute that memory with the colours and well-defined margins of everything in bloom; she recognizes the place first through her body, nose and skin, and only later with her head.

An entire year has gone by since Bianca's arrival. At twenty years old, it seems like a lifetime. It has taken her this long to call this place, populated by strangers, home. That other house, the one at the lake, is far away. This house, with its wide-open windows, seems to want to embrace her.

Minna leaps on her when she sees her, and then steps back, lowering her chin to her chest in embarrassment. She has grown an entire foot, as children and plants often do between seasons, and her face has taken on certain features that have not been present before.

'Shall I put your clothes away, Miss Bianca?' she whispers, eager to get back to her place.

Bianca takes her by the hand and twirls her around.

'First let me look at you. Go on, stand up straight. Look me in the eyes. Do you know that you truly are a good-looking girl?'

Beautiful, too, are the round faces of the kitchen maids, suddenly illuminated by gleeful curiosity. They greet her with due reverence and then run off.

'Miss Bianca, how elegant you are.'

'You look like a lady, Miss Bianca.'

To Bianca it is as if they are saying, *How could this be? Weren't you merely one of us? Or just slightly more?*

Then, as soon as Pia descends from the second coach, Minna jumps into her arms. Pia lifts her up and laughs.

'You're as heavy as lead, doll face. You didn't get fat now, did you?'

'What a beautiful dress! What a lovely hat!'

'I'll let you try it on later.'

There is laughter of relief and rediscovered complicity. Now everything can go back to normal.

But there is little time for pleasantries. Donna Clara has arrived and descended from her personal stagecoach. Giulietta, who's had the privilege of travelling with her, throws herself out of the carriage in a frenzy, almost knocking her grandmother down.

'Giulietta! Is that how a young lady behaves? I want to see all of the domestic help immediately, in the east courtyard. Call Ruggiero for me . . . Ah, here you are, I didn't see you there, as skinny as you are. My goodness, the hedges. Why has no one pruned them? And what about the lawn? What are those yellow splotches? Does everything stop when I am not here? And move that cart – it's offensive.'

As always, nothing is right, and will be fixed only when she asks for it to be done.

Donna Julie passes into the house delicately and unobserved. It seems as though she is better, but she is still pale. She smiles at everyone, almost gratefully, and everyone smiles back at her. The children run off, Nanny chasing after them. She needn't have bothered, as they will certainly not let themselves be caught, but she doesn't know where else to go. The men will arrive later, in time for dinner, and the wave their arrival will cause will be cushioned by habit. It will be an intimate dinner, serene, *en famille*, before the holiday rituals attract neighbours and friends to them like flies to honey. People will flock to them, summoned by the serenity that radiates from their small world, hoping to catch this infectiousness as if it is a desirable illness.

❧ ❧

Pia seems to have forgotten the encounter that was supposed to have amounted to glory, but which is instead now buried under the sand. Bianca watches how the young maid focuses on reclaiming her place in that world. Bianca wishes she could have her to herself but she feels she needs to let her go. And yet, it occurs to Bianca that she must have planted some seed of doubt because shortly thereafter she sees Pia immersed in conversation with Don Dionisio. They keep being interrupted by every kind of disturbance – the voice of Donna Clara, a servant who walks too close by – but they always take up again where they left off, whether it is an hour later or the following day. It is as if they never get tired of telling each other things. Perhaps Pia seeks approval from her protector. Perhaps she expects to learn more from him. Perhaps truth has to be brooded over like an egg, before it will hatch in all its awkward beauty. Perhaps – and this hypothesis feels like an oncoming headache and Bianca does not want to admit it – not all truths deserve to be revealed. She wishes she could listen to those exchanges, though. She wishes she could *understand*. For someone who thinks that she has understood everything, not knowing is complete torture.

❧ ❧

She is not tired and cannot sleep. It is warm and the novelty of her surroundings keeps her awake, even when an unnatural yet perfect peace has settled over the house, broken only by the song of the cicadas that rises over the gentle sound of crickets. She imagines everyone sleeping: the maids in their quarters upstairs, stretched out on the wooden floor close to the tiny windows; the poet in his loose nightshirt, the sheets kicked to the end of the bed; Donna Julie, pale as the pillow on which she rests her head, the sheets tucked under her chin; Donna Clara, freed from her corset, her mouth slightly open, breathing with difficulty; the little girls, their hair sticking to their foreheads with sweat, their eyelids threaded with pink and blue veins. A house asleep. She imagines Minna and Pia awake, though, their eyes bright and vigilant, the spell finally broken, intent on telling each other stories in whispered voices.

She doesn't feel like reading. Instead, she gets up to take in the beautiful stillness of the garden. It is a beauty made up of blacks and greys; the only white the marble contour of the fountain and the gravel splashed with moonlight. A nocturnal bird cackles mockingly. Silence.

There is the rustle of shifting pebbles and light, careful footsteps. And then, two small, quick shadows come out from behind the corner of the villa and cross the path cautiously. Once on the great lawn, which swallows up the sound of their feet, they run to its centre, where a new sycamore tree has just been introduced to replace the one struck by lightning. Enrico is ahead and runs faster; Pietro follows behind with a bundle under his arms.

Bianca smiles and remembers when she used to play with her own brother Zeno and his friends Berto, Tiziano and Tilio. Once, at night, they even climbed to the top of La Rocca. It was an easy trek during the day along a path shadowed by oak trees, but scary and dangerous at night. They couldn't see where to step, the stones were slippery with moss, and there was a heavy curtain of leaves above their heads that shut out the moonlight. But in the end, holding each other's hands, they made it and were able to look down at the lake from above, sitting together on the stone throne built for an ancient queen.

The two boys are happy to be out on the lawn. Pietro puts down the bundle and gives it a kick. It is a white ball and looks like it is made from strips of silk. When they kick it, it gives off a thudding sound, which seems odd. Is it leather? Bianca, now curious, goes downstairs and walks outside. She won't scare them. She'll promise to be silent. And maybe they will let her play with them.

When they see her approaching, the two children stop running and freeze in their places. Bianca is unable to read their expressions. She tries reassuring them and promising complicity.

'But . . .' Her words fade into nothing.

The thing has rolled towards her. It is not a ball. It is not made of fabric or leather. It is a skull. A human skull. It smiles at her impassively before rolling over to display its white nape.

The moment feels like an eternity. Bianca brings a hand to her mouth to stop herself from screaming.

Pietro comes to her side. He is breathing heavily. He flips his hair with an almost effeminate gesture. When he speaks his voice is coarse, breathy, and yet authoritative.

'You'll be sorry if you say anything. You'll be sorry if you tell on us. You'd better keep quiet. Otherwise I will tell on you and then you'll be in big trouble.' He smiles a frightening, adult sneer.

Bianca turns and walks away without saying a word. She is ashamed to have something to be ashamed of.

❧ ❧

Another night, after dinner, Tommaso takes her by the hand and pulls her up off the sofa, possessive and insistent.

'Let's go for a walk. It's warm, and the moon is out.'

She refuses. She isn't in the mood.

'Oh, yes, you must go. You kids should have fun, not sit around with us old folks, listening to us say the same old things.'

Bianca hears Donna Clara's bass line of malice, that old strain of envy. Innes excuses himself. As he leaves the room, it is useless to try to make eye contact with him. When he is like that, Bianca has learned, it is better just to let him be, and wait for the clouds to clear.

Once they get outside, Tommaso is silent, as if he is a wanderer of the moor. The silence makes her feel uncomfortable so she starts a conversation.

'I would have thought that you preferred literature to nature at night.'

'He rejects me. He has something else on his mind, and it's not his devoted puppy. Dogs have a basic defect: they die of loyalty. I think I've decided that I'd rather live.'

Instinctively, Bianca moves further away from him, as much as she can while remaining polite; he must feel her coldness because he adds: 'You shouldn't believe everything I say, my dear Bianca. And don't worry, you aren't a substitute. If literature is everything, nature is even better.'

His expression is impossible to read. Every so often he turns and looks back at the house, as if he wants to flee from its gaze. They walk for about a mile down the gravel path and then turn up a little hill. The dark grows darker. She sees steps: sheets of stone, as white as dragon's teeth. She is about to rest her foot on the first step, and tries to loosen her arm from his, but he doesn't let her go. He actually pulls her towards him and pushes her up the stairs.

'I want to show you something,' he says. It is the ice chamber. 'Have you ever been in there?'

'No, and I don't think I ever will,' Bianca says.

'Ah, but it's worth it,' Tommaso replies, turning the key in the lock. 'Another of the amazing secrets of Brusuglio to discover.'

Inside, he rummages about with a flint and a lantern that seems to have been placed randomly on the floor. But there is nothing random about it, she realizes; he has wanted to bring her here. Her heart skips a beat. Is she scared? Scared of Tommaso? The door is still ajar, she can still escape. But curiosity gets the better of her.

The dim light reveals a low brick vault. It is surrounded by alcoves and inside there are blocks of ice wrapped in clean cloths. She can see the squares of paralysed deep green water; they are opaque and have the same colour as the lake. The place feels like a Roman catacomb. She shivers not only on account of the cool air, which makes the room as cold as a cellar, but for what lives within. It smells strange. It reminds her of the mix of dust and bones she had inhaled during archaeological visits, when not even a handkerchief in front of her face had been sufficient to suppress the musty air. Here, the cool air enters her nostrils and rises to her head. It is the coolness of the abyss.

Bianca blinks. She feels like she did when she needed to rise from the depths of the lake's dark waters that she remembers with love. She is almost amazed to see Tommaso still by her side. He lifts the lantern and shines the light all the way around.

'Nice, huh? In its own way, of course. This place is full of surprises. You should come to see my home, one day. Up in the attic . . .' Then he stops and suddenly becomes serious, almost bitter. 'I can't even go there any more. They treat me worse than a mouse. Do you know why I have brought you here?'

Let him speak, Bianca tells herself. And he does.

'Of course you know why I brought you here. I am sure of it. A young, bright woman such as yourself. Sharp and cold as a blade. You are the ice queen. Why are you so cold, Bianca, why?' He places the lantern carefully in one of the alcoves and kneels down before her. He takes her by the hand and gazes at her with the expression of a transfixed martyr. How ridiculous he looks. The dim light gives him the appearance of a wax statue. 'I kneel here before you as humble as an ancient cavalier, ready to serve you, prepared to dedicate myself to you.'

Bianca takes her hand out of his with a small laugh.

'Go on, laugh at me,' he continues. 'But I am serious. Do you understand me? Serious! Is it possible that only other people's seriousness attracts you? Mine is not an insurmountable wall or a deep trench that separates. It is the opposite: it is a solid link, a bridge of souls, an arch in the sky that begins at your feet.'

What is he talking about? What does he mean? Does he have a fever? Without thinking, Bianca feels his forehead with her fingers, as she would a child. He looks at her with a calm smile.

'There. You see how easy it is to take pity on me? And how little it takes to make me happy? I can do the same: I can make *you* happy, today, here, on this earth. If you let me. Let go of fantasy, forget about them, and choose me. For some time now, I have worshipped you from the shadows.'

Bianca is dumbfounded. She hears the alarm of danger, a voice in her head. It is freezing in here. She wraps herself tightly in her shawl and takes a step back as he goes on.

'Ah, I see the shawl I gave you. May you always be enveloped in my passion. Did you realize it was me?'

Heavens, no, she thinks. She was convinced that the gift came from somebody else. What about the other things? Instinctively, she jerks the fabric off her shoulders. It is the shirt of Nessus, poisonous when it is recognized as such. He watches her and mutters.

'You torture me. Does it bring you pleasure? What pleasure could there be in other people's grief?'

Bianca is tired of this. It is cold. She turns around and walks out. Tommaso stands and follows her. She begins to run. She hears him close the iron door behind her and turn the key, as if to close in his prey, though it has already fled. Or has it?

❧ ❧

The following day, in the sunlight, all that cold air seems never to have existed. It feels only like a vague aversion, a mosquito bite that has almost healed, but then reawakens, the venom still pulsating under the skin. An irresistible bother.

Nothing has happened.

And yet it feels like everyone knows. Donna Clara sings an old love song; Nanny smiles faintly; Innes reads his newspapers in silence and doesn't pass her tea. What do they know? Bianca thinks, growing annoyed. There really is nothing to know.

But every time she runs into Tommaso, she blushes. And it seems like he bumps into her on purpose: in the living room, the greenhouse, the garden. Always with no witnesses around. Even when there are witnesses, it doesn't matter. He keeps at his game. He will kneel down, put his hand on his heart, over the lightweight batiste shirt that he wears unbuttoned at the top, like a true romantic, as if posing for a portrait. As quickly as he appears, he'll then disappear, swallowed by the folds of a curtain, a door, or a hole in the ground. Bianca feels like there might be an entire army of Tommasos, ready to jump out in front of her, disrupt her train of thought and make her blood boil. Why? For what? In the end he is just fooling around. No one ever takes him seriously and she will not be the one to start. But her irritation begins to mix with something else too: for truthfully she likes it. She likes it a great deal.

He hasn't tried to kiss her. Bianca doesn't realize it then, but this is how he wins. Now all he has to do is wait.

He hasn't pronounced the word 'love', either. Not even once. Bianca doesn't pay any attention to that. She doesn't even think about it. She doesn't think about the gifts or about the gift-giver. She understands the shawl, but the rest of them? They are too elevated to be the fruit of the intelligence of this boy. He hasn't claimed them, even if he could have. And so Bianca keeps on deceiving herself, and keeps nurturing a small certainty, which is good for her.

⁂

And then the heat comes: the white heat of summer, impossible to escape from, except in the early hours of the morning. It lasts all day and deep into the night and it isn't even summer yet. Everyone is irritable, the children most of all. They are tired of the same old nursery games and forbidden from going outdoors during the peak hours. After only a few minutes outside, they are drenched in sweat and covered with dust. Soon they have violet circles under their eyes, as if they have been persecuted by insomnia. Their cheeks are as pale as winter.

Bianca doesn't have time for them. She feels sorry for this, but she has to finish a series of hydrangeas before they lose their freshness. She knows that in August the plants will be faded and although she prefers them that way, rather than as they are now, with their big, tousled pink and green heads, her portraits are meant to capture subjects across their lifespan, not only during one interesting state of decay. If it had been up to her, she would have willingly set aside the assignment in favour of a brief holiday. She can think of many ways of entertaining the little ones far better than Nanny is doing.

Bianca smiles to herself as she prepares her colours. She remembers how easy it had been to say goodbye to a governess once she had been used up, and how exciting it had been to wait for a new one to arrive, descending from the sky, equipped with a flowery carpet bag of new tricks and distractions. It is time for Nanny, the poor thing, to change her lifestyle and get married. But how will she find a husband? She should forget about Innes. Tarcisio is the one. Tarcisio would be perfect for her. He is a peasant, yes, but a landowner. He is independent, not shy and clumsy like the others, and he has a certain rugged handsomeness thanks to his impossibly blue eyes. What magnificent children they would have – with Nanny's copper-coloured hair, the only remarkable thing that she possesses. Bianca shakes her head, scolding herself. But then she starts in again. The game is irresistible. The pair could live in that little house beyond the town walls. It is small but fair. All it needs is a fresh coat of paint, maybe a nice pink, like the shade they use for homes at the lake. She wonders how pink will look against that landscape. Surely Nanny could afford to buy a new outfit too, perhaps in a light grey, a skirt with a fitted jacket that accentuates her waist and plumps up her flat chest. Bianca begins to draw the outfit she envisions: the skirt fluttering at the bottom, a braided row in front, on her head a simple hat held in place by a knot under her chin, and a small bouquet of three blossoming peonies surrounded by magnolia leaves.

If I ever grow tired of flowers, Bianca thinks, *I can devote my time to fashion.*

The problem with Bianca's work is that when she finishes the flowers, she has too much time left over for thinking. And desiring. She wonders what the watermill is like at this time of year, if the water is still green and translucent like the fountain of Melusina. She has no time to go there though, no time at all. The hydrangeas call out to her.

Sometimes, at dusk, a small procession of carriages come from the city, friends in search of cool air, who pass the evenings fanning themselves and watching the ice gems from the ice chamber melt in their glasses. Even their conversations seem limp and tired. By the end of the season, all the gossip has dried up. Not even Bernocchi is able to scrape a scandal together. Don Dionisio gets older and sicker. He has to stop every three steps to catch his breath. Pia is always nearby, ready to offer him a cool beverage.

Essentially, nothing really happens. If Bianca was a little older, she would know that this is how a storm announces itself. A bubble of still air pushes forward, a river of emptiness is created, and then things fall apart. Attention is lax and omens fade. Later, she will say that it has all been predictable, and therefore avoidable. Later still, she will tell herself that no good comes of thinking that way. It has happened and nothing can be made right again.

֍ ֍

It is an accident. These things happen in a household full of children. A ball made of Florentine leather – this time a real one – flies through the open French window and crashes into the glass bell jar that sits on the mantelpiece above the French fireplace. The objects under the bell jar are also French. Donna Clara has told their stories countless times; they are relics from a life that seems to belong to someone else, far off in the distant past. They are neither beautiful nor ugly, and of value only to the person who owns them. They are small, motionless things of questionable taste. There is a stuffed dove, its marble eyes fixed on nothing. There are some gesso flowers and fruit created by Garnier Valletti of Turin, based on certain garden fruits of the Hesperides. And finally, there is a miniature tree, which in reality is merely a small branch shaped like a tree trunk. From it hang three small, straw-like garlands in pale, almost unnatural colours: one blonde, one nearly grey, and one almost white. They are three locks of Carlo's hair that have been cut at different times of his life. The last lock of hair was cut shortly before his death.

The ball crashes into the room and sends these grim relics and shards of broken crystal flying across the floor. The little dove is bent out of shape but continues to clutch at its branch with an odd arrogance. The strands are scattered, and the fruit chipped. Donna Clara, attracted by the clamour like a fly to honey, stands immobile in the doorway. She covers her ears with her hands, as if she does not want to hear any explanations. The maids come running and then disperse to find brooms and dust pans. Bianca, who has been arranging flowers in the foyer, finds Donna Clara on the floor like a bent black tulip. In trying to retrieve the hairs, she has scratched her finger and her blood drips on the white strands, resealing an ancient pact.

The cause was a naughty child. Though it was not done deliberately, Pietro is sent to his room without dinner, even if it is only three in the afternoon and dinner still an eternity away. He stays in the nursery until the following day. When he emerges, he is not at all penitent. It was just an old decoration, wasn't it?

Giulietta asks for the white dove before it is thrown away, and it is given to her. From that day forward, she carries it in the pocket of her smock or between her fingers. She doesn't want it to fly off, as birds have a habit of doing.

❧ ❧

The weather changes. A heavy nocturnal downpour brings forth the summertime in its full force but the following morning the park is in ruins. Broken branches, flower heads, and torn leaves sprinkle the great lawn. Matilde comes running.

'Look what I found,' she says, proudly dangling a small dead country mouse by the tail. Nanny draws back – *quelle horreur* – but she is the only one to do so. Everyone else is spellbound by the creature's perfect little body, its damp fuzz, the delicate pink fringe around its closed eyes, and its miniature paws.

'Should we give him a funeral?'

Enrico manages to obtain a gold-bordered chasuble from the church sexton. He runs back to them wearing it, holding up the long tunic with one hand so as not to trip. He stops, lets go of the folds, and recomposes himself, opening his arms and broadcasting pagan blessings for the deceased.

'Can I say a prayer?' Francesca asks. 'Dear Mouse, I hope that you are happier in Paradise than you were here. You died young and you didn't know very much. I hope a piece of cheese waits for you in heaven. Amen.'

'Amen,' everyone replies and they bury the little mouse in a box beneath a bush of *Olea fragrans*, where he will not be forgotten.

Besides this small loss, the world cannot be better aligned.

In the time it takes the gardeners to tidy up after the storm's damage, the sun has dried the garden. The rain leaves everything green and crisp, as if it is springtime. Nature is restored to a glistening state and the timing cannot have been better: they have to prepare for the estate's annual reopening festivities. Truthfully, the ladies would choose not to have a party, but their friends are expecting one.

'It has to take place,' the poet says in his strict manner. 'And I have a reason for it. It is a secret reason. Be patient, and you will find out.'

Everyone does their part to help. Donna Clara, pleased to be in charge once again, declares that the house, although it has been properly cleaned after their arrival, needs to be scrubbed again from top to bottom, eliminating every hint of dust and spider's web.

Donna Julie is still tired. The heat has taken its toll on her and the thunderstorm hasn't been enough to restore her strength. In any case, taking charge is not something she is good at. Instead, she relaxes in the shade of the sycamore tree, resting beneath its sweeping, low branches on a new chaise-longue made of braided straw and light-coloured wood – a homecoming gift from her husband. Bianca has sought refuge in that spot many times herself before the arrival of the chair. The location makes it easy to forget about the surrounding world.

The children run off in all directions to rediscover the estate, which still appears surprisingly new to them, though a tad smaller. In the back of the house, through half-open windows, Donna Clara can be heard commanding her troops through organized chaos.

Bianca seeks out her own hiding space. The greenhouse has suffered damage from the hail and many of the windowpanes have been shattered. She sweeps up the pieces of glass and moves the plants around, which leaves her a luminous, ventilated and sheltered space. It is one of those rare instances where a loss becomes an advantage, at least until the windowpanes are replaced and the greenhouse will go back to serving its intended purpose as a warm, damp, stifling place. At that point Bianca will have to find another refuge. Meanwhile, she stays there and works. She feels somewhat lazy, which is unusual for her and which she blames on the tantrums of the weather, just like everyone else.

She is in the greenhouse when she receives a letter. The big celebration is only two days away and the letter announces that she too will have a visitor. Bianca reads it, looks around, rereads it, and puts it away. She fixes her hair as if to organize her thoughts, picks up the missive, and goes to search for the mistress of the house.

❦ ❦

'He will be our guest of honour,' is Donna Clara's dutiful answer to Bianca. But there is also a vein of sincere curiosity. 'Are you saying that he will bring his military attaché with him? Interesting. Just so you know, I have always preferred Minerva to Mars. As far as my son is concerned, I am sure you know how he feels . . . and one of these days he's going to get all of us into trouble with his crazy ideas. But of course, your brother will be welcome in our household, whatever his uniform may be. Did you say that you look alike? No? That's too bad. Attilia, two more bedrooms need to be prepared in the west wing. Now, if you'll excuse me . . .'

Bianca listens as Donna Clara gives more orders.

'You have plates to dust and silverware to polish. Be careful of the Chinese vases! Have the floors been waxed? And what about the quails' eggs? Can someone please tell me if the quails' eggs have been delivered?'

※ ※

Zeno looks so handsome in his uniform. He had brought it with him in his trunk, neatly folded away, so he could secretly show it off to his sister. The red jacket accentuates his blond hair and the blue of his childlike eyes. *Or perhaps*, thinks Bianca, pushing him back so she can get a better look at him, *I will always see him as a child*. Tassels and ribbons on his cap create a crown of almost feminine complexity that borders on the ridiculous and must surely be uncomfortable. But perhaps one actually goes to battle in rags, half naked like savages, leaving those lofty hats behind.

'You seem happy,' she says and he takes her by the waist and spins her around.

'I am, dear sister. This is what I wanted. You, on the other hand, seem as light as a fairy. Don't these barbarians feed you?'

She places a hand on his mouth to silence him and together they laugh. She hasn't felt so happy in centuries, it seems. So much at home, and at ease. But there isn't much time for intimacies. He and his friend, Paolo Nittis, a tall and slender soldier with a coiffed moustache and shiny hair and who cannot take his dark eyes off her, have arrived in the middle of the afternoon and at the height of the preparations.

'Have you a nice room for me, my trusted valet?' Zeno asks with a smile as she accompanies them to their quarters.

Because of the heat, she has left all the flower arrangements until last. The cut flowers wait for her in a washtub full of water and ice. She dips her hands in fearlessly, allowing the cold to move up her wrists through her body, like a long shiver, until it reaches her head. *I will do the flowers,* she thinks, *then go upstairs, get changed, come back down and celebrate.*

⁂

It is the beginning of summer, the night of San Giovanni, the night damsels wait for a sign from the heavens to tell them their lot in love. A year ago she felt out of place and ran away from that celebration to follow the calling of another. Now she will do differently. She is more at home in this small world. She can allow herself to have some fun, can't she?

Once she is back in her bedroom, she peels a small pear that she has stolen from a triumphant display in the house's entrance, throws the peel over her shoulder, turns around, and attempts to decipher the letter that the peel forms. Is it a P, B or D? She would appreciate some help in understanding. Then: *What of it?* she thinks. *My little brother is here and we will laugh and dance. It doesn't matter if there are no other cavaliers for me. We will talk together on the great lawn in the torchlight; we will drink sparkling wine, and in silence we will promise each other things, as lovers do. And it will be all right if the promises are not kept.*

Before leaving the city, Bianca made time to visit Signora Gandini's shop to order two summer dresses. She has paid for them with her hard-earned cash and because of this they seem like the most beautiful dresses in the entire world. It is difficult for her to decide now which one to wear. She almost misses the days when she owned only one elegant gown, the one she wore for her eighteenth birthday. Perhaps she should wear it: the white muslin double-skirted dress of plumetis. Although it is starting to become a bit tight across her chest. No, no, she will wear one of her new gowns. Should she wear the antique rose or the jade green? She knows that the pink one makes her features softer – even the milliner has said so. She has unstitched some of the roses that the seamstress placed at the neckline because she finds them too girly. The other dress accentuates the colour of her eyes, though, and she is almost certain that no one else will be wearing that style.

'Very few girls can wear this sort of dress. It makes most of them look like fish, or ghosts. But not you. You were born to wear green.'

And so she opts for the jade. It has a high waist in the Paolina fashion, which seems destined to last forever, and a thin, triple-braided ribbon that falls down her side for almost the whole length of the dress, becoming untied at the very end.

'You are the perfect model for this dress,' Signora Gandini had said. The neckline is square, generous, almost daring. 'Only girls with a little bosom can wear this.'

Et voilà, a defect has been transformed into a virtue by way of fashion. She's had three minuscule flowers for her chignon made from tightly rolled-up pieces of the same fabric. She needs Minna or Pia to help her with them. But where are they?

Bianca draws closer to the window, still barefoot and impatient. She is just in time to see Count Bernocchi descending from his coach, making it rock dangerously from side to side. He looks up towards the facade, sees her, smiles, and gives a quick bow. Bianca draws back, hoping he might mistake her for a curtain. Perhaps he hasn't recognized her and only wishes he had seen her. She feels her cheeks burn. Bernocchi has become so insistent of late. He calls her a 'beautiful little flower'. He even sent her a complete garden of sugared almonds, replete with petals and leaves, which had aroused admiration from them all, especially from certain hungry family members who had wolfed them down. He tries to make time with her alone, and Bianca avoids him as much as possible. She flees from his ambushes in the corridors. And when they are in the presence of others, which is almost always, he stares at her with big, rheumy eyes that make her almost miss his sardonic look. Even Donna Julie notices his strange silences.

'Did the cat get your tongue?' she asked once.

Now Bianca turns her attention back to the pear skin lying on the floor. B for Bernocchi, with a big belly, she thinks. But P for Paolo, Zeno's tall friend. Solemn and composed, the soldier's gaze burned straight through her. He had one of those dark stares that are hard to read.

'Did you know, my dear sister,' her brother said, 'that all Sardinians are dwarfs except this one? Where do you come from, my friend, the land of Snow White?'

Paolo's answer was a blinding smile.

P is also for poet. But the poet only stares at her in silence. Behind his impenetrable eyes is an entire world, a world in which there is no dancing, only fighting for causes worth fighting for. His weapons are words sharpened in anger.

There is a letter for everyone's name and yet not one is right. Bianca's heart sings the easy song of youth, of blood coursing through her veins, of a new dress and beautiful new jade-green shoes. She wears a bracelet of tiny white roses which she has made herself, and which she, without the help of Minna or Pia, has to tie around her left wrist. *No one will have jewels like this; I am the lady of the flowers.* And she wears one more thing: her mother's earrings, tiny pearls like droplets falling from two golden knots. 'Knots of true love,' her father said when he handed her that gift, 'the love of which you are a sign.'

That night, Bianca skips down the stairs as if she is flying. She slows down as she reaches the foyer with its hundreds of candles and takes one step at a time, as though the dancing has already commenced. Outside, the dusk creates puddles of near darkness where the trees are low and thick. Happy swallows scribble across the still light-blue sky above the sycamore tree.

Bernocchi, thankfully, is out of sight. Zeno and Paolo look up and watch her descend the stairs, as one does for a young woman. And when she reaches the last step they bow to her and take her by the arms, one on each side, two glowing escorts in white and blue.

'You are truly enchanting,' whispers Paolo, his eyes fixed on her.

'That's enough, you. She's just a girl,' Zeno says, his voice rising. It is the first time he has ever protected her. He is the younger of the two, after all.

'Shh.' She silences both of them, feeling superior and exquisite.

Bianca frees herself and walks in front of them to the dining room, where, by Donna Clara's instruction, a modern buffet has been prepared. She has done well in choosing her green dress, she thinks with a hint of frivolity, because the room, which is two or three tones darker, is an ideal background for her. She has to stop thinking like this. It isn't her party. It is an occasion to celebrate the beginning of summer, the reopening of the house, and the secret announcement – which is no secret at all – regarding the upcoming publication of Don Titta's novel.

Indeed, it is really a party for the poet-turned-writer and for his wife, who has patiently stood at his side through turbulent times, almost dying while doing so. But that's what a writer's wife has to do, is it not? Or perhaps that is the role of any wife.

Donna Julie looks ravishing in an ivory silk gown that contrasts sharply with her dark hair, which she wears down for once, straightened with care in two *bandeaux* with only a couple of rebellious curls. Fixed to her hair is a small bunch of tiny flowers (so that's where Minna and Pia have been). The whole effect makes her look like a delicate bird. Hanging from her long, white neck – devoid of the usual foulard that protects her from the cold – is a cross of diamonds, her only adornment.

Donna Clara, on the other hand, parades all of her rings and pendants, including a long *chevalière* that hangs over the generous shelf of her chest before falling into nothing.

'Are those the keys to the heavenly kingdom?' Bernocchi asks, covering his venomous mouth with one hand, his eyes enraptured by the perpetual movement of her golden key pendants. He is far enough away for Donna Clara not to hear him, but the others do.

Bianca feigns indifference but secretly she smirks. Everyone knows that they are in fact the keys to the now-silent harpsichord and to the crystal box in which Donna Clara keeps her most precious relics. Or so they say. Who knows if she has now added the dead man's hair to that pile, Bianca asks herself with a shiver of horror.

And then she stops thinking. She laughs, dances, drinks, dances again, drinks again, laughs, drinks some more, runs, blushes, pales, and dances. She travels from one cluster of guests to another, tirelessly. She talks, answers and quips, as lively as ever. During the formation dancing, Zeno whispers to her.

'Is this really you, sis? I didn't think you were so worldly.'

'I'm not, in fact.'

'I thought you had come here to work, not to learn new dances or how to become a coquette . . . Who is that man pouting over there? He's been staring at you all night.'

Tommaso's face floats over the large knot of his white tie. He stands to the wall as if nailed.

'The dances aren't new. And I'm not a coquette!'

'But you are new indeed.'

'Hush, hush.'

And yet, perhaps Zeno is right. It was one of those moments that make her feel as though something has just changed, or has to change. She gallops forward in dance.

Am I really altered? she asks herself in a moment of rest, fiddling with a lock of hair that has fallen out of her chignon, standing in front of one of the tall nebulous mirrors at the entrance. Perhaps it is the stain of time on the glass, or the light from the chandelier, but she really does look different. She looks back at herself impudently, without ceasing to fix her hair. This Bianca is less *bianca* and more lively and green, like one of her rare hellebores. She is a winter flower: she has survived the frost, and has lifted her nonchalant head from the cold to look around, deciding she likes the world the way it is and that she will stay a while.

All this takes place in a moment. Suddenly, a tall shape appears in the reflection behind her. A man wrapped in shadow or perhaps a cloak. No, it isn't a cloak. This isn't the season for cloaks. Who is it? The shadowy figure disappears but not before giving her an indiscreet look, a look that disturbs her greatly, even if her shoulders are covered, her neckline is conservative, and her ankles are not visible. For a moment, Bianca feels stripped bare. She blushes to the roots of her hair and waits for the flush to subside before rejoining the guests.

Her embarrassment lasts only a moment, though, and she soon feels the pleasurable warmth that rises when one has danced much, drunk a great deal and been admired by many. Thanks to her slight intoxication, Bianca jokes with self-confidence. She flees artfully from Signora Villoresi with a polite curtsey. The lady wants to commission a set of dead leaves – that's exactly how she says it, a set, as if she is dealing with a service of dessert forks. No work tonight. But Bianca forgets that the reason she is there, and not dressed as a Nanny or a tutor, is thanks to those dead leaves. Foolish Bianca, for whom one glass of sweet wine and a sugared compliment are enough for her to forget who she is. But who is she really? She is a girl on her own who feels like having fun. Who can blame her? Donna Clara and Donna Julie would warn her if they could read her heart. With the wisdom gleaned from the experience of the one and the calm erudition of the other, they would tell her that too much light is deadly for nocturnal butterflies. But she wouldn't listen. She would nod her head, yes, but close off her heart. Her ears hear the music summoning her again. She contemplates the couples whirling across the large stage of smooth wood, positioned at the foot of the stairs.

'Care for another dance, Miss Bianca?'

It is too late to avoid Bernocchi without being rude. She shouldn't be, it wouldn't be proper. And she has to admit, he does know how to dance. He focuses so hard on it that he doesn't have time to chat, which is helpful. Bianca eyes his chubby ankles, his shoes of yellow damask that look as though they have been cut from the coat of a reptile, and feels his perspiring hand tight on her back, even through the shield of her clothes. Now it is time to change partners. Her new partner places his hand on her waist – light and airy this time. He doesn't dance as well, but he is handsome and tall. It is Paolo Nittis from Sassari, which has to be a city full of snakes and stones, with all those S sounds to its name. She wonders if all Sardinians have eyes the colour of spilled ink. Since he is the first she has ever encountered, which feels a little like seeing an exotic bird in an enclosure, she asks him. He blinks, as though he hasn't understood, and then smiles, revealing his white teeth.

'Come see for yourself with your own eyes,' he laughs. 'My land is wild and untamed.'

'And you?'

He seems to find her question amusing.

'I'd say I have been domesticated, by now. My uniform has helped a great deal.'

'Oh, what a pity. I have enough domesticated puppies around here to keep me company.'

Nittis casts a quick glance around the room at the men dressed in the latest style of frock coats, their hair combed back. Everyone looks the same, a pack of hounds.

'Woof!' laughs Bianca. She feels Nittis's hand release her and suddenly she is in someone else's more familiar grasp. She has never danced with Innes, but it is as if she has always done so.

'Tonight I like you more than usual, Miss Bianca. You are bold.'

They share that same sublime, dry precision of the language.

Bianca looks up towards the facade of the house, certain that Nanny is peering out of one of the windows, protected by the darkness. Governesses, poor creatures, are only invited to parties in novels. They wear new dresses and flowers in their hair, and stay seated all night long. They lose their gloves and stain themselves with lemonade. *I am not a poor thing. I am not a governess. I am a free woman, I know how to read, how to write, how to do arithmetic, how to draw, how to uncover mysteries and solve riddles . . .*

'What are you thinking about?'

The question seems banal, but Bianca has had enough practice in navigating salons to know that banal and silly questions do not really exist. Only banal answers.

'I am thinking about how fortunate I am,' she answers, looking up at Innes both because the difference in height requires her to do so and because she wants to see his reaction.

'I think so too,' he says. 'But fortune is cultivated in the greenhouse, you know. It is a rare flower that doesn't last.'

'Please do not speak of flowers. Not tonight, I beg you.'

'Is our gardener on her way out? Has she hung up her gloves and apron?'

Together they smile. It is lovely to be made fun of without needing to take offence. How different that same phrase would be if Bernocchi had spoken it. But Innes can say anything to her. Why is this so?

'What are we, you and I?'

He understands her immediately and grows serious.

'Brothers. Neighbours of the house and of the spirit. Accomplices.'

'Friends?'

'That's different.'

She bites her lip and then curtseys, as required by the dance. If she could, she would hug him. *Perhaps this is the first time, in all my life, that I feel at home*, she thinks. *Does that mean this is the right place for me? Is this my place in the world?* Thoughts scatter, like frightened birds. A moment, and then all that is left is a lingering intuition and the disappointment of not having seized it.

Suddenly, the master of the house bows before her briefly and formally, as is his manner.

'May I have this dance?'

What an absurd question, Bianca thinks, letting herself be guided towards the centre of the stage. She would accept even if she were exhausted, even if all the guests had left and the house were empty, even if there was no more music. Sometimes, one doesn't have the right to say no. And anyway, a dancing poet?

'It's almost an oxymoron,' she thinks out loud. He looks at her without understanding. Thank goodness a good deal of the phrase had been lost to the orchestra.

He is, in fact, a decent dancer with a natural ability that can only have come from intense practice and habit at some point in his life. It is as if he ceased to dance only yesterday and is now ready to take it up again, although Bianca knows very well that this isn't the case.

She looks around her and everyone's faces appear the same: dilated smiles on dolls' heads. She sees Donna Clara's acute and questioning eyebrows, Donna Julie's innocent smile, Bernocchi's smirk, Don Dionisio's mild indifference, Tommaso's paleness, and all the others – perplexed, curious, ironic.

'What about your wife?' Bianca asks suddenly, worried about conventions. He still hasn't asked Donna Julie to dance. He started off the evening by accompanying his mother.

'She never learned to dance,' he replies.

She thinks about Donna Julie: her modest ways, her sober clothes, her lowered gaze, prayers and fasts. Bianca has heard the story many times in the maids' quarters. His mother chose this wife for him, a fresh young girl ready to marry; she was young and rich, from a good and pious family, ready to move from one cloister to another. He loves her, though. It is evident. He looks for her now, they exchange a spark of understanding, and he keeps on dancing.

Earlier, when he made his announcement, it was the same. Donna Julie did not stand by his side. She placed herself in a part of the salon that allowed her to survey everyone and everything. Invisible, yet always present. He gave her a look before signalling to the musicians to fade out the polka. The guests interrupted their dancing and gathered around the French window. He made his way forward, creating an empty space at the centre of the hall.

'Friends,' he said, 'you are here because it is the beginning of summer, because we have returned to our much-loved Brusuglio and because we want to share with you the joys of the season before they turn to suffering – the light kind of suffering that nature inflicts on us. In fact, I am pleased to say that we were able to eliminate all the mosquitoes for tonight's celebration.' People laughed and he continued.

'We have also been able to summon a light breeze to comfort the warm bodies of those who love dancing. We know that it won't last. There will be heatwaves and crops to think about. But those are my concerns. You know that I am a country poet – and perhaps more country than poet – that's up to you to decide.' More laughter.

'But there's another reason I have invited you here. Many of you know that for years now I have been working on a project that has absorbed my days and nights. Some people called me mad, and perhaps they are right. But my feat is finally over, and I will now begin the second part of my adventure. In September, my historical novel will be published.'

Applause.

'And then I hope that someone will read it.'

Laughter.

'Actually, no, I hope that people will purchase it – either out of curiosity or simply to see what has gone through this madman's head. Ultimately, I only want people to buy it. I don't even care if they read it!'

More laughter.

'I know that many of you appreciate me as a poet. Recently, the poet in me has become a sort of youthful brother to consider with the kind of indulgence we tend to reserve for young people. Let us bid him farewell. Let us say that he's leaving for a journey abroad, from which he will return changed, unrecognizable. Or perhaps he won't come back at all. I invite you now to discover the writer, the older brother, raised by the severe schooling of life and certain to have at least one story to tell.'

'And you – where are you in all this?' someone called out, bringing more laughter.

'Oh, at the moment I am in Brusuglio, where the land and my family summon me and ask me to be both of the soil and father of family.'

Applause followed and trays of drinks were passed so that they could toast.

'To our friend Titta, who always knows how to amaze us.'

'To the poet we won't forget.'

'To the novelist we want to get to know.'

Other whispered sentences were hidden behind sips of white wine, phrases uttered in a tone that showed more concern than criticism.

'Is he sure about what he's doing?'

'How much will it cost him? To self-publish, what an idea! It will be his ruin, trust me.'

'And his family? How will he maintain them while he waits for his glory to arrive?'

'With what it costs to keep up this house . . .'

The comments she heard expressed mild unease but were not malicious. The poet truly has many friends, Bianca thinks as they dance. She wishes she could ask him, as one friend to another, if he really is serene. She wants to know if he thinks he has done the right thing. She wants to ask what the novel is actually about. She wants to tell him that Enrico, more than any of his other children, needs him as a guide and a companion; that he is being spoiled by his mother and grandmother and turning into a whiny brat. She wants to tell him that the girls shouldn't be mollycoddled and should have more independence. They are fun and intelligent. They deserve more attention and more ample horizons than the ones framed by the windows of their nursery. But it isn't the right moment to do so. If he is really going to dedicate himself to the countryside with vigour, there will be other opportunities. Everything is possible and even more so now. She should be happy to have him close by. He ends the dance with a bow and a farewell, but holds onto her fingers for a moment longer than necessary.

'Thank you. Really,' he whispers.

What is he thanking her for? Bianca will never know.

࿇ ࿇

He takes her by the hand without saying a word, imperiously, like someone with the right to do so. She says nothing. He leads her quietly up the stairs, careful in his movements so as not to bump into columns or the decorative objects on top of them. He opens the door to a room that is bound to be empty at this hour and then closes it behind them. Windows of moonlight illuminate the pavement. Someone has forgotten to draw the curtains, which is not new for this room. The shadows in the darkness are phosphorescent, luminous. The lightness of his first kiss melts her lips like a snowflake in a child's palm. The fabric roses in her hair get caught in a cuff. They are ready to come undone and surrender, one petal at a time. *Where should I put my nose? Here.* That is good. His mouth is good too. She imagines the secret obscurity inside, the flash of her tongue on his teeth; she can taste traces of tobacco and alcohol – an aroma light enough to be pleasing. *Do I taste good?* She thinks back to when she was little and how she would bite flower petals to see whether they tasted the same way they smelled. They all tasted like green. *I'd like to taste like a flower. It would be logical.*

Should I stop and defend myself? Should I? I still can. I should shield myself with armour. Armour – what a metallic-sounding word. She imagines a flimsy sword. She pictures herself brandishing a flower for protection. From what? From a kiss? No, he isn't dangerous. *It* isn't dangerous. It isn't. When one kisses one ceases to think. And that's all.

But this isn't love. This is something that resembles it, a copy, a surrogate. Love, the real thing, has to be something else. It *is* something else, something impossible; it belongs to that other man, the man that belongs to another woman, the master of the house, unattainable. *That which we cannot have is perfect, intact and incorrupt.* For now, she will take what comes her way, what she is offered, because this is youth, it is frightening, and it makes her feel good. Because: yes.

What follows is not what she expected or even wanted. She wants to say no at that point, to leave, deny everything, and return to the coy games, glances, or even just to the kissing. By the time this occurs to her, it is too late.

No, this isn't love, this rubbing of fabric against fabric, this warm and rugged fumbling. Fingers, fingers everywhere. Hands touching places where no stranger's hand has ever been. A strained gasp. To want and not to want. Here, this, where, what, why. And then the pain: piercing, tearing, leaving her breathless, unceasing, insistent, like pain without compassion, a rasping of flesh inside flesh. *No, not like that, no.* But words are useless. Nothing changes.

Her other self, silent and composed, watches from afar. Her eyes are pools of pity. *Why pity? What if this is actually what it is like? What if it is supposed to be like this?* She doesn't know any more.

She continues to listen to the agony stampeding inside her, nailing her to the wall, snatching from her very throat a sound that doesn't belong to her. It isn't her voice; it is neither laughter nor lament. It is a horrible sound, the sound of a wild beast suffering, nothing more. *How long will it go on for? Will it ever stop?*

And later, when it is finally over and the folds of her dress cover her wound, the question lingers: is this love?

Of course not. It is what it is.

He rests a hand on her cheek almost out of pity. She would feel anger for that if only anger could make its way forward through the thick confusion. And then he leaves, shutting the door behind him soundlessly. She is alone in the semi-darkness, somewhere between the doll's house and the window's luminous rectangle. She slides down the wall to the floor and slumps over like a wilted flower. And then she cries.

※ ※

Everyone has left. The house sleeps a satisfied sleep charged with success. But here and there is work to be done. The musicians drink mulled wine outside the kitchen. Bianca can smell its sharp wintry scent from the dark hallway.

'It's June but it doesn't feel like it,' one of them says. 'We shouldn't have played outdoors. My violin has rheumatism and so does my shoulder.'

'True, but in rich people's houses it is always summer,' comments another musician.

'Only us poor folk know about seasons.'

A female voice speaks, low and rugged, from inside the kitchen. 'You really think of what you do as work?'

'It depends on one's point of view,' says the first violinist in a tired tone. 'May we have some more wine? And a warm pie, one of the leftover ones? Or have you eaten them all up? You cook for an army at these parties. It's as if they never ate. Thank you, you're a good woman, and an excellent chef. Don't you, perchance, desire a husband who can play?'

'I have one already, but I am the one who plays the instrument, when needs be.'

Laughter and then silence.

Bianca slips into the darkness. She would like some mulled wine. Or maybe not. No more wine. Never again. She opens the French window and walks down the steps. At this hour, the forest has not yet made up its mind about what it will become. It has the purity of a print scored with ferocious black shadows. Not even the forest can promise or guarantee peace. Is there peace on this earth?

No.

Bianca turns around, thrown by a presence behind her. It is Nanny. She is evidently very worked up as she has forgotten to put her robe over her flannel nightgown. Nanny, who always feels cold, now stands barefoot. Bianca notes all the details, including the two fleshy shells that poke out of her braided hair: Nanny has big ears. Bonnets, however silly they seem, serve their miserable purpose.

Nanny claws at Bianca's arm and shakes her.

'Have you seen her?'

She cannot imagine which of the three girls is missing.

'Francesca has disappeared,' Nanny adds coarsely. 'I heard a noise; I got up and went to look in their bedroom . . . She's nowhere to be found.'

෨ ෨

They find her body in the brook. She has been carried downstream by the current for more than two miles. Unable to drag her any further, the water has left her there, like a broken doll, her head bumping against the wooden dyke, her nightgown sticking to her skin. Her eyes are open, her tiny face serene. It is not yet dawn.

❧ ❧

Later, Giulietta tries to explain.

'We went down to the brook together yesterday afternoon. Alone. There was so much confusion and no one was looking after us.'

Everyone glances at Nanny but it isn't her fault. They recruited her in the kitchen and she couldn't be in two places at once.

'She wanted to learn how to swim like me so that she could show everyone and prove that she was a big girl. She had almost learned. She almost didn't sink under the water any more.'

And then? The questioning continues as if adding more details will help clarify, correct and soften.

'And then we got tired. Matilde didn't want to walk any more and I had to carry her. She even fell asleep. We changed our clothes. Nanny came and fed us dinner early and then we went down to greet the guests.'

The girls wore identical mauve dresses tied at the waist with violet ribbons. They left their hair down, which was unusual for them, and wore headbands. Francesca's band kept slipping down onto her face like a pirate's bandana. Her hair was very fine and had recently been washed by the fresh water of the brook.

'Mamma let us have one dessert each. I chose the pastry with the raspberries and she chose a *petit four* with a pistachio on top. She got her whole face messy with cream but no one scolded her.'

Children get lost in the details. Adults are indulgent when they have something else on their minds. *Oh, Franceschina, what a messy girl you are! You look like a clown. You're so funny. Isn't that right? Isn't she funny? Our little star. Now up you go. It's bedtime, girls.*

'And then Nanny came down to get us,' she continues.

Bianca remembers how Nanny came out of the shadows in her ugly, dark silk dress, not at all fit for a party.

'And she brought us to bed. I fell asleep right away. I was so tired. Matilde, too.'

There is a pause. She looks at their tense faces, searching desperately for approval.

'Then the dark man came in. It must have been him.'

If only there had been a dark man. If only one of the statues had awoken and descended from its pedestal to vindicate some ancient wrongdoing. If only there had been a faceless monster that could be held responsible for all of this.

Bianca has no difficulty imagining what happened. The little girl was restless and couldn't fall asleep because of the sounds from the party: the music, the chatter, the laughter. She got up and went to the playroom window, the one protected by bars – a prudent yet useless measure – and sat on her knees and watched. She looked down on the great lawn from above; a splotch of darkness delineated by stains of light. There was beautiful Mamma, and Miss Bianca in green (a play on words like the ones she always enjoyed). There was Papa, at the centre of the crowd. Everyone looked as tall and dark as he did, as they laughed, drank and talked. *Sometimes, my papa makes other people laugh,* she must have thought. *If I learn to swim, he will be happy. Miss Bianca will be happy too. Everyone will be happy because it's something only big boys do. I could go and practise and stay up all night trying. No one will see me. I will learn*

*how and then tomorrow I will show everyone. I will say: I have a
surprise for you. Come, come and watch me, and everyone will
follow me like the children of the Pied Piper, and then I'll jump
in and everyone will tell me how good I am, and that I was brave
to learn all by myself. I can do it. The others are sleeping but I'm
not scared. It's a bit dark but I'm not scared. The moon is bright
enough for me.*

❧ ❧

It rains for a full two days. It is as if the sky is crying. If the sun
dared come out, someone would extinguish it or shut it down,
such is the sentiment in the air.

On the afternoon of the second day, Bianca finds herself in
the nursery playroom without realizing how she has got there.
It is empty. Donna Julie and Donna Clara don't want to leave
the children. Bianca, though, doesn't think that being with two
crying women will be good for them. If adults cry, there are no
more rules; the world is upside down. Innocence is gone from
the nursery. No one feels safe anywhere. Nothing is sacred;
nothing can remain untouched, not even childhood. Bianca
straightens an overturned chair. She closes the doll's house by
shutting one of its facades onto the bewildered faces of its
inhabitants. She goes over to the window with bars on it. There
are fingerprints on the glass, a small hand, a palm print and five
little fingers, open wide. There is no need to measure it to know
that it is Franceschina's. She is the one who, on the night of
the big storm, found the courage to look out at the world. Her
sisters covered their ears with their hands, trying to shut out
the sounds of thunder. Bianca tried to calm them down.

'It's just angels moving furniture. Even they get tired of the
sky and like to change things around sometimes.'

Francesca was the only one who listened to her.

'What is their furniture like? Is it made of clouds? And if it is made of clouds, why do they make so much noise?'

She pushed the chair forward to test its own sound, until it bumped into an uneven brick and tipped over.

Farewell, Franceschina. You died young. You didn't have time to learn much. If you ever feel like moving a bedside table or chair, we will listen for the soft, distant thunder, not the frightening kind, and know that it is you.

For a moment Bianca thinks of calling in the child's mother and grandmother to show them that last trace of her, but then decides against it. There are already so many signs to erase: her doll, Teresa, with her dishevelled head of hair; her clothes in the wardrobe; her little shoes under the bed. Traces of her that need to disappear. They lead nowhere; there is no mystery to solve. They only speak loudly and boldly of the little girl's absence.

Bianca returns to her senses. As if awakening from a difficult sleep, she feels a moment of confusion. She senses that something is not right. There is something else, she remembers, and she feels embarrassed. She feels like a monster. That death, ugly and unjust to the umpteenth degree, is, in that instant, merely a painful distraction. It is like a terrible headache, the kind that makes her eyes hurt, that forces her to press her index fingers into her lids in order to feel more pain, hoping that one grief will cancel out the other.

By thinking about Franceschina, she does not think of herself. And, of course, there *is* no comparison. Franceschina is gone. There will never be another Franceschina. She, on the other hand, is alive. Thank God. Alive. Everything is still possible – forgetting and forgiving. Although these both seem so remote, she thinks of them as old accomplices that support and encourage one another. *Certain wounds heal*, she thinks.

And some do not. Downstairs is a woman with a wound that will never heal.

❧ ❧

Guilt hits her again like a backhanded slap, a kick in the stomach, a hand clenched around a heart. These feelings come to her cruelly and regularly. When it seems as though her cheek has lost its sting, her eye burns in its socket. When the depth of the punch has tapered off, her stomach is seized by anxiety. Although no one has ever accused her, she cannot forget that single playful swim that took place almost a year ago. Once she thinks she sees a slight look of disapproval in Pia's eyes. Although perhaps it is just fatigue. The meeting of two exhausted beings. Her eyes burn constantly. As soon as she finishes crying she is ready to start up again, to spill tears that can never wash away the grief, tears that fall like alcohol onto an open wound; that burn like fire in her flesh.

❧ ❧

'What does the death of a child really mean? When they're little, they're all the same: all children are promises. Whether the promises will be maintained, no one can know for certain. And how many did Donna Julie lose already? Two? Three? That didn't prevent her from bringing more life into this world. Isn't this a woman's trade? Everyone, ultimately, is capable of being a mother. So come now, all of us, let us remember that life awaits us.'

Fortunately, very few people actually hear Bernocchi's grim funeral oration. He mumbles it in a low voice from a pew at the back of the church. A few do hear, though, and no one wants to add anything.

Francesca was unique, as we all are. She had the right to

become her own person, as we all do. Bianca casts a glance at Bernocchi, who looks as empty as the void she feels inside. She then goes back to staring at the backs of the people in the front row, their shoulders hunched over, locked in their grief. Visitors have come from the city in a melancholic procession similar to the one of two nights earlier, wearing crêpe instead of muslin, black instead of white and pink. They come with puffy eyes, burning eyelids, and irritated skin due both to their suffering and to the cruel light of morning. But they will leave their grief there, with the flowers, the too-many flowers, all of them white and destined to wither under the too-brilliant sun. Once the guests return to their homes, they will feel discomfort mixed with relief; they will throw themselves with new vigour into everyday tasks because Death has passed them by. Father, mother and grandmother speak to no one after the ceremony. They walk slowly to the cemetery behind the coffin, which has been hoisted onto the shoulders of four peasant men but which is so small that one of them alone could carry it under his arm. Don Dionisio shields the family and shakes his head.

'I beg of you, please. The family wishes to be alone.'

Some guests climb back into their carriages immediately, a touch disappointed by the lack of show. Others linger in the church piazza, engaging in brief circumstantial conversations – they can't even remember which one Franceschina was. As Bernocchi has said, she was only a little girl.

'Shall we go to the tavern to drink something and refresh ourselves?' Signor Bignamini proposes.

Attilio is pleased to receive so many clients at such an odd hour. He hasn't even opened, but he quickly pulls the chairs down, pours some wine, and slices up some bread.

Bianca stands to the side with Innes and Minna. Pia whispers something into the elderly priest's ear. He nods and they hug farewell. He goes then to the cemetery while she stays behind.

'He says we should pray for acceptance,' she says. 'That the Lord sometimes does things that we can't understand. Things that not even he understands.'

The four of them quietly make their way back towards the villa. What is there left to say? Afterwards, the pall-bearers are given a glass of wine in the kitchen. They recount the devastating story of the cemetery. The tomb, which already houses the children Bernocchi spoke of that Donna Julie has lost – Battista, Andreina, and Vittorio: which makes three, not two as Bernocchi had suggested – had been opened to make room for the small coffin. Donna Clara gasping with tears and Donna Julie and Don Titta's frightening silence. The good-hearted maids cry when they hear this. The image of the little one, her habits and her fixations, is all too clear in their minds.

'She loved my almond pudding so much,' sighs the cook. 'She could have lived off it. She ate barely anything else, poor babe.'

'Do you remember when she didn't want us to break the chicken's neck? Remember how she tied a bow around it and looked after it as if it were a puppy?'

'And what about when she asked me if I would make a dress for her dolly that was identical to hers?'

Children's fancies are different, and yet all the same. Bianca walks out then and sits on the steps, her elbows on her knees, and looks at the garden and its unresponsive beauty. A small cloud hovers alone above the sycamore tree.

'What are we going to do?' she asks Innes, who in the meantime has sat down next to her.

'I don't know. We will keep on, I suppose. He has his novel, and thank goodness for that. A big world to fill his mind. She will become all the more apprehensive, poor thing. And Donna Clara . . . well, she will reclaim her post at the rudder. It will come easily to her. It's a big estate – there is so much to watch over and debts to oversee. She will put on her accounting gloves and her owl eyeglasses. That will be her distraction.'

Bianca wishes she could smile. She tries to but she feels as though her lips would crack. So she stops.

'And what about you?' she asks.

'Let's talk about you. Are you all right?' he says, changing the subject. Bianca feels him staring at her. She knows his gaze well. Without waiting for an answer, he continues. 'Sometimes the best way to confront grief is to stand still and wait for it to subside. To agitate oneself, to flee, is not worth it; it doesn't get rid of grief. It is better to give oneself time. Often, time can cure a wound that reason can't bring back to health. Seneca said that, not me,' he concludes and then looks straight ahead.

What if it really was that way? What if we could go back to our previous lives, to our habits, and to the natural rhythm of things, and let the tears slowly dry? In that very moment, Bianca wants only for nothing else to change. She wants her world to freeze, to be held still under a sheet of glass, like her leaves and flowers. The two of them look at each other. Perhaps he understands. Maybe not. He must be thinking back to her first question.

'I think that it would be a bad idea if I left now. But that doesn't necessarily mean that it is a bad idea in itself.'

Ah, here we go. Bianca knew it.

'You will be the first to know my decision, if this is indeed the case,' he concludes. 'We are fortunate: we can leave when we like, if we want to. This isn't our life. Turning our backs on all of this will be painful. But possible.'

He takes her hand and squeezes it. She does not pull away. She loves this tall, long-limbed man with his tumultuous thoughts and distracted gaze. She loves him and she trusts him more than any other man in this world.

Zeno, her adorable little brother with eyes as bright as the buttons on his uniform, left the night of the party, avoiding the tragedy. Nittis, with eyes like spilled ink, promising and elusive, left with him. Perhaps soldiers are all like that: they grab what they can find, take it with them, and run away. They are forgivable thieves, aware that sooner or later a bullet could catch them. We have to let them go. Innes, too, is a soldier, only he is in a dress shirt. He won't flee though; he is heading towards something that he desires, that still does not exist but which is possible. That is the difference. And Don Titta, so carefully drawn to his own standards, can go nowhere.

Bianca recalls a fragment of a conversation that took place one spring afternoon in the living room when all the windows were open.

'A writer or a poet possesses words, and for this reason he also possesses the things his words define,' Tommaso said, pressing the fingertips of his hands together in concentration.

'Correct,' Don Titta replied. 'If to possess is to know, then we who work with words understand and possess the world, or at least we make this ambition our daily goal. But to give things a name, my friend, makes us neither wise nor happy. If anything, it only makes us more aware.'

'You don't really think that we are put on this earth to be happy?' Tommaso asked almost scornfully.

'Every so often,' Don Titta replied, staring at his children as they ran on the gravel path. 'Every so often I like to deceive myself that it is so.'

'But if your happiness depends on others,' Tommaso countered, following his gaze, 'then you have little chance of preserving it.'

'What are you suggesting? That's it's sufficient for a stylite on top of a column to be happy? Or a monk in his hermitage? I want to be happy in the world,' Don Titta said.

'I, on the other hand, am content with the small world that is my study,' Tommaso replied.

'And here,' concluded Don Titta, 'our thoughts diverge. Believe me, we are nothing without love. And I speak of pure love, not the love that asks or deceives, but the love that gives and commits. We end up depending on it, it's true. And it depends on us. It creates connections. And connections are complications. But I want to be complicated, and of this world.'

He then stood up, opened the French window, and called out to Giulietta, who stopped what she was doing and ran into her father's arms.

In 'this world' Don Titta is the master of words, but in love he isn't any more a master of himself. He cannot go anywhere. Maybe he would like to, but his world is calling him, holding him back – it needs him. And now that world is inhabited by one small shadow more.

❧ ❧

Bianca leafs through her folders, prepares her charcoals, ties on her apron, and sits down at the table inside the greenhouse. Nobody has repaired the damage to the glass yet and therefore it is still miraculously cool with currents of fresh air. But what is the point of portraying the lightness of the honeysuckle now? There are other things out there: the stain of lichens on the stone cheek of a *putto*; the sick symmetry of mushrooms that crawl like insects on a severed trunk; the vibrations of a spider's web, magnified and yet endangered by droplets of rain. A dirty, fragile, poisonous kind of grace. She wished that nothing would change; instead everything has been transformed.

Maybe it is her perspective, but suddenly she sees other, darker things where before there was only the pure, mild grace of a garden, cultivated with love. Beauty does nothing but take risks.

❧ ❧

It is strange how time ungoverned dilates and expands indifferently, stretching out and emptying the hours. Whereas before it was so important to fill time with rituals and rhythms that are just and necessary, now nothing matters. There is no work, there are no errands to run. They wait.

It is too early for people to force themselves to forget; the grief is so fresh that one can only relive it, amazed by its everlasting energy. Days and weeks go by. Not one event can disturb the surface of this void. What matters lies beneath and within, and it grows incessantly.

❧ ❧

Then, one evening, something happens.

There is the sound of confusion at the front door but no one pays it any attention. Everyone has taken a seat: one here, one there. It is an empty shell of an evening, just like the others, but Donna Clara has insisted and so they arrange themselves as directed. Only Donna Julie is missing, rightly excused from all obligations and formalities. Bianca looks towards the doorway. She thinks she is the only one who sees Ruggiero peek in, but no. Innes jumps to his feet and approaches the butler, who delivers a message to him in a whisper.

'We have visitors,' Innes announces. He looks at Don Titta, who raises his head sluggishly, as if it is unbearably heavy, and then lowers it again in silence. 'We need to get ready.'

Tommaso rises, walks towards the closed window, and

gently moves the curtain back. Donna Clara, hostile, watches him, as if it is his fault.

'Visitors? We were very clear when we stated—'

'I'm afraid these men won't listen to your requests,' Tommaso says, glancing back at the others. He is strangely vigilant, almost excited. He stands tall, with his hands in his pockets. The door to the sitting room opens.

'Lieutenant Colonel Steiner, of the Royal Imperial Army,' Ruggiero announces, stepping aside to present a blond, fairly young official with blue eyes and a neat appearance.

The master of the house rises slowly. Instead of walking towards the visitor, he turns to Tommaso, who stands looking out the window still, his back to the scene.

'May I help you?' Donna Clara spits from her place on the sofa, looking the official up and down.

'Good evening,' he says. His accent is heavy. He articulates every word. It takes a long time to put together a full sentence. 'In the name of his Majesty . . . information . . . search . . . documents . . .'

Bianca hears the man's speech emerge fragmented, with little meaning. She cannot tell if she is distracted or if the Colonel's Italian is truly pitiful. She looks at Innes and then at Tommaso: they both appear calm. Don Titta keeps his back turned, as if none of this concerns him. The moment feels long and drawn out, suspended in the air. Nothing happens. And then two soldiers appear behind the official, awaiting their instructions. From the clinking noise in the foyer, it is clear that there are others, too. They will spread out through the house, open drawers, throw books and flip over tables. It happened at the Maffei home, at the Confalonieris', the Galleranis', and even at Bernocchi's country house. It is a vicious game of dominos:

search, discover, and condemn. It is both expected and unavoidable. Bianca feels herself grow cold. The slow chill wraps around her, starting at her legs and fixing her to the sofa.

And then, just before the soldiers start to move in, a figure dressed all in white and ignited by pure willpower appears among the soldiers. It is Donna Julie. She ignores the strangers and walks straight past them, a tiny creature amid robust, meaty men.

'Titta,' she says. 'The children need you.'

It is as if he doesn't hear her.

'Titta,' she repeats, slightly louder this time. He finally turns and slowly walks towards his wife, puts an arm around her shoulder, and leads her away. The official stares at the couple, speechless. Who do they think they are, ignoring him like that?

'Perhaps I wasn't clear enough,' he says, then repeats his message. This time any hint of kindness has vanished from his voice. It is an error. It is Donna Clara's turn now to speak.

'This family,' says the old woman as she struggles to get up from her seat, clutching the armrest with both hands, 'has recently been struck with a loss. Look at us.' And with her hand she makes a wide gesture across the living room: dark clothing and despair. The official has a brief doubt: if this is a farce, it is well played. But what if it isn't? 'How could you have the gall to come here at a time like this?' Donna Clara continues. 'I will be sure to let the governor know. The Milanese nobility still counts for something in this tortured, upside-down world that doesn't even honour death. Leave us in peace. Leave, now. Immediately. Go.'

Lieutenant Colonel Steiner doesn't know how to respond. His informers are trusted sources; the spying took place weeks ago and in the meantime they have undergone all the necessary checks in order to avoid diplomatic incidents, in case the accusations turn out to be unfounded. Although they clearly aren't unfounded. And so Steiner has decided to act. Perhaps, if Donna Clara cried and wrung her hands, he wouldn't have pity on them. But their stone-like faces, the heavy dignity of grief that has brought the household to a standstill, their eyes – including those of the domestic help, who stare straight back at him instead of looking down in fear – cracks his self-confidence and zeal.

'I didn't know,' he says finally. 'I apologize.'

Much later, troubled by the thought of having made a mistake and thereby wasting an opportunity, he wonders whether it has all been staged. These Italians, he thinks, with their tendency to dramatize everything, you can never fully trust them. But he only needs to leaf through the newspapers to learn it has all been true and that he has behaved as a wretched slave of duty. But justice will take its course. How much time will he allow them to grieve? Not long. He needs to pound down his iron fist on these discontented traitors. They have everything and they have risked it all. It is too bad for them. They don't know what they are about to lose. If only they stayed in their living rooms and protected their young, there would be less trouble for everyone.

Meanwhile, at the house, the message has been received, loud and clear. The inevitable has arrived. Things will have to change, and not in the definitive and brilliant manner that they have worked towards in the darkness. Governments aren't toppling and declarations won't be made. No, this is not the time for a compromise. This is the time to perfect the art of the getaway. Only in this manner can order be restored, at least temporarily, at least for those who can get away. How much time do they have? No more than a week.

Many things happen in that week.

❧ ❧

'Young Tommaso left like a thief in the night.'

'He must have got scared.'

'He must have gone home to his mamma.'

'But they don't even talk to each other! He told me as much when he brought me his shirts. Rich people are strange, I tell you. I think that boy cared more for this family than for his own mother.'

'Well, why did he go back to his family in the end, then?'

'You know how it is: families unite in times of difficulty.'

'Oh, don't be a know-it-all. Tommaso was just a coward. In this house, rebels sip tea in the living room. In Tommaso Reda's house, they kiss the Austrian flag, so soldiers don't go there at night to knock things about and make a mess.'

'You're right. And guess who would have to clean up the mess?'

Voices bounce off one another, intersecting, insinuating, supposing, sentencing. The farmer speaks elegantly, the cook always knows the details, and the others, the extras, become animated only when no one else is looking at them. There is an indistinct hubbub of gestures and sounds. Bianca tries to soothe her headache by staying in bed, but in order not to hear them all she would have to close the window, and the fresh morning air feels good.

So, he has left. At night, like a thief. In this, the help's verdict is painfully correct. He has taken what he wanted. Thief. Bianca buries her head in her pillow and cries tears that the fabric quickly absorbs. Thoughts run through her like clouds rushing past, high in the sky. *I should have known. I could have held back. I should have trusted myself. What a monster. I hate him, I liked him, I wanted him, I didn't want him . . . well, not like that, or maybe . . . yes, it was my fault, his fault, mine, his, mine, mine, his. Mine.* She is certain of only one thing: no one can ever find out.

❧ ❧

There hasn't been a day in my life when I haven't expected this kind of grief.

On one of those days, which pass like all the others, when he neither eats nor sleeps, Don Titta writes three short pages. It is Innes, Bianca later discovers, who takes the ink-stained papers out of his master's hand. He is the first to read them. He is the one who waves them gently in the air and says, 'Titta, we must publish this.'

Don Titta doesn't want to, but he is too spent to resist, and in any case, he no longer cares about anything.

'I know you wrote this for yourself, Titta, to flush out your soul, but this is precisely what the people need. Clean words, clear words, words that show the world who you really are.'

'I am nothing,' Don Titta replies, resting his forehead against the windowpane. 'I am nothing, and I care about nothing.'

'You are a grieving father who is not afraid to show his suffering. That's all.'

'They will think that I'm taking advantage of the situation.'

'So it isn't true that you don't care. And anyway, they will think the same thing that they think about your poetry: that it is good for the heart because it says what no one can put into words. This is why you are here, you poets and writers. To find the right words, the words that everyone would like to be voiced and that no one else can. I am going to see Marchionni. I'm sure he will agree.'

And Marchionni, who is a publisher as well as a loving father of three small children and an experienced businessman, understands very well. Soon the city newspaper stands and bookshops are inundated with the inexpensive light blue pamphlet. Actually, it cannot even be described as a pamphlet, more of a broadside. No one will get rich from it, but it certainly helps Don Titta's fame. The title, *On the Death of My Child, My Daughter*, repulses and attracts at the same time. People stand in queues to get it; there are discussions in the cafes; they print a second run. It is so popular that it arouses the suspicion of the imperial authorities. They are convinced that it is actually a coded message, a subversive leaflet cunningly edited by one of the most dangerous and deceitful conspirators, known for his connection to the inglorious cause for independence; and who has, up until now, escaped from the claws of investigation. It is said that the police even use decoders to read between the lines for something that is not there. Instead, that miniature diary of enormous loss leaves them teary-eyed and with a lump in their throats.

Perhaps Innes is right: everything in this family has ended. Only art still counts for something. And if the vocation of a writer is to extract art from life, then Don Titta does what he can with what he has. Maybe there will never be a novel published now. Maybe the poet's lucky star has burned out just as he is preparing to become a great writer. But these pages exist. These pages are memorable because they are courageous and alive, because they pulsate with a suffering that everyone can recognize – those who have known it and those who fear it. Sorrow makes people feel. This unnameable beast is always lying in wait, far away and yet nearby, too. It never leaves anyone in peace. Don Titta's writing also captures something else, something that Donna Julie supports and that an anonymous critic of *Rivista delle lettere* notices: a new way of being a parent, a way that erases the mechanical indifference of continuity of the species in favour of choice. *Everything that we choose*, the anonymous critic writes in conclusion, *is moral responsibility first and social responsibility second.*

֍ ֍

What about the things that we don't choose? What about the things that are imposed on us through force? Bianca broods over this as if it is an illness, as if she has caught some kind of repulsive infection by chance or by mistake, because she hasn't known how to defend herself, or because she is weak. What would Tommaso say about these things? Nothing. His silence is heavy. And he passes on to Bianca the nauseating feeling of an unasked-for presence. The idea of him taking responsibility would make her laugh if she had the desire and strength to do so. She would gladly choke that critic. He thinks he knows everything, but he will never have to carry a child in his womb, whether he wants one or not. He is only good for creating one and then leaving, paying off his lover with a satchel of coins and ignoring the child's existence. He might be asked to pay for its education in some squalid, provincial boarding school. He might legitimatize the child or disown it. He might even love it, if he so desires, if he is inspired to, if the fashion of the times dictate it. He will do what the nobles and the rich always do: whatever he pleases. But some people cannot do as they please and must only do what they can.

Nothing can go back to the way it was. This new, unknown and unwanted person makes its way forward, leaving only signs. Bianca has a sour flavour in her mouth; deathly exhaustion catches her by surprise; gone is her desire to do anything; she sleeps at all hours of the day; and her breasts swell painfully. These are the symptoms of the thing she fears. Bianca is sharp enough to recognize them. She will have to do everything on her own. But what can she do?

I didn't know any better, the ghost, Pia's mother, had said. That crazy woman had been humiliated by life itself. It all comes back to Bianca now. For the first time, instead of anger, she feels pity for the woman, which in turn becomes pity for herself. *It was easy to think I knew everything. I felt like I was on top of the world. And then the bubble burst. It wasn't the world; it was merely a soapy illusion full of beautiful, false colours.* She has fallen. Bianca is a fallen woman. Suddenly the phrase takes on an entirely new meaning, so literal she can see it. It is easy to stay fallen, to cake yourself with mud and hope that no one will recognize you, especially if nobody holds out their hand to help you get back up on your feet. Bianca remembers herself on the night of the party, descending the staircase and being greeted by Zeno and Paolo. It is all too vivid, almost false in its gaiety. A couple of weeks earlier, which now feels like a century ago, she didn't need their hands, she knew how to walk on her own. Bianca doesn't want anyone to know about what has happened, but now everyone will.

If only she could make a switch and exchange the life of this child, whom no one has asked for, with the life of Franceschina, who was called forth from the honest love of matrimony, who had a place, who knew how to be loved. But these kinds of bargains don't exist. They aren't conceivable. There's no logic in the drawing of one's destiny, just scribbles in the margins, ink spilling from a quill, clumsily, incompetently, by mistake or by chance. Then the mark left on the paper is clear, while the quill returns to a lake of blackness.

As if Bianca's own story – the story of her flesh, the narrative that weighs under her skin and in her heart like a stone – isn't enough, there is that other story, the one that has already been played out. It only adds to her grief. Of all the places she could go, the church seems to be the most suitable refuge: no one is ever there. It will be silent. It is there that Bianca learns that she needs silence to speak to the departed, and that they need it too, to be able to speak to the void inside her. All her beloved and departed come to her now. No one is missing: her mother, with her heavy gaze of reproach; her father, his hand pressed against his heart as if to stifle the sorrow; Franceschina, her little feet running, in an echo of her brief race through the world. She hears Don Dionisio arriving, his breath raspy. He doesn't know. But he can keep a secret. What difference will another mistaken child make? In this world children are almost all the results of mistakes. Bianca is startled when the old man places a hand on her shoulder. He slips onto his knees beside her and starts to pray. She does the same, but without believing for a moment that somewhere, someone is listening.

What if the baby is Franceschina's ghost and she has returned to avenge herself or just to get a second chance at life? What if the baby is Bianca's punishment or a ransom? Maybe she needs to accept this second-hand being, raise her and let her destroy her life in order to reclaim her own. In so doing, might she settle the score? Bianca's grim fantasies allow for every possible hypothesis, with the cruellest one being the simplest. She needs to die and, in so doing, kill it. She needs to finish them both off at once, without making a show of it. Parsley concoctions, rusty irons, a pool of blood and it will all be over. Who will care? She no longer has a father who, like Don Titta, will cry at the absurdity of his own survival. Her brothers have their lives to live; she is merely a childhood memory to them, a gracious figurine frozen on that distant moor. And no one ever cries for long about the death of hired help. Bianca feels alone in the world and therefore is. She sees herself float away in a boat made for one, with a trunk full of colours, drifting away over pewter waters towards a steely sky. She watches herself from above; she feels pity; she cries. She is cold. Nothing can ever warm her now, now that shame moves inside her. Shame, and life too.

❧ ❧

She and Innes sit in a stagecoach, alone. They are taking a quick trip to the city to retrieve forgotten and indispensable things for Don Titta and Donna Julie; it is a way of getting away from the house's heavy, oppressive grief. Bianca feels these parents need to open the doors of their emotions and let them out, allow them to evaporate, but the voices of the children on the gravel are almost unbearable.

The carriage moves beyond the confines of the estate and the odd statue of seven nymphs dancing in a semicircle that has always made the guests and Bianca smile. But not now. The orderly fields of modulated greens speak of the sober beauty of hard work and good land. But there is no one there to listen to their words.

'I'm leaving,' Innes says suddenly.

'But . . .' Bianca mumbles. *What about those things you said? How will I manage without you?* These unspoken thoughts press at Bianca's lips but don't surface, held back by the remains of dignity.

'I'm going back to London. I have some friends there. A small family of exiles is building up around them. Apparently, they have this incredible tendency to love failures.' Innes smiles weakly. 'For me, the land here is starting to burn.' He speaks distantly. It is as though he can see himself from the outside and finds himself to be hopelessly lacking.

'What if I came with you?' Bianca says.

It just pops out, without thought. But it feels right. It is the only possible decision. Innes looks at her, somewhat worried.

'All of Nanny's darkest fears would come true,' he says with a smile.

'Yes, you're right,' says Bianca, returning the gesture weakly. She sighs wearily and continues. 'I'm expecting a child.'

She cannot read Innes's expression in the half-light, but she can imagine it: lips pursed together, frowning. The questions, the conjectures. She is about to offer an explanation, but is defeated by her humiliation. This is the time for honesty. She waits. He is quiet. The sound of the horses' hooves grows excessively loud and then distant, as if she is underwater. She will have to say something, explain things, explain herself. Answer questions. Shame herself. But she is better off holding her breath. His voice brings her back to the surface.

'Then we shall get married.'

Bianca struggles. She no longer knows where she is. She wants to go under again. She tries to but cannot. It is as if her body is telling her to stay afloat, life grasping life.

'Do not fear,' Innes continues. 'I shall only ask you to be my friend. And I will be your friend. It will be our pact. You will like London. I realize that you know it a little, but the London I am thinking of is a completely different city. We'll have to settle down, grow accustomed to the fog, and forget the sun and this blessed land. And we'll have to work. Seriously, I fear that we've been spoiled here. It won't be easy in the beginning. But we'll make it. We know how to do things and there are two of us. And soon there will be three.' He takes her hand, opens it, and gives her palm a quick, dry kiss, after which he clasps it gently and places it back on her lap. 'And perhaps, over time, there might be more.'

Bianca does not dare look at him. She allows herself to be jostled by the rhythm of the coach. That small kiss burns her skin. She would like to rub it out but she cannot. She doesn't want him to misunderstand. She doesn't know if it is burning from torment or because it feels confusingly joyful. Is it the poor elation of relief or is it something else? Enough questions. Whatever the answer, at this point it doesn't matter.

※ ※

When it comes time to pack their cases, Bianca agonizes. She feels caught between being gone and having not yet arrived. She doesn't know what to do with her time. Her gloves don't match and her things are in disorder. She thinks about how messy her hair will be during the journey. This is not a holiday; she should feel contrite and oppressed. But amid the feelings of guilt, fear and melancholia, she also feels the flutter of a bird taking flight. Somewhere inside; not in her heart, though. Her heart is unfeeling, petrified, or perhaps just absent. It has been crushed and has disappeared into her veins through a flow of blood.

She thinks back to the sycamore tree she saw with her father in Padua. She pictures the great tree clearly – the black fissure at its centre, and yet the branches laden with leaves that were shady, fresh, alive. In the same way, she feels alive and yet heartless. But it is her head that is fogged up with worry. This is what guides her through her final hours as she collects her things. She takes the essentials, the items that make us who we are, or who we'd like to think we are. Things she cannot leave behind: a box of coloured pencils, her brushes, a stack of sketches. She takes her precious keepsakes: her mother's earrings, her letters, miniatures, a diary. She takes the money, hard earned and in satchels, so that the wheels of their coach will slide across tracks of gold. She doesn't take the gifts: the white stone egg, the shawl, the pomegranate, the box of seeds. She leaves them on her vacant desk to be dispersed among people to whom they mean nothing.

❧ ❧

'I'm coming with you,' Pia says calmly.

Bianca notices a bundle at the girl's feet: a raggedy, red blanket that likely contains her few things.

'But Pia, you have a home here. A family,' Bianca says.

'He . . .' She bites her lip in silence. 'He is sick, he is going to die soon, he told me. And then I will have no one. The others, they don't need me. But you do. And when the baby is born . . .'

The baby. Pia knows. Without realizing it, Bianca glances down at her stomach. It is the same as it has always been, the fabric of her dress covers it and holds it in. So how did Pia find out? Maybe everyone knows. It is better not to ask. It is better to believe that the young girl who looks at her so patiently and assuredly from top to bottom possesses the intimate gaze of a Cassandra. The baby. Bianca can no longer hold her stare. She buries her head in her hands and hates herself because she cannot think of anything else to do. *How much do I detest him?*

As if reading her mind, Pia takes a step forward and places her hand on Bianca's arm. 'The child will need to be loved. He isn't the one to blame. Children should never carry the blame.'

You, of all people, know this, Bianca thinks. She is overcome by a wave of tenderness that allows her to forget herself. *You, of all people.* Bianca rests her hand on Pia's arm. It is all set.

❧ ❧

The last trunk is shut. She glances around the room at its orderly emptiness. There is the sound of rapid footsteps on the gravel. The window is half open. It is very early. There are voices: subdued but crystal clear.

'Take it. It's the least I can do.'

'About time.'

'Oh, come now, don't judge me. I can do that on my own. I cannot change my life; I've never been capable of it. Allow me at least to contribute to changing the life of another.'

'Your quasi-divine omnipotence is too much.'

'Do I appear arrogant? I apologize. For once, I assure you, it isn't arrogance that moves me to act this way. Enough, stop being difficult, you cannot afford to. You know very well that you will need it, all of you. Don't worry. It's nothing personal. You won't have to think of my august profile each time you spend some of it. And when you settle down, send me your address.'

'What if I direct her towards an improper profession and use your money for myself? For gambling or opiates or any other form of degradation available to us?'

'Come now! I know and trust you, Innes. In any case, this money is also for the cause. I cannot say it is "our" cause, for I give it no honour. I deny it every day with what I am and my inability to act. But this way, from afar, in silence . . . I can make a contribution.'

'So, basically, I have to leave with a burden – a debt to you. That's not light luggage, you know.' Innes's voice is sarcastic but his tone is serious.

'Not even all my money can make good what I am contracting with you today.'

'So handle your fortune with caution, because we will need it. Goodbye . . . and thank you.'

She hears footsteps on the stairs. Outside there is silence. And then she hears Young Count Bernocchi walk back down the gravel path, slowly and heavily. Not young any more.

※ ※

It is a torment to say goodbye. Things go unsaid, the grief is challenging, blessings and smiles and questions are uttered and hinted at. Don Titta embraces Innes tightly and gasps with emotion. Donna Clara's eyes are glassy and almost frightening. Nanny, with tears in her own eyes, whispers, 'In the end you managed to take him from me.' Minna stands shyly behind everyone. She holds a silk kerchief with a handful of coins in it under her apron. The others are awkwardly absent. They won't have understood. What will they choose to believe? Bianca no longer cares.

Soon after they have said their goodbyes and just before departing she turns to Innes, won over by a crumb of her old curiosity, which lifts her spirits.

'What did Bernocchi want from you?'

'He wanted to commend me his soul. Not his own, of course. And anyway, since I am no priest, I suggested that he look elsewhere.'

'And what about the money? He did offer you money, didn't he?'

'Bianca, you are incorrigible. Let's say that it was his modest contribution towards the creation of a better world. It was just a start. The rest of it will come a little at a time, once we settle down. No, he hasn't converted to our cause; he likes his world the way it is. It was an act of contrition, late but well timed. I doubt that he could ever consciously be generous: he would find it too banal. He feels only slight regret.'

Bianca stares at him without understanding.

315

'Enough with the secrets,' Innes says clearly. 'The money is for Pia.'

A spark flares in Bianca's mind. Is it possible? Is young Pia pregnant, too? That's why Pia had understood. If only she had been more vigilant, wiser, more careful. Bianca's expression must reveal her thoughts, because Innes is staring at her, perplexed. He shakes his head.

'No, Bianca. No, no. What on earth did you think? Pia is Bernocchi's daughter.'

So she is *his* daughter. The truth hangs like an empty nest in the bare branches of a tree in winter. It has been there all along, well hidden, but there. *You didn't see it*, she thinks. *That possibility didn't even exist to you.* But when finally it comes forth in its naked simplicity, she recognizes it, nods, and accepts it. It is no less true because she hasn't thought of it. She leaves the fact suspended there, austere and pure. And everything goes back to its place. *Pomo pero, dime'l vero. Dime la santa verità.* (Apple-pear, tell me the truth. Tell me the blessed truth.)

'You really didn't know?'

It is all so simple in the end. All she needed to do was look at things with the right perspective, without letting herself be blinded by the light of misunderstanding. Don Titta could never have been an unknowing father, or even worse, a knowing accomplice. Don Titta is a man who honours his children, although perhaps a little more in death than in life.

Innes looks at her indulgently and with mild surprise. She hopes he cannot read her mind. She has been so silly. She has been stupid. She has no defences now and carries the burden of nobody's child.

'For what it's worth . . .' Innes says, and then turning around, he asks, 'You are in agreement, aren't you, Pia?'

She comes towards them from the kitchen with two heavy

baskets of provisions for the first leg of their trip: fruit, biscuits, cordial. Without knowing what they have been discussing, the girl smiles at them. Innes takes her burden and she curtseys her thanks.

Of course Pia is in agreement. All that has happened before means nothing, even if it has led to her being there now. She might never have been born. She might have been sent back to where she came from when she was still an infant. She could have remained entangled with her destiny as a servant. She'd be lining up with the rest of her peers for that sad and indifferent goodbye, and then she'd have to hurry back to her poorhouse duties. Instead Pia now stands on the right side of the wall. She climbs in, situates herself in the corner, fixes the folds of her skirt, and waves her hand out the window even before leaning out to show her face to whoever wishes to remember it. It is as if she has rehearsed this act of liberation thousands of times. She is going out into the world and the world is ready to unfurl before her. This is only the first act. Pia is going to London. She, who has never been anywhere, is going to London. So everything truly is possible after all.

❧ ❧

Everything *is* possible, including dying in an ice storm in the Alps, the coach tipping over on one side, like a ship on a wave, the wind whistling by them, the wheels barely making it through the two feet of snow, the cold scratching deep into the dark cabin. Snow in summertime is far worse than in winter because it is unexpected.

They could be caught by a band of French highwaymen in their capes and cone-shaped hats, grim characters who come down from the mountains with their rifles to impose a harsh sentence in the name of black hunger. They could be chased and finally captured by the Austrian forces, the kind that shows no compassion, and sent to Spielberg.

Everything is possible. But nothing happens. These three beings have already been part of a storm; they have already confronted and defeated their own bandits, let themselves be manipulated by suspicion, ill will, and hearsay. The trip is as smooth as the crossing of multiple borders can be, with exhausting interactions at customs, exchanges of documents and money; with the lice in the cold inns, the greasy food and greasy bowls; with drunkards' songs that sound the same in all dialects. The late-summer rain diligently beats its meek song down on the rooftop of their carriage; they see the occasional comrade whose eyes are sharp and who wants to peer in. Outside, postcard images roll by, postcards no one cares to write. There are damp rice plains, solid mountains and pure blue skies. There is France, with its damp haystacks and fairy-tale castles surrounded by woods of marzipan.

Bianca has been sleeping through a great deal of the journey. She blames it on travelling sickness, but is seized by a strange sort of lethargy. Her body has advised her to rest because she knows that later on the creature will steal her sleep away. Therefore, in the final scenes of this story – or of this episode at least – we shan't look at the world as we would normally, over her shoulder, trying to make sense of things through her eyes. No, Bianca's eyes shall remain shut in an imitation of rest that absolves her from the effort of paying attention. Ultimately, it is better that she does not look outside. Otherwise her memory might tease her into remembering that she has seen these lands before with an unnameable, now-departed companion, and she would feel sadness, great sadness. In recompense, she now has a different companion inside her, an unknown parasite who has turned her life upside down. She doesn't know where she is going. Or rather, she knows but doesn't want to imagine it. She will have all the time in the world soon, and more. Is it any wonder that she avoids looking out at the landscape? This journey isn't one of pleasure. It is necessary. Let's leave her to rest, or pretend to sleep, and let's move quietly away so that we can obtain that tiny bit of perspective that changes everything.

At last, the moment arrives. As if in a dirty dream, the dusty profile of a thousand rooftops and a million chimneys appears outside the sweat-glazed windows of their final coach ride.

'Is this London?' Pia asks, with a dazed look.

'This is London,' Innes replies without even looking out of the window.

It feels to him like the trip has been far too short. He will never go back. He can't. It is only a small consolation to know that he is now safe. He didn't even go to Rome. He would have liked to die in Rome. Not deliriously lost, like Keats. He's had his fill of poets. No, he wishes he had become the head of a group of intrepid, uniformless men, out waving a flag that has yet to be imagined. It is still early days, though; he needs to be satisfied with being alive and elsewhere.

'Where are we going now?' asks Pia.

'Home,' Innes says.

Pia draws closer to the window.

He thinks back to what he has left: a locked door, a few things, things he can't have and can't be, now or ever. He looks over at Bianca, who is as pale and parched as a flower that has been without water for too long. She is alive, though. Alive for herself and for the unnamed creature. Pia's not even pretending to be tired. Her eyes shine with the future. A young woman, a girl, and an unborn baby – for the first time Innes feels old. The three of them need him. And he, a new kind of man, will always be there for them.

A Note from the Author

The Watercolourist was inspired by voices and places, by the voices that places own. Places are characters. First of all, the garden at Villa Manzoni in Brusuglio, near Milan. As the plaque at the front gate indicates, this was the summer residence of Alessandro Manzoni: writer, poet and statesman. The novelist of Italian literature. The villa was a place of leisurely activities and bucolic interests, where the writer grew cotton, planted rare grape cultivars that he ordered from afar, attempted to make wine, took an interest in silkworms, tended to exotic plants, and christened his favourite catalpa tree 'Hippopotamus', due to its enormous size. It is a fascinating place for children, who have always wished to trespass, to climb the wall and enter that charming park, as vast and as obscure as a jungle.

The Watercolourist was also inspired by a town house: Casa Manzoni, on Via Morone in Milan, the winter home of Alessandro Manzoni. Here, people skilled in the art of conversation gathered to discuss the future: whether it was the Great Novel that Manzoni was working on, or the Republic of Italy, a daring idea which was taking shape at that time.

A third inspiration came from the city of Milan, and in particular those neighbourhoods where so little has changed that it is easy to imagine what life was like two hundred years ago. A city of brick that was transformed into a city of marble; a 'city of contradictions', as the keen traveller Lady Sydney Morgan once described it.

A Note from the Author

Fifteen years ago, while working on a children's book project about foster parents, I had the chance to visit the historical archives of the Brefotrofio, the former orphanage of Milan. There, inside those large sliding shelves, surrounded by the smell of metal, moisture and dust, rest the traces of many lives, summarized in the dry language of bureaucracy. Everything had its origin there: the church documents that attest to a state of poverty, which in turn justified the need to resort to institutions; the requests and promises of parents ('that she may be named Luigia', 'we are giving her up out of poverty; I beg your kindness; we will come back and get her'); and especially the tokens and keepsakes – medals and medallions, little images cut in half, embroidered pillows, crucifixes, anything that would allow the parents to deposit and reclaim their children in months or years, and always under the mask of anonymity. Sometimes, when the parents were finally ready, it was too late. The children might have died as infants of smallpox or infection, or from an epidemic or ailment in the distant homes of those who raised them. The antique pages of those ledgers are misshapen and deformed by the objects they contain; they press at the pages as if struggling to tell their own stories.

It was a place where one didn't want to be alone. Both Pia and Minna's stories started there.

It took me about ten years to pull the stories together, to let them breathe, to find a way to cut, paste and sew them, and to understand how they could become a work of fiction. Everything finally clicked in place thanks to Bianca Pietra. Twenty years old at the beginning of the nineteenth century, Bianca is the true creator of the story, which takes shape in her hands; literally, as she is the watercolourist.

A woman of flowers, Bianca is devoted to her ephemeral subjects, but she is neither ephemeral nor frivolous. She is deeply committed to her work, and to the occupation we all share: the building of self-awareness. Finding one's place in the world. Discovering one's purpose. She is not a solitary soul lost on the moors, nor a porcelain doll nodding and smiling in a drawing room while waiting to be whisked away by a decent husband. Half English by blood, she is Italian, *Italianissima*: passionate, chaotic and dynamic. A truly romantic girl for a romantic novel.

I must say I took some liberties in weaving all these stories together. It is not likely (though not impossible) that a lady of the Milanese bourgeoisie of the early 1800s would have personally taken her illegitimate child to a centre for public assistance. She would probably have used a go-between such as a midwife, trusted servant or priest. It is even more likely that she would have had the child raised by other family members or individuals close to the family, and would have supervised the child's development from a distance. But Pia needed to be a girl of non-humble origins who had been entrusted to public care. This led to some slight stretching of the customary habits regarding abandonment at the Ospedale Maggiore, a sad but powerful institution that alleviated many family hardships in the Milan of the past. Minna's story is more typical: she was first entrusted to a wet nurse and then sent to a family in the country to be raised until her own family had the means to retrieve her.

I admit I made some deliberate 'mistakes'. The names of the ballerinas at La Scala who affected Bernocchi so deeply are all invented. Some types of flowers and plants I mention were not yet known in that period of history, at least not in the form described, and derive from later grafts and cultivations. The regular flower trade along the coast of Liguria only began in the middle of the nineteenth century.

A Note from the Author

And finally, the kidnappings. 'What good are kisses if they are not given?' is a line from a poem by Vivian Lamarque. Other citations are more or less obvious: Homer, Ronsard, Shelley, Prévert, Grossi, Foscolo, Mallarmé, Auden, Tagore, Neruda, Barrie, Meneghello. Don Titta's poems are entirely his own creation.

Ten years is a long time, but it flew by, as time tends to do. Writers of historical fiction need to take breaks for research, need to deviate from the path now and then. And I enjoyed my detours so much. Writing-time is different from clock-time, anyway. When we write, it is as if time becomes a place. It is that house in the country where you wish you could live but cannot; each time you return there, you have to open the windows to air out the rooms; it is an orderly, empty space you would like to complicate with your dearest clutter. Then, once you are settled, you never want to leave. It's where you want to be. When you're there, filled with the lives of others, you wouldn't want to be anywhere else in the world. Nor you could.

January 2016, Milan

extracts reading groups
competitions books new
discounts extracts
competitions
books new
events extracts
events books
extracts new titles reading groups
interviews
new books events
discounts
events new
discounts extracts discounts
www.panmacmillan.com
extracts events reading groups
competitions books extracts new